## ALONE WITH MARY

Mary kicked off her flip-flops and curled her toes around the short grass beneath her feet, favoring her right foot and her injured toe. Her ankles were swollen and her face carried the puffiness of a woman who was going to have a baby, but Andrew couldn't imagine that Mary could get more beautiful. She glowed as if lit from within by her own propane lantern. Was it this way with all women about to give birth? Was there anything closer to Gotte than bringing a child into the world? No wonder she looked like an angel.

The urge to kiss her seized him like a trap with razor-sharp teeth. He clamped his fingers around a clump of grass and held his breath.

Kiss her? He couldn't kiss her. Couples weren't supposed to kiss until they got married. The bishop made that clear with *die youngie.* Of course, everybody knew that everybody broke the rule, and if there was no choice to say yes, was it really a choice?

Andrew leaned closer to see if he could tell if Mary might be thinking the same thing . . .

## Books by Jennifer Beckstrand

*The Matchmakers of Huckleberry Hill*

HUCKLEBERRY HILL

HUCKLEBERRY SUMMER

HUCKLEBERRY CHRISTMAS

HUCKLEBERRY SPRING

HUCKLEBERRY HARVEST

HUCKLEBERRY HEARTS

RETURN TO HUCKLEBERRY HILL

A COURTSHIP ON HUCKLEBERRY HILL

HOME ON HUCKLEBERRY HILL

*The Honeybee Sisters*

SWEET AS HONEY

A BEE IN HER BONNET

LIKE A BEE TO HONEY

*The Petersheim Brothers*

ANDREW

*Anthologies*

AN AMISH CHRISTMAS QUILT

THE AMISH CHRISTMAS KITCHEN

THE AMISH CHRISTMAS CANDLE

AMISH BRIDES

Published by Kensington Publishing Corporation

# ANDREW

## JENNIFER
## BECKSTRAND

ZEBRA BOOKS
KENSINGTON PUBLISHING CORP.
www.kensingtonbooks.com

ZEBRA BOOKS are published by

Kensington Publishing Corp.
119 West 40th Street
New York, NY 10018

All Kensington titles, imprints, and distributed lines are available at special quantity discounts for bulk purchases for sales promotion, premiums, fund-raising, educational, or institutional use.

Special book excerpts or customized printings can also be created to fit specific needs. For details, write or phone the office of the Kensington Sales Manager: Attn.: Sales Department. Kensington Publishing Corp., 119 West 40th Street, New York, NY 10018. Phone: 1-800-221-2647.

Zebra and the Z logo Reg. U.S. Pat. & TM Off.
BOUQUET Reg. U.S. Pat. & TM Off.

First Printing: July 2019
ISBN-13: 978-1-4201-4771-1
ISBN-10: 1-4201-4771-4

ISBN-13: 978-1-4201-4774-2 (eBook)
ISBN-10: 1-4201-4774-9 (eBook)

10 9 8 7 6 5 4 3 2 1

Printed in the United States of America

# Chapter One

A muscle pulled tight across Mary's abdomen, creating a line of pain from her hip to her belly button. The tightness made it difficult to walk. She didn't care what that website said. Three miles was too far for a pregnant girl to go in one day.

Not that she had a choice. Mary's *mamm* had slammed the door in her face before Mary had even gotten a word in edgewise, and Mary hadn't known when the next bus was scheduled to come down the deserted road. She had turned her back on her parents' home and cried good and hard for about a mile before talking herself out of her self-pity. She couldn't blame her parents for reacting the way they had. She'd even been expecting it. After not seeing her family for two years, she'd shown up wearing jeans and a Maroon 5 T-shirt. And pregnant. Mamm couldn't very well overlook that inconvenient fact. Mary should have taken out her earrings. Mamm might have at least listened if Mary hadn't been wearing earrings.

Mary huffed out a breath. She should have thought

that one through a little better. Mamm was hurt and angry. The community might be even less forgiving.

Did she really want to raise her child in such a place?

If a wayward daughter wasn't welcome in her own house, how could Mary hope to be accepted by the community? Would the Amish treat her child like an outsider for the rest of his life? By mile number two, it was safe to say that Mary's hopes had fallen in the ditch. But Mary wasn't one to slosh around in her own tears. She'd made a lot of mistakes, bad ones, but she wasn't afraid to own up to them and get on with her life.

Finally, the Honeybee Farm came into sight as Mary rounded the next bend in the road. A big sign painted with flowers and butterflies stood right in front of the property. BEWARE THE HONEYBEES, it said. It wasn't a very friendly message and Mary didn't know Bitsy Kiem well, but something told Mary if anybody would take her in, Bitsy Kiem and her three nieces would. Bitsy had once been an Englischer. Surely Bitsy would feel sympathy for Mary's plight. Then again, Mary had been away a long time. Maybe nobody here would feel anything for her, not even obligation. Maybe she'd have to walk back into town and find a park bench to sleep on for the night. She hoped not. Her feet were going to fall off.

Mary clomped clumsily over the small wooden bridge that spanned an even smaller pond at the front of Bitsy's property. She passed several beehives on her left and nearly a dozen on her right. The hives hummed like a Corvette, and a cloud of bees flew in and out and around the hives. It was late spring, and they were busy. Mary inhaled the glorious scent of the flowering bushes lining the little lane that led to the house. The Honeybee Farm was the best-smelling property in Bienenstock, Wisconsin. The Honeybee Sisters had planted hundreds of trees, bushes, and flowers to attract and feed their bees. It was a heavenly place. Mary thought she could be quite happy here if Bitsy didn't throw her out before she even got in the door.

Mary climbed the porch steps, swallowed hard, and knocked. Her heart pounded against her ribs, and not just because she'd walked the three miles from her parents' house in flip-flops. Maybe Bitsy would have pity on her and give her a drink of water before kicking Mary off her property.

The door cracked open an inch, and the barrel of a shotgun appeared through the gap. Mary sucked in her breath. She had jumped the fence two years ago, but surely Bitsy didn't think she deserved to be shot for it. Mary took two steps back and raised her hands over her head like she'd seen people do in the movies. "I'm going. I'm going," she said.

The shotgun drooped, the door opened even farther, and Bitsy Kiem stuck her head outside. Under a red bandanna, her hair was a pleasing shade of blue, not too bright, not too faint. She wore a purple dress, pink earrings, and her usual frown. "Mary Coblenz? Is that you?"

Keeping her hands high above her head, Mary nodded slowly.

Bitsy grunted, propped her shotgun against the wall, and folded her arms across her chest. "I thought you were that magazine salesman. That boy won't leave me alone."

"I'm-I'm sorry," Mary stuttered.

"Don't apologize. I'm glad you're not the magazine salesman. I might have had to shoot you."

Mary giggled in spite of her racing heart. "I'm glad you didn't have to shoot him."

Bitsy's frown deepened, and she waved her hand in the air like she was swatting a fly. "I wouldn't shoot anybody unless they deserved it. I don't believe in guns."

For a woman who didn't believe in guns, Bitsy certainly treated hers like it was an old friend. And maybe she'd pick it up again as soon as she heard what Mary had to say. "Bitsy, I know this is strange—"

Bitsy stepped onto the porch, curled her fingers around Mary's arm, and nudged her into the house. "You look like you've had quite a time of it yet. *Cum reu* and sit down. I've got muffins fresh from the oven, and cold milk."

Nothing in the world sounded so good as muffins and cold milk. Mary closed her lips and sat down at the table. What she had to say could wait. She'd like to eat a muffin before Bitsy made her go. Maybe Bitsy hadn't noticed she was pregnant.

"Those shoes are the most impractical things I've ever seen," Bitsy said, taking a plate from the cupboard and putting two muffins on it.

"They are," Mary said, because the space between her right big toe and the next toe was growing a blister, and bits of caked dry mud stuck to her feet like moss on a rock.

Bitsy set the plate of muffins on the table with a knife, a spoon, and a jar of raspberry jam. Mary sighed out loud. She couldn't remember the last time she'd had homemade raspberry jam. Bitsy went to the fridge and poured the most delicious-looking glass of milk Mary had ever seen. "They're bran muffins, but don't worry. They're delicious. You can even make bran taste good if you use enough sugar, and Yost needs bran to stay regular."

Mary didn't know who Yost was, but bran muffins sounded like about the best thing in the world right now. Her stomach growled. She hadn't eaten anything since about five this morning except a bottle of water, and that definitely didn't count. She cut a muffin in half, spread on a generous dollop of jam, and took a bite. It was the best thing she'd ever tasted and probably the best thing she'd ever taste again.

Bitsy set the glass of milk on the table. "Good?" she asked.

Not wanting to talk with her mouth full, Mary smiled, nodded, and took a drink of milk. It tasted so good, she finished off a third of the glass before taking a breath. "It's *appeditlich*, Bitsy. *Denki*."

Bitsy studied Mary's face. "I've got some peanut butter in the pantry. You look like you need some protein. Or I could fry you up a steak right quick. I have a special seasoning."

"*Nae*. Of course you don't need to fry up a steak."

"I don't *need* to do anything, but I don't mind cooking a steak. It's not that hard."

"Please don't trouble yourself." Mary finished off her first muffin and started in on the second. She needed to get it down before Bitsy started asking questions.

Too late.

Bitsy pulled out the chair next to her and sat down.

"My muffins are famous, but I don't expect you came because you heard I'd made a batch today."

Mary looked down at her hands. "*Nae.* I didn't come for the muffins."

Bitsy nodded as if she already knew what Mary was going to say. "Well, it's lucky I had some on hand."

Might as well get it over with. Mary drank the rest of her milk and stuffed the last of the muffin into her mouth, taking a few seconds to chew before she explained herself.

She should have known Bitsy would be four steps ahead of her. "When's the *buplie* coming?"

Mary instinctively rested her hand on her growing abdomen. "August sixth."

Mary hadn't expected Bitsy to smile—she rarely did, at least since Mary had known her. Bitsy laid her hand over Mary's. "It's *wunderbarr* to have a baby, you know. I never got that chance."

Mary pressed her lips together. She'd spent so many months worrying about being pregnant. It was almost a relief that someone was happy about the baby. Of course, Bitsy probably didn't know Mary wasn't married. She might feel differently if she knew.

"They say your bladder will never be the same," Bitsy said, "but it's a small price to pay to bring another soul into the world. Boy or girl?"

"I don't know."

"We'll have to do the needle test on you. If it circles, it's a girl. If it goes back and forth, it's a boy. I've never seen it fail yet."

Mary nodded. "I . . . I'd like to try that. It would be . . . fun to know."

"Well, it's nice to be able to make blankets and

booties the right color before the *buplie* comes. Have you had any heartburn? They say if you have bad heartburn, your baby will have lots of hair."

Mary couldn't speak past the lump in her throat. It was such a commonplace conversation—two women talking about having a baby, making plans, actually getting excited about it. Mary had missed so much.

Bitsy tilted her head and eyed Mary with all the understanding of a woman who'd raised three nieces. "That boy you ran off with, did he marry you?"

Mary shook her head and braced herself for Bitsy's indignation.

"Thank goodness."

Mary's eyes nearly popped out of her head. "Thank goodness?"

"It's easier when you don't have to unstick yourself from a sticky situation. The lawyers get rich, and you get nothing but heartache." Bitsy poured Mary another glass of milk. "So. You're pregnant, you're unmarried, and you've completely lost your sense of fashion."

A laugh escaped Mary's lips, and droplets of milk shot out of her mouth and splattered the tablecloth. "You don't like my T-shirt?"

"It's a bad color on you and the earrings are all wrong, and since when does a self-respecting young woman wear holes in her jeans?"

Mary didn't dare take another swig of milk. Bitsy was so unexpectedly brash. "Everybody wears holey jeans these days."

Bitsy handed Mary a napkin. "You've got your *mamm*'s smile."

"*Denki*," Mary said, not feeling all that much like smiling anymore. Mamm hadn't smiled this morning.

Bitsy heaved a great sigh. "I suppose she kicked you out."

Mary's shoulders sagged. "She didn't even let me in."

"So you came here?"

Mary caught her bottom lip between her teeth. "I should have known she wouldn't let me come home. *I* wouldn't have let me come home. I was foolish, *deerich*, not to have another plan when I left Green Bay, but I only had enough money to get here. You were once an Englischer. I thought maybe you wouldn't mind if I stayed here for a few days until I can make arrangements to go back to Green Bay."

"Do you want to go back to Green Bay?"

She might as well be honest, even if it made her sound pathetic. "Not really."

Bitsy leaned forward. "I need to know a few things first, Mary Coblenz. Are you afraid of bees?"

"*Nae.*"

"Are you allergic to cats?"

"Not that I know of."

Bitsy frowned. "Too bad. It would have given me an excuse to get rid of them. I have four. People at church call me 'the cat lady' behind my back." She pointed to a fuzzy white cat lounging on the window seat. "Farrah Fawcett is as useful and as pleasant as a bowl of Brussels sprouts." Bitsy wiped at a spot of milk on her tablecloth. "This is the most important question. Will your parents be mad if I take you in?"

Mary's heart sank. And just when she was starting

to feel a tiny sliver of hope. "I don't think they'll like it."

Bitsy smiled again. That was twice in less than fifteen minutes. "*Gute.* People need something to get worked up about. It's so much fun for everyone if I give them a reason to gossip."

"You don't care that my parents will be mad?"

"All my nieces are married, and I have three empty beds upstairs. You can spread out over all three if you want. And I won't hear talk about going back to Green Bay. Stay here as long as you like. This house needs a baby."

Mary had already bawled once today and she wasn't usually a crier, but tears pooled in her eyes. "That . . . you don't mind if I stay here?"

"Of course not, and Yost will be thrilled."

"Who is Yost?"

"My new husband," Bitsy said. "He agrees with me on just about everything, and if he doesn't, he knows enough to admit that he's wrong. Yost is around about half the time. He works his farm as well as mine. He's a treasure." A shadow passed over her features. "I only have one request. If any boys come poking around, don't feed them. Boys are like stray cats. If you feed them once, they keep coming back."

Mary giggled. "I think we can safely assume that no boys are going to come poking around. I jumped the fence, I'm pregnant, and you have a shotgun."

Bitsy grunted. "Don't be so sure. Boys are very determined when they want to be."

Mary brushed crumbs into her hand from the table. "Bitsy, I don't know how to thank you."

Bitsy waved away any mention of gratitude. "You're

welcome, and never mention it again. If the truth were told, I'm being selfish. I like it when people gossip about me."

"They're more likely to gossip about me."

"That's double the fun as far as I'm concerned. Now sit tight. I'm going to fry you a steak."

# Chapter Two

Alfie Petersheim was only eight, but he was old enough to know that Mamm had pulled one over on him.

*Sleeping in the cellar will be a grand adventure,* she had said. *It will be like sleeping in your own cave, and you and Benji will have it all to yourselves.*

Alfie should have known it was a trick. A dirty, dirty trick.

He lay on his back on the hardest air mattress in the world staring at the ceiling, which he couldn't see. The cellar was so dark, he wouldn't even be able to see his hand if he held it right in front of his face—although he hadn't tried it because he didn't dare let go of the blanket that he clutched for dear life around his chin.

The cellar smelled like dirty socks and moldy peanut butter. What had Mamm been thinking? Everybody knew mold was poisonous. Willie Glick even said so. And Alfie was sure a spider had crawled across his hand not one minute ago.

The ceiling creaked as if it was going to fall on him

and his brother. Or maybe it was a ghost sneaking around upstairs waiting for Alfie to go to sleep so he could attack.

"Benji?" Alfie whispered, risking pulling his hand out of the covers to tap his twin *bruder* on the arm. Benji responded by rolling over and jabbing his knee into Alfie's side.

*It will be fun,* Mamm had said. *You will love sleeping down there.* It was the first time that Mamm had lied straight to his face. At least he hoped it was the first time. How many other lies had she told him? Had his hamster really run away?

Alfie was not happy that Benji could sleep through anything, even a ghost attack. "Wake up." Alfie shoved his *bruder* so hard that Benji slipped off the air mattress and thudded onto the cement floor.

"Hey!" Benji protested. "Stop it."

"We've got to make a plan," Alfie said, pulling the covers tighter around himself. It was almost summertime, but how hard would it have been for Dat to build a small fire in the stove so his youngest sons didn't freeze to death? Alfie heard some shuffling on Benji's side, then Benji fell hard onto the mattress as if he'd tripped trying to find it in the dark. His hard fall bounced Alfie into the air—not far, but high enough to wake all the spiders lurking under the mattress. There was a small pop and a hiss, and Alfie slowly started to sink. "Benji, what did you do?"

Benji sat up again. "I didn't do nothing, but I think there's a hole in here."

They both fell silent. A low hiss came from Benji's side of the air mattress, and no doubt about it, they were sinking like a leaky boat.

Mamm had told them not to turn on the electric

lantern unless it was an emergency because it wasted the battery. Their mattress was flattening like a pancake, Alfie had probably already been bitten by a spider, and he was going to die from mold poisoning. As far as he was concerned, this was an emergency.

Alfie felt around the edge of the bed until his hand found the lantern. He flipped the switch, and the cellar flooded with light. There were some spooky shadows in the corner where monsters could be hiding, but Lord willing, the lantern would keep them safe.

"Come on, Alfie," Benji said, rubbing his eyes. "I want to sleep."

"You popped our mattress. Mamm said not to jump on it."

Benji sat cross-legged on the slowly shrinking mattress, squinting into the light. "I didn't jump on it. I fell." Benji was still wearing the trousers he'd worn during the day with nothing on top.

Something shiny in his back pocket caught the light. "What's that?" Alfie said.

Benji twisted his body to look at his pocket. He reached back and pulled out a fork. "This is in case I woke up and wanted a piece of pie. Then I wouldn't have to go upstairs to get a fork."

Alfie rolled his eyes. "You still have to go upstairs to get a piece of pie."

Benji grinned, reached down to the other side of the mattress, and lifted a plate from the floor. On it was a thick slab of snitz pie from dinner last night, and Benji had somehow missed squishing it when Alfie had pushed him off the bed. He stuck his fork into the slice and took a bite.

"Me," Alfie said, motioning for Benji to give him some.

Benji picked up the pie with his fingers and shoved it toward Alfie. Alfie took a big bite. "You didn't need a fork."

Benji frowned. "I guess not."

"And it poked a hole in our bed."

Benji frowned harder. "I didn't think of that."

The mattress continued to hiss, and Alfie and Benji continued to sink. Alfie growled. They'd die if they had to sleep in the cellar for the rest of their lives. He picked up Benji's pie and took another bite. "We've got to make a plan, and it has to be super secret."

Benji's eyes darted from left to right, and he smiled so wide, Alfie could see the gap where one of his back teeth was missing. "What kind of plan?"

"We need to get our room back."

Benji stopped smiling. "But Mamm and Dat kicked us out."

"Look, Benji, our air mattress is dead, and when it gets all the way to the ground, the spiders will start crawling on us. And Mamm killed a mouse in here just last week."

"Mice are cute, and spiders eat bad bugs. Mamm said so."

"It's so dark. What if Mamm forgets we're down here and leaves us in the cellar forever?"

Benji nodded, eyes wide. "The window is too high to crawl out."

"We need fresh air. It stinks down here."

Benji took the last bite of his pie and stuffed his fork back into his pocket. "But Mamm and Dat have to sleep in our room because Mammi and Dawdi are in their room. Dawdi can't climb the stairs since his stroke."

Alfie scratched his head. "We can't kick Dawdi out. He can't hardly even talk."

Benji got sort of weepy all of a sudden. "I love Dawdi so much, but Mamm says he can't remember who I am."

Alfie shook his head. "He remembers, all right. Just cuz he don't say nothing doesn't mean he doesn't know us. He smiles with his eyes. Yesterday I heard him say *jah*."

"I miss him. He used to tell us stories and help us catch pollywogs."

"He'll do that again, Benji. Mamm says he'll get better if he does his exercises every day. That's why he's living with us, so Mamm and Dat can help him."

Benji slumped his shoulders. "We'll never get our room back."

Alfie scrunched his lips together. "We have to get rid of Andrew."

"Andrew? Why Andrew? He's my favorite *bruder*, next to you."

Alfie sighed. "We have to get rid of all three of them. Mamm wants to turn Andrew's room into a sewing room when he moves out, so we'll still be in the cellar. Abraham and Austin will have to go too. Then we can have their room."

"But how do we get rid of all three of them? They're way bigger than us," Benji said.

Alfie couldn't help but agree. Their three older *bruderen* would never take orders from Benji and Alfie. "They should move out and get their own houses. That's what Aunt Beth says." Alfie leaned his head close to Benji's. "She told me not to tell anyone."

Benji licked up the crumbs on the pie plate. "I don't see how to get them to move out."

"We need a plan."

"A really *gute* plan." Benji fished a piece of wax from his ear. "We could play a trick on them."

"What do you mean?"

"Most boys move out when they get married."

"You mean we can trick them into getting married?" Alfie said, a slow smile growing on his lips.

Benji nodded. "We could find Andrew, Abraham, and Austin each a wife. But I don't know who."

Alfie looked up to the ceiling like he always did when he thought deep thoughts. A long, thin cobweb dangled directly over his head. He squeaked, slapped at it, and scrubbed his hand across the blanket to get rid of it. They had to come up with a plan or he was going to have an attack of the heebie-jeebies. He didn't know exactly what the heebie-jeebies were, but you could catch them from spiders and girls. That's what Willie Glick said. "We need to think of some-body right quick. I hate this cellar."

"We should do Andrew first because he's the oldest."

Alfie heaved a sigh. "He doesn't like anybody in Bienenstock. He said so himself."

"What about Mary Coblenz? She's new in town, so Andrew hasn't met her."

"Who is Mary Coblenz?"

Benji pulled the fork from his pocket and twirled it in his fingers. "She's living with Bitsy Weaver—you know, the *fraa* who paints her hair. And she"—Benji looked around to make sure no one was spying on them, leaned close, and lowered his voice—"she's going to have a baby."

Benji leaned too far and bonked Alfie in the forehead. Alfie pulled away and rubbed his sore head. "There's no need to whisper."

"That's how Mamm said it, like it was a secret. I didn't think it was proper to say it out loud."

"*Ach, vell,* girls have babies all the time. If it's that big of a secret, why did Mamm tell you?"

Benji shrugged. "She didn't. She was talking to Aunt Beth. They never think us little kids listen."

The more Alfie thought about it, the more he liked the idea. "Mary Coblenz is a *gute* choice. She's already going to have a baby, so that would save time for all of us. It wonders me if we won't get rid of Andrew in three or four weeks."

Benji chewed on his bottom lip. It was what he did when he was thinking real hard. "We'll need some supplies. Walkie-talkies and binoculars for sure and certain."

"We can break our piggy banks."

"But I like my piggy bank. He smiles at me."

"Benji, do you want to get our room back or don't you?"

Benji sniffed and swiped the back of his hand across his nose. "I guess so."

"Dawdi has binoculars. He won't care if we use them."

"How do you know? Dawdi can't even talk."

"He won't care," Alfie said, with a confidence he didn't really feel. He *hoped* Dawdi didn't care, because Benji would never go along with the plan if he thought it might upset Dawdi.

Benji pressed his lips together and looked sideways. "We could ask Mammi Martha."

Alfie squished his face into a terrible, awful frown just so Benji would know what he thought of that idea. "We can't tell Mammi Martha. She told Mamm we stink."

Benji looked up to the ceiling and thought about it long and hard. "Let's ask Dawdi. Sometimes he gives me secret messages with his eyes. I'll know if he says yes." Benji slid off the air mattress, which was now so low not even a small child would trip over it. "I'll sneak upstairs and get a paper and pencils so we can write down what we need."

"*Nae*, Benji. What if Andrew found our plans? Or Mamm? We have to memorize them and keep our lips shut. The only people who can be in on our secret are you, me, and Dawdi. Agreed?"

"Agreed." Alfie and Benji shook hands. They could always count on each other—brothers to the death.

Alfie smiled to himself. They'd have their room back before harvest time.

# Chapter Three

"Alfie Benaiah Petersheim, get that cat off my table!"

Andrew hadn't even walked in the house yet, but he could hear Mamm loud and clear in the kitchen. The neighbors could probably hear her too—not that this was anything unusual. Mamm tended to raise her voice to one of her boys on a regular basis. She had mostly quit shouting at Andrew, Abraham, and Austin since they'd grown up and didn't get into much mischief anymore.

But the twins, Alfie and Benji, were another story. If they were awake, they were either making trouble or planning trouble, and Mamm was diligent about keeping all that funny business under control. She ruled with a firm hand, knowing that if she let up for even a minute, they'd probably kill themselves trying to do something stupid like lighting a fire in the house or scaling the barn roof in their underwear.

Grinning, Andrew's *bruder* Austin poked Andrew in the ribs with his elbow. "It sounds like the twins are in trouble again." Austin was twenty-one years old and didn't seem to have a care in the world—especially if Mamm was mad at someone else besides him.

"Don't even think about it," Mamm growled, loudly enough to spook the chickens in the yard.

Abraham folded himself onto the porch step where he sat to take off his muddy boots. Of the three older *bruderen*, Abraham was the tallest—six-foot-three—and even though he was twenty-two years old, he hadn't shown any signs of stopping. He'd grown an inch last year. "I think it's gotten worse since Mammi and Dawdi moved in." Abraham was quieter and more pensive than either Andrew or Austin. He noticed things like *why* Mamm was in a bad mood instead of just *when* she was.

Not that Andrew hadn't noticed it too. Mammi and Dawdi had moved in a couple of weeks ago after Dawdi's stroke, and while Mamm and Dat were happy, even eager to help, two new guests in the house hadn't been easy on anybody.

Andrew and his *bruderen* left their muddy boots by the door and filed into the house. Mamm held the broom aloft, pointing the broom head in Alfie's direction. The kitchen table stood between Mamm and Andrew's twin *bruderen*, Alfie and Benji, and Alfie was wrestling with the sorriest cat Andrew had ever seen. It was black and white with lopsided whiskers and one ear split right down the middle. Part of its tail was missing too. Alfie held the cat at arm's length to avoid getting scratched, but the cat hissed and bared its fangs while trying to claw its way up Alfie's arm.

"Get that cat out of my house this instant," Mamm said, raising her broom in case of an attack.

"But, Mamm, he's so cute," Alfie said, forcing a smile before shoving the cat in Benji's direction.

Benji took the cat from Alfie and cuddled the pitiful animal close to his chest. The cat hissed and scowled, but surprisingly, it didn't go for Benji's throat. Maybe it didn't like the way Benji smelled. Or maybe it did. The cat stuck out its tongue and licked Benji's wrist. "He's lost, Mamm. We need to take him back to his rightful owner," Benji said.

Mamm blew a strand of hair from her eyes. "You need to take him behind the barn and put him out of his misery, that's what."

Benji's mouth fell open. "You want us to kill him?"

Mamm half sighed, half growled. "*Nae*. I don't want you to kill him. Just take him back to the woods where you found him and let him loose. He can take care of himself. And whatever you do, don't feed him."

Benji gave Mamm a sheepish grimace. "We opened a can of tuna fish."

"*Ach*," Mamm said, throwing up her free hand, but Andrew knew better than to think she'd surrendered. "He still has to go. You know the rule. No pets allowed. Look what he did to my table." Her voice rose in irritation. "Look what he did to my chair."

Andrew wasn't quite sure how it had happened, but the table was dotted with little flour paw prints, and stuffing poked out from the upholstery on one of the old kitchen chairs. "I can make a whole new set of chairs for you, Mamm," Andrew said, trying to keep the eagerness out of his voice.

Abraham nodded. "He could make the finest chairs you ever saw, Mamm."

Mamm waved away the suggestion. "We don't need new chairs. What we need is a kick in the seat of the pants and to be rid of this cat."

"But, Mamm, someone loves this cat, and we need to help him find his home." Alfie's eyes filled with tears, and Andrew might have thought he was truly upset if he didn't know any better. Alfie was very *gute* at turning on the tears when he really wanted to get Mamm's attention.

Apparently, Mamm wasn't fooled either. "Save your tears for your sins, young man."

Austin dampened a piece of paper towel and started wiping the paw prints from Mamm's table. "You can search all over town, but you won't find anyone who loves that cat."

Benji seemed a little more sincere than Alfie. "He's one of Gotte's creatures."

Mamm wasn't about to give in, but she wasn't completely insensitive to the poor animal. "All right. You can take him to the animal shelter in Shawano, but I don't know how you think you're going to get there."

"We don't have to take it to Shawano," Alfie said, scratching at what looked like a mosquito bite on his arm. "This is Bitsy Weaver's cat. If Andrew will drive us, we can take it back tonight."

Mamm's face became a brewing storm. "You knew it was Bitsy's cat all along?"

Alfie bit his bottom lip. "Well, um, *jah* . . . I suppose."

"Why did you carry on and on like you didn't know?" Mamm said.

Alfie shrugged, widening his eyes in artificial innocence. "You never asked us."

Mamm gave Alfie the stink eye and chased him around the table with the broom. Alfie ran for his life, and they both ended up laughing by the time they'd made a complete circle around the table.

"Alfie Petersheim, don't think you can pull your shenanigans on me," Mamm said, laughing and frowning at the same time.

Andrew couldn't help but smile. It had always been that way with Mamm. She did her share of shouting, but there was affection behind every word. All her sons knew that Mamm loved them enough to give them correction, even if it meant ruining her singing voice.

"Now get to Bitsy's before I tan your hide," Mamm said.

Benji turned to Andrew. "Will you take us tonight?"

Andrew glanced at his brothers. Why didn't the twins ever ask Abraham or Austin to do things for them? It was one of the consequences of being the oldest. "I suppose. We can go after dinner."

Mamm stomped her broom on the floor. "Go now, Andrew. I want that cat out of my house. You have an hour before dinner."

Alfie drew his brows together. "But, Mamm, that won't give him enough time to . . ."

Mamm started sweeping the floor. The cat had apparently been there too. "Enough time to what?"

"Nothing," Alfie said quickly, as if he wanted Mamm to forget he'd said anything.

"Then get going." Mamm tapped Alfie's bottom with the broom, then caught Benji as he passed.

"I'll sweep, Mamm," Andrew said, nudging the broom out of her hands. She moved as if her back was hurting her again. Either that or Mammi Martha had really gotten on her nerves today.

Mamm took back her broom and gave Andrew a peck on the cheek. "You'll do me a better service by getting rid of that cat. Austin can sweep."

"Ah, nuts."

Mamm gave Austin a quick and sharp look. "Watch your language, young man." She handed Austin the broom and looked at Andrew. "Did you ask the vet about Snowball?"

Andrew glanced at Abraham. "Didn't need to. Abraham took a look at her."

Abraham had a talent for caring for animals. "I don't think it's a tick bite, so we still have to talk to a vet. She's had all her shots."

"You'll do that tomorrow?" Mamm said.

Abraham nodded.

Mamm turned back to Andrew. "And what about the peanuts? We need them in one week."

"I took care of that too," Andrew said. "They should be here by Wednesday, and jars by Thursday."

She patted his arm. "*Denki.* I can always depend on you."

Andrew smiled back because he truly was glad to please his *mamm,* but he didn't dare tell her how he really felt. He was sick, sick, sick of peanut butter.

Andrew and his *bruderen* still helped Dat with the hay and corn, but a *gute* part of their time was spent making peanut butter and selling it to Amish markets and food shops. This enterprise had earned them the nickname Peanut Butter Brothers, which Mamm thought was adorable and Andrew thought was just a little too cute.

The name wasn't the worst part of it. Andrew hated making peanut butter. It was mundane, mindless work. He wanted to work with his hands, building chairs and tables and other pieces of art out of wood, but Mamm wouldn't take it well if he up and quit the business. He couldn't upset her now, not when

Mammi and Dawdi Petersheim had moved in for what looked to be several months, if not permanently. Mamm had enough to worry about as it was. Andrew wouldn't make Mamm's life harder just to gratify his own selfish desires.

For sure and certain, he should count his blessings. He still had a room of his own to retreat to when Mammi Martha started handing out cleaning assignments. Mamm and Dat had moved into the twins' room because Dawdi David couldn't possibly climb stairs. Alfie and Benji had to sleep in the cellar on an air mattress—although they probably loved it. They got the whole cellar to themselves. It was the perfect place to plan mischief.

Mammi Martha walked in the house carrying two large grocery sacks. Andrew and Abraham rushed to her side to take them from her. They were heavy, too heavy for an eighty-year-old woman to be carrying by herself. "Well, bless my soul," Mammi said, after taking a short look around. "That cat looks like something the cat dragged in."

Mamm grunted her displeasure. "It won't be here long."

"It's just as well," Mammi Martha said. "Keeping up a litter box is a chore. Tidy Cat is the only brand that will keep away the smell."

"Where's Dat?" Abraham asked.

Mammi waved her hands in no direction in particular. "*Ach*, he's unhitching the horse and buggy."

Dawdi took a two-hour nap every morning and a three-hour nap every afternoon. Mammi spent naptime in the mornings rearranging Mamm's cupboards and organizing her spices. She spent the afternoons shopping. Once a week she hired a driver to take her to Walmart, and the other days—except Sunday— Dat drove her somewhere in the buggy. Usually it was to Glick's Family Market in Bienenstock or Lark Country Store in Bonduel, but she always came back with a "gift" for Mamm.

Mammi was eight years younger than Dawdi, but she seemed even younger than that. She could run circles around most women her age. She sighed, took off her black bonnet, and hung it on one of the hooks by the door. "Now, would you like to see what I bought?"

It wasn't really a matter of "liking." Mammi's purchases tended to be practical and burdensome—at least for Mamm, who not only had to figure out a place to store them, but she had to use them or risk hurting Mammi Martha's feelings. Mammi was only happy if she thought she was being helpful.

Mamm gave Mammi Martha probably the best smile she could manage. Mammi pulled a shiny metal cookie sheet from one of the bags. "What do you think?"

"It's so clean," Mamm said.

"*Jah.*" Mammi beamed as she set the cookie sheet on the table. "I bought nine of them."

Mamm's smile faded to nothing. She was probably wondering where to keep nine cookie sheets.

"They're not for cookies." Mammi went to the cupboard and retrieved a plate and a cup and set them on the cookie sheet. "From now on, we're going to eat on these trays. They'll keep the crumbs off the table yet, and if Benji or Alfie spill their milk, we won't have to mop the floor."

Mamm's stunned look meant she was either counting how long each of those trays would take to wash or imagining how attractive her blue plates would look nestled inside the cookie sheets. Judging by the look on her face, they didn't seem to be happy thoughts. "*Denki*, Martha. That was very thoughtful of you."

Mammi shook her head. "Don't mention it."

"We should get this cat back," Andrew said, not wanting to see Mamm's distress when Mammi Martha set the trays on the table for dinner.

Mammi held up her hand. "Wait one minute." She went to the cupboard under the sink and pulled out a bottle of pink liquid. "You little boys almost forgot. What do we do every time we come in the house?"

Alfie slumped his shoulders so low, his knuckles almost scraped the floor. "Spray with a breath of spring."

"*Gute*," Mammi said. She went to Benji, who was the closest, and held the nozzle up to his neck. "Lift your chin." Two spritzes for Benji and two for Alfie. Alfie made a face that would have done a sucker fish proud. The cat hissed like water on a fire, but that didn't deter Mammi from spraying him too. Austin was next. Mammi kindly invited him to stop sweeping so she could give him a spray. Andrew could see the muscles in Austin's jaw twitch as Mammi sprayed his neck and arms.

Seeming a little more willing, Abraham clamped his eyes shut and held out his arms and let Mammi spray him. Andrew did the same. He was twenty-four years old, for goodness' sake, but he wasn't about to hurt Mammi's feelings for the sake of a little rose water. If he didn't smell like a man, at least he didn't smell like a pile of manure. Mammi replaced the bottle under the sink. "I've never found anything better than rose water for hiding those bad smells."

Andrew and the twins hurried outside, but Dat had been too fast. The horse was unhitched and munching hay in its stall. "Sorry, Snapper," Andrew said, patting the horse on the neck. "We have to go one more place."

Dat was spraying the outside of the buggy with something from a yellow spray bottle. He lifted it so Andrew could read the label. "Your *mammi* recommended it."

"Do you mind wiping it down when we get home? We have to run one more errand for Mamm."

"Okay." Dat put the lid on the spray bottle. "How did your *mamm* like Mammi's present?"

"Oh, I think it went just fine."

Dat grimaced. "Oh, dear. That's what I thought."

Alfie helped Andrew hitch up the buggy with more enthusiasm than usual, while Benji tried to keep the cat from escaping.

"Willie Glick's cousin Paul just got married," Alfie said as he handed Andrew the harness. "Did you know that?"

"We went to the wedding, remember?"

"I don't think his wife is all that pretty, do you? She has a big mole on her cheek."

Andrew wasn't about to tell Alfie what he really thought of Paul Glick and his new wife. "It doesn't matter what someone looks like on the outside, Alfie. The Lord looks on the heart."

Benji rocked the cat back and forth like a baby. "But you want a pretty wife, don't you?"

Andrew chuckled. "I suppose I'd prefer a pretty wife over a plain one."

Benji nodded eagerly. "Maybe someone with yellow hair?"

Alfie snapped his head around to glare at Benji. "It doesn't matter what color her hair is." He turned to Andrew and gave him a painful smile. "But there aren't any girls in Bienenstock you like, right? You told me they're not good enough. Right?"

Had he really said that? *Nae*, of course not. Andrew wasn't that arrogant. It was just that he was tall and strong, a hard worker and a godly man who knew the Bible as well as some of the ministers. Mamm had said so herself: *Any girl would be blessed to get Andrew for a husband.* "I didn't say they're not good enough. I only said I haven't found anyone in Bienenstock who interests me."

Alfie glanced at Benji, and they grinned at each other as if sharing a private joke. Andrew didn't really care that he wasn't in on it. He just wanted to get to Bitsy Weaver's, get home, and spend a little time in the woodshop before bed. *Ach*, *vell*, it wasn't really a woodshop, just a corner of the barn with a bench and a few tools, but they were his tools and far away from the peanut butter.

Bitsy Weaver's farm was a tidy assortment of orchards, flowers, and beehives. Most people in the *gmayna* considered Bitsy a bit odd, but she made excellent cakes and cookies, and she was always the first to visit a sick neighbor or help with someone's *kinner*. About a year ago, Bitsy had surprised everybody and gotten baptized and married in the same month.

Yost Weaver was an unlikely match for Bitsy, but they seemed to get along right well.

Andrew didn't know Bitsy and Yost that well. He only saw them at *gmay* and an occasional *singeon*, but Aunt Beth liked to gossip, and she had mentioned the Weavers more than once in her weekly visits.

Andrew drove the buggy over the narrow wooden bridge that marked the front of Bitsy's property. Alfie and Benji hadn't stopped talking since they'd left home. They acted as if they were going to see the fireworks instead of returning a runaway cat. *Ach*, what Andrew wouldn't give to be that excited about life again.

He drove the buggy up the long lane lined with flowering bushes. The odor was so strong, he could almost taste it. Andrew stopped the buggy at the end of the lane between the barn and the house. The twins hopped out before Andrew had even set the brake.

The boys were halfway across the flagstones when Alfie turned back. "Come on, Andrew. You don't want to miss this."

Andrew raised an eyebrow. What didn't he want to miss?

The boys stopped and eyed him expectantly. "You have to come," Benji said, "or you'll ruin everything."

"What will I ruin?"

Benji looked down and nudged a dandelion at his feet. "Everything."

"Okay," Andrew said, slowly forming the word between his teeth. His *bruderen* were eight years old, which had to be their excuse. Andrew didn't ever understand more than half the things they said anyway.

He slid out of the buggy, stepped between his *bruderen* and wrapped a hand around each of their shoulders. "Okay. Let's take this cat home."

You would have thought he'd offered to buy them double-decker ice cream cones. Alfie practically skipped up the porch steps. Benji might have skipped but the cat started struggling in his arms as if it knew where they were taking it.

Andrew knocked on the door. Bitsy was known to greet people with a shotgun. Lord willing she'd be so happy to see her cat that she'd forget about shooting anybody.

They waited for a few minutes, and Alfie knocked. No answer.

Andrew peeked in the window next to the front door. He couldn't see much past the curtains. "I don't think they're home."

"Benji," Alfie hissed, "they're supposed to be home."

Benji lifted his chin and scrunched his lips together. "It's not my fault. Mamm was in a hurry."

"Now, Alfie. How could Benji know if Bitsy would be home or not?" They'd done their duty. That was enough for Andrew. "Let's just leave the cat on the porch. Bitsy will find it."

"We can't just leave it. They have to meet us," Alfie said.

Andrew was already halfway down the porch steps. "They already know us. We can tell them about the cat when we see them at *gmay*."

Alfie leaned against the front door as if he wasn't going to budge until that cat was reunited with its family. "It would be rude to leave without saying hello."

Benji joined his *bruder* with his back against the

house. "Bitsy will be wonderful sad if we don't say hello."

Andrew trudged back up the stairs and squatted so he could look his *bruderen* in the eye. "I don't know what you want me to do. Mamm will have a fit if we bring it home, and she'll have a fit if we're late for dinner."

Alfie stuck out his bottom lip. "We have to wait."

Andrew wasn't quite sure what to do with his little *bruderen*. They were stubborn, like Mamm, and if Andrew insisted on going home, they might just insist on staying here all night—all over a stupid cat.

Benji nudged himself from the wall, his face brightening like a sunflower in full bloom. "Look, Alfie. There she is."

Andrew turned and looked where Benji was pointing. A girl in a navy-blue dress strolled up the lane toward them, carrying a square board in front of her like a shield. It looked like it might be a frame from one of Bitsy's beehives. The girl's hair was tied up in a fluorescent pink kerchief, and her white-golden strands caught the late afternoon sunlight. With the yellow hair framing her face, she looked very much how Andrew imagined one of heaven's angels would.

Alfie whooped like a wild man, and he and Benji bolted off the porch and ran toward the girl, which was quite a feat for Benji with a cat in his arms. Andrew gathered his wits and took off after his *bruderen*. "Slow down," he called, but if they heard him, they didn't pay him any heed. The poor girl would think she was under attack.

Andrew had longer legs, so he caught up with his

*bruderen* just as they caught up with the girl. "Hallo, Mary Coblenz," Alfie said.

The girl raised a puzzled eyebrow and smiled as if Benji and Alfie were her favorite nephews. "Do I know you?"

Benji held the cat aloft, if by chance she hadn't noticed it hissing in his arms. "We brought back your cat. And we brought our *bruder* Andrew."

Alfie reached back, grabbed a handful of Andrew's shirt, and pulled him forward. "This is Andrew."

She took half a step backward. "Nice to see you again, Andrew."

Did he know her?

The name sounded familiar, but he couldn't place the face. She looked to be no more than nineteen or twenty. She might have gone to school with him, but he hadn't paid much attention to the younger kids. Oy, anyhow. He should have paid attention. Mary Coblenz was as pretty as a picture.

Alfie seemed to wilt like a spring flower in the heat. "You already know each other?"

Mary's smile twitched on her face. "I went to school with Andrew, but he's four years older. I remember him because the younger girls were always in love with the older boys." She tilted her head teasingly to one side. "You don't remember me, do you?"

He hated to admit it. "*Nae*, I don't." He wished he would have remembered her, but what did it matter now? They'd met again, and he wouldn't waste a second chance to get to know her better. Something told him she was someone he wanted to know very well.

She didn't seem offended. "Maybe there's not as

much gossiping around here as I feared. I thought you would have heard my name by now."

Alfie smiled with his whole face, obviously overjoyed that Andrew and Mary didn't really know each other. "Mary jumped the fence, and she just got back. You said you don't like any of the girls in Bienenstock."

Andrew frowned and pulled his gaze from pretty Mary Coblenz. "I already told you. I never said that."

Wait a minute. What was that other thing Alfie said? Jumped the fence? Did Alfie even know what *jumping the fence* meant? Mary had left the community to go out into the world? How long had she been gone, and why hadn't he heard any gossip?

*Ach, vell,* that wasn't hard to explain. He'd missed *gmay* last week to stay home with Dawdi, and he'd been pretty busy with the wood and the peanut butter to have much to do with his friends lately.

Mary's smile faded as her eyes flicked in Alfie's direction, then she turned her steady gaze on Andrew. He found her look unnerving and fascinating at the same time. Mary may have jumped the fence, but he certainly couldn't hold that against her. She'd come back, hadn't she? And she had the most interesting blue eyes he had ever seen.

"Where should I put this cat?" Benji said.

Alfie poked Benji with his elbow. "Don't interrupt. They're talking to each other."

"But it keeps scratching me."

Mary smiled again, as if there was no such thing as an annoying eight-year-old boy. Andrew liked her better and better. "I was just going to the house. Let's take him in."

"He's not a very nice cat," Benji said.

Mary laughed. "That's what makes him such a *gute* mouse cat. He's mean enough to catch a mouse every day. His name is Billy Idol, after one of Bitsy's favorite Englisch singers."

"Here," Andrew said, holding out his hand, "I'll carry that frame for you."

She handed over the frame she'd been holding in front of her, and Andrew nearly lost his balance. Mary Coblenz was pregnant! Very pregnant. Pregnant enough that he could tell she was pregnant.

An involuntary gasp escaped his lips, and he felt as if he'd been socked in the head with a basketball. The frame slipped from his hand and fell in the dirt.

Mary eyed him, a mixture of hurt and defiance in her expression. "*Ach.* I thought you knew." She folded her arms and scrunched her lips to one side of her face. "No wonder you were so nice."

Alfie had no sense of the awkward situation. "And look, Andrew. She's going to have a baby."

"Do you . . . do you have a husband?" He knew it was rude the moment it came out of his mouth. Besides, he already knew the answer. Of course she didn't have a husband. She had left the community, she was living with Bitsy Weaver instead of her family, and Andrew probably would have heard about a wedding.

Benji grinned like a cat—well, like any cat but the one he was holding. "She's not married. What do you think about that?"

"I'm not married," she said, as if she wanted to be sure Andrew had heard Benji correctly.

In an effort to escape her piercing, unembarrassed gaze, Andrew reached down and retrieved the frame he'd dropped. He handed it back to Mary. "We need to go."

Alfie groaned. "Come on, Andy. We just got here."

He didn't have any other explanation but the truth. "I don't want you boys to be uncomfortable."

Mary cocked an eyebrow. "Are you boys uncomfortable?"

Alfie shook his head. Benji squinted in Andrew's direction. "The cat scratched me and I have a pebble in my shoe. I'm in pain, but I'm not uncomfortable."

"We like you," Alfie said, stuffing his hands in his pockets. Alfie tried to pull on Andrew's shirt again. "Andrew likes you too."

Mary glanced at Andrew, and her look made him squirm, as if he was the one who was guilty instead of her. "Are you uncomfortable, Andrew?"

"One of us should be."

"And why is that?" She was purposefully goading him. Did she want to embarrass him or justify herself?

Andrew stepped between his *bruderen*, put one hand over each of their ears, and nudged them so their other ears were pressed against his sides. "Because you're in a family way," he whispered.

One side of her lips curled upward. "*Ach*, I don't think you have to cover their ears. They seem to be aware."

"Hey," Alfie said, wriggling free of Andrew's grip.

Benji did the same. "What did you do that for?"

Andrew tried to swallow around the lump in his throat. Mary didn't seem sorry for what she had done. What kind of girl didn't even feel remorse for . . . for doing that? She acted as if she didn't even care, as if she didn't see the need to repent. It didn't matter about Mary. Andrew's first responsibility was to protect his *bruderen*. They shouldn't see things that would give rise to questions that Andrew had no intention of answering.

Andrew turned at the sound of Bitsy Weaver's open-air buggy coming across the small wooden bridge. Bitsy's dress was bright pink like Mary's kerchief, and her hair glowed a light shade of blue. The color was completely out of place for an Amish *fraa*, but the bishop hadn't made a fuss about it, so the community put up with her. Most people liked Bitsy too much to be concerned about her hair color or the occasional nail polish she wore. Those who didn't approve whispered behind her back and avoided her at *gmay*. Bitsy seemed perfectly content with herself, no matter what other people thought of her.

It was no wonder Mary was living with Bitsy. There weren't but a handful of people in the community who would have taken in Mary in her condition. For sure and certain Mary's parents hadn't allowed her back in the house.

Andrew frowned. Mary had done something terribly wrong. She should rightfully be ashamed, but it didn't seem right that her parents wouldn't let her come home. Of course, she didn't seem all that sorry. Maybe her parents wanted her to show some remorse.

Bitsy stopped the buggy next to them. "If it isn't the Peanut Butter Brothers, come for a visit. What have you got to say for yourselves?"

"We're not here to visit," Andrew said, wanting to make it clear that he would never intentionally come to visit Mary Coblenz.

Bitsy puckered her lips as if his words tasted like a lemon. "Did you come to pester Mary? Because if you did, you can just march right back the way you came. I won't allow it."

Mary sighed and glanced in Andrew's direction. "I'm fine, Aunt Bitsy. It's only to be expected."

Bitsy climbed from the buggy, positioned herself between Mary and Andrew, and looked Andrew up and down like he was a lame horse for sale. "You're handsome enough, Andrew Petersheim, but that don't make you better than anybody. Just you remember that. He who is without sin can cast the first stone. The rest of you can keep your comments to yourself."

"Don't worry, Aunt Bitsy," Mary said. "He's been very nice."

Andrew resisted the urge to lower his gaze. There was no reason to feel guilty. He had been nice, as nice as he could be to a girl who'd been taken in sin. Bitsy didn't need to lecture him.

Once again, Benji held up that stupid cat. He was no doubt ready to be rid of it. "Here's your cat."

Bitsy propped her hands on her hips. "Well. If it isn't Billy Idol. He disappeared this morning." She narrowed her eyes in Benji's direction. "It's a wonder he made it all the way to your house."

Benji clutched the cat to his chest and took a step back. "He's a fast runner."

"Hmm." Bitsy nodded slowly, thoughtfully. "I thought maybe he'd been stolen, but I shouldn't have got my hopes up."

Alfie laughed a fake, uncomfortable laugh. What was wrong with him? "Who would want to steal this cat?"

"Who indeed?" Bitsy said. She looked from Benji

and Alfie to Andrew. Her gaze lingered on Andrew a little too long. "Well, I should feed you something to show my appreciation for bringing back my cat, even if I don't like him all that much. *Cum* to the house. I made honey buns."

Alfie caught his breath. He and Benji smiled at each other. "With honey?"

"*Jah*, with real honey."

"Where do you want me to put this cat?" Benji said.

Bitsy pointed to the fields behind the barn. "He probably wants to hunt. Put him down anywhere. He always finds his way home. Well, almost always. Except this morning."

Benji relaxed his hold on the cat, and he immediately jumped from Benji's arms and bolted behind one of Bitsy's sheds.

Benji breathed a sigh of relief and Alfie put a brotherly arm around him. "You did a good job, Benji."

Benji grinned. "*Denki*. I didn't know this would be so hard."

"Don't dawdle," Bitsy said. "My honey buns will get stale."

Andrew had no intention of staying to eat honey buns. "We need to go. Mamm expects us home for dinner."

Alfie was a champion whiner. "Aw, come on, Andrew. Mamm won't care."

Bitsy wouldn't stop looking at Andrew, as if she was trying to read his mind. "So, Andrew Petersheim, you don't want to stay."

Of course he didn't want to stay. Mary Coblenz was

making him wonderful uncomfortable. "Mamm would be unhappy if they ruined their dinner."

Bitsy thought about that for a minute and nodded. "How is your *dawdi*?"

"He is coming along, but Mamm and Mammi still have to do most everything for him."

Would she quit looking at him like that? "Your mamm says she couldn't get along without you. She says you lift him out of bed every morning because your *dat* isn't strong enough. And you help him in the bathroom."

"He's my *dawdi*. For sure and certain he used to clean up after me."

Bitsy looked up into the sky. "*Denki*, Lord, that you never blessed me with boys. I wouldn't have any hair left to color." She finished her prayer—Bitsy was known for praying out loud—and looked at Andrew again. "How is your *mamm* doing with Martha?"

"She's doing just fine," Andrew said, because it was hard to explain the cookie sheets and the rose water, and Mamm wouldn't like it if Andrew thought she wasn't "doing fine."

Bitsy smirked. "*Ach, vell.* Tell her she's always welcome to come to my house and just sit. She'd have to put up with the cats, but at least the cats don't say anything."

Andrew didn't know quite what to say to that. Any reply would mean they'd have to have a conversation and stay longer than Andrew wanted to. He was feeling increasingly uncomfortable with Mary Coblenz, pregnant and standing not five feet away from him. "I'll tell her," he finally said. Bitsy could take that any way she wanted.

Benji took Andrew's hand. "Can't we stay?"

The boys were persistent, but they usually did what Andrew said when he was firm. Besides, they didn't want to risk Mamm's wrath. She truly would be irritated if they ruined their dinner. He shook his head. "Get in the buggy."

Both boys groaned as if they'd been asked to muck out the barn, but they turned and trudged up the lane, looking like scholars on the first day of school.

Andrew followed them, turning to give Bitsy and Mary a swift goodbye nod. He should have offered to carry that frame to the house. It was heavy, and Mary was in a family way. Even though he should have helped her, he couldn't regret getting out of there as quickly as possible. He didn't want to have anything to do with Mary Coblenz ever again.

He climbed in the buggy, turned Snapper around and down the lane, passing Bitsy and Mary one more time before he drove over the bridge and off Honeybee Farm.

Benji and Alfie were both beaming like a pair of headlights, as if they'd completely forgotten how dejected they were not two minutes ago.

"She's pretty. Don't you think she's pretty?"

Andrew wasn't about to admit anything like that. "Who, Bitsy? I like her blue hair, I guess."

Alfie rolled his eyes. "Not Bitsy. Mary. She's prettier than any girl in Bienenstock."

"Pretty is as pretty does," Andrew muttered.

Benji nudged the buggy floor with the toe of his foot. "You should take her to the *singeon*."

"You don't take a girl to a *singeon*," Andrew said.

Benji pulled back his sleeve and studied a small scratch on his wrist. "Then take her to the next gathering."

Andrew frowned. "It wouldn't be appropriate for Mary to go to a gathering."

"What does appropriate mean?"

"It means right or good." Neither of which applied to Mary.

"Why wouldn't it be appropriate?"

Benji asked too many questions. How could Andrew explain that it wasn't right for Mary to be seen in the community, broadcasting her sin like that, behaving as if she'd done nothing wrong? "It just wouldn't, that's all. Ask Mamm when we get home."

"Okay," Alfie said. "But when are you going to visit her again?"

Andrew jerked on the reins and almost ran the buggy off the side of the road. "Visit her? I'm not going to visit her."

"Why not?"

"Because I'm not."

Both Benji and Alfie eyed him with puzzled concern. "Don't you like her?" Benji said.

"Like her? Of course I don't like her."

"Not even a little?" Alfie asked.

Andrew shook his head. "Not even a little."

Unlike Alfie's fake tears, Benji never pretended to cry. That's why the water that pooled in his eyes surprised Andrew. "But she's so nice, and I got all these cat scratches."

"She's nice, Benji, but I don't want to ever talk to her again."

A small sob escaped Benji's throat. "Why not?"

Andrew wasn't quite sure why Benji was so upset, unless he liked honey buns a lot more than Andrew thought he did. He reached out and messed up Benji's already unruly hair. "She's a very nice girl and very pretty, but . . . I'm just not interested."

"Not interested?" Alfie's voice rose in pitch with every word. "After all that, you're not interested? What's wrong with you?" He stomped his foot on the floor of the buggy. "You are a *dumkoff*, Andrew. A *dumkoff*."

"That is uncalled for, young man." *Ach.* Andrew sounded like his *mater.*

"It's true," Alfie said, glaring at Andrew as if he'd taken the last helping of mashed potatoes. "Our air mattress is flat, there's a ghost in the cellar, and we could get eaten by spiders for all you care."

"Your air mattress is flat?"

Benji swiped a tear from his cheek. "I popped it with my fork."

"Did you tell Mamm?"

Alfie shook his head. "She'll get mad."

"I get hungry at night sometimes," Benji added, as if that explained everything.

Andrew hated to see his *bruderen* so upset, even if he wasn't quite sure of the reason. A flat air mattress had probably done it. "Okay, boys, I will come down after dinner to patch and fill your air mattress. But don't go poking it with any sharp objects."

Benji nodded, a look of earnest regret on his face.

"And I want both of you to stay away from Mary Coblenz. Do you understand?"

"But why?"

"I don't want you getting any ideas."

"Ideas about what?" Benji said.

"Just ideas."

Alfie would not be mollified. He folded his arms and stared out the side window. "I'm not giving up."

Benji looked at Alfie then at Andrew, scooted ever so slightly in Alfie's direction, and put his arm around his twin *bruder*. "Me neither."

Alfie's mouth twitched upward.

Andrew didn't like that expression. It always meant trouble.

# Chapter Four

Alfie sneaked a peek into Dawdi's room. Dawdi's eyes were open, even if it wasn't time for his nap to be over. He was awake!

Alfie motioned for Benji to follow, and they slid into the room and shut the door as quietly as possible. They'd have to hurry. Mammi Martha would be home from the store any minute now, and they needed to have a serious talk with Dawdi, and since Dawdi couldn't talk, it was going to take a long time.

"Hi, Dawdi," Benji whispered, as if trying not to wake him, even though he was already awake.

Dawdi turned his gaze in their direction and smiled.

"Hey, Alfie," Benji said, forgetting all about whispering. "He smiled. Did you see him smile?"

"Of course I did. I got eyes."

Benji got real close to the bed and laid a hand on Dawdi's arm. "Hey, Dawdi. You learned how to smile."

Alfie sidled next to Benji. "Do you know how to frown too?"

Dawdi's lips twitched, and he looked like he was

concentrating hard. His smile disappeared, but you couldn't exactly call his expression a frown.

"That's okay, Dawdi," Alfie said, taking his hand. "You're doing real *gute*."

Benji nodded. "Nobody needs to know how to frown anyway. It doesn't matter if you never learn how."

Alfie nudged Benji. "Don't say that. Mamm says we have to be encouraging." He looked at Dawdi. "You're going to learn how to frown, Dawdi. And then you'll learn how to walk and talk, and you can take us to the stream to hunt for pollywogs."

Dawdi smiled again. He was the best pollywog hunter in the family, even if he was really old.

Benji sniffled and rubbed his nose with the palm of his hand. If Benji started crying now, Dawdi would think he wasn't going to get better. They had to show him a *gute* face, like Mamm always said. Besides, they didn't have time for crying. Mammi would be home soon. Alfie stepped on Benji's foot. Hard.

"Ouch," Benji said, scowling like it was Alfie's fault he'd been about to ruin all of Dawdi's hopes and dreams. "Stop it, Alfie."

Alfie squeezed Dawdi's hand and pretended that Benji hadn't said anything. "We know you're going to learn how to talk, Dawdi, but we don't have time to wait for that. We need your help now. We want to find Andrew a wife so he'll move out and we don't have to sleep in the cellar."

Benji patted Dawdi's arm. "Even though it's your fault we have to sleep in the cellar, we don't want you to feel bad about it."

Alfie stomped on Benji's big toe.

Benji jumped and shoved Alfie away from him. "Stop that, Alfie."

They were wasting time, and they hadn't even asked Dawdi any questions yet. "Dawdi," Alfie said, rubbing the spot on his arm where Benji had shoved him, "we need to borrow your binoculars so we can find Andrew a wife. Is that okay?"

Benji nodded encouragingly. "Can you show us your answer in your eyes?"

Dawdi kept smiling, but Alfie couldn't tell if his eyes said yes or no. He turned to Benji. "What did he say?"

"I don't know."

"You said he sometimes gives you secret messages with his eyes."

"Sometimes," Benji said. "Not every time. It looks like he's saying 'I love you, Benji.' His eyes aren't saying anything about binoculars."

Sometimes Benji was not a *gute* partner.

Benji's face brightened like a shiny penny. He patted Dawdi's arm again. "Dawdi, we are going to ask you some questions. If the answer is yes, give us a smile. If the answer is no, give us a frown."

Alfie tried to step on Benji's foot again, but Benji was too quick and scooted it out of the way. "Benji," Alfie whispered through gritted teeth, "Dawdi doesn't know how to frown."

"But if he doesn't smile, we'll know it's supposed to be a frown."

Alfie furrowed his brow. That sort of made sense. "Okay, let's try a fake question first." He leaned on Dawdi's leg so he could look closely at his face. "Dawdi, is my name Captain Haddock?" Dawdi quit smiling, which was as good as a frown to Alfie. His heart beat faster.

"Dawdi," Benji said, "what is my name?"

Alfie growled. "It has to be yes or no, Benji. *Ach*, don't you know anything?"

"I forgot. Dawdi, did we catch a snake in your garden once?"

Dawdi burst into a smile. Alfie and Benji paused in silence, threw their arms around each other, and jumped up and down.

"Dawdi," Alfie said, "can we use your binoculars to find Andrew a wife?"

Another smile. They had their answer.

Benji scrunched his lips to one side of his face. "Are they in the shed at your old house?"

No smile. Uh-oh. Where were Dawdi's binoculars?

"Are they at our house?"

A smile.

"In this room?"

Dawdi's gaze traveled to the chest of drawers across from the bed. Benji searched through the drawers until he found Dawdi's huge pair of black binoculars. Alfie couldn't contain his excitement. He let out a war whoop and gave Dawdi a big hug.

Benji tried to stuff the binoculars into his pocket, but there was no way they were going to fit. They'd have to take their chances sneaking them into the cellar without being seen. They both kissed Dawdi on the cheek. "This will do the trick for sure and certain," Benji said, as they hurried to the door.

Alfie turned back. "Do you promise not to tell anybody, Dawdi, even when you learn how to talk?"

Dawdi had never smiled so wide.

* * *

Alfie's walkie-talkie crackled like a campfire. "Do you see her, Alfie? Pancake."

Alfie put his mouth right against the front of the walkie-talkie where all the dots were. "Benji, you have to hold down the button all the way before you talk. And you have to say *over*. Over." The lady at Walmart told them you had to say *over* so the person on the other walkie-talkie knew when you were done talking. It hadn't made sense to Benji. He wanted to say *pancake* instead because it was more like a secret code word, but how could they be real spies if Benji insisted on saying *pancake*? He sounded like a little kid.

Alfie shifted on his branch in the tree and tried to see through the binoculars while holding the walkie-talkie to his ear. There was silence on the other end. *Now* what was Benji doing?


The Memorial Day auction and bazaar was always a big day for Petersheim Brothers Peanut Butter. Andrew and family spent two solid weeks making peanut butter while also trying to sow the fields and keep the farm going. This year, with Mammi and Dawdi living with them, the days had been even longer and tempers had worn even thinner, especially Mamm's. She couldn't very well lash out at Mammi Martha when she was irritated, so she tended to take out her frustrations on her sons and the peanut butter. Andrew didn't mind it. If yelling at her sons helped Mamm keep her sanity, then let her yell.

Andrew loved Mammi Martha, but her rose water was, for sure and certain, a trial.

Andrew and Abraham quickly set up the blue canopy that they'd had specially printed in big vinyl letters: Petersheim Brothers Peanut and Almond Butter. The almond butter had been Austin's idea. He said it was the new, popular thing to eat among the Englisch. Once the canopy was up, Andrew, Abraham, and Austin set up their tables and arranged several jars of peanut and almond butter on the tablecloths.

"Slide the box under the tablecloth," Mamm said, fussing like a hen and smiling like a cat. "It looks better if there are levels." Mamm was in a very *gute* mood today. She loved market days, and they gave her an excuse to get out of the house. They'd left the grandparents home with Dat. Dawdi wouldn't have been able to sit through more than a few minutes of the bazaar.

Englisch and Amish alike flocked to the auction every year. The Englisch loved to buy anything Amish. Tourists came from out of state just to see what it was all about. Some Amish didn't like the tourists. They tended to be nosy and tried to take photos when they thought no one was looking. But tourists spent money, and like Mamm said, there was nothing wrong with that.

Something bright caught Andrew's eye, and his stomach churned as he turned to see Mary Coblenz in a sunny yellow dress, looking more pregnant than ever, pulling a wagon full of honey jars. She was as pretty and as appealing as the first time he'd seen her, as if she was a magnet that pulled Andrew into her orbit.

He shook his head to clear it. He shouldn't be thinking such thoughts about a pregnant girl. Mary was the one who should be ashamed. She should be sitting quietly at home reading the Bible and thinking upon her sins. She was going to make a lot of people uncomfortable today just by being here. Didn't she have any consideration for the feelings of others?

Andrew furrowed his brow. Bitsy and Yost Weaver trailed behind Mary empty-handed, with apparently nothing better to do than to let someone in her condition pull the heavy load. She was going to hurt herself, or possibly the *buplie*.

He took two steps toward her before he saw Junior and Ada Herschberger out of the corner of his eye. Ada and Junior didn't look as if they were selling anything at the bazaar today. Maybe they were just here to buy. Ada said something to her husband and pointed in Mary's direction, her eyes alight with indignation and . . . what was that emotion on her face? A gaping hole opened up in Andrew's stomach. Ada's expression looked almost gleeful, as if she rejoiced in Mary's sinful ways—or rejoiced in being better than the pregnant girl who'd come crawling back to the community. Ada's brother Perry Glick stood nearby, and he turned to stare at Mary as she walked past.

*Bruder* and *schwester* Sol and Treva Nelson were under the next canopy over helping their *dat* with his wooden baskets and Amish trinkets the Englisch liked so much. Treva nudged Sol with her elbow, and Andrew was close enough to hear her outrage. "How dare she show up here, as if she hadn't done nothing wrong?"

Sol froze when he saw Mary, as if, like Andrew, he

wasn't sure what he should do, then he looked away, pretending he hadn't seen her.

Treva didn't notice Sol's hesitation. "Does she think she has as much right to be here as decent people?" She smirked. "Because she's not decent people."

Heat traveled up Andrew's neck. He didn't know if he was more embarrassed for Mary or Treva. For sure and certain Mary had heard her. Treva had said it loud enough to carry into the next county. Maybe he didn't need to feel sorry for Mary. She had made the choice to come to the auction, and she had to expect that people were going to treat her like this.

Andrew pressed his lips together. Whether or not she deserved it, Andrew bristled at the looks people gave Mary and the whispered conversations that were taking place in plain sight. It seemed cruel and not at all what Jesus would do.

It was too much to hope that Mary hadn't noticed the disdain that was as thick as mosquitoes in springtime. Her steps faltered briefly as she scanned the crowd for a friendly face. Thank Derr Herr, she couldn't see Andrew lurking in the shadows of his canopy. She glanced behind her at Bitsy, who gave her a reassuring nod. Mary squared her shoulders and marched on, as if she was one of the martyrs going to her own execution.

Andrew took a halting step back. Would people think he approved of Mary if he helped her with her honey wagon? Would they whisper about him behind their hands and assume that he was a sinner because he'd helped? Every muscle in his body pulled taut as he balled his hands into fists and watched Mary drag that wagon over the dirt and through the gauntlet of disdainful gazes and scornful church members. What should he do? And why did his heart ache for a girl he barely knew and didn't want to have anything to do with?

To his utter relief and shame, his *bruder* Benji appeared right in Mary's path wearing no hat and a wide grin. Andrew was too far away to hear what Benji said to her, but he reached out his hand and took the handle of the wagon. Mary shook her head, but Benji smiled up at her and flexed his muscles. Mary's laughter tripped lightly over the breeze, and Andrew thought it was the happiest sound he'd ever heard. She pointed to one of the canopies a few hundred feet away, took Bitsy's arm, and let Benji lead the way. The wagon really was heavy. Benji strained to get it rolling but did okay once it was moving.

Andrew wanted to burst his buttons and then crawl under a rock. His eight-year-old *bruder* had shown more Christian kindness today than Andrew had ever seen and had made Andrew ashamed that he hadn't had the courage to do it first. No matter what Mary had done, he should have acted like a Christian. Benji was going to get as much ice cream as he wanted today, and Andrew didn't care if it ruined his dinner.

Andrew couldn't tear his gaze away as Benji pulled that wagon all the way to Bitsy's honey tent. Benji pulled a tiny, crushed wildflower from his pocket and gave it to Mary, who smiled as if he'd given her the world. Andrew could have had that smile, if he wanted it—which he didn't.

The sensation of warm syrup spread through Andrew's chest when Hannah and Mary Yutzy practically raced to Bitsy's honey tent and each gave Mary an enthusiastic hug. Hannah and Mary were the best kind of girls—maybe a little too loud—but friendly and kind to everyone, even pregnant girls who shouldn't have come today.

Neither Mamm nor his other *bruderen* had seen what had happened. Austin, who was the most excited about peanut butter, was laying crackers out on a plate while Abraham scooped samples of peanut butter into bowls so people could taste. Abraham seemed distracted by something across the way and accidentally dribbled some peanut butter on the tablecloth. Mamm swiftly wiped it up.

"Sorry, Mamm," Abraham said.

Mamm tossed the paper towel in the garbage. "No harm done. There's bound to be spills before the day is through."

She *was* in a good mood. Of course, Mamm was never as hard on Abraham. She didn't need to be. He was always so hard on himself.

"Mamm?" Benji wriggled between Andrew and Abraham, laid his hands flat on the table, and studied the identical jars of peanut butter as if deciding which one he wanted to buy. "Can I have a jar of peanut butter?"

"Your hands better be clean, young man, or get them off my tablecloth."

Andrew glanced at Benji's hands. There was black dirt under every nail, a scab on one of his index fingers, and blood seeping from under his thumbnail. Benji snatched his hands from the table and put them behind his back. "Mamm, can I have a jar of peanut butter?"

Mamm lifted an eyebrow. "You want a jar of peanut butter?"

"*Jah.* I want to give my friend a taste."

Mamm shook her head. "Oh, no, young man. I'm not wasting a whole jar of peanut butter so your friend can have a taste. You'll have to buy one like everybody else."

"But I don't have any money," Benji said. To his credit, there wasn't even a hint of a whine in his voice.

"Then your friend will just have to imagine what our peanut butter tastes like."

"But I want them to taste it."

"Bring him over here, and he can have a sample." Mamm held up her index finger. "One sample. That's all. And don't bring twenty hungry boys. One friend, one sample."

"But, Mamm . . ."

Andrew suspected he knew who Benji's "friend" was, and he still owed Benji his gratitude. "I'll buy Benji a jar," he said, fishing in his pocket for the twenty-dollar bill he had there.

Mamm shrugged. "It's your money."

Benji looked up at Andrew and there was so much happiness in his face, Andrew couldn't help but smile. He gave Mamm the money, she gave him his change, and Mamm let Benji pick which jar he wanted, which took way longer than it needed to since they were all the same. With jar in hand, Benji shoved his way past his *bruderen* in the direction of Bitsy's honey tent. Maybe Mary would be impressed with their peanut butter. Maybe she wouldn't. It didn't matter to Andrew.

After twenty minutes of selling jars of peanut butter, Andrew got curious about Benji. Why hadn't he come back yet? Where was Alfie? Did Mary like the peanut butter? He'd better at least check on his *bruder* to make sure he wasn't making a pest of himself with Bitsy. "Mamm," he said, "I'm going to have a look around."

"Be back for the lunch rush."

Many of the Amish and some of the tourists bought a block of cheese or a loaf of bread and a jar of peanut butter to eat for lunch. People always wanted their smaller jars for lunch.

Andrew stepped out from under the shade of the canopy and tightened his jacket around him. It was only Memorial Day, and the air was still a little chilly. The auction would be going on all day in the big field to the west. They sold everything from livestock to farm implements to quilts.

Andrew glanced in the direction of Bitsy's canopy. Bitsy was there with her husband, Yost, and two of her nieces, but Mary and Benji were gone. Andrew strolled to Bitsy's canopy, trying not to act too eager. Benji shouldn't be alone with Mary. She was a bad influence.

*Ach, vell,* Mary didn't seem like a bad person, but Andrew didn't want Benji getting any ideas about marriage and babies and what order they were supposed to come in. It might confuse Benji that sin could wear a pretty face and seem perfectly nice even when it wasn't. Benji needed to understand that wickedness made you miserable, and Mary didn't seem miserable at all. It was too much for one little boy to sort out.

Andrew ducked into Bitsy's canopy. Her niece Poppy had a small child in her arms and was expecting another one. Rose, the youngest Christner *schwester,* was also expecting, and it looked to be any day now.

What was it about Bitsy and expectant mothers? Did she collect them like stamps?

"Hello, Andrew," Rose said. She was practically glowing.

"Hello, Rose. How's Josiah doing?"

"He's growing some sunflowers this year, if you're interested. Mashed sunflower seeds make a *gute* spread."

Andrew nodded. Mamm might be interested, but Andrew definitely was not. He needed less nut butter in his life, not more. "Bitsy, have you seen Benji?"

Bitsy was making faces at the toddler in Poppy's arms. Her hair was purple today and there was a tattoo of a daisy on her neck. "He and Mary went to buy a pretzel. They took a jar of honey and a jar of peanut butter with them."

That might be relatively harmless, but Benji shouldn't get attached to Mary. "Okay. *Denki.*" Andrew turned to look for the pretzel stand. He could peel Benji from Mary's side and give him a lecture about not hanging out with unsavory individuals.

Bitsy stood up straight and eyed Andrew as if she'd just now noticed him. "You're nice enough, Andrew Petersheim, but sometimes you should look past the end of your nose."

Andrew frowned. He didn't understand half the things people said to him nowadays. "Okay," he said, because everybody knew Bitsy was odd.

Bitsy waved her hand in no direction in particular. "Benji and Mary went that way. I hope you find them."

He walked in the direction of the heavenly smell of pretzels, but Mary and Benji weren't anywhere to be seen. Andrew stood with his thumbs hooked around his suspenders and surveyed the crowd. Where had they gone?

A small body crashed into him and knocked his breath away. "Alfie, watch where you're going. What's the big hurry?"

Alfie snatched Andrew's hand. "You've got to hurry. Benji and Mary are sitting over there at the picnic table. I told Benji he was supposed to stay away from Mary, and he said he didn't care if he got all sorts of ideas because you couldn't stop him."

Andrew narrowed his eyes. That ungrateful little trickster. After Andrew had bought him a whole jar of peanut butter, no less. "Show me."

Alfie pulled him around the back of the Yutzys' pretzel and donut stand where six or seven picnic tables sat under a stand of trees. Mary and Benji sat at the farthest table eating a pretzel. Andrew would deal with Benji right quick.

He strode toward the table but had second thoughts about halfway there. He didn't want to offend Mary, and he certainly didn't want to hurt her feelings. Maybe she'd had enough pain for one day. All he had to do was sit and wait for Benji to finish his pretzel and then casually coax him from Mary's table and back to the Petersheim Brothers Peanut Butter canopy. Nothing could be easier. Mary wouldn't suspect a thing.

She looked up as he approached, with the guarded expression she'd worn the last time they'd parted. Well then. How did she expect people to react to her? She was the one who was pregnant. He'd done nothing wrong.

Benji's back was to Andrew. "You take a piece of pretzel," Benji said, tearing off a section of the pretzel that sat between them on the table. "Then you dip it

in the peanut butter and then the honey, like this."
With those grimy hands, Benji dipped the pretzel
into the open jar. It came out thick with peanut
butter. Then he dipped it into the honey. Some of the
peanut butter got left behind in the honey jar, but
Mary didn't seem to notice. She also didn't seem to
notice the sticky, gooey honey trickling down Benji's
hand as he handed Mary his messy pretzel concoc-
tion. She popped it into her mouth without even
stopping to consider where those hands had been.

"Mmm," she said, closing her eyes and savoring
her mouthful. "*Appeditlich.* I love crunchy peanut
butter."

"We make creamy too. Alfie likes creamy. I like
crunchy."

Alfie pulled Andrew to sit next to Benji at the
picnic table across from Mary. Then Alfie went
around the table and sat next to her. "Are you one of
the Honeybee Sisters now?" he asked. "Because we're
called the Peanut Butter Brothers. It's like we're
family."

"I like that," Mary said. She tore off two pieces of
pretzel and handed one to each of the twins. "Try it."

Benji and Alfie dug right in, making sure they got
generous helpings of peanut butter and honey before
popping the pretzels into their mouths.

Mary ripped off a bigger piece and held it out for
Andrew, smiling at him as if she harbored no ill will
toward him. "Do you want to try it?"

He scrunched his lips to one side. "I don't think
so. I can guess where Benji's hands have been."

She clicked her tongue at him. "Dirt gives it extra
flavor. Don't be such a scaredy-cat."

He grunted. "I'm not going to risk a stomachache just to prove my manhood."

"Come on, Andrew," Benji said. "It's really good with Honeybee Sisters honey."

Mary daintily dipped the pretzel into the peanut butter and honey, then leaned over the table. "Open up."

Completely disarmed and more than a little unnerved, Andrew opened his mouth, and Mary stuffed the pretzel into his mouth. His pulse quickened, and he could hear his heartbeat inside his head. No wonder his first impulse was to avoid her. Mary Coblenz felt like trouble—right down to his bones.

He stood so fast, he cracked his knee on the table leg. Ignoring the pain, he said, "It's time to go back. We've got to help Mamm with the lunch rush."

Benji stuffed another piece of pretzel into his mouth. "Thust a bimute, Anbew."

"Don't talk with your mouth full." Yep, he was definitely turning into his *mater*.

Alfie grabbed Mary's hand. "We can't go back yet. We have to show Mary something."

Andrew tried to subtly massage his knee while Mary wasn't looking. "You can show her another time. We have to get back."

Alfie was already on his feet, pulling Mary along with him toward one of the bigger tents. Alfie and Benji were oblivious to the sideways glances and veiled hostility that followed them as they walked alongside Mary, each holding one of her hands. How many steps behind could Andrew walk without being rude? He didn't want people to get the wrong idea about him and Mary. He didn't want people to get *any* idea about him and Mary. They certainly weren't friends. They weren't even really acquaintances. Surely people knew him well enough to know he'd never associate with someone like her—so obviously wicked and shamelessly unrepentant.

Andrew was more than puzzled when he realized exactly where they were headed. From a safe distance, he followed Mary and the twins into the large tent where chairs and tables, desks and chests were waiting to be auctioned off. There toward the back, sitting next to a cradle, was Andrew's little piece of woodwork. How had Alfie and Benji known, when Andrew hadn't even had the courage to tell Mamm and Dat?

Benji pointed to the child-sized chair that Andrew had spent two weeks making in his little shop in the barn. He'd sanded it so smooth that no child would ever get a sliver, and the deep walnut stain made the chair seem to glow from the inside. He'd finished it two days ago and asked Luke Bontrager to bring it to the auction for him.

"Andrew made it," Alfie said.

"*Ach, du lieva,*" Mary whispered. Despite her condition, she knelt down beside his chair and ran her fingers along the curved armrests. "Andrew, it is beautiful."

His heart banged around in his chest and nearly came up his throat. "It's not much."

"Not much?" she said. "Andrew, it's *wunderbarr.*"

Even though he was trying to remember she was a sinner—and a big one—a ribbon of warmth curled around Andrew's gut and pulled itself tight. It shouldn't matter what Mary thought of his chair, because he was determined to avoid her from now on and forever. But the way she almost reverently stroked the seat and ran her fingers along the spindles made him think that maybe she was being completely sincere and maybe he did have some skill after all. Maybe he could make a living making furniture instead of peanut butter, and maybe Mamm wouldn't even dream of being cross with him about it.

"Andrew sneaks in the barn every night and makes stuff," Alfie said.

"Don't rattle on like that, Alfie."

"But it's true. The window in the cellar . . ." Alfie's voice trailed off to nothing, as if he'd forgotten what he was going to say.

How did he know such things? Mamm knew about Andrew's tools, but she didn't know how many hours he spent shaping scraps of wood into something beautiful. She didn't pay attention to the times he'd gone to Luke Bontrager's workshop to use the power tools. She just didn't know.

Mary's face clouded with concern. What had brought on that reaction? "You sneak?"

"I don't really sneak, but Mamm thinks it's a waste of time. I don't want to have to explain to her every time I go out."

Alfie walked all the way around the chair as if he was inspecting it. "He doesn't want Mamm and Dat to know about it."

Mary nodded, never taking her eyes from his face. Her gaze was a little unnerving. "Sometimes it's hard with parents. I can understand that."

She didn't think that her situation and his were similar, did she? She'd run off and gotten herself in trouble. Her parents were understandably upset. Mamm wanted his mind on peanut butter, not wood-working. He didn't want her to be mad, so he kept it from her.

Mary ran her hand along the back of the chair. "You have real skill, Andrew."'

He hung his head like any man would do who was tempted to be proud. "I'm nothing, really. Luke Bontrager makes chests and tables and rockers."

"I'm only being honest. Honesty is not a sin, Andrew."

"Pride is."

Benji sat on the ground with Mary. "Andrew made me a box for my rock collection."

"Did he?"

"*Jah.* It has a secret way to open it."

Mary smiled. "I'm sure he's very clever."

It alarmed Andrew that he liked that smile so much. He cleared his throat and pushed away that warm, fuzzy feeling that threatened to overcome his *gute* sense. He and the boys shouldn't even be talking to Mary. They were all going to stay away from her, starting now. "We need to go. It's almost the lunch rush."

Alfie made a face. "Abraham and Austin are there. We'd only be in the way."

Andrew couldn't look Mary in the eye. "Mamm needs us back for the lunch rush."

Mary's smile faltered. Andrew didn't know how he knew, but Mary saw right through his ploy. Guilt nagged at him like a pesky mosquito. Fortunately, the buzzing was faint and easy to ignore.

"*Denki* for showing me Andrew's chair, and *denki*

for teaching me the secret trick of the peanut butter and honey." She held out her hand to Benji, and they shook on it as if they were doing a business deal.

Benji shrugged. "That's not really a secret trick, but most people don't know about it. Alfie made it up."

She shook Alfie's hand as well. "*Denki* for making up the secret peanut butter and honey trick. I'll never eat my pretzels the same way again." She was still sitting on the ground next to Andrew's chair. Taking a deep breath, she squared her shoulders. "Leave now, and I will count to twenty—no, thirty—before I come out. That way no one will know that we were in here talking together. I'll even take the long way around to Bitsy's tent. Then no one will suspect we even know each other." Andrew hadn't felt this ashamed since Mammi Martha had caught him dumping her asparagus casserole in the garbage. The shame was worse because there was a small part of him that felt relief at not being forced to walk all the way to the Petersheim Brothers Peanut Butter tent in the company of Mary Coblenz—the pregnant, un-married girl who couldn't seem to muster any shame for herself.

"But, Mary," Benji said, his gaze flicking in Andrew's direction, "we can't leave you. Mamm says you're in a delicate condition."

Mary studied Benji's face, perhaps wondering what else Mamm had said about her. "Do you know what that means, Benji?"

Andrew had to put a stop to this conversation. The twins might get the idea that it was normal to be preg-nant. *Ach, vell,* of course it was normal to be pregnant. Lots of women were pregnant, but it would be best not to give Alfie and Benji any ideas. "We need to go."

"I know what a delicate condition means," Benji said, loud enough that the few people milling about the tent paused and perked up their ears while pretending not to listen.

"We are not going to talk about this," Andrew hissed, but Benji didn't seem to hear him. He probably had too much dirt in his ears, even though Mammi Martha had bought each of them their own special washcloth.

Benji only knew how to speak at one volume, and it was not soft. "It means you're going to have a *buplie*, and Mamm says it's a disgrace that your *mamm* won't take care of you. She thinks I don't listen." Benji squinted out of one eye. "But I don't know what *disgrace* means."

Andrew was taken aback. That was Mamm's opinion of Mary's *mater*? Didn't she think Mary should be punished for her sins?

Mary's face turned a dark shade of red, sweat beaded on her upper lip, and she pressed her lips together as if she'd never speak again. Andrew barely knew Mary. He'd spent maybe twenty minutes with her altogether, but this was the first time he'd seen her genuinely upset.

Benji scrunched his lips like a prune. "Who's going to help you off the ground? You're too fat to get up yourself."

One side of Mary's mouth curled upward. "I'll try not to be offended." She held out her hands to Benji and Alfie. Benji jumped to his feet, and the twins each took one of her arms to pull her up.

Andrew nudged Benji and Alfie away. "Stop, stop. Someone's going to get hurt." He braced his feet and took Mary's hands in his. They were surprisingly soft.

That ribbon of warmth around his gut returned with a vengeance, and he found it nearly impossible to draw a breath. He yanked more than pulled Mary to her feet. Even as pregnant as she was, she hardly weighed a thing. Was she getting enough to eat? She had to think of the *buplie* as well as herself now.

Andrew clamped his teeth together. No good would come of worrying about Mary's baby. Mary was obviously someone who could take care of herself. Besides, she lived with Bitsy Weaver. Bitsy wouldn't let her starve, and she would give away all her cats before she let any harm come to that baby.

"*Denki,*" Mary said, her expression guarded as she smoothed her hands down her apron and straightened her dress. "Now you go along. I promise not to follow you."

Andrew felt like a jerk, but if Mary was going to make it easy for him, he'd be a fool not to take the opportunity. "*Cum,* boys."

Alfie folded his arms across his chest. "We wait for Mary."

It was the right thing to do, and Andrew knew it. Was he more concerned about reinforcing *gute* manners for his *bruderen* or about how he looked to the *gmayna*? Unfortunately he had to pick one or the other. Why were his *bruderen* doing this to him? And why had they chosen Mary as their method of torture?

Mary, Benji, and Alfie stared at him, unmoving like a trio of statues, and he felt more than a little perturbed. Alfie wasn't going to budge, Benji looked as if he wouldn't be persuaded, and Mary seemed curious but not particularly concerned either way. His *mamm* had taught him to watch out for those who were weaker than he, but she had also taught him to avoid sin and stay away from bad company. What would she want him to do?

He knew that answer without even thinking about it. *Always do unto others, Andrew, as you would want them to do to you.* He'd never be pregnant and unmarried, but he was pretty sure what he should do anyway. "Come back with us, Mary. You don't want to miss the lunch rush."

Alfie and Benji whooped like something amazing had just happened, and Andrew told them to hush, as they had already drawn the attention of every person in the tent.

A smile grew on Mary's lips like a sunrise, gradual and stunning. "I don't think the honey tent has a lunch rush."

"Come to ours," Benji said, as if he was inviting her to a party.

They paraded out of the tent, Mary and Benji in the lead, Andrew and Alfie behind. It was all Andrew could do to hold his head high. He'd made his choice. He'd live with the consequences.

A thick, chunky chest of drawers stood near the exit, and Andrew heard a thump as Mary's foot knocked into it. She gasped and hurried from the tent. Hissing in pain, she limped around and around as if the quick movement made her foot feel better.

"What happened?" Benji asked.

Without stopping her little walk of pain, Mary took four or five deep breaths and winced with every step. "I stubbed my toe something wonderful."

Andrew would have to help. She was going to fall over and really injure herself. He cupped his hand around her elbow and led her to the nearest place to sit, which providentially happened to be on a long crate sitting just behind the furniture tent. No one would notice them there. He could be a Good Samaritan and help Mary, and no one in the *gmayna* would have to know.

Benji and Alfie followed them as Andrew led Mary to the crate and helped her sit down. Alfie pointed to her foot. "Look, Mary, you're bleeding," he said, as if her injury was better than an ice cream cone. Little boys were like that. Blood was always a cause for excitement.

Andrew knelt on the ground to get a better look. Her pinky toe stuck out from her foot at an awkward angle and it looked like the entire nail had been ripped clean off. It oozed with deep, red blood, and the skin around her toe had already started turning purple. "Oy, anyhow, Mary. I think you broke it."

Andrew frowned. She should have been wearing shoes. And a sweater. A woman with child should always bundle up and wear shoes.

She took several deep breaths, propped her elbow on her knee, and cradled her head in her hand, taking a peek at her foot. "*Ach, du lieva.*" She pressed her fingers to her forehead and closed her eyes, obviously concentrating on the pain. It must have been excruciating.

Alfie and Benji both leaned in for a closer look. "That's a lot of blood," Benji said. "Does it hurt?"

"Terrible," Mary said breathlessly.

Benji bit his bottom lip. "We should take you to the hospital."

"I can't walk just yet, Benji, but I don't think I'll need a hospital."

"We should get Mamm," Benji said.

Mary still had her head buried in her hands. "It's

okay, Benji. Once the pain dies down, I'll only need a Band-Aid."

"And some Motrin," Andrew said. "It's going to hurt something wonderful. And you'll need to wrap it in some gauze. Alfie, go see if they have a first aid kit at the pretzel stand."

Alfie poked Benji in the ribs. "We'll go find a first aid kit, but it might take us a very, very long time. You two will have to sit here and wait for us and talk." Benji glanced at Alfie, and they burst into smiles as if it was the first day of summer vacation. They didn't have to be so happy about it. A broken toe might be something to brag about to your friends, but Mary wouldn't be smiling anytime soon.

"Hurry as fast as you can. If they don't have a first aid kit at the pretzel stand, ask someone else. Maybe Mamm brought hers."

The boys strolled away, apparently with nowhere important to go. What was wrong with them? They liked Mary. They should have been in a great hurry to help her out. "Alfie, Benji," Andrew barked. "Hurry it up."

His brothers looked back, glanced at each other, and took off running. At least they still obeyed him when it was urgent.

Andrew eyed Mary's face. "Do you mind if I have a closer look?"

She shook her head, still cradled in her hands. "Just don't do any poking without warning me."

"I'm just going to see . . ." She winced as he took her foot in his hands. "Sorry." Her foot was ice-cold, which was only to be expected on a cool day. The nail was halfway off. It would have to be ripped out the rest of the way if she didn't want to risk catching it on things. "Do you want me to pop your toe back into place?"

She didn't lift her head. "It sounds so innocent."

"It will hurt worse than when you stubbed it."

She wryly curled one side of her mouth. "Why would I want you to do that?"

"*Vell,* it's quick and you wouldn't have to go to a doctor."

"I'm not going to a doctor."

Andrew nodded. "Then you have two choices."

"Which are?"

"Let me pop it into place or walk funny the rest of your life."

She looked up into the sky as if weighing her options. "*Ach.* I think I'm going to cry, it hurts so bad. It might be worth walking funny. I already waddle like a duck."

He pressed his lips together to stifle an unwanted smile. "I think that is a temporary condition of being with child."

She grunted. "I hope so."

He sat with her foot cupped in his hand and watched several emotions play on her face, the chief one being pain. He hated to see anyone in pain, even Mary Coblenz. He rubbed his other hand up and down the front of her ankle, hoping to soothe some of her discomfort.

She tensed and sat up straight. "You seem very confident in your ability to fix my toe, Andrew Petersheim. How do I know I can trust you?"

"When I was fourteen, I popped Abraham's middle toe back into place. He'd been jumping from the haymow when Mamm had warned him not to. Then last year, Alfie dislocated his finger trying to open the window to sneak out of the house. You just pull real hard until you hear a pop. Works every time."

Mary grimaced. "Oy, anyhow. I think I'm going to be sick."

He sat next to her on the crate. "Do you need a drink?"

"Of course I need a drink." She buried her face in her hands once again and her next words were muffled. "A *gute*, stiff drink." She lifted her head and gave him a pained smile. "I didn't mean it. That foolishness is definitely in the past."

He had no idea what she was talking about. "I'll find a water bottle."

She grabbed his wrist before he could leave. "*Nae*, don't go. I think you should pop my toe back into place before it heals wrong."

"You want me to do it?"

She took a deep breath. "*Jah*, but please don't mess up. I'd rather not be a cripple."

"I don't think you'd be crippled. You probably wouldn't miss your toe even if they had to amputate it. Mahlon Zook lost three of his toes in a threshing accident and—"

She held up her hand. "Maybe you can tell me the story later. My head is already spinning."

"Okay. Sorry."

"I have a low pain threshold. At least that's what Josh told me."

"What does that mean?" And who was Josh?

"It means I don't endure pain well."

Andrew shrugged. "You're doing fine. I think my head would be spinning too." He knelt down on the ground and lifted Mary's foot.

"Wait!" she yelled. "Tell me before you do it."

"Of course."

She made a face. "Don't say *of course*, like you weren't going to do it without warning me."

He couldn't help but chuckle. Mary wasn't afraid to say exactly what she thought, but she wasn't rude about it. She was in pain, that was plain enough, but she was handling the situation with good humor, almost as if she was laughing at herself, even through her discomfort. Well, she wasn't laughing at herself now, but Andrew could see that she was the type of person who would laugh about it later, and thank him profusely for the pain he was about to cause her.

He crossed his legs and set Mary's heel on his knee, examining it closely for the best way to grip it so that he could do the job quickly and with the least amount of discomfort to her. There was too much blood. "I can't get a good grip on it. The blood makes it slippery."

She huffed out a breath and fished inside her apron pocket. "Will this do?" She pulled out a crinkled tissue and handed it to him.

"That should do the trick." He wrapped the tissue carefully, painstakingly around her toe. It soaked up the blood and lent enough friction to make his grip nice and secure.

"*Ach*," she shouted, nearly jerking her foot from his grasp. "Don't do it until you warn me."

He lifted an eyebrow. "Of course."

She narrowed her eyes. "Of course."

He gently wrapped his fingers around her toe. She winced and braced her hands on the crate. "This is going to hurt something wonderful," he said. "You might want to scream, but if you could hold it in, that would be better. I don't want to alarm anyone."

She made another, more comical face. "I won't promise anything. I'll probably scream, just to warn you. We can tell people it was a passing chicken."

"A passing chicken?"

"Those passing chickens are real squawkers."

"I'm going to do it now," he said, tightening his grip on her toe.

She nodded and drew in a deep breath. *Ach*, this was going to hurt. He squeezed her toe hard so it couldn't slip out of his fingers and yanked it in the direction it was supposed to point. Andrew both heard and felt the toe pop back into place.

Mary gasped and pain traveled across her face like a bull charging across the plains. She took a full minute to speak. "Is it done?" she asked, her voice trembling like a match in the wind.

"It's done, and I didn't do half bad."

"I like your confidence. It makes a patient feel secure." Once again, Mary slumped over and held her head in her hands as if her neck didn't have the strength to hold it up.

"Do you want that drink now?"

"That would be *gute.*"

Andrew ducked into the furniture tent and asked Mahlon Mast for a bottle of water. Mahlon handed him one without even asking why.

Andrew hurried out to Mary, who was leaning back on her hands and looking at her toe. "It's a mess."

"How does it feel?"

"Awful. But I feel better knowing it's fixed. At least you got it pointing in the right direction." Andrew handed her the bottle of water, and she took a long, thirsty swig. "I don't even want to think about having to tear out that toenail. Maybe I'll leave that for another day. Would you pour water on my toe, try to wash off some of the blood?"

Andrew knelt down and let the water trickle over Mary's foot. She winced, and he pulled back. She shook her head. "You have to do it, even though it stings something wonderful."

He kept pouring until half the bottle was gone. It didn't seem to make much difference with the blood. It was already too caked on to wash off with a little water. Andrew put the lid back on the bottle and handed it to Mary. "When the boys get back, we can wash it better with a piece of gauze and some soap. Or we might have to soak it."

She got another funny look on her face. She must have hundreds of funny looks for several different occasions. "I don't think *die kinner* will be back for quite some time."

"I told them to hurry."

"*Jah*, you did." She winced again and placed a hand on her abdomen.

"Did the water make it worse?"

Mary shook her head. "It's the *buplie*. She's kicking me. In all the fuss, I think I made her mad."

Andrew didn't know what to say—didn't want to have to say anything. He stood up and turned his face from Mary, as if he were watching intently for his *bruderen* to return with that . . . what was it they were bringing? The first aid kit. For Mary's foot. Mary, the unwed pregnant girl.

"You don't have to act that way, Andrew. I'm going to have a baby. You know it, and I know it. What's the use in ignoring it?"

Andrew refused to look at her. "I suppose you can't ignore it, but you shouldn't be proud of it either."

"Andrew," Mary said, the exasperation evident in her voice, "look at me."

"I should go see where the boys have gone."

Mary stood up and gathered the fabric of Andrew's sleeve in her fist. She shouldn't be standing up. She was going to hurt her toe. "Sit down and talk to me, and for goodness' sake, look me in the eye like I'm a normal person instead of a vile sinner."

He snapped his head around to look at her. Maybe she was more willing to own up to her sins than he had expected she'd be. "So you admit you're a sinner."

"Absolutely."

"Then why don't you act like one?"

Mary's eyes grew as round as dinner plates, and she gaped at Andrew with pure disbelief on her face. He frowned back. Was this all a joke to her? A giggle tripped from her lips. "Did you hear what you said?"

"Sin is nothing to laugh about."

She didn't seem to care. The giggle turned into laughter, rich, unbridled laughter that she couldn't seem to stop. She stepped back to keep her balance, inadvertently putting weight on her injured foot. She winced, sucked in a breath, and plopped down hard on the crate.

Andrew anxiously slid next to her. "Are you okay?"

Breathing heavily, she propped her ankle on her knee and made a face that landed somewhere between agony and amusement. "*Ach, du lieva.* I shouldn't have done that."

"You need to be more careful of your toe."

She took a few seconds to catch her breath, then carefully examined her foot. "It's your fault, you know."

"My fault?"

"You shouldn't have made me laugh. I forgot about my toe for a minute, and it led to disaster."

He raised his eyebrows. "It's not my fault if you take your sins lightly."

Mary sighed, as if she was barely keeping her patience with him. "You said I should act like a sinner. It struck my funny bone. How would you suggest I act like a sinner?"

Andrew puzzled over that for a second. "I suppose that came out the wrong way. I only meant that you should act sorry for your sins."

She puckered her lips and eyed him as if he were a magazine salesman. Another one of her faces. "*Ach, vell*, I am sorry, for sure and certain, but I've never been a good actor."

How could he make her understand? "But you're so cheerful all the time, as if you're happy that you sinned."

She huffed out a breath. "It's useless to try to make any of you understand, but I see repentance as a gift, not a burden. Jesus has washed away my sins. It makes me happy."

She was right. He didn't understand. Of course Jesus washed away her sins, but sin never was happiness.

But what did it matter? He never had to talk to her again after today. Let her go on wallowing in her sin, and he would go on living his life as if he'd never met her. She was just another girl in the *gmayna* like the dozens of other girls who held no interest for him. Her eyes were bluer and her hair more golden than any of the other girls, but that didn't mean he couldn't ignore her. Mary Coblenz was trouble, and Andrew steered clear of trouble.

He stood and looked around the corner of the tent. "Where are those boys?"

Mary lightly brushed some dirt from her injured foot and tried to wiggle her toes. She winced and gritted her teeth.

"*Ach*, Mary. We need that first aid kit."

"A few pain pills might be nice." She glanced in the direction the twins had gone. Had they taken a buggy to Walmart? "My *schwester* Suvilla broke her finger once, and the doctor taped it to the next one over. I think if Benji and Alfie ever come back, we should tape my pinky toe to the next one."

"That's a *gute* idea."

Andrew didn't want to talk about sin or repentance or *buplies* anymore. Those subjects were better left for *gmay* and the ministers. Instead, while they waited, he told Mary about the time Abraham slammed his finger in the door and about the summer when Austin was attacked by a swarm of yellow jackets. She made more than one funny face and smiled a dozen times.

He was glad he could help keep her mind off the pain.

A girl with that pretty of a smile was going to be wonderful hard to ignore.


"What are they doing now? Pancake."

Lying flat on his stomach on one of the lower branches of the maple tree, Alfie clamped the thick antenna of the walkie-talkie in his teeth to free his hands for one more look in the binoculars. Andrew helped Mary from the crate. They were on the move.

Alfie let the binoculars dangle from the strap

around his neck and grabbed the walkie-talkie. "I think they've given up waiting for us. Time to move in. Over."

No reply. Benji got easily distracted.

"Benji? Are you there? Over."

*Crackle, crackle.* "This first aid kit is heavy. Pancake." It sounded like he was in a cave.

"Hurry. They're done talking. Over."

The walkie-talkie slipped out of Alfie's hand and fell to the ground, landing in a patch of weeds. He should get a strap for that too. He didn't have money to buy another one. He lifted the binoculars to his eyes. Mary and Andrew were gone. Alfie searched the surrounding area but couldn't see them. *Ach.* Benji had been too slow. If he had arrived in time with the first aid kit, Andrew would have had a chance to fix Mary's toe. That would have made her fall in love with him for sure and certain. Lord willing, they had gotten more than enough time to get to know each other. Alfie wouldn't be surprised if Andrew was taking Mary to the Petersheim Brothers tent right now to introduce her to Mamm and set a wedding date.

Ach, *Andrew, she is the perfect girl for you,* Mamm would say. *We'll have fireworks for your wedding. And she's going to have a baby! Think of the time that will save. I'll plant a whole patch of celery, and as soon as the wedding is over, we'll move Alfie and Benji out of the cellar.*

It was obvious that Gotte wanted Alfie and Benji to get their room back. Hadn't He made Mary stub her toe at just the right moment?

The plan was working nicely.

Now it was time to work on Abraham and Austin.

Gotte helped those who helped themselves.

# Chapter Five

Alfie sat on the air mattress, his arms folded tightly around his chest, his eyes fixed on the dark shadows directly in front of him. Mamm had scolded him when she had to change the batteries on the lantern for the third time, but Alfie couldn't care less—or could care less—he never knew which was right, but tonight he could care less or couldn't—who cared? If Mamm didn't want him using up all the lantern batteries, she shouldn't have put him and Benji in the cellar. But she couldn't care less about her youngest sons. Why should Alfie care any more . . . or less?

Alfie would have slept with the lantern on all night to keep the spiders away, but he was beginning to wonder if the light attracted the bugs instead of scaring them. There were already four moths fluttering around his lantern, and that was inside the house. He'd watched a spider crawl up the wall two minutes ago, but hadn't dared get out of bed to smash it. Didn't Mamm even care that they were going to be eaten by a giant butterfly or caught in a spider's web?

For sure and certain, some spider would suck out all of Alfie's blood before Mamm came down to wake him in the morning.

How could Benji sleep at a time like this? Their plan wasn't working out at all, and Benji slept as if all their older *bruderen* were already engaged. Benji gave a little snort and rolled over. Alfie wouldn't stand for it. He poked Benji, being careful not to knock him off the air mattress. They'd ended up with a hole the last time Benji had fallen off.

Benji rolled over again and scratched his nose, but he didn't wake up. Alfie poked him harder.

"Hey," Benji said, his eyes still closed. "What are you doing?"

"Wake up, Benji. We need another plan."

Benji propped himself on his elbow and rubbed his eyes. "I don't have any more money."

Alfie groaned. "We don't need more money. We need to make a plan."

Benji sat up and reached for the stack of nine shiny cookie sheets on his side of the bed. The stack was sort of Benji's nightstand. He'd put a plate of cookies there after dinner for a midnight snack. Benji grabbed two cookies—peanut butter—and gave one to Alfie. "I thought we already had a plan."

Alfie took a big, mad bite out of his cookie. "It didn't work. Andrew isn't even close to being engaged."

"For sure and certain, I thought the pretzels and peanut butter would work."

"She really liked Andrew's chair yet."

Benji nibbled on his cookie. He liked to make it last, even if he had three more sitting on Mammi Martha's cookie sheets. "When Mary stubbed her toe, I thought we had them for sure."

"But you got there late. She would have fallen in love with him if he'd fixed her toe."

Benji frowned until his bottom lip stuck out. "It was heavy, and I had to carry it all the way from the buggy."

"Well, it made things worse. Andrew says we are never to talk to Mary again, and if we see her coming, we're supposed to run away."

Benji scratched his head and watched Alfie through bleary eyes. "Where does he want us to run away to?"

"He's such a *dumkopf* sometimes."

"He fixed our air mattress," Benji said.

"He might be nice, but he is still a *dumkopf*." Mamm would have given him the spatula if she had heard Alfie call his *bruder* bad names. Alfie couldn't have cared less. He was madder than a hen in the river.

"What should we do now? We could try to find a wife for Abraham."

Alfie finished off his cookie and did some deep thinking while he chewed. "I'm not giving up on Andrew yet. I want him to marry Mary."

"She doesn't talk to us like we're little kids."

Alfie nodded. They wanted to get their room back, but Mary as a sister-in-law would be a nice benefit. "There's a gathering next week. People fall in love at gatherings all the time."

"How will we get Andrew to go? He thinks he's too old."

Alfie sighed clear down to his toes. He didn't want to have to do this, but they were desperate, and another spider was crawling across the floor straight toward their bed. "We're going to have to get Mammi Martha."

* * *

Mary sat in Bitsy's buggy, took a deep breath, and let the air seep from her lips as her shoulders sagged. She could still go home. She certainly didn't have to subject herself to the humiliation.

Bitsy held the reins at the ready and stared at Mary. "You don't have to go, you know."

"I know."

"Some of them will be very nice, but others will try very hard to make you feel ashamed."

"They don't have to try very hard. I can feel their sharp looks with my eyes closed."

Bitsy shrugged her shoulders. "I say, if you can't find any fun in being the subject of all the gossip, you might as well come home with me and make cookies."

"They don't like being in the presence of a sinner."

"Some of them have forgotten that we're all sinners."

Mary cracked a smile. "Andrew said I should act like a sinner."

Bitsy scrunched her lips together. Mary could tell she was trying to keep from smiling. "What in heaven's name does that mean? If every sin were as obvious and visible as yours, there'd be a lot less judgment and a lot more love."

"I'm not so sure. Maybe there'd just be a lot more outcasts."

Bitsy nodded. "You're right. Might as well come home and save yourself the trouble."

"*Nae*," Mary said. "If my time away from the community taught me anything, it's that I need to be brave. I won't let someone else decide where I go or how I should feel. Andrew Petersheim and the likes of Treva Nelson aren't going to keep me from attending a gathering. I'll go if I please and show them I won't be shamed or bullied into staying home."

"*Gute* for you," Bitsy said.

Mary pretended to have more confidence than she felt. "If that won't win me any friends, then the way they treat me will give me a very *gute* reason to leave the community for good this time. Josh would say it was a win-win."

"I don't know. Josh said a lot of stupid things. But at least you have a cake to help you be brave. And if they're hostile, you can always throw it at them."

Mary didn't feel brave or defiant as she limped across the lawn into the Kings' backyard. Mostly she just felt sick. Bitsy had taken her to the doctor this morning. He had numbed her toe and ripped out her dangling toenail. She definitely should have stayed home. Her sore toe would have been the perfect excuse. Instead she had put on her best pair of flip-flops, determined to let nothing stop her.

Frieda King had been one of her best friends in school. Mary had played for many hours in this very backyard as a little girl. A dozen walnut trees lined the edge of the yard, and a little patch of pansies surrounded each tree. The yard was especially beautiful in autumn when the trees were bright yellow and the chrysanthemums were in full bloom. Mary and Frieda had spent hours helping Frieda's *bruderen* crack walnut shells with hammers. The nuts went into Edna King's big metal bowl and the shells fed the fire during the winter. Mary still loved the bitter taste of walnuts in October. She'd always get at least one canker on her tongue from eating too many, but it was a small price to pay for such deliciousness.

Mary strolled into the backyard as if she hadn't a care in the world. Several of *die youngie* played volleyball in the center of the yard. Others gathered around the eats table where an overflowing plate of pretzels sat next to bowls of honey and cheese sauce. She smiled to herself. She preferred pretzels with peanut butter and honey. Benji had shown her his trick.

No one seemed to notice her as she made a bee-line for the eats table, clutching her cake in front of her like a shield. *If you insist on going,* Bitsy had said, *you should at least take something to soften them up. No one can resist my bee-sting cake.*

"Why, Mary Coblenz, how nice to see you." Edna King stood on the other side of the table with a genuine smile on her face. Mary had always liked Frieda's *mater.* She was a tall, sturdy woman with hair that had been dirty gray for as long as Mary had known her. Edna was naturally reserved and quiet, but she had always seemed sure of herself, even though she didn't ever say very much.

Mary returned Edna's smile and felt some of the tension in her neck lessen. Edna didn't seem reluctant to talk to her. "Edna, *vie gehts?* Is Frieda here? I'm eager to see her."

Edna shook her head. "She married in November, and her husband took her to Indiana. I told him he is now my least favorite son-in-law."

"Aaron Borntrager?"

"*Jah.*"

"I thought as much," Mary said. "They were pen pals for almost seven years." Frieda and Mary had shared all their secrets. Except one. Mary hadn't dared tell Frieda about Josh. That way, Frieda could honestly have said that she knew nothing about Mary and her Englisch boyfriend and that she had no idea that Mary had been thinking of running away. Frieda must have been quite hurt when Mary had jumped the fence without breathing a word of it to anyone, not even her best friend.

Betraying a cherished friendship was one of the things Mary regretted the most. Four months after she had left, she wrote a long letter of apology to Frieda, but she'd never heard back. Maybe the letter had never reached her. Maybe Frieda hadn't cared to answer. Maybe Mary had burned too many bridges. Was it any wonder that everyone hated her?

"I'm . . . I'm sorry I left without telling her."

Edna glanced up from the pretzels and smiled. "I am too, Mary. But there's no use pining for the way we wish things had been."

Mary nodded. "We can only move forward as best we can."

"That's right. Keep moving forward. Frieda understands."

Mary got an update on the rest of Edna's family, left her bee-sting cake on the table, and turned to face her doom. *Ach, vell,* she didn't really know if it was her doom, but she was prepared for the worst. After her icy reception at the auction last week, she expected a few daggers and knives. And neither Bitsy Weaver nor Benji Petersheim was here to rescue her.

Still, she refused to let anyone else decide how she was going to behave. She pasted a wide smile on her lips and looked for someone, anyone, to smile back at her.

She hobbled around the perimeter of the yard, saying hello to the many young people lounging under the trees. Some said hello back, but as soon as she tried to engage them in a conversation, they seemed to have somewhere else they needed to be, or they acted as if they were completely and fully occupied with some other conversation and couldn't spare the time to talk to her. Mostly, she got whispers and dirty looks as she passed. Treva Nelson gave Mary a stink eye that would have done any skunk proud. Treva's *bruder* Sol didn't even lower his voice as he leaned to say something in Treva's ear. "What does she think she's doing here, trying to fellowship with decent folks?"

Perry and Peter James Glick stood side by side like twin pillars, looking Mary up and down, unashamedly ogling every last inch of her body. Were they trying to make her uncomfortable or giving in to their baser desires? Mary had seen plenty of men's baser desires in the Englisch world. She should have known it would exist in the Amish community as well. Maybe the Amish just hid their passions better—except for Perry and Peter James. They didn't seem inclined to hide anything.

Mary made her way clear around the yard, but no one, not one person besides Edna King, would fellowship with her. Most wouldn't even look her in the eye. It felt as if a whole buggy full of anvils was pressing on her chest, making it nearly impossible to breathe and nearly unthinkable to smile. Why had she come back to Bienenstock? Besides Bitsy, Yost, Edna, and Benji and Alfie Petersheim, there was nothing but rejection for her here.

*Ach, vell.* That wasn't exactly true, but the thought

made it easier to wallow. Mary and Hannah Yutzy had been nothing but kind at the auction, and two or three others in the *gmayna* were nice.

Mary drew in a deep breath even though the pain was almost unbearable. She had come back because there had been nowhere else for her to go. She'd come back because she had hoped that maybe, just maybe, she would find a beautiful, safe place to raise her baby—a place where bonds of a family were stronger than death.

Maybe she'd been mistaken.

At the very least, these old friends needed to see that she would not be bullied or humiliated. She would not crawl into the hole they thought she belonged in. She would show them happiness and a glad heart, even if it killed her. Maybe she'd teach them a thing or two in the process.

It was pure foolishness, but she half marched, half limped into the middle of the volleyball game, chose a team, and positioned herself on the front row. Alvin Miller, one of the boys she had known in school, dropped the ball mid-serve and stared at her as if she'd arrived from another planet, like the alien in *Close Encounters of the Third Kind.* It was a terrible movie, but Josh had insisted on showing it to her.

Mary hunkered down and clasped her hands together in the set position, pretending that she had no idea why Alvin had dropped the ball.

Everyone, in the game and out of it, seemed to freeze like upright popsicles. Every eye was on her, and it took supreme effort not to crumble into a million pieces. Instead, she smiled at the player next to her, clapped her hands, and called, "Let's play," with a sickening amount of enthusiasm.

The girl across the net from her drew her brows together in a look of confusion. "I . . . I don't think you're supposed to be here," she whispered, glancing at her teammates as if fearing she'd get in trouble for talking to the enemy.

"You could get hurt," someone right behind her said, still whispering, just in case anything louder would be overheard. "You're going to have a baby."

Mary valiantly kept that smile ironed in place, even though her lips ached and her heart felt like a lump of coal. "I'm okay. Volleyball isn't a hard game."

"We don't want you here," someone behind her hissed.

"You don't want to hurt yourself."

"You need to get out of our game." That was Sol Nelson. She had made the unfortunate choice of joining his team.

The oppressive weight of their hostility smothered her. What should she do now? If she walked away, they'd win, and she would rather move back in with Josh than let them win. If she stayed, they'd probably heap more abuse on her head. She wasn't strong enough to bear it.

She hadn't seen him come, but suddenly Andrew Petersheim was by her side, gazing at her with a mixture of concern and irritation in his eyes. She didn't even know if he was mad at her or irritated that she was messing up the game, but she thought she might faint with relief. It was nice to see a friendly face— well, sort of a friendly face. He thought she was proud and a sinner, but at least he hadn't called her some of the nasty names being whispered behind her back.

Andrew tried to smile but couldn't quite form a believable one on his lips. "Mary," he said, his eyes darting from volleyball player to volleyball player, as if he hoped none of them would notice that he was standing in the middle of the game holding a plate of cookies. "Mary, remember how you told my *mamm* that you would help me cut these cookies for the gathering?"

She took a shuddering breath. He was trying to give her a way out of the game, and she would be a fool not to take it. Her knees were about to buckle under her, and if she didn't get out soon, she'd be in a heap on the ground and *die youngie* would, no doubt, rejoice over her. "*Ach*, I forgot. *Cum.* I'll help you right now."

She led the way, as if this had been the plan all along. Without meeting her eye, Andrew followed her to the eats table, where he dumped the plate of cookies, handed her a butter knife, and promptly walked away. Okay, he was irritated—or more likely embarrassed to be seen with her. She pressed her lips together and tried to ignore the ache in her chest. For some ridiculous reason, his walking away hurt worse than anything Sol Nelson had said to her or any harsh look Treva had shot at her.

Andrew had popped her toe back into place. He'd brought her a drink of water and shown her the chair he'd made. He hadn't wanted to be seen with her at the auction, but he *had* smiled at her and actually been willing to have a conversation with her. She had hoped that maybe he was different than the others, that maybe he didn't think so badly of her. But it didn't matter. They were all the same—resentful, unforgiving, and judgmental. And as rigid as telephone poles.

Mary blinked back the tears and forced a pleasant,

aching smile onto her face. She couldn't blame them. She used to be one of them, and she knew how hard it was to see the world in a way different from what she'd been taught. Still, Andrew's rejection stung like a fever blister. She'd hoped to find a friend tonight. There was nothing but heartache for her here.

She could still feel dozens of pairs of eyes boring into the back of her head. Maybe she should cut the cookies so they wouldn't get suspicious of Andrew. Although if she touched the cookies, for sure and certain, no one would want to eat them, even if they were Andrew's *mamm's* famous peanut butter cookies.

It was good the cookies were soft enough to cut with a butter knife, because that was all she had, although where Andrew had gotten a butter knife on such short notice was anybody's guess. She couldn't stop her hands from shaking as she cut, but she was determined not to lose her smile. They couldn't see that they had gotten to her. The knife slipped and nicked her finger. She hissed and popped the finger in her mouth. A butter knife wasn't especially sharp, but it did have those tiny grooves like little teeth, and they had enough of an edge to draw blood.

Great. Now she had a sore finger, a broken toe, and an aching heart. This day was getting better and better.

She didn't know how Andrew managed to appear from thin air like that, as if he'd learned a few tricks from a magician, but suddenly he was at her side, though he had his back to the table and his arms folded as if he just happened—not on purpose—to be loitering on her side of the table. "What did you do?" he said.

"I thought maybe they would let me join their

game," she said, wincing at the little hitch in her voice. "I tried to force them to accept me, but no one likes to be forced. I was too proud to run away."

"I mean, what did you do to your finger?"

Surely her face must be turning six shades of purple. "*Ach.* Nothing. Just a little cut."

"You're going to bleed on my cookies."

"There isn't even enough blood to speak of."

"*Nae,*" he said, sliding the knife out of her fist. "Go in the house. I'll come help you find a Band-Aid."

"I'm okay."

He turned his head and looked at her, even though who knew what that would do to his reputation. "You're shaking like you've got palsy, and I don't think anyone's going to volunteer to catch you if you faint." He took all the pretzels off one of the plates, piled them on top of another plate, and handed the empty plate to her. "Here, take this into the house. Then no one will think you're running away, especially since you can't go very fast with that toe."

She wouldn't have done his bidding for the world, except her legs were shaking violently and she'd be lucky to make it into the house with her dignity intact. She pushed the cookies in his direction and ambled around the table, across the lawn, and up the back steps into the kitchen.

Thank Derr Herr, the house was empty. She slid the empty plate onto the counter and eased herself onto the sofa next to the door. The *buplie* poked her foot into Mary's ribs, as if chastising her for even thinking about doing something so *deerich*, foolish, as playing volleyball. *Ach, du lieva.* What had she been thinking, throwing herself into the middle of a volleyball game like that? Maybe some of her teammates had genuinely been concerned for her safety. They probably hated her too, but some of them might have been concerned.

She rested her head against the back of the sofa. No good had come of her being here. Even though she told herself she wouldn't let her former friends and neighbors humiliate her, that's exactly what had happened. She felt like a coward, but as soon as she stopped shaking, she was going to go back to Bitsy's house and never show her face again.

Maybe.

Then again, maybe she would gird up her loins and try again. Everyone deserved a second chance to show some kindness.

*Ach, vell*, maybe not Andrew Petersheim. He'd had his chances. First and second. Nope. She was finished with Andrew.

The back door opened, and Mary craned her neck to look behind her. *Ach*. Maybe if she closed her eyes and pretended to be napping, he'd go away. She peeked through barely open eyes to watch him hang his hat on one of the kitchen chairs, then rummage through Edna's cupboards. Did he know how rude that was? He pulled out a glass and filled it at the sink, then brought it to her. He gently nudged her arm, and she pretended to wake up.

"Here," he said. "You need to drink. You look flushed."

She wasn't going to forgive him, even though he'd apparently come to check on her. "For your sake, I hope nobody saw you come in."

He frowned, but whether he felt guilty or worried, she couldn't tell. He sat next to her and handed her the glass of water. He smelled of fresh, clean cedar and peppermint. And . . . maybe just the slightest hint of roses.

"How is your toe?"

It was nice of him to ask, even if he didn't really care. She looked down at the thick bandage wrapped around her toe. "Black and blue, but it hurts less every day." She didn't realize how thirsty she was until she touched the glass to her lips. She emptied the glass and handed it back to him. "*Denki.* You can go now."

"I'm not leaving you like this. I've seen you when you're hurt. We can't risk you screaming like a passing chicken."

To her dismay, she felt the corners of her mouth curl upward involuntarily. She pushed them down again by sheer force of will. "I don't want anyone to catch you in here with a sinner."

He lifted his chin. "You don't have to get all huffy about it. You are a sinner. Might as well admit it."

"I've admitted it several times already." She sighed. She was already losing patience with him, and he'd been in the house all of three minutes. "I am a sinner. Aren't we all sinners?"

He drew his brows together. "We are all sinners, yes, but you don't seem to understand that's no excuse for what you've done."

She leaned back and looked up at the ceiling. Was it worth trying to make him understand? Hadn't she tried hard enough already? Did she even want to give Andrew another chance? "I'm not trying to make excuses for what I've done, Andrew. I'm willing to talk about my sins."

"I don't want to talk about your sins."

"*Jah*, you do. You said I'm proud of my sins. At least let me defend myself."

Andrew's eyes flashed, and the muscles of his jaw twitched as if he was ready to call Mary to repentance and help her get there all by himself. He'd never looked so handsome. Or so fierce. "You can't defend yourself, Mary. You've done something terrible."

She sighed again, loudly. "I admit I'm a sinner, Andrew. So, what now?"

"What do you mean?"

"Is that enough for you? Can we be friends, or are you still determined to avoid me?"

"I'm not as petty as you believe I am," he said. "People will say things, draw conclusions about me if they see me with you. Can you blame me for trying to avoid you?"

"I suppose not."

He cleared his throat and wrapped his hands around her empty glass. "Someone needs to help you understand your place, Mary. You act as if you're not sorry, as if you're proud of breaking your parents' hearts and jumping the fence and then getting pregnant without marriage. You walk around town as if you have nothing to be ashamed of. You upset many *gute* people when you came to the auction last week. You've ruined the gathering. Is it any wonder people avoid you? Don't you care about their feelings? They're just trying to protect their children and teach them the ways of righteousness. It makes it harder when you blatantly parade your sin in front of them."

Mary wasn't upset by his admonishment or his ignorance. His zeal just made her tired. She sighed a third time, almost too weary to explain. "Andrew, do you think I'm proud of being pregnant?"

"*Jah.*"

She hesitated. "I'm not proud of being stupid." She thought of Frieda and her parents. "I'm not proud that I hurt so many people along my way. But no amount of groveling on my part is going to change what I've done."

"But you should at least show some remorse."

"Who says I haven't?"

That made Andrew stop for a second. "I haven't seen any remorse."

"Believe me, Andrew, if my remorse were feed corn, it would fill ten silos and three barns."

"But, what about consequences? We should all suffer consequences for our sins."

Mary placed a protective hand on her stomach. "You don't think this is a big enough consequence?"

Andrew had nothing to say to that, but she thought maybe she saw a softening around his eyes.

"Maybe you think I haven't suffered enough, that I need to be punished."

He looked away. "Maybe. It doesn't seem you've suffered enough."

"But didn't Jesus suffer for our sins?"

Andrew furrowed his brow and shifted on the sofa as if trying to get more comfortable. "You're twisting things around. Jesus suffered for our sins, but how will the sinner learn to do right if he isn't punished?"

"Why do you assume that I haven't already paid a high price for my deeds?" Mary smiled sadly and shrugged. "Or maybe it's not good enough. How much punishment do you think I deserve? Was stubbing my toe enough punishment? When bad things happen to people, are they being punished for their sins?"

"I don't know. Maybe."

"What sin did your *dawdi* commit to cause Gotte to send him a stroke?"

Andrew stiffened and his knuckles turned white around the glass. "We're not talking about my *dawdi*."

"*Nae.* I forgot. You want to talk about me and my sins." She leaned her elbow on the armrest. "Let's assume being pregnant is not a punishment for my sins. It's a consequence, and I have come to terms with it. I truly believe that Gotte would never send a precious baby as a punishment. You may believe differently."

His eyes momentarily flashed with something like compassion. The emotion didn't last long. "I . . . I don't think a *buplie* is meant to punish anyone, but I do think it should make you think on your sins."

She fell silent. If he only knew how a baby changed every thought, every dream she'd ever had. "It does make me think on my sins. But my sins aren't what you think they are. Don't you see, Andrew? No amount of shame or guilt my parents or you or Treva Nelson want to heap on me will make me want to change. The community wants to humiliate me."

"They don't mean to be cruel. It will take time to forgive you for what you've done."

Mary truly felt no ill will in her heart for Andrew Petersheim. She had been where he was. She placed a hand on his arm. "Do I need their forgiveness?"

He locked his gaze on her hand. "I thought I was sure, but now I don't know."

"It is my understanding that I only need Gotte's

forgiveness. I don't need yours. I've done nothing to offend you. How long do you think I'll want to stay in the community if I'm treated like an outcast every time I go out? The way you treat me is more likely to drive me away, don't you think?"

"*Jah*," he said, his voice inexplicably cracking in a dozen different places.

"My parents, who are supposed to love me, want me to suffer. They want punishment, as if that will induce me to return to their loving arms." She couldn't keep the bitterness from her voice, though she'd done her best to forgive her parents. She had hurt them deeply. "My *mamm* and *dat* won't allow me in the house. I came back almost three weeks ago, and Mamm took one look at me and slammed the door in my face. Do they want me to grovel or come begging at their window in sackcloth and ashes?" He wouldn't look at her. "What do I have to do to satisfy their demands for justice?"

He looked truly troubled for her. "I don't know."

Mary's parents had been furious with Bitsy and Yost for taking her in. Her *dat* had come to Bitsy's house and argued with Bitsy and Yost for over an hour. Mary had been sitting at the top of the stairs listening to the entire conversation. Dat had demanded that Yost throw Mary out of his house—as if cruelty would nudge her toward repentance. Mary smiled to herself. Bitsy had even threatened Dat with her shotgun. Yost had defended Mary and Bitsy, and Mary had never been more grateful to any man in her entire life. No man had ever taken Mary's part before.

Yost had called her *dat* to repentance before inviting him to leave. It had been truly unforgettable, but she took no pleasure in the memory. "You might not believe it," she said, "but I've thought a great deal about how I could make my parents love me again. I could sit at the stop sign with a poster tied around my neck that says *I'm sorry for what I've done.* Or even better: *Here is a horrible sinner. Shun her, punish her. She doesn't deserve love or forgiveness.* People could throw tomatoes at me."

Frowning, Andrew scrubbed his hand down the side of his face. "You shouldn't . . . that's not what I think."

"Isn't it?"

"I don't know."

Andrew had seemed so sure of himself at the auction. Maybe he was humble enough to consider what she was saying. "Believe me, Andrew. I have wrestled with the weight of my sins. I have shed many tears in the middle of the night, praying for Gotte's forgiveness. I spent five nights sleeping in a Laundromat with nothing but newspapers for a blanket. Believe me, I have suffered the weight of my sins. You say I'm too cheerful, but Jesus has washed my sins away. I can't help but rejoice in Him. Should I spend the rest of my life wallowing in my shame, letting it grind me to dust? How do you think a sinner should be treated?" She leaned toward him, hoping he saw sincerity in the question instead of scorn.

She sensed the tension in his neck, his arms, his strong hands and long fingers. He turned his back on her and leaned his hands on the counter. He stood that way for several silent minutes, and his shoulders moved up and down with the rhythm of his lungs. It was as if he was fighting some sort of battle inside himself. Finally he spoke in a soft, intense whisper that stole her breath away. "I have treated you poorly, Mary."

"Better than some."

"*Nae.* Not better than anyone."

"You fixed my toe."

"I didn't want to be there."

She wished he'd turn around so she could see his eyes. "You stayed anyway."

"I saw the disgust from my neighbors. I heard the whispers. I . . . I agreed with them. When you showed up pulling that wagon, I watched, indignant that you had dared to show up. I thought you were the worst kind of sinner, undeserving of my help. I didn't want to help you for fear of what the others would think."

Mary smiled at the memory, though Andrew wouldn't understand why. "That was Bitsy's idea, to see if anyone would find some Christian charity and help the poor pregnant woman."

He turned around, and his gaze pierced right through her heart. "Benji made me feel ashamed."

Mary tried to hide her surprise. Maybe Andrew's heart wasn't so hard as she thought if he had been ashamed even then. Maybe there was hope for the rest of them, and maybe there was a chance that Mary would find a place here. "Benji is a *gute* boy. He sees when no one expects him to be looking, and he hears when no one thinks he's listening."

Pain flashed in Andrew's eyes. "I shouldn't have treated you the way I did. Jesus ate and fellow-shipped with sinners, but he saved his wrath for the hypocrites, who fancied themselves so righteous but couldn't show love and forgiveness. I am the worst kind of sinner."

"Andrew," she said. She stood and took the three short steps toward him. Her head began to spin. She had been trying to slay too many dragons today, as Josh would have told her. She pressed her hand to her forehead.

Andrew grabbed her arm and steered her back to the sofa. "Are you all right?" He snatched the empty glass from the counter and filled it again. "Here, drink this."

"Too much volleyball excitement," she said as she drank down a second brimming glass of water. At this rate, she'd be floating back to Bitsy's house.

"You shouldn't be playing volleyball in your condition."

She gulped down the last swallow. "I'm too proud."

"Is that why you were playing—for your pride?"

"I suppose so. I wanted them to notice me, to acknowledge me instead of pretending I don't exist or making faces at me behind my back. It was *deerich*."

"But everyone has treated you so unfairly, I can see why you'd want to do it."

She glanced at him. "You shouldn't be so hard on yourself. In spite of how you felt about me, you helped me get out of that volleyball game with my pride intact, even though pride is a sin."

He lowered his eyes and stared at his hands. "I couldn't let them treat you like that, not after my failure at the auction."

"So you came up with the story about needing to cut cookies."

He cracked a smile. "It was all I could think of, though Gotte is surely not happy that I lied."

"I thought it was very clever of you. It got me out of the game, and I could still hold my head high."

"I saw something fierce in your expression. I could tell that you wouldn't surrender even though everyone was against you."

She smiled. "Not everyone."

He looked away, the faintest smile playing at his lips.

"See? You do have a *gute* heart."

"But even then I wanted nothing more than to get away from you. I handed you the knife and walked away."

"You came back," she said, resisting the urge to touch his arm for a second time. The Amish weren't apt to do a lot of touching. They thought it was inappropriate. She'd learned many useful things from Josh—like the fact that the smallest touch could convey a thousand warm emotions. She wasn't about to teach Andrew those kinds of lessons.

"Do you need more water?"

She shook her head.

He took the glass from her and set it on the counter. "Why did you come tonight? After the auction, you had to know how people would treat you."

"I'm a little dense that way. I don't know when to quit."

"Quit what?"

"I came to see if people would behave like Christians," Mary said. "I came to prove to them that they can't scare me off with a few nasty looks and *hesslich*, ugly words. I want them to see I'm stronger than that, and I won't be bullied." She sighed and shook her head. "*Nae*, that isn't entirely true. This community, these people, they are who I am. I came back to see if there is a place for me here, to see if these people are still my people. I'm beginning to wonder if maybe I don't belong here. Maybe I never will."

"You should give it more time," he said.

"I want my baby to grow up in a place of love and security. I just don't know if I can find that here, and I don't have forever to decide."

He pressed his lips together. "I hope you'll give us a chance to prove ourselves. If I can change, anybody can change."

"*Ach, vell*, I don't know about that. You are not just anybody, Andrew Petersheim. You have some very *gute* qualities." She gave him a teasing smile. "I can't think of any just now, but it will come to me."

His frown deepened. "I don't have any *gute* qualities."

"You can admit when you're wrong."

"No, I can't." His own words made him grin, and the grin gave way to laughter. "Not very often."

His smile was like a flash of light in the darkness, almost as if she should shield her eyes to keep from going blind. She'd never seen anything so extraordinary. She caught her breath as something warm and pleasant washed over her like a summer rain. Who knew a smile had that kind of power?

She needed to say something before he suspected he'd made her lose her wits. No doubt he could hear her heart beating against her chest like an Englischer's drum. She was not going to drink another glass of water, no matter how giddy she felt. "Why did *you* come to the gathering?"

He threw up his hands in mock surrender. "I'm too old. I told Mammi Martha, I'm too old."

"Your *mammi* made you come?"

"She bought me, Abraham, and Austin some teeth-whitening toothpaste especially for the gathering. She said it would help us get a wife and insisted that we come tonight. Abraham and Austin are still young enough to enjoy a gathering, but it's pure torture for me."

Mary laughed. Benji had told her that Andrew refused to look at any Bienenstock girls. "Couldn't you have explained it to your *mammi*?"

He shook his head. "Mammi lives to be 'of help,' as she says. If she had any inkling that we didn't appreciate her gifts, she'd be devastated. So, I used the toothpaste and came to the gathering so Mammi wouldn't be upset. I try not to smile directly into the sun. I don't want to blind anybody."

Mary averted her eyes. He already had. She pointed to a strange strap dangling from his straw hat. "Is that from your *mammi*?"

He grinned sheepishly. "I forgot to leave it in the buggy. I'm supposed to wear it around my chin so my hat doesn't blow off in the wind."

Andrew's *mammi* must not have cared how ridiculous her grandsons would look with chinstraps on their straw hats. "How thoughtful."

He chuckled. "Mammi Martha thinks everything is a problem just waiting for her solution."

"I'm glad you came, even if just to spare your *mammi*'s feelings."

His eyes filled with tenderness. "I'm glad you came too. I'm sorry you got your feelings hurt."

Mary wasn't sorry she'd come. She'd finally found a friend—maybe. She didn't dare say the word *friend* to Andrew. He might throw up his hands and run screaming out of the house. It was one thing to own up to your mistakes and show Christian charity. It was quite another to commit to being a friend. Andrew probably wasn't ready for that.

She sighed inwardly. Maybe he never would be.

# Chapter Six

Mammi Martha sniffed the air as Alfie and Benji stormed into the house, ran past her, and hurried down the cellar stairs like a two-cattle stampede. "Someone hasn't been using the special rose water, Rebecca. Dinnertime would be much more pleasant if all the boys sprayed the rose water on themselves three times a day and used my special soap."

Mammi had grown suspicious that Andrew and his *bruderen* weren't using the special rose-scented soap she'd put in each of the bathrooms, so on Monday, she'd hid all the regular soap so they'd be forced to use the smelly stuff. It had been an agonizing choice for Andrew. Either smell like sweat and manure all day or get strange looks from his friends because he smelled like "a bed of roses in the bathtub." Two days ago, he'd sneaked over to Glick's Family Market and bought a bar of deodorant soap, which he hid in the bottom of the trash can in the bathroom. Lord willing, Mammi wouldn't get a notion to empty the trash cans anytime soon.

Mamm stood at the cupboard with her back to the

table, putting together a meatloaf for dinner. "Truer words were never spoken, Martha." Mamm had taken to giving Mammi the same noncommittal answer for everything. *Truer words were never spoken.* That way she didn't have to lie to Mammi but neither did she have to follow every well-meaning direction Mammi gave her.

Of course, if Mammi bought something for the house, Mamm was forced to use it or risk hurting Mammi's feelings, but what Mammi didn't know wouldn't hurt her. Unless she took a shower with every last one of her grandkids, she'd never know that they were hiding the good soap at the bottom of the trash can.

Dawdi David sat at the table with his head slumped over his chest and a dishtowel draped around his neck. Mammi Martha was getting ready to trim his hair while giving Mamm pointers at the same time. "Now, Rebecca, you have boys, so it's normal that everything in the bathroom is going to carry the faint smell of urine, but all you need to do is spray the toilets twice a day with Clorox Disinfecting Bathroom Cleaner. But use the special cleaning rags I bought. Don't use the washrags. It's too easy to spread hand, foot, and mouth disease."

Mamm pounded down the hamburger in her bowl. "Truer words were never spoken." She was extra grumpy. Andrew had heard her ask Mammi not to cut Dawdi's hair in the kitchen where she could get hair in the food. Mammi hadn't paid her any heed.

Dawdi hadn't said any words since his stroke, but it was obvious he could follow what was going on. He widened and narrowed his eyes in Andrew's direction every time something interesting happened and smiled whenever something really interesting happened. Andrew, Abraham, and Austin each spent an hour a day taking care of Dawdi and helping him with his exercises. More than twenty minutes of exercise a day left him exhausted, but he was making progress. Yesterday he had squeezed Andrew's index finger with his hand. That was a new skill.

Alfie and Benji stormed up the stairs, tromped across the kitchen, and out the back door again without a second look at anybody. Something dangled from a strap around Alfie's neck. Were those binoculars?

"Boys," Mammi called. "Where are your shoes?" For sure and certain the boys hadn't heard a word she'd said. "Now, Rebecca, those shoes won't do any good sitting in their closet."

"Truer words were never spoken."

Andrew didn't dare tell Mammi that the boys didn't have a closet in the cellar. She might go out and try to buy one.

Dat and Abraham were in the fields, and Austin was milking their four cows. They didn't get a huge amount of milk, but enough that a milkman came by every night to collect what they'd milked and take it to a processing plant. It was a little bit of extra money every month.

Andrew had come into the house to wash peanut butter jars, but with Mammi cutting hair, he'd decided he'd better wait. No food inspector would take kindly to pieces of hair that could easily float into a jar of peanut butter. Andrew glanced at Mamm, who was still trying to pound the hamburger into mush. "Mammi, would you like me to cut Dawdi's hair? I'll take him outside so we don't have to wear out the special broom on the floor."

Mamm stopped pounding. She'd probably give Andrew a kiss if he could talk Mammi into letting him take Dawdi out of the kitchen for a haircut.

"That's a very nice offer, Andrew, but I already told your *mamm*, I don't think it's wise to take David outside. He could get a chill."

"I stopped by the thermometer on my way in, Mammi. It's seventy-five degrees outside."

"He can't do the porch steps."

"I'll cut it on the porch and drape a blanket over Dawdi's legs."

Mammi raised her eyebrows. She liked to have her way, but she wasn't too stubborn to consider other options. "All right. Some time outside might do your *dawdi* good."

Andrew carried a kitchen chair out to the porch along with a smooth blanket that wasn't as likely to catch all the hair trimmings. Then Mammi held Dawdi's elbow with Andrew on the other side, and they helped him shuffle out to the porch with his walker. Mammi brought out a chair and the comb and scissors. "It won't hurt to cut it shorter than normal," she said. "No one at the *gmayna* is likely to see him." She patted Andrew on the shoulder before she slipped inside. "You've always been the most thoughtful young man."

Dawdi smiled at Andrew, and it made him feel ashamed. "Don't believe it, Dawdi," Andrew said, opening and closing the scissors in his hand. Dawdi's smile faded. "I know you love me, Dawdi, but it's true. I used to believe I was a thoughtful young man, but now I can barely stand to live with myself. Plain and simple, Dawdi, I'm a hypocrite, and Mary sees right through me."

Dawdi lifted one eyebrow. That was something Andrew hadn't seen for a very long time. Dawdi used to lift his eyebrow like that when he questioned the intelligence of one of his grandchildren.

"I met this girl. Her name is Mary Coblenz. Do you remember her? She jumped the fence and came back about a month ago. She's with child, unmarried, and living with Bitsy and Yost Weaver because her parents won't let her in the house."

Dawdi might have given Andrew a slight nod, but he couldn't be sure.

The thought of Mary Coblenz sent several emotions swirling in Andrew's head like a pile of hair trimmings caught in the wind. "Benji and Alfie love her, but I was mad at her at first. She seemed so sure of herself, like she wasn't sorry for her sins. I told her to stop being so proud because I wouldn't tolerate her sin—and neither would anyone else in the community. I hoped she would feel the shame that Gotte wanted her to feel so Gotte could lead her to repentance."

Andrew was staring at the back of Dawdi's head, but he heard a faint grunt from Dawdi's throat. Andrew pressed his lips together. Dawdi wasn't happy with him. He wasn't all that happy with himself.

"I thought I was right, but my own sins nagged at me. No matter what Mary has done, I should have helped her with that wagon." He stepped around to face Dawdi. "There was this wagon. Benji pulled it for her, but I was afraid of what other people were going to think. I should have had the courage to be the man Mamm taught me to be."

Dawdi smiled. He agreed.

Andrew's heart sank. Dawdi was never going to respect him again. "I went to this gathering and Mary was there and people were being so mean to her. She made me see how bad I had been treating her too, and I was ashamed to call myself a Christian. Jesus said to love the sinners. I thought I was so much more righteous than she was, but I was just being proud."

It had taken Mary to make Andrew see how blind he had been, but his thoughts had been so heavy and his discomfort so acute at the gathering, he had barely been able to look her in the eye for shame.

"I'm sorry, Dawdi. I've soiled the family name."

Dawdi twitched his head back, and Andrew nearly poked him with the scissors. It was plain Dawdi didn't like that thought. Maybe he wasn't so ashamed of his grandson after all.

There were other emotions that he'd tried to banish from his mind for a whole week. "There's something else, Dawdi. I've been trying not to think about Mary at all. She's nice and everything, but I'm not part of her world and I don't want to be. I've just never had such a struggle getting a girl out of my head before. It doesn't matter how many cold showers I take or how many peanut butter jars I wash, Mary Coblenz just keeps creeping into my thoughts. It's like my head is a house, and she's moved in. I wish you could give me some advice. I've tried singing hymns and whistling tunes, even shouting songs while I'm in the barn, but they don't do anything to drown out Mary. She's like a tune in my head I can't get rid of." There was no possible way to stop thinking about her. "Has that ever happened to you?"

Dawdi's smile got so wide, Andrew could see his

gold tooth. It probably happened to every man at some point.

This was a very bad thing.

He liked Mary. And this was a very bad thing too. She had a tiny scar on her right eyebrow that danced when she smiled, and rosebud lips that were inviting even when she made one of her funny faces at him. What defense did he have against that? How could he possibly resist eyes the color of a crisp autumn sky or the way she smoothed her hair from her face or how she rested her chin on her hand when she was thinking deep thoughts? He even liked her toes and the way her lips twitched when she was in pain but she was trying to be brave.

Andrew pulled the comb through Dawdi's hair. "It's just that Mary is with child. And she has a broken toe. And she's completely unsuitable in every way, no matter how much I like her smile."

Her pregnancy was the mountain that stood between them, and Andrew didn't have enough faith to move it, didn't *want* to move it. He'd rather remain safely on his side of the mountain and leave her safely on hers. And for sure and certain he wasn't about to scale a mountain only to fall off a cliff on the other side.

"Jesus may have forgiven her, but even Mary admitted there were consequences to what she's done. You can see the consequences, can't you, Dawdi? No man in the *gmayna* would ever consider marrying her. It isn't fair, and I feel like a bigger hypocrite than ever, but there it is. I'm sorry, Dawdi, but there's nothing I can do about how I feel."

Dawdi sort of pinched his lips together and squinted at Andrew as if he were studying the thoughts in Andrew's brain. Dawdi understood. There were probably only about five people in the community who didn't understand how Andrew felt.

For about the hundredth time, Andrew resolved to avoid Mary. He could be her friend from a distance. It wasn't like their paths crossed all that often except at *gmay.* As long as she didn't come to any more gatherings or break any more toes, they could be indifferent acquaintances who barely had a word to say to each other. Surely she would understand his hesitation.

*Ach, vell,* she wouldn't like it. She wanted to be accepted, not ignored. Andrew could bear Bitsy's shotgun, but he didn't know if he could bear Mary's cold looks when she realized he'd be ignoring her from now on.

But maybe he wouldn't tell Dawdi about his plans. He couldn't be sure Dawdi would approve.

Andrew finished cutting Dawdi's hair and let Dawdi watch as he threw the cut pieces of hair into the air and let the breeze carry them away. Dawdi seemed to enjoy that. Then Andrew helped his grandfather inside to the sofa. Dawdi was getting better with his walker, able to hold on to the handles and shuffle his way across the floor. Andrew had to place his hand over Dawdi's left one to help him maintain a tight grip, and he always placed a firm arm behind Dawdi's back to help him keep his balance. It wasn't likely that Dawdi would ever be as robust as he was before the stroke, but Andrew could see the improvements every day.

After Dawdi was settled on the couch with a blanket over his legs, Andrew went out to the porch and swept up Dawdi's hair clippings with the new hand broom Mammi Martha had brought home from

e's really stuck, and all of Bitsy's cats climbed up
ith him and they're stuck too."

"Alfie's on Honeybee Farm?"

"And stuck in a tree."

Andrew tried not to grunt his exasperation. Alfie
could get himself into trouble with a spoon and a
rubber band. It took almost no effort at all. "Honeybee Farm is pretty far."

"We ran. Then I ran back."

There was no time to ask why Alfie and Benji had
run to Honeybee Farm or why Alfie had wanted to get
stuck in one of their trees. With two eight-year-olds,
there was probably no good answer. "Let's take the
horse. It will be faster."

Benji sniffed and nodded. "I don't want him to
die. And Bitsy will be mad about her cats, but we
didn't ask them to come with us."

Andrew saddled the horse and sat Benji in front of
him as they trotted to Honeybee Farm. Andrew's
heart pounded in his chest like a drum, but it didn't
have anything to do with the fact that he might see
Mary Coblenz.

A row of tall basswood trees stood along the east
side of Bitsy's farm. They were in full bloom with tiny
white blossoms and a sweet fragrance that filled the
air. A dull hum came from each of the trees. Bitsy had
planted trees and flowers her bees liked. It was a good
bet that those trees were teeming with bees.

"Which tree is it?" Andrew said, peering up into
he tall basswood trees. Surely Alfie hadn't climbed
ne of those.

Whining and sniffling, Benji pointed to a tree right
the middle of the row. Of course Alfie had chosen
tallest one. "There."

Walmart—horsehair bristles with a blue rubber
ergonomic handle. While Dawdi recovered from his
stroke, Mammi Martha was renting their house to
Cousin Moses, and she seemed determined to spend
all the rent money on improving Mamm's house.

Just to make Mammi happy, Andrew went in the
house, got down on his hands and knees, and swept
the kitchen floor. She loved it when anyone used one
of her house gifts.

Benji burst into the kitchen and stopped right
inside the door, letting the screen door slam behind
him. His face was bright red, and he glanced around
the kitchen as if he didn't want to make a scene but
had something important to say. "Benji," Mamm said
without turning around, "you know better than to let
the door slam. Go back out and try again."

"But, Mamm, I need to tell Andrew something."

"It can wait. Go out and show me how a nice young
man shuts the screen door."

Benji groaned and dragged his feet, but he went
outside, came back in again, and held out his hand
so the screen door gently swung shut behind him. "I
need to talk to Andrew."

"Three more times," Mamm said, "just to be sure
you learned your lesson."

Benji acted as if Mamm had asked him to clean the
toilets for a whole year with his toothbrush. "Come
on, Mamm, someone might die."

Mamm raised an eyebrow. "Someone might die?
Well, someone might get the spatula if he doesn't
stop whining."

Andrew looked away to hide a smile. Benji and
Alfie practiced shutting doors at least once a week.
They didn't seem to be learning anything.

Benji went outside three more times and carefully shut the door all three times when he came in. "Okay, Mamm?"

"Okay," Mamm said. "Now give me a kiss."

Benji sighed like a dying cow but gave Mamm a peck on the cheek before turning to Andrew and tugging on his sleeve. "You've got to come, Andrew. There's something very important I have to show you outside."

Andrew knelt down and swept the last of the crumbs into the dustpan, in no hurry to see what Benji had to show him outside. What his *bruderen* were convinced was important could turn out to be a pile of deer droppings or a dead bird in the yard. And lately Benji and Alfie acted as if Andrew was their only *bruder*. They asked him to do everything for them and talked nonstop about Bitsy Weaver and cats and what kind of girl they wanted to marry. It was sweet, but sometimes Andrew wished they'd pick on someone else. "What do you want to show me?"

Benji narrowed his eyes into slits and pressed his lips into a trembling line. "I can't tell you until we get outside," he whispered. "It's really bad."

Something in Benji's expression told Andrew this wasn't about deer droppings or dead birds. "What's wrong?"

"You have to come outside."

One of the unwritten rules among the *bruderen* was that none of them ever tattled to Mamm. If one of the *bruderen* was in trouble or had made trouble, they tried to keep it to themselves and help each other out because Mamm was happier when she didn't know. "Okay, Benji," Andrew said, glancing at his *mamm.*

She was grating carrots into the meatloaf a willing, oblivious to Benji's distress.

Benji took Andrew's hand and practically y him toward the door. "Just a minute, Benji," M Martha said. "Have you had your spray of rose v today?"

Benji let out a quiet yelp, like a puppy caught i trap. This was no time for rose water.

"We'll do it later, Mammi," Andrew said, guidi Benji out the door and down the back steps. H cringed when the door slammed behind him.

"Benji!" he heard Mamm yell.

They both looked behind them and ran like the wind. Mamm could make them practice their doors later.

Andrew followed Benji to the front of the house and out onto the road. Benji stopped and waited for Andrew to catch up with him. "What's the problem?" Andrew said, hoping it didn't involve Alfie or blood.

To Andrew's surprise, Benji puckered up his whole face and burst into tears. "He was doing it on purpose, and then he got stuck. He's going to die. Wit all the cats."

Feeling more than a little anxious, Andrew squat and steadied Benji's shoulders. "What happen Where's Alfie?"

"Don't tell him I told you," Benji said, w away his tears and smearing dirt and water his cheek.

Andrew had no idea what Benji was talkin but if he was going to get anything useful fr he'd have to be agreeable. "Okay, I won't t

"Alfie was going to pretend to get stuc Bitsy's trees and then he climbed too h

Andrew felt like a little whining and sniffling himself. His chest tightened. Those basswood trees were nearly sixty feet high. He spurred Snapper to go faster until they made it to the base of the tree, where Andrew vaulted off his horse and helped Benji down. Andrew stared up into the branches, but the tree was thick with leaves and blossoms. He couldn't see any sign of Alfie or Bitsy's cats. "Alfie? Are you up there?"

He heard a rattle from an impossibly high branch about forty feet up. "I'm here." Alfie's voice floated down like a dried leaf, shaky and weak. "I can't get down."

"We came to save you," Benji yelled. "And the cats."

"The white one won't let go of my shoulder," Alfie called. "If he let go, for sure and certain, I could climb down."

Andrew's heart did a sickening flip as he pictured his *bruder* tumbling from the tree. "Don't try to climb down, Alfie. I'll come and get you. Hold on."

Andrew jumped over the wire fence that snaked around the front of Bitsy's property. Gazing up into the tree, he backed up until he caught a glimpse of Alfie sitting on a very thin branch clutching another branch above his head for dear life. A fat white cat did indeed sit on Alfie's shoulder, probably digging its claws into Alfie's skin, making it harder for Alfie to hold on. An orange marmalade cat perched on the branch next to Alfie, but Andrew couldn't see the other two cats.

It didn't look good, and it only took Andrew about five seconds to realize there was no way he could climb that tree. The branches toward the top wouldn't hold his weight, and there wasn't enough leverage to grab on to Alfie and guide him down.

Andrew ground his teeth together and growled under his breath. What had Alfie been thinking?

That was the problem. Alfie hadn't been thinking, and as soon as he was safely on the ground, Andrew was going to kill him.

Benji ducked under the fence and stood next to Andrew, sniffing back his tears and peering into the tree. "He got wonderful high."

Wonderful high and Andrew was going to kill him.

"We could get a ladder."

"There isn't a ladder high enough, Benji."

"I could climb up with a rope."

"*Nae*," Andrew shouted, his irritation shooting to the surface. The only thing worse than his *bruder* stuck in a tree would be two *bruderen* stuck in a tree.

Alfie shifted on the creaky branch, and Andrew nearly had a heart attack. That branch could only hold his *bruder*, and who knew how many cats, for so long. They had to get him down immediately.

"Benji, Bitsy has a phone shack. Do you know where it is?"

Benji slumped his shoulders. "Alfie and I have never been able to find it."

Andrew didn't know if he should be grateful for that or not. "Run to the house and ask Bitsy where her phone shack is. We need to call a fire truck."

Benji's eyes nearly popped out of his head. "A fire truck?"

Much as Andrew hated the thought that he couldn't help his own brother, he'd rather no one, including himself, broke his leg. "They're going to have to get Alfie down."

Benji cupped his hands around his mouth. "Alfie," he yelled, "hold on. We're calling the firemen."

"Go," Andrew said.

Benji ran toward the house like he'd been shot from a hunting rifle.

Andrew glued his eyes to Alfie, as if he could keep him in the tree by staring hard enough. "We're going to get you down, Alfie, but you've got to be really still and hold on tight."

"Billy Idol keeps growling at me."

Billy Idol? *Ach*, that was one of the cats. The ugly one. "Just ignore Billy Idol. He's trying to make you nervous."

"And three bees landed on me already."

Bees were everywhere. "They won't sting you if you just leave them alone."

"But what if they won't leave me alone?"

Oh, no. The rose water. Bees probably adored the smell of rose water. He wouldn't mention rose water to Alfie. It would only make him more agitated, but Andrew prayed that just this once, Alfie had disobeyed Mammi Martha and hadn't sprayed rose water on himself this morning. He let out the ragged breath he'd been holding. Surely Alfie had neglected to spray rose water on himself. He hated that stuff.

There was rustling in Alfie's part of the tree, and Andrew's heart jumped like a bullfrog. Alfie could bring down the whole branch by swatting at the bees. "Alfie, you've got to hold very still until the fire-fighters get here."

"It's hot and itchy up here. And one of the cats keeps licking me."

*Maybe you should have thought of that before you decided to climb that stupid tree.* Andrew didn't know if fear or anger was his strongest emotion at the moment. Mamm was going to hear about this. Alfie deserved a good hide tanning, even though Mamm had never actually tanned anybody's hide. She preferred a swift smack on the *hinnerdale* with the spatula. It didn't hurt, but it got her point across.

Andrew chastised himself for thinking of punishing Alfie at a time like this. Just being up in that tree was punishment enough. Alfie was frightened and all by himself—if you didn't count the growling cats. Not only that, but he was in terror of being stung every minute, and there was the very real possibility that he could fall and break several bones. All that mattered was that Alfie got down safely. He'd already been punished amply for his carelessness.

Hadn't Mary told Andrew the very same thing?

Mary was experiencing the unforgiving consequences of what she had done. Jesus died for Mary. The punishment had already been meted out. Was the community so callous as to demand more from her?

Maybe now all that mattered to Gotte was to get her home safely.

Mary, Bitsy, and Benji jogged across the lawn toward Andrew. Well, Mary wasn't jogging. It was more of a very fast walk, but she shouldn't go so fast in her condition. She always looked like an angel with that golden hair framing her face like a halo. And why did she have to wear that blue dress. It made her eyes look like a clear sky right after a thunderstorm. Andrew shouldn't stare. He shouldn't even look. Mary Coblenz was not for him, and he was not for her. It would be best to ignore her altogether. Mary need never know he thought she was pretty. No good would come of it.

In her own way, Bitsy was as hard to ignore as Mary, so to avoid looking at Mary, Andrew trained his gaze on Bitsy. She'd dyed her hair an emerald green color, which clashed horribly with her bright pink fingernail polish. She was scowling, which wasn't unusual, but her eyes were directed at the ground below Andrew's feet.

Bitsy tried to talk while catching her breath. "Get off the dandelions, Andrew Petersheim. Have you no shame?"

Andrew raised his eyebrows and tried to position himself so he wasn't standing on any dandelions, but it was impossible to do. There were more dandelions than grass.

Bitsy obviously wasn't pleased with his efforts. "We can talk about dandelions after we've saved your *bruder*. Much as I hate to admit it, he's more important than dandelions. What has he gotten himself into?"

"He's stuck in that tree and can't get down. Your cats too." He mentioned the cats just in case it would give Bitsy a greater sense of urgency.

Bitsy looked up into the tree and shaded her eyes even though the sun was behind her. "Alfie Petersheim, you have no business being in my tree."

"I didn't mean to," Alfie called, his voice trembling with desperation and irritation. He was obviously desperate to be down, but maybe also irritated that Bitsy would lecture him at a time like this. "Your cats are stuck too."

Bitsy swatted away sympathy for her cats. "Serves them right for following you up the tree on a fool's errand."

"The white one won't get off my shoulder."

"Alfie," Andrew called, "you've got to keep still."

Bitsy's brows practically crashed into each other.

"Farrah Fawcett climbed up with you? I find that hard to believe."

"Can you get us down?" Alfie said, obviously not in a position to argue with Bitsy Weaver.

Bitsy squinted into the tree. "I can't get you down. I quit climbing trees a decade ago."

Mary cupped her hands around her mouth. "Don't worry, Alfie. Everything is going to be okay. Do you know any songs you could sing to the cats? Maybe they won't be so scared if you sing to them."

"We need to call the fire department," Andrew said, more than a little annoyed that it was taking Bitsy and Mary so long to come to that conclusion. "Can you take me to your phone shack?"

"Don't get your knickers in a knot, Andrew Petersheim," Bitsy said. "They're on their way."

Andrew stopped short. "Who's on their way?"

"The fire department. Mary has a cell phone."

Of course she did.

"We called them before we came outside," Bitsy said. "That's what Benji told us to do, and I always try to do what Benji tells me. He's as smart as a whip."

Andrew hid his irritation that someone hadn't informed him of the phone call, but at least help was on its way. He was grateful for that.

Benji was a mess. Tears ran down his cheeks, his hair stuck out in about four different directions, and he couldn't seem to keep still. He paced back and forth under the tree with his hat in hand and scratched his head as if he had about a hundred lice chewing on his scalp. "Alfie," he yelled, "one time, I ate your pumpkin chocolate chip cookie, the one you were saving. And I was the one that broke that wooden horse Andrew made you, even though I blamed it on the cow."

Bitsy glanced at Benji. "You blamed it on the cow?"

Benji nodded, looking pale and pitiful. He was a very distraught eight-year-old. "I blamed Ivy Bell, who never hurt a soul in her life—except that one time when she stepped on my foot."

Mary knelt down and gathered Benji into her arms. "I'm sure Ivy Bell has forgiven you. And I'm sure Alfie will forgive you too. We all do things we regret."

Benji glanced above his head and whispered, "But what if Alfie dies before he forgives me?"

Mary smoothed a lock of Benji's hair. "Alfie is not going to die. The firemen will get him down."

Benji burst into tears all over again. "I'll sleep in the cellar for the rest of my life if Gotte will save Alfie."

Andrew thought his heart might break right there on Bitsy's lawn. Benji was inconsolable, but Mary was trying anyway. She whispered soft words in his ear and cooed and hummed as if Benji was her own son and she wanted nothing more than to comfort him.

Every unkind thought Andrew had ever harbored about Mary flew out of his head. No hardened sinner could treat someone with such exceptional kindness. If Mary was a lost soul, then there was no hope for any of them.

The mammoth fire engine rolled around the bend and slowly made its way down the dirt road. Couldn't they have at least pretended to be in a hurry? Where was the siren? Wasn't it supposed to be an emergency vehicle? It was probably a *gute* thing there were no flashing lights or blaring noises. Nothing drew a crowd like a siren. Mamm didn't need that headache in her life. She never had to find out. Andrew climbed over the fence and flagged the truck down, motioning for them to stop directly under Alfie's tree.

Three firefighters jumped from the truck. Andrew smiled in relief. One of them was Jerry Zimmerman, from Andrew's *gmayna*. Last year, Jerry had gotten permission from the bishop to volunteer with the fire department. It was *gute* to see a familiar face.

Jerry took off his hard hat and reached out for Andrew's hand. "They said there was trouble at Bitsy Weaver's house. I didn't expect to see you."

"My *bruder* is stuck in that tree," Andrew said, pointing to the spot where Alfie was trapped. "He's too high for any of us to reach him. And there are three cats."

"Four cats," Bitsy said from behind the fence. "And you don't have to save them if it's going to cost extra."

Four cats? No wonder that branch creaked like a rusty hinge. He leaned toward Jerry and lowered his voice. "I would appreciate it if you didn't tell my *mater*."

Jerry made a show of buttoning his lips. "I won't tell anyone."

"But you need to hurry. I'm worried that branch won't hold much longer."

Jerry turned to talk to the other two firefighters. They stood side by side, gazing solemnly up into the tree. One of the other ones pointed and said something Andrew couldn't hear. The two others started tinkering with their truck, hopefully getting ready to quickly hoist that ladder into the tree.

Jerry came back to Andrew. "Which of your *bruderen*?"

"Alfie. Abraham and Austin wouldn't be so *dumm*."

Jerry nodded, a teasing glint in his eyes. "Just checking." He glanced over Andrew's shoulder and practically exploded into a smile. "Mary Coblenz, I was hoping I'd see you. *Vie gehts?*"

Something about Jerry's smile set Andrew's teeth on edge. It was so genuine, so unreserved, as if he was truly happy to see Mary back, pregnant and all. Andrew hung his head and tried to swallow the lump in his throat. This was the way he should have treated Mary all along.

"I am *gute,*" Mary said, standing up but keeping hold of Benji's hand. "Will it be hard to get Alfie out of the tree?"

Andrew appreciated her sense of urgency. Alfie was the most important person right now, no matter how Jerry Zimmerman was looking at Mary.

Jerry took several steps backward. "Alfie," he yelled. "Are you okay?"

"I think Billy Idol wants to eat me."

Jerry glanced at Mary. "Billy Idol?"

Mary shook her head. "One of Bitsy's cats. He's harmless."

Jerry looked up again. "Don't be afraid, Alfie. We're going to get our long ladder and come up and get you. Hold on tight and try not to move." He turned back to Mary. "Make sure he stays as still as possible. We don't want him to fall."

Jerry seemed to have abandoned Andrew altogether and talked to Mary as if she was in charge. In charge of what, Andrew didn't know, but he was still a little put out by it. Jerry should be doing his duties, not making eyes at Mary. Mary was pregnant, for goodness' sake. Andrew wasn't sure what that had to do with his irritation, but it sounded good in his head and made him feel better about himself and the times he'd treated Mary like a leper instead of an actual person with feelings.

One of the other firefighters signaled to Jerry and pointed to Bitsy's bridge. Jerry smiled apologetically at Mary. "I'm afraid we're going to have to drive to this side of the fence. The angle will be better and safer."

"I beg your pardon, young man," Bitsy said. "What about my dandelions?"

Jerry signaled for his partners. "We're going to run over quite a few of them."

Bitsy huffed out a loud, long sigh. "I suppose it can't be helped."

"Dandelions will grow back, Aunt Bitsy," Mary said.

"Alfie is going to get a good talking-to when they bring him down here. It's lucky for me he's so wiry. There's not a chance he's going to fall. If he fell, I'd feel too guilty to scold him."

It was oddly comforting that Bitsy seemed so unruffled. She knew these trees and her bees and cats better than anyone. If she wasn't concerned, surely Alfie would be okay.

One of the firefighters drove the truck across Bitsy's small wooden bridge. Andrew feared it might collapse under the weight, but it held strong long enough for the truck to pass. The truck made deep ruts as it lumbered across the grass, and Andrew knew just what Alfie and Benji would be doing for the next few days. They'd need two shovels, a rake, and lots of elbow grease, but they'd even out Bitsy's grass or face the wrath of Mamm.

Once the truck was in place, the rest of the operation went quickly and smoothly, much to Andrew's relief. Jerry and one of the other firefighters stood in the basket while the third firefighter sat at the bottom as they went higher and higher into the air. Mary gasped, and Andrew held his breath when Alfie let go of his branch, obviously unwilling to wait for the harness Jerry held in his hand. Jerry grabbed Alfie under his arms and hauled him into the basket. The white cat—what had Bitsy called her? Farrah Fawcett?—tumbled off Alfie's shoulder and into the basket. It was a *gute* thing cats always seemed to know how to land.

They lowered Alfie and deposited Farrah Fawcett on the ground before going back for the rest of the cats. As soon as Alfie was safely on firm soil, he and Benji ran toward each other and crashed into a grunting hug, the only thing between them a pair of binoculars hanging from Alfie's neck. The binoculars were extremely suspicious, but questions could wait.

Mary and Andrew reached Alfie and Benji at the same time, and they ended up in a four-way hug with Mary's arms partially wrapped around Andrew and his arms sort of touching hers. It would have felt *wunderbarr* if Andrew hadn't decided it should feel awkward.

He shrugged away from Mary's touch and scooped Alfie into his arms, hugging him tightly enough to squeeze the wind out of him. He could feel Alfie's heartbeat vibrating like a hummingbird's wings. *Jah*, Alfie didn't need any punishment, even if he did deserve a *gute* scolding. "Are you okay?"

It was only when Andrew set Alfie on his feet that he noticed the red, bleeding welts on both arms.

Mary saw them too. She knelt down, took Alfie's wrists, and turned his arms over. It would be a lot

easier to avoid Mary if she wasn't so kind to his *bruderen*.
"*Ach*, Alfie, did Billy Idol scratch you?"

"*Nae*, but he hissed at me every time I tried to
climb down."

Andrew furrowed his brow. Maybe that cat wasn't
such a menace after all. "What happened?"

Alfie shrugged. "I got too high and tried to climb
down. I slipped and scraped against the tree trunk."

Andrew pursed his lips. With scratches that deep,
Alfie had slid hard. Thank Derr Herr he'd been
strong enough to catch himself.

"Poor Alfie," Mary said, cooing and clicking her
tongue. "It must hurt something wonderful."

Benji's lips formed into an O. "That looks bad. Do
you think you'll have a scar?"

Alfie wasn't in too much pain to puff out his chest.
"At least twenty, all down my arms."

Benji suddenly wanted to know everything. "Why
did the cats follow you? Could you see everything
from up there? Did you get stung by a bee?"

"*Nae*, but I killed seven mosquitoes. And I dropped
my walkie-talkie."

"I missed you so much, Alfie."

"I missed you too, Benji. And I forgive you for
breaking my horse."

Yost Weaver came tromping across the grass from
the direction of the barn. "What in the world is
going on?"

Bitsy didn't look at her husband as she was watching the firefighters save her cats. "Alfie Petersheim
got himself stuck in one of our trees. Mary had to call
the fire department."

Yost put his arm around Bitsy in plain sight of
everybody. Bitsy took her eyes off the tree long enough

to give Yost a gruff, affectionate smile. Yost used to be the most buttoned-up Amish man in Wisconsin, happily pious and unwilling to step one foot outside of the rules. Folks gossiped, wondering what Bitsy had done to trick Yost into marrying the most headstrong, unconventional woman in the district—the woman who painted her fingernails and kept a shotgun.

But the reason was as plain as the smell of rose water on Mammi Martha.

Bitsy and Yost loved each other, madly. They weren't like most old married couples. Yost couldn't seem to take his eyes off Bitsy, and Bitsy seemed to tolerate Yost just fine, which was the highest compliment she ever paid anybody. And she smiled at him more often than she smiled at anybody else—which wasn't saying much. Bitsy didn't smile at anyone unless it was a special occasion.

"Alfie needs a few Band-Aids," Yost said.

Bitsy turned her eyes to the firefighters who were being lowered to the ground. Jerry held an orange marmalade cat, and the other firefighter held a light-and-dark-brown striped cat. Should there have been three cats?

The first firefighter handed his cat to Yost, who immediately put her down and let her run off to find adventure. Jerry handed his cat to Mary with that smile that was really starting to annoy Andrew. He was grateful for Jerry's help with Alfie, but he didn't have to hang around when he was no longer needed.

Mary's smile was radiant and completely unnecessary. "*Denki*, Jerry. We are all so grateful."

"*Jah*," Andrew said, nearly choking on his own saliva, "we're wonderful grateful."

Benji and Alfie both gave Jerry a hug. Alfie's hug smeared blood on Jerry's firefighter shirt. Jerry messed up Alfie's already unruly hair. "Stop climbing trees. You could break your arm or your neck next time."

Alfie scrunched his lips to one side of his face. "I won't break anything."

It was plain that Alfie had no intention of staying out of trees. Andrew would have scolded him, but it would have done no good. Trying to keep a boy out of a tree was like trying to stop a river with your arm.

Jerry reached into his pocket and pulled out two Tootsie Rolls, which he handed to the boys. "Just remember to be careful."

Mary pointed to the trunk of the tree about ten feet off the ground. "Look, Aunt Bitsy. Billy Idol climbed down by himself."

Bitsy grunted. "He's not very fond of people. He has some trust issues." Billy Idol let go of the trunk when he was about four feet off the ground and landed gracefully on his feet. Bitsy picked him up and gave him a pat on the head. "Good job, Billy Idol. Good job." She set him on the ground, and he bolted in the direction of the barn. Andrew hoped there was a juicy mouse waiting for him there. He deserved it.

"*Cum*, Alfie," Mary said, holding out her hands to both boys. They took her hands as if she could save them from drowning. "Let's go into the house and get your arms fixed up, Alfie. I have a whole bee-sting cake that needs eating."

The boys looked at Andrew, who felt his face flush with heat. The last time Mary had offered them a treat, he'd refused to even step inside the house. Surely Mary hadn't forgotten.

Mary eyed Andrew with a guarded expression, as if

this was a test and she expected him to fail it. "There's lots of bee-sting cake," she said.

"Does it have bee stings in it?" Benji asked.

"*Nae*, it's called bee-sting cake because it's so sweet bees would eat it if we let them in the house."

"I want some bee-sting cake," Alfie said, sticking out his lips and showing Andrew his blood-encrusted arms. "I deserve a treat for being so brave."

Andrew narrowed his eyes, but he was unable to keep a smile from creeping onto his lips. "You deserve a spanking for being so *deerich*." He put a hand on Alfie's shoulder. "Come on then. We'd better go see what all the fuss is about this cake."

"Hooray!" Benji yelled, doing a little jig and almost stepping on the orange cat.

"It must be *gute*," Andrew said. "Mary brought one to the gathering."

Mary's lips twitched upward sheepishly, but there was just a hint of something unhappy in her eyes. "It *is* the cake I brought to the gathering."

*Ach.* Andrew's stomach dropped to his toes. No one had touched Mary's bee-sting cake at the gathering, even though there were plenty of hungry boys and that cake could have stopped traffic on the highway. *Die youngie* didn't want to have a thing to do with Mary or her cake. Andrew's stomach dropped clear to China, or whatever was on the other side of the world from Wisconsin. He'd passed by Mary's cake at the gathering for the very same reason. He didn't want anyone to think he'd even consider eating a sinner's cake.

He forced a smile and pretended not to understand the significance of an uneaten cake. "Well,

Alfie, you should be grateful no one ate it at the gathering."

Mary nodded. "Not quite as fresh, but we kept it in the fridge and it's still *appeditlich*."

Bitsy headed toward the house. "They can soak it in milk, if they're picky." She turned, and her gaze flicked from Andrew to Jerry. "Can you stay for a piece of cake, Jerry? You and your friends or mates or comrades or whatever it is you call them?"

Jerry seemed pleased by the invitation. Andrew could only be annoyed. What was wrong with him? Jerry had just saved his *bruder*. He should feel nothing but grateful. Jerry asked the other two firefighters, and they all agreed to a slice of bee-sting cake.

"Brady is going to drive the truck back onto the road, and then they'll come in." Jerry fell in step beside Mary, and Andrew felt compelled to abandon Alfie and walk with Mary and Jerry. *Ach*, their names rhymed. They were the perfect couple.

Except that they weren't.

Mary was going to have a baby, and Jerry would never consider someone like her as a suitable wife, would he?

"I'd heard you were back," Jerry said. "I'm sorry Alfie got stuck in that tree, but at least it gave me a chance to see you." Jerry glanced at Andrew. "My *dat* never has to find out."

Andrew knew exactly why Jerry didn't want his *dat* to find out, but did Jerry have to come right out and say it? Didn't he care about Mary's feelings? Andrew felt about two inches tall. In all his righteous indignation, he had said much worse things and felt perfectly justified. Who was he to find fault with anybody?

Mary laughed as if she found everyone's disapproval

endearing. "I'm going to become the best-kept secret in Bienenstock. They gossip about me, but no one wants to admit they've talked to me. Andrew sneaks around like a fox prowling the henhouse."

"I do not," Andrew said. Hadn't he followed her into Edna King's house in plain view of about thirty of *die youngie*?

"I'm sorry," Jerry said. "I'm as much of a coward as any of them, keeping it from my parents. It's just easier, if you know what I mean."

"I know," Mary said. "I used to be one of you."

"You still are," Jerry said. It was a kind thing to say, even if it wasn't entirely true.

"That's nice, Jerry, but I know how they feel about me." She peered at Andrew. "I can't expect anyone to understand what I've gone through. People here don't know what I know. They haven't had the experiences I've had. I can forgive them for being less than kind. They can't make sense of it."

Jerry slowed his pace as they approached the house. "Where did you go? I heard you were in Milwaukee."

"Nothing quite that grand. I went to Green Bay and lived in my boyfriend's stepmom's basement."

Andrew wanted to speed up, but Jerry slowed to a crawl. "Josh?"

Mary nodded.

They shouldn't be talking about such things, but his curiosity was like a raging fire. Who was Josh, and why did Jerry know about him? Andrew swallowed past the lump in his throat. It was none of his business, and he hoped they'd keep talking about it.

"Green Bay has a *gute* football team," Jerry said.

Football team? Who cared about football when there was so much more to know about Josh?

Benji and Alfie walked ahead of them. Benji had his arm draped around Alfie's shoulder, their heads together as if they were already planning their next adventure. Alfie glanced back at Andrew and whispered something to Benji. Benji looked back at Jerry and bit his bottom lip. They were planning something, for sure and certain. Andrew could only hope it wasn't a climb to the roof of Bitsy's barn.

Benji broke away from Alfie and grabbed Jerry's hand, pulling him forward and away from Mary and Andrew. "Do you have a gun?"

Andrew smiled at Mary. "At least Benji and Alfie got some excitement out of the whole thing."

"I thought it was very exciting," Mary said.

Andrew shook his head. "I thought I was going to have a seizure."

Andrew didn't know why, but he liked it very much when he could make Mary smile. Had Josh made Mary smile? "You watch out for your *bruderen.*"

"It's what the oldest does, I guess."

"Most *bruderen* your age ignore their younger siblings. My oldest *bruder* is ten years older. I hardly know him."

Nobody seemed to have been in a hurry to get to the house, but even moving like snails, they had to get there eventually. They walked up the porch steps, Benji still chattering with Jerry about guns and fire hoses. Alfie had grown silent, probably finally feeling the full pain in his arms and wondering how he was going to explain two bandage-covered arms to Mamm.

Bitsy invited them to sit around her heavy wooden table and served everyone a piece of cake. Jerry and his two firefighter friends, Brady and Rob, got the biggest pieces. Andrew tried not to be offended. Maybe Bitsy was just grateful to them for saving her cats. Maybe she liked Jerry better than she liked Andrew. What did it matter who Bitsy or Mary liked better? Andrew didn't care one bit.

Mary sat Alfie at the head of the table and pulled up a chair next to him. She filled a bowl with water and got some first aid supplies, then carefully poured water over Alfie's arms and gently scrubbed away the dirt. Alfie hissed and flinched, but he wasn't one to make a big fuss. Mary went upstairs and came back with a pair of tweezers. "We're going to have to get out all the slivers."

Alfie clamped his eyes shut and held his breath.

"You have to breathe, Alfie, or you'll pass out."

"Okay," Alfie said, sucking in a deep breath and holding it again.

Mary smiled at him and did her best to move quickly. While Alfie shut his eyes, she pulled out six slivers and deposited them on a paper towel on the table. One sliver was nearly an inch long. Alfie picked it up and examined it from four different angles. "Look, Benji. Look at the size of it."

Benji took the sliver from Alfie. "Oy, anyhow. Won't Willie be jealous?"

Every life-threatening, terrifying experience was worth it if you could brag about it to your friends.

Alfie deflated like a leaky bicycle tire. "We can't tell Willie. His *mamm* will tell Mamm, and we'll never get dessert again." He eyed Jerry across the table. "You won't tell anybody, will you?"

Jerry took a swallow of his milk. Bitsy hadn't given

Andrew any milk. "Andrew already asked me to keep it a secret. I won't even tell my *dat*."

He wouldn't tell his *dat* for more than just Alfie's sake.

Andrew took a bite of cake. It was like heaven in his mouth. "I don't think you're going to be able to hide this from Mamm," Andrew said. "Mary is going to have to bandage both your arms all the way up. Mamm will see that a mile away."

Alfie flinched as Mary smeared ointment on his skin. "I'll wear my long sleeves."

"All summer?"

Mary layered gauze pads all the way up Alfie's right arm. "Even when it's safe to take off the gauze, you'll have scabs for weeks," Mary said. "If I were your *mamm*, I'd notice for sure and certain."

Benji grimaced. "Mamm will know. She sees everything, except that one time when Alfie and me . . ." He trailed off, no doubt realizing he had nearly revealed a deep, dark secret. His face suddenly brightened. "We could pick off all the scabs."

Mary made one of her many faces, puckering her lips into a wrinkled frown. "Then he'd need bandages again."

Andrew watched Mary as she loosely wrapped medical tape around and around Alfie's arm to hold the gauze in place. He was quite taken with the lines of her fingers, the curve of her hands as she tended to Alfie. He'd once touched those hands, and they were petal soft. "I'm afraid Mamm is going to find out," Andrew said. "You might as well tell her what happened."

Alfie didn't like that answer. "I can do it. Mamm never notices what I wear."

"She notices everything," Benji insisted. "Do you remember when we snuck candy before dinner, and she smelled chocolate on our breath?"

"She checks behind my ears, but she's never asked to check my arms."

Jerry, Brady, and Rob stood in unison. "We've got to get back to the station," Jerry said. "*Denki* for the cake."

Bitsy swatted away his compliment. "Don't thank me. Mary made it."

Jerry turned his annoying smile to Mary. "*Denki*, Mary. I don't think I've ever eaten something so delicious."

Really? In his twenty, twenty-one years of eating, Jerry had never tasted anything as delicious as Mary's bee-sting cake? He had stooped to shameless flattery. Mary would see through that like a thin window curtain.

Her cheeks turned an attractive shade of pink, which was probably from the exertion of wrapping Alfie's arms. Jerry looked sharp in his fireman's uniform, but a smart girl like Mary could surely see past a nice smile and a uniform.

Bitsy opened the door for them. "Come by anytime. Mary's always got something baking."

"I will," Jerry said, as if Bitsy had invited only him. Andrew had never known Jerry to be the arrogant type, but he was certainly getting on Andrew's nerves today. "Stay out of trees, Alfie." Jerry was down the porch steps before he finished his sentence.

Alfie motioned to Benji, who went to the open door and waved. "*Denki*, Jerry. You did *gute* helping Alfie." He leaned his head out the door and whispered loudly enough for everyone to hear him. "But Mary's already spoken for."

Already spoken for? Did Benji mean the father of Mary's child? How did Benji know such things? Andrew was going to have to quit underestimating his little *bruderen*. Benji, especially, had keen ears and a fruitful imagination.

Bitsy shut the door and plopped into the chair next to Yost, who was on his second piece of cake. "I've had enough excitement to last an entire year. It's lucky I dye my hair, because I think the rest of it turned white today."

"Did you think I was going to die?" Alfie said, eagerly leaning forward with his eyes as wide as saucers. What boy didn't want to tell his friends that he'd almost died?

"I didn't think any such thing, young man," Bitsy said, stabbing her uneaten piece of cake with her fork. "That fire truck ran over a half acre of dandelions and almost toppled my beehives, and Farrah Fawcett left her window seat for the first time in a decade. I won't even need to go to the Fourth of July fireworks. I've had enough thrills today to last me all summer."

Alfie turned to Mary. "I could have broke my neck. I could have."

Mary patted Alfie's hand. "Were you scared?"

"I wasn't scared, but Benji was."

"I wath not," Benji protested, with a double forkful of cake in his mouth.

There were so many lectures Andrew could have given Alfie, he didn't know where to begin. The no-bragging, no-lying, no-sneaking-around lectures would have to wait. He gave Alfie the stink eye. "That was a very *deerich* thing to do, Alfie. You could have been badly hurt."

Mary tore the last piece of tape and let go of Alfie's wrist. Alfie turned his arms every which way so he could get a good look. He was covered from bicep to wrist in bandages, as if his blue shirt had long white sleeves. "*Ach*! I look like I fought with a bear. Willie won't think he's so tough when he sees me."

Alfie obviously had a short memory. A very short memory. A memory the length of a mealy bug. Maybe he wouldn't be so cocky when Mamm caught sight of him.

"You know, Alfie," Mary said, "you have a wonderful nice *bruder*. Andrew came running when you needed help, and he stayed by the tree the whole time and made sure we called the fire department. I'm sure he would have rescued you himself if you hadn't been so high and the branches hadn't been so thin."

Andrew clamped his mouth shut on scolding Alfie. Mary was smiling at him as if he was one of the blessed saints. He didn't want to burst her bubble.

Alfie studied Mary's face, bloomed into a grin, then turned his gaze to Andrew. "*Jah*. Andrew is wonderful brave. You should see him with his shirt off. He has big muscles."

Andrew thought his face might catch on fire. He vowed never to be in the same room with Alfie again, unless it was in his own house and there were no girls present. He didn't dare look at Mary. Was she as embarrassed as he was? Or was it commonplace to a girl who'd already . . . well . . . had already seen a man's chest before? *Ach*. That thought made him want to shrivel into a little ball, crawl beneath the floorboards, and never come out.

When he heard her laugh, he worked up the courage to glance in her direction. She was making a funny face at Alfie as if he'd just said something *dumm* and typical of an eight-year-old—nothing more serious than that. Andrew relaxed a little. If Mary didn't feel awkward, then he wouldn't either.

He liked that about her. Even in the most uncomfortable situations—like someone finding out she was pregnant—she didn't get flustered. For sure and certain everyone would feel comfortable around her if they gave her a chance.

Bitsy's lips vibrated as she blew air from between them. "Big muscles aren't nothing. I prefer nice teeth and a lot of money."

Yost's mouth fell open. "You married me for my money?"

Bitsy raised her eyebrows. "How much do you have?"

"Hardly any."

"Then I married you for your teeth," Bitsy said.

Yost smiled. "I'm glad I still have a few left."

"You have just the right amount." Bitsy's brows inched together. "But what do you say, Mary? Do you like muscles or teeth?"

Mary laughed, unembarrassed and unconcerned. "I like a *gute* heart." If Mary wasn't bothered by this conversation, Andrew wouldn't be either.

Bitsy groaned as if one of her cats had jumped on her lap and asked to be petted. "Go ahead. Make the rest of us look shallow."

"I like a *gute* heart too," Andrew said, just so Bitsy wouldn't think he was one of the shallow ones.

Bitsy eyed Andrew as if he were a door-to-door

salesman. "But I bet you wouldn't mind a *gute* set of teeth."

Andrew couldn't help but grin at the skeptical look on Bitsy's face. "I suppose not."

Bitsy finished her cake, pulled her chair around the table next to Alfie, and pointed her fork at him. "Now that the dust has settled and you didn't break your femur, I want to know what you were doing in my basswood tree."

Benji, who was sitting next to Alfie, clamped his lips together and shook his head as if Bitsy had asked him the question. His eyes nearly bugged out of his head.

Alfie nibbled on his bottom lip for several seconds, obviously choosing his words very carefully. Lord willing, he wasn't making up a lie. Everyone would know. "I can't tell," he finally said.

"Because it's a secret and he doesn't want to lie." Benji gave Alfie a reassuring nod. "Alfie would never tell a lie."

Hmm, Andrew wasn't sure about that, but he was proud of Alfie for not making up a story about why he was stuck in the tree, and he was proud of Benji for having so much faith in his *bruder*.

"Were you spying on my beehives?" Bitsy said.

Benji had always had a hard time keeping a secret. "We were spying, but not on the beehives."

"Benji!" Alfie scolded. "Don't say anything."

"Sorry."

Bitsy leaned back in her chair, folded her arms, and glanced in Andrew's direction, the fork still in her hand. "Whatever spying you were doing, I appreciate that you had some consideration for my dandelions, though it didn't matter in the end because that fire truck ruined the whole field."

Andrew gave his *bruderen* a stern gaze. "The boys and I will come early tomorrow to fill in the ruts, even if it takes all day."

Alfie burst into a smile. "Really? We're going to spend the whole day here?"

Benji leaped off his chair, jumped up and down, and clapped his hands in delight.

Andrew had no explanation for the excitement, except that maybe they were hoping for another piece of bee-sting cake tomorrow. It was wonderful *gute.*

Bitsy's piercing gaze could have drilled a hole through Andrew's skull. What was she looking for? And why did she seem to be picking on him? "All right," Bitsy said, after a long pause. "But you can't step on the other dandelions while you smooth out the ruts. That would be a disaster."

"We'll be extra careful," Andrew said, though he couldn't guarantee the safety of all of Bitsy's dandelions. He was working with two eight-year-olds.

Bitsy was still looking at him as if she wanted to read his mind. "It was nice of you to help your *bruder,* Andrew. Most brothers couldn't have spared the time."

"Andrew's nice," Benji said. "He doesn't yell at us."

Bitsy pursed her lips. "He stepped on my dandelions. He still has to prove himself."

Why did he need to prove himself to Bitsy? It was hard enough just keeping up with Mamm and Mammi Martha and the peanut butter. Bitsy was concerned about her ruts. Andrew could only do his best.

Bitsy stood and gathered the plates from the table.

Mary followed suit and started gathering forks. "Leave them, Mary," Bitsy said. "Alfie and Benji are going to help Yost and me clean up and get dinner started. You and Andrew are going to walk out to the field and examine the ruts and the beehives. Make sure Andrew knows enough not to get stung tomorrow."

Mary glanced at Bitsy, then at Andrew, and shrugged. "Okay. I'll show Andrew the hives."

"And be careful of the dandelions."

"Always."

If Bitsy was anything, she was single-minded. The dandelions seemed to be the only thing she cared about, and they were a common weed. Surely there were more important things in her life.

Mary smiled and led the way as she and Andrew strolled down the porch steps and over the grass to the deep ruts in Bitsy's lawn. Andrew had to tiptoe to avoid the thick clumps of dandelions. "For sure and certain Bitsy cares about her dandelions," he said.

Mary nodded. "Bees love dandelions. She's very protective of her bees."

"But there are lots of other flowers on the farm. And look at those trees. It looks like the bees are getting plenty."

"It's true," Mary said. "Maybe it's because Bitsy has a heart for the downtrodden, and there's nothing more common and less valued than a dandelion. Most people try to get rid of them. But Bitsy looks beyond what most people can see. Dandelions take no effort to grow. They are hardy, even if you step on them, and the bees like them just as much as they like roses or tomatoes. I think bees like them better because they're so easy to find."

Andrew swallowed hard. Jerry had started the wheels in his head turning, and Andrew couldn't stop them. Jerry hadn't been afraid to ask questions, and Mary hadn't seemed ashamed to answer them. Andrew had confused Mary's open, unembarrassed way with pride and an unrepentant heart. But maybe it was as Mary said, she'd made peace with what she had done and invited Gotte's forgiveness into her life. "Is that . . . is that why you came here after your parents kicked you out? You knew Bitsy would take you in?"

Mary eyed him as if trying to decide why he was asking, but she kept walking and answered anyway. "Bitsy lived as an Englischer for almost twenty years. I knew if anybody could understand me, it was her. Bitsy isn't afraid to love people who don't fit in."

His curiosity overtook him, even though that little voice inside his head screamed at him to be careful. It might be wonderful dangerous to get to know Mary better. She could pull him into her sinful ways. "Were you happy in Green Bay?"

She paused and looked at him out of the corner of her eye. "Nobody but Bitsy has asked me that. Nobody wants to know."

Andrew couldn't imagine that more than a handful of people had said more than three words to Mary in all the time she'd been back. The subject of Green Bay had understandably never come up. "I want to know."

Mary seemed hesitant, which wasn't what Andrew had come to expect. "It might be hard to hear."

Hard to hear? "Okay."

"I lived with my boyfriend, Josh, in his stepmother's basement."

"Okay."

"Josh got us both jobs. He's a *gute* mechanic. I worked in a bakery. They hired me because they found out I was Amish. I wore my Plain clothes every day to work. It brought in more customers. They think the Amish have some secret to good baking."

"Were you happy?"

She raised her eyebrows in his direction. "Are you sure you want to know?"

"What do you mean?"

"Because you've been taught your whole life that living in the community and strictly adhering to the Ordnung is the happier, safer way. The way to salvation. It's hard to accept that other people might have found happiness outside our way of life."

Andrew frowned. "I still want to hear it."

Mary sighed. "I felt guilty to be living in sin with Josh, but he told me that was the way all Englischers did it. They lived together before they got married to make sure they truly wanted to be with each other. It made sense, so I put it out of my mind. It's the only thing that still makes me ashamed. I believed a lie Josh told me because I wanted to believe it. I couldn't have made it in the Englisch world on my own. In some ways, I was using Josh to get what I wanted."

"What did you want?"

"Freedom." Her eyes filled with concern, as if she worried she was going to upset the balance of Andrew's entire life. "The truth is, Andrew, I was very happy. For the first time in my life, I could choose what I wanted to do. I could choose what I wanted to wear. I could choose whether or not to go to church.

I started going to school because I wanted to be a nurse. I had no knowledge beyond the eighth grade, Andrew. It was like a whole new, *wunderbarr* world opened up to me."

Mary was right. Andrew didn't want to hear that. The right way was supposed to be obvious. The sinner was supposed to be miserable and let that misery lead her to repentance. How would anybody learn obedience if disobedience was so attractive? "*Ach, vell,* I can't imagine any happiness that would compensate for living a life of devotion to Gotte and the church."

"Of course you can't, and I honor that. Safety is more important to you than freedom."

"Safety and righteousness."

She nodded vigorously. "Of course you are right. But what is righteousness? Is it keeping my head covered as a sign of humility? Is it wearing suspenders instead of belts or forbidding buttons on dresses?"

"Those are traditions that point our thoughts to Gotte."

"*Jah,* and to a seventeen-year-old girl, they were restrictions I couldn't live with."

"That seems short-sighted," Andrew said.

"*Ach, vell,* I was seventeen, and I've learned a lot."

"What have you learned?"

Mary stopped about four yards from the beehives. "My idea of freedom was an illusion. I am free to make my choices, but nobody is free to choose the consequences. I worked two jobs, sixty hours a week to pay for my freedom. What kind of freedom is that? My family rejected me, which didn't surprise me, but it was one of the consequences of leaving. Josh's stepmother liked to stick her nose into our lives, but we were living in her house. I was never free of her."

Andrew had to shove his hands in his pockets to keep from caressing that silky cheek with his thumb. Something warm and swelling pressed against his rib cage, and he found himself aching to understand her. "I thought you were happy?"

"I was." Her lips turned upward. "When you choose one path, you also reject all the other paths you could have taken. It's never an easy decision with anything that matters."

"I guess that's true, but you made the wrong choice to begin with." He probably shouldn't have said that, but it was so obviously true.

Mary's eyes were turned from him, gazing at the beehives and the small pond beyond. She didn't answer him for a few seconds. Then she turned, and her smile took his breath away. She pointed to the nearest beehive. "They won't bother you if they don't think you're a threat." And just like that, they were done with freedom and consequences and choices, and Andrew couldn't help but think he'd missed something important and opened his mouth when he should have kept it shut.

Ten beehives stood in a row, like a line of rag-tag scarecrows. Some beehives tilted slightly, as if winter had made them weary. Each box had been painted with flowers or farm scenes, but the colors had faded, weathered with age, snow, and rain, until the paint had peeled and flaked and gray wood was exposed at the corners. Still, they were a sight to see with what must have been thousands of bees flying in and out and all around. Each hive was so thick with bodies that it looked as if a cloud hovered over every one. And the hum of a thousand wings was like an approaching train, pleasant and mighty at the same time.

"Wear long sleeves." Mary grinned. "Although I probably don't need to tell Alfie that. It appears he's going to be wearing long sleeves for the next three months. And don't wear brown. If you look like a bear, the bees will sting you."

"Will the bees think we're flowers if we wear colors?"

"Maybe." Mary's lips twitched sheepishly. "And you can't smell good."

"Can't smell good?"

She shifted her weight. "I mean, well, mostly you smell like cedar or walnut or leather, but sometimes you smell like roses. I like it, but the bees do too."

Andrew's heart beat double time. Mary liked it when he smelled like roses? Maybe Mammi Martha knew something Andrew didn't. "*Ach.* Okay. No smelling like roses."

Mary gave him a curious smile. "There must be a story behind that."

"My *mammi* thinks rose water is the cure for smelly boys."

"I'm guessing the twins are against rose water."

"*Jah.* But Mammi is persistent."

He really liked Mary's laugh. "Persistent with you too?"

Andrew shrugged, and he felt his face get warm again. "Sometimes. Usually I don't smell as bad as Alfie and Benji, so she forgets to make me use it."

"You smell like cedarwood."

"I'm making a cedar chest for the next auction."

Keeping a safe distance, she slowly walked around

the beehives. He followed her. "You said your *mamm* doesn't want you to build things."

"Well, not exactly. She knows I have the tools. She doesn't know how much of my spare time is spent in the barn with the wood. She doesn't like anything that takes away from making peanut butter and helping on the farm."

"But you'd rather work with the wood."

"Mamm would be heartbroken if I told her I want to be a carpenter instead of a Peanut Butter Brother," Andrew said. "The business wouldn't survive without my help."

"Your *mater* seems like a reasonable person. Maybe you should tell her."

Andrew shook his head. "I couldn't do that to Mamm. She's done nothing but sacrifice for our family. If the twins are awake, they're into some sort of trouble, and now that Mammi and Dawdi are living with us, her burdens are three times as heavy."

Mary's brows inched together. "I'm sorry."

The look she gave him sent warm chocolate pulsing through his veins. "It's okay." It was more than okay. Mary Coblenz actually cared.

Mary grew quiet as they finished circling the hives. "I know why Alfie was in that tree," she finally said as they headed back toward the house.

"You do?"

"He was spying on me."

Andrew pulled down the corners of his mouth. "You? Why?"

"*Ach, vell,* I'm the strangest girl Benji and Alfie have ever seen: pregnant, unmarried, and forbidden. They're curious."

Andrew always got tense when she mentioned she was pregnant. "It's a dangerous way to be curious."

She cleared her throat and looked away from him. "You told them to stay away from me, so they were spying."

His heart sank. "They told you that?" He should never say anything to an eight-year-old that he didn't want repeated. And he never should have said that about Mary. He'd been terribly unfair.

"I don't blame you, Andrew. You're a *gute bruder*. I'll have a talk with them tomorrow and tell them they need to obey you. Disobedience got Alfie into a lot of trouble."

This would be a good time to crawl under the dirt. "*Nae*, Mary. I'm the one who was wrong. That first day, I was taken by surprise." He couldn't tell her how much her golden hair had distracted him. "I didn't know you had come back and then I saw that you were pregnant."

"I still am."

"*Ach*, I was shaken up. I was afraid you'd be a bad influence on my *bruderen*."

"You're not the only one who feels that way."

"It doesn't matter how everybody else feels," Andrew said. "As a Christian, I know better than to judge someone by how they look."

"But it's not just how I look, Andrew. I've obviously done something very sinful. It's normal that you would warn your *bruderen* against me."

He wasn't going to let her make it easy on him. He stopped walking, cupped his fingers around her arm, and tugged her to a stop. "It might be normal, but it wasn't nice. It was mean and cowardly, and I'm sorry."

She scrunched her lips and regarded him with raised eyebrows. "That's . . . that's a very nice thing to say, Andrew."

But.

He could tell she didn't quite believe him. At least she was nice about it. He couldn't blame her for not trusting him. He hadn't given her a lot of good reasons. How often had he called her a sinner to her face? How often had he called her to repentance? How many of his self-righteous words had cut her right to the heart? He'd helped her out of the volleyball game, but he had also stood by and let Benji pull the wagon for her. And he had practically done somersaults and back flips to avoid being seen with her.

"I'm sorry, Mary," he repeated, unsure if he'd ever convince her to believe him. "I'm going to tell the boys that they don't have to stay away from you."

"Maybe that will keep them from climbing trees."

"I hope so. Bitsy might call the police if her dandelions get stepped on."

Mary smiled, but it didn't quite reach her eyes.

# Chapter Seven

It would be safer if Alfie never took his shirt off again, except to take a bath, and even that was risky. Last night, he'd dressed in the T-shirt he wore as pajamas, and Mamm had come downstairs to tuck him and Benji in bed. She hadn't tucked them in bed since the first night they'd slept in the cellar. Something was up.

Maybe she was getting suspicious.

Alfie had dived under the covers so fast he'd popped another hole in the air mattress. Luckily Mamm hadn't noticed the air hissing from beneath him or the bandages on his arms. He had clamped the blankets right up against his chin when Mamm had knelt down to kiss him. She couldn't have pulled those covers off with a crowbar.

Tonight he decided to go to bed with his long-sleeved shirt on. That way if Mamm came down to tuck him in, she wouldn't see a thing. And if she sneaked down in the middle of the night to spy on him, his sleeves would keep him from getting caught. Mamm was smart for a girl, but Alfie was on to her plans.

He'd been tricked into moving into the cellar. She'd never trick him again.

Alfie lay down on his back and stared at the ceiling, doing his nightly check for attacking spiders. He forgot about his arms for a second and tried to tuck his hands under his neck. Bending his elbows made everything sting, and he accidentally smacked his hand on the bookshelf Mamm had put next to his bed this morning.

Mammi Martha bought the bookshelf because she said Benji and Alfie didn't do enough reading. Mammi probably thought that if she got a bookshelf, Alfie and Benji would fill it with books. Alfie liked to read, but Mammi only approved of books like *Martyrs Mirror* and *March Forward with the Word!* Alfie liked Scooby-Doo, and Benji read Tintin. They got them at the library and hid them under their pillows so Mamm wouldn't know. Mamm had never actually told them they couldn't read Scooby-Doo, but better to be safe than sorry. What she didn't know couldn't get them in trouble.

When two Englischers had delivered the bookshelf this morning, Mamm got that look on her face like when you stuff a deer and give it marbles for eyes. Alfie was beginning to wonder if Mamm didn't appreciate Mammi Martha's gifts. For sure and certain, Alfie didn't appreciate them. Mammi forced him and Benji to read for half an hour every day— In. The. Summer!—and he'd just smacked his hand on her bookshelf.

He was beginning to think that the cellar was where Mamm put all her unwanted things.

Alfie's arms still hurt something wonderful. Raking and shoveling Bitsy's grass today had made them feel worse, even though Andrew had let Alfie and Benji sit under the tree half the time and drink lemonade with Mary while Andrew did all the work.

Andrew was as *dumm* as a fish. Alfie had done a lot of spying, but for all he could tell, Andrew hadn't even held Mary's hand yet, and it was going on five weeks knowing Mary. Andrew had done a lot of looking at Mary yesterday when he thought no one was paying attention, but looking didn't do squat. They needed a wedding. What was Andrew waiting for?

There was nothing wrong with Mary. She had let Alfie and Benji eat as many sugar cookies as they wanted, and she didn't even get mad when Benji spilled his drink on her leg. Her toe was still wrapped up with tape, and her foot was a spooky, jiminy-critters color of purple. She didn't ever cry about it, even though Alfie could tell it hurt her cuz she limped when she walked, along with waddling, which she said she was doing because she couldn't walk straight with a baby in her tummy.

Maybe it was Mary's fault. Maybe she wasn't all that excited about Andrew. Andrew was pretty nice and he was tall, but Jerry Zimmerman had a real fireman's hat and a coat with yellow stripes and the neatest truck Alfie had ever seen. Mary had smiled at Jerry after he helped Alfie from that tree. What could Andrew do to impress a girl that Jerry couldn't?

Andrew would never have a *wunderbarr* red truck like Jerry. Maybe it was a lost cause. Or maybe they'd have to try harder if they wanted their own room. They might need some firecrackers, and they'd definitely have to consult with Dawdi.

The cellar door opened, and Alfie could hear footsteps on the stairs. He almost dived under the covers until he remembered he didn't need to because he had long sleeves. They didn't need another hole in the air mattress. Andrew had already fixed two. Of course, if Andrew was married, they wouldn't have to sleep on the air mattress, so Alfie couldn't see it in his heart to be grateful.

Benji didn't dive under the covers, but he did stuff the whole cookie in his mouth that he'd been saving for a midnight snack. Mamm didn't like food in the cellar. She said it attracted bugs. She didn't know that there were already too many bugs to count, and enough spiders to eat them all. What was she thinking anyway? All there was in the cellar was food—and Mammi's bookshelf. Canned spaghetti sauce, chow-chow, green beans, Mammi's cookie sheets, and stewed tomatoes. If Alfie and Benji ever got stuck down here, they could live for five years on salsa and canned cheese.

Sure enough, Mamm appeared at the bottom of the stairs with two mugs of something steamy hot in one hand and a lantern in the other. *Jah*, she was up to something. She never made them a bedtime drink. Alfie made up his mind then and there not to drink it. It was another trick.

"All ready for bed?" Mamm asked, with pretend happiness in her voice. For sure and certain it was a trick. She could very well see they were ready for bed.

"Ready, Mamm." Alfie tucked his arms under the covers, just to be safe, and smiled as if he didn't know what Mamm was up to. *Ach, vell*, he didn't know what Mamm was up to, but he knew she was up to something.

Benji's cheeks bulged with the force of his cookie,

and he chewed as fast and as secretly as he could. It was a big cookie.

"It's getting crowded down here," Alfie said, to take Mamm's attention off Benji's chewing.

Mamm glanced at the bookshelf and sighed. "I brought you some hot chocolate to help you sleep." Maybe she hadn't understood him. Maybe she was ignoring the bookshelf. Maybe she was hoping Benji and Alfie hadn't noticed she'd stuck it down here.

They'd noticed, all right. If there was an earthquake, it would fall over and kill both of them.

She handed Benji a mug, and he drank three big gulps to wash down his cookie. Alfie pulled one hand from under the covers.

"Sit up, Alfie. You'll spill all over yourself."

Mamm would get suspicious if he tried to drink lying down, and she'd get suspicious if he told her he didn't want any hot chocolate. It was his favorite drink, except for the fizzy punch Mamm made for Cousin Ira's wedding. Alfie sat up, pulling the covers with him so they reached his chin. Mamm smiled as if she thought he was so cute and patted the covers down, ripping them from his hands, and leaving him out in the open. "Why, Alfie, you're still wearing your shirt. You'll be more comfortable in your pajamas."

"I like sleeping in my shirt," Alfie said, which wasn't really a lie since he liked sleeping in his shirt a lot more than he liked getting caught. He'd better drink fast before Mamm guessed his secret. He grabbed the mug from Mamm, and a little hot chocolate dribbled on his blanket. Mamm didn't seem to notice.

"*Denki*, Mamm," Benji said, swallowing the last of the cookie and another gulp of hot chocolate.

Mamm reached across Alfie and smoothed Benji's hair out of his eyes. "I love you, Peanut."

Mamm hadn't called Benji *peanut* since he was seven. Something was definitely up. Mamm was being too nice. Alfie's gut clenched. When Alfie least expected it, she was going to pounce like Billy Idol on a mouse.

Alfie took the tiniest sip of hot chocolate and gave Mamm a fake smile that made his lips hurt. "This is wonderful nice, Mamm."

"Drink the whole thing. It's good for you." She pinched Alfie's cheek, which she hadn't done since he was in diapers. "I love you so much, Alfie Benaiah."

Now he was getting really worried. She never used his middle name unless she was mad at him. *I love you* and *Alfie Benaiah* were never used in the same sentence.

He stretched his lips tighter across his teeth. "I love you too, Mamm."

"Me too," Benji said, hot chocolate dripping down his chin. He looked a little worried.

Mamm smiled. "That's nice." She smoothed her hand along the bottom of the bookshelf. "Maybe you boys can put your rock collections and other things here. You'd like that, wouldn't you? Your own private place to store things."

What Alfie really wanted was his own private room, but Mamm was acting strange so he didn't mention it.

"Mammi Martha wants us to put books on that shelf," Benji said.

Mamm pursed her lips. "Truer words were never spoken." She kissed both of them on the forehead, took their empty mugs, and went upstairs.

For sure and certain, Mamm was up to something, and she might explode at any minute.

Jiminy critters. The suspense would kill him.

# Chapter Eight

Before getting out of the buggy, Mary practiced her deep breathing, which seeing as she was seven and a half months pregnant, wasn't very deep. Bitsy watched her doubtfully. "You're either in labor or having a panic attack."

Mary giggled between breaths. "Neither. I'm practicing biting my tongue."

"I never developed that talent," Bitsy said.

Yost set the brake and squeezed Bitsy's hand. "It's one of my favorite things about you."

Mary stopped trying to use up all the air in the buggy. "I'm not really hopeful that *die youngie* will be nice to me tonight, but the benefit haystack supper is a *gute* place to practice. I can at least try not to return railing for railing, like it says in the Bible."

Bitsy smirked. "Returning railing for railing is definitely one of my talents." Mary slid out of the buggy, and Bitsy followed her. "You're limping," Bitsy said.

"*Ach.* My right leg aches clear up to my thigh, my little toe is still sore, and the flip-flops hurt my feet. Am I too young for varicose veins?"

"Probably," Bitsy said. "But there are no rules when you're pregnant. Everyone is different. We should have brought our honey wagon. Yost would have pulled you."

"I'm in my fifties, Bitsy. I can't pull a face."

"That's not true, Yost. You're stronger than most men ten years younger. All that farm work makes for big muscles."

Yost flexed his biceps. "This is all yours, *heartzley*."

Mary looked under the canopy, and dread squeezed at her heart. "I wish I didn't have to pretend to be so strong."

Bitsy rolled her eyes and shook her head. "You're not pretending. You really are strong."

"It would be so much easier to stay home and let them turn up their noses at me from a distance."

"Much easier." Bitsy put her hand on the buggy door as if she was going to open it again. "Let's go home, but I'll warn you. I'm not making dinner. We were supposed to eat here. We'll have to settle for coffee soup. Yost's recipe."

Mary smiled at Bitsy. She'd never force Mary to do anything she didn't want to do. But as Mary had told Andrew, actions had consequences, and she wouldn't avoid consequences simply because they were harsh. "I need to know if I will ever be accepted here, Bitsy. I want to see if I can make a home with the people I grew up with, and the only way to do that is to give them a chance to love me or reject me."

The way things were going, she'd be back in Josh's stepmother's basement by Halloween. How appropriately spooky.

Bitsy handed the saucepan of cooked rice to Yost.

"I suppose you're right, but playing tag at home with my cats might be a lot less painful."

"No doubt." Mary squared her shoulders and made her best attempt at a smile. Not everyone had rejected her. Hannah and Mary Yutzy were always more than kind. Edna King had invited her over for dinner three times since she'd been back. Bitsy's nieces, their husbands, and their husbands' extended families included Mary in everything they did.

Hadn't Andrew apologized for all those things he'd said to her? She had forgiven him, but didn't necessarily believe he'd had a change of heart. Words were easily tossed around, like dandelion parachutes on a summer breeze. She wouldn't believe a word Andrew said until he actually did something about it.

Still, he had treated her kindly when most people either ignored or rejected her. Kindness was hard to resist. As were blue eyes and broad shoulders.

Mary frowned. Josh had chocolate-brown eyes and broad shoulders, and look where that had gotten her. Andrew might have a fascinating, slightly crooked smile and dark eyebrows that brooded over his face like storm clouds, but Mary was well aware of the consequences of giving her heart away to the wrong person—to any person. She wouldn't do it again. Falling in love left her powerless, and if there was anything Mary craved, it was the power to make her own choices.

No falling in love for her. She'd learned her lesson.

A huge canopy had been set up in the Zimmermans' side yard. The Zimmermans' house got used a lot because their yard had thick, green grass that made for a nice place to have a benefit supper. This benefit supper was to raise money to help pay Lily

Rose Zook's hospital bills. Englischers, mostly from Shawano and Bonduel and surrounding areas, came to eat, donating however much money they wanted to pay. It was called a haystack supper because you went down the line and stacked different things on your plate—rice then chicken and sauce then lettuce and onions and the like.

Mary had always loved haystack suppers growing up. She got to choose whatever she wanted to put on her plate, and Mamm was always too busy helping her siblings to notice when she skipped the broccoli. And there had always been brownies with mint frosting.

Bitsy had steamed a huge pan of rice, and Mary had baked a pineapple-coconut cake, even though no one had asked her to. She thought it might be fun to add it to the desserts and give people something to choose from besides cookies. The Englisch wouldn't care that an unmarried pregnant girl had made the cake. Maybe it would get eaten.

Yost took Bitsy's pan of rice to the serving table. Bitsy smirked at Mary. "Do you dare try to do the rice? I usually wash pots and pans in the back because Englischers get upset when they see an Amish woman with blue hair."

Mary nodded. "I can serve rice."

There was just a hint of concern in Bitsy's eyes. "Okay. Never let them see you sweat."

"What does that mean?"

Bitsy looked sideways at Yost. "It's an old TV commercial. Don't let them get to you, or at least don't show it if they do. Just smile and pretend you don't know how offended people are. It's an old trick I still use."

Mary smiled in spite of herself. "I'll do my best."

"I'd wish you good luck," Bitsy said, "but the Amish don't believe in luck."

Mary raised a teasing eyebrow. "The Englisch do."

"*Gute* luck, then. You'll need all the help you can get."

"*Denki* for the vote of confidence."

Bitsy pinched Mary's earlobe between her thumb and index finger. "You'll always get my vote, even though the Amish don't vote."

Mary went straight to the dessert tables, trying valiantly to ignore the stares and whispers cast in her direction. They'd had plenty of time to get used to her appearance, hadn't they? Apparently not. There wasn't a lot of excitement in their small Amish community, and Mary was an easy subject of gossip every time she set foot outside the house.

Women and girls were busy spreading out the food and preparing the tables, but a few of them weren't too busy to shoot Mary an unfriendly glance or to nudge their neighbor to make sure everybody saw who was invading their haystack supper.

Mary took a deep breath, reminding herself that this was an experiment. She was trying her neighbors, not the other way around. If they couldn't find it in their hearts to show love for a misfit, then she didn't want to be one of them anyway. But it did nothing to take away the sting of loneliness that made her feel as hollow as an empty warehouse.

Mary marched up to the treats table and smiled at the two women arranging plates of cookies. One was Ada Herschberger, who seemed to have a particular dislike for Mary. Ada pursed her lips so tight, a crowbar wouldn't have been able to pry them open. Even though Mary was a few inches taller, Ada looked down her nose at Mary, as if studying a fly that had landed on one of her cookies.

Mary didn't know the other woman. She was about Ada's age, midtwenties, with a round face and curly hair that didn't seem to want to stay in place under her *kapp*. She burst into a smile when she saw Mary's cake. "You brought a cake? *Ach, du lieva!* They are going to love it."

Mary couldn't help but smile, even though this woman would probably run for the hills when she found out that Mary was a vile sinner.

The new woman took Mary's cake and set it smack-dab in the middle of the treats table. "This will get eaten first, no doubt about it. The early bird gets the worm, as they say." Her laughter tripped easily from her mouth, as if she spent most of her life seeing the happiness in everything. She reached across the table and shook Mary's hand. "My name is Serena. I'm from Appleton. I married Stephen Beiler last fall and moved here. I've seen you at *gmay*, but just from a distance."

Ada's indignation was written in the lines around her narrowed eyes. For sure and certain, she'd yank Serena aside as soon as Mary turned her back and make sure Serena knew not to be so kind next time.

But Mary would enjoy the goodwill while she could get it. "Stephen's dog used to follow him to school every day, like Mary's little lamb in the nursery rhyme. He got in trouble for it more than once."

Serena's eyes danced. "I don't wonder that he did. Stephen loves that dog."

"Well, welcome to Bienenstock. I hope you like it here."

"*Jah*," Serena said. "It takes time to get used to a

new place, but everyone has been so nice. Ada has been teaching me how to make homemade rolls like they serve in her family's restaurant."

Mary did not let her smile falter. The Glicks owned a market and restaurant in town, but Bitsy and her nieces didn't shop there anymore. Bitsy's niece Lily had once been Paul Glick's girlfriend, but she'd broken it off with him, and according to Bitsy, Paul was still a little bitter about it, even though he'd gotten married to someone else not long ago. The last time one of Bitsy's nieces had tried to buy something at the market, Paul's *bruder* had refused to help her. Maybe Ada wasn't so mad about Mary being pregnant as she was about Mary living with Bitsy Weaver. The Glicks held a grudge tightly with both hands.

This actually made Mary feel a little better. She'd probably never win over Ada Herschberger, considering she was a Glick, but maybe others would see it in their hearts to forgive her—even though it wasn't their forgiveness to give.

"I hear Glick's rolls are *appeditlich*," Mary said. "How nice of Ada to teach you how to make them."

Serena widened her eyes. "You haven't tasted them?"

Mary glanced at Ada and shook her head. No use bringing up that subject.

Serena clicked her tongue. "Let's go to the restaurant next week. I'll buy you a roll. You'll think you've gone to heaven."

Mary didn't quite know what to say to such a kind invitation. She wasn't going to pull Serena into an old family feud. "That would be nice. We'll talk later."

An errant curl at Serena's forehead bobbed up

and down when she nodded. "You've got to taste those rolls."

Mary didn't dare look at Ada. She didn't want to see the outrage or the self-righteousness. Mary turned around and pretended to be searching for someone. The haystack supper started at five, and people were already lining up. Serena was kind, but Mary didn't expect Serena to seek her out again. It would take Ada less than five minutes to set Serena straight, and Serena would stay far away until the haystack supper was over.

The ache in her chest wasn't unexpected, but it still took her breath away. She had made herself unfit for the Amish community, but she certainly didn't fit in Josh's world either. Maybe there wasn't a place for her anywhere.

Benji and Alfie rushed under the canopy and each snatched one of Mary's hands. "We hoped you'd be here," Benji said. "We got plans."

Alfie nudged Benji with the palm of his hand. "Benji," he hissed.

"Oh, really?" Mary said. "What plans?" Hopefully they didn't include climbing trees.

Benji glanced at Alfie. "It's a secret."

Mary couldn't resist tousling Benji's unruly hair. "You boys keep a lot of secrets." She bent as far over as she could to whisper in Alfie's ear and caught a scent of something ripe and moldy. "How are your arms?"

Alfie instinctively slid his hands behind his back. "Mamm doesn't even know."

"He's worn the same shirt for two weeks," Benji said. He swished his hand in front of his nose. "He stinks."

"I do not."

Mary did a quick inspection. There were smudges and stains and dirt marks all over Alfie's shirt. Even if she hadn't seen the dirt, she would have been able to tell Alfie hadn't changed his shirt for days. Alfie smelled like wet dog. "Don't you have another shirt with long sleeves?" For sure and certain, his *mamm* wasn't going to allow him to wear that one much longer without washing it. Andrew's *mamm* seemed like someone who would be particular about her laundry and her boys' smells.

Alfie picked at something on his shirt that looked suspiciously like a dried booger. "Mamm got mad."

Benji nodded. "She told him to take it off or we wasn't going to the haystack supper, but then Mammi Martha came home with a new vegetable chopper. She had to show Mamm how to use it, and Mamm forgot about Alfie's shirt."

"She's not going to forget for long," Mary said.

Alfie scrunched his nose. "I could wear my coat."

"In July?" An eight-year-old should never look so sad. Mary looked at Benji. "Do you have a long-sleeved shirt you could let Alfie borrow?"

Benji widened his eyes. "I never thought of that. Alfie, you can borrow my shirt until Mamm washes yours."

"You're so smart, Mary," Alfie said.

Benji squinted at her. "Do you like Andrew or Jerry better?"

Andrew or Jerry? Where in the world had Benji come up with that question? "I like them both just fine."

Alfie slumped his shoulders. "Jerry has a fire truck."

Benji pointed in the direction of the road. "We

brought Mamm and our *bruderen*. Dat stayed home with Mammi and Dawdi and our new vegetable chopper."

Mary tried to act mildly interested, but her pulse betrayed her. Why would she get worked up about seeing Andrew? He was just a typical Amish boy who had been nice to her. Was she that starved for friendship?

*Ach, vell*, maybe that wasn't the only reason her heart pranced along her rib cage like a nervous horse. Andrew was more than typical, and she was more than interested—which she shouldn't be. She'd only get her heart broken again.

Benji and Alfie raced out of the canopy and returned dragging their two other brothers, Austin and Abraham. Austin had been two years ahead of her in school, so she knew him the best. Abraham was between Andrew and Austin in age, and as quiet as a church mouse.

"This is Abraham," Benji said, pulling his *bruder* forward with both hands.

Abraham blushed, probably to his toes, but looked Mary in the eye and gave her a strong handshake. "*Gute* to see you again, Mary."

He might have been painfully shy, but at least he knew his manners, and he didn't seem to care at all that Mary was a sinner and that others were casting resentful glances in her direction. Mary smiled widely. "I'm *froh* to see you too."

Alfie jabbed his thumb in Austin's direction. "This is Austin."

"She knows us, Alfie," Austin said. "We see her at *gmay*." Austin was as outgoing as Abraham was shy. He couldn't have smiled any wider without stretching his lips beyond the breaking point. "Benji and Alfie can't talk about anything else but Mary Coblenz. Have you been sneaking them candy in the middle of the night?"

Mary laughed. "We are best friends. Benji taught me the pretzel trick, and Alfie has been very *gute* to Bitsy's cats."

Austin's eyes danced. "Andrew doesn't talk about much else either. I think at least three of the Petersheim boys are smitten."

She might as well ask, or get an ulcer fretting about it. "Where is Andrew?"

Austin waved his hand behind him. "Helping Mattie Herschberger with her sauce. She's got seven gallons of it."

There was definitely a family resemblance among the brothers. Andrew's hair was the darkest, but his eyes were the color of Abraham's. Abraham had a tinge of red in his hair, while Austin could almost be called a redhead—dark auburn with enough chestnut brown that no one could call him a ginger outright. Austin shared Benji and Alfie's brown eyes, but nobody but the twins had freckles.

"Alfie, what did I tell you about that shirt?"

Andrew's *mater*, Rebecca, marched right up to her sons, and it was immediately apparent who was in charge. Through her wire-rimmed glasses, she gave Alfie the stink eye. Mary couldn't blame her. Alfie looked like every self-respecting mother's nightmare. His hair was always somewhat unkempt and there was a smudge of dirt down the side of his face, but it was his shirt that really stood out. It stunk to high heaven and had too many stains to count. It might be easier for Rebecca to buy Alfie a new shirt. This one didn't look as if it would ever come clean.

Alfie took two steps backward. "I forgot, Mamm."

"You can remember what I said three years ago, but you can't remember what I told you half an hour ago? Your shirt smells like something died in it."

"But, Mamm, I love this shirt."

"And I love my underwear. That doesn't mean I never have to wash it again."

Mary covered her mouth to stifle a giggle. How many people talked about underwear right out in public? Rebecca had definitely been living in a household of boys too long.

Rebecca was a no-nonsense, wiry woman with a ready smile that somehow managed to make her seem grumpy and cheerful at the same time. She appeared young for her age with not a speck of gray in her hair, but she also looked tired, as was only to be expected from someone who had five sons and her in-laws living with her.

Rebecca looked at Mary as if she hadn't noticed her there before. She closed her mouth on whatever chastisement she was going to give Alfie next and bloomed into a smile. "Why, Mary Coblenz, what a nice surprise. I haven't had a chance to talk to you at church. Did you get your cat back okay?"

"My cat?"

"Benji and Alfie found one of your cats. I told them to take it back."

"*Ach*, yes, it was very nice of them," Mary said.

Rebecca smoothed her hand over Benji's hair. "*Vell*, they are required to do at least one nice thing a month. It's a real hardship."

"It is not, Mamm. We do lots of nice things."

Rebecca was teasing, though if you weren't looking closely, you'd wonder if she didn't think much of her boys. But the glint in her eye was there, like a little fire glowing in the woodstove.

"Benji helped me pull my wagon at the auction," Mary said, "and Alfie saved one of Bitsy's cats from falling out of a tree."

Rebecca propped her hand on her hip and eyed Alfie. "And how did you do that?"

Oy, anyhow. Sometimes her *gute* intentions got her in trouble. Alfie looked at Mary as if he was going to pop a blood vessel in his neck. "Benji let me try some of your peanut butter. It's *appeditlich*."

Rebecca seemed to have to pry her gaze from Alfie. She hesitated. "What? Oh, *jah*. One-hundred-percent natural. The Englisch love it. We sell hundreds of jars a year, and we can sell as much as we make. Next year, we're going to expand, and all the boys will be working on peanut butter full time. Benaiah is going to rent out some of our land to another farmer, so there's not so much to do in the fields."

"The business must be going well."

"It is," said Austin. "We sell it as far as Milwaukee."

Rebecca again turned her attention to Alfie, but his shirt was so dirty, Rebecca must have forgotten Mary's little slip about the cat. Rebecca pointed a stern finger at Alfie. "You will go home immediately after supper and change that shirt."

Alfie gave Benji a sly look. "Okay, Mamm. I will."

"And don't forget, or I might forget to make breakfast in the morning."

The deacon started taking money for the dinner.

Mary glanced at Bitsy's rice pan waiting for her on

the table. "I need to help serve, but it was *gute* to see you all again."

"Can you serve us first?" Benji said.

Rebecca shook her head. "You'll wait in line like all the other polite little boys."

Mary walked to the other side of the long row of tables, took a place next to Millie Hoover, and started scooping rice onto people's plates. Millie glanced at Mary as if Mary had done something very surprising, then she tried to pretend Mary wasn't standing right beside her. The Englischers, however, smiled at her as if they found her fascinating and not at all offensive. Englischers liked the Amish, and they had no idea how wicked Mary was. They didn't even care.

A man with a chin full of stubble held out his plate for some rice. "How do you folks get away with this? Do any of you have food-handler's permits? What does the health department think?"

Millie turned beet red and lowered her eyes, staring into her rice as if she was trying to read it. Mary had lived as an Englischer for two years. She wasn't quite so timid. "I think because we ask for a donation, the health department doesn't care."

The man narrowed his eyes but seemed good-natured about it. "So eating here could be hazardous to my health?"

Mary scrunched her lips to one side of her face and looked up at the ceiling of the canopy. "Maybe. But I've eaten at some pretty suspicious burger joints in Green Bay. This can't be as dangerous as that."

The man chuckled. "I suppose not."

Millie raised her gaze to Mary's face. "You're . . . you're so brave. I thought he was going to get mad."

Mary nudged Millie's shoulder with hers. "*Nae*, Englischers aren't so bad."

One side of Millie's mouth curled upward. "I'm still glad he didn't yell at us."

"Me too."

Millie had been in the grade behind Mary. "You were always so nice to the little kids at school. And so *gute* at math," Millie said.

Not when she had taken the GED. "And you were the best speller. I still don't know how to spell chrysanthemum."

Millie scooped rice onto another plate. "Did you . . . did you hate us?"

Mary frowned. "Hate who?"

"I shouldn't ask. Never mind." Millie turned her face away and smiled at the next person in line. Considering she hadn't smiled at anybody up to this point, it was quite a feat.

Mary put a hand on Millie's shoulder. "You can ask me whatever you want, Millie. I'm not mad."

"They say you hate us," Millie stuttered. "That's why you left."

Mary nearly dropped her spoon. She wanted to ask who had been saying such things, but it was no use. Gossip spread like the flu. No one knew how anything started or what it would look like once it passed through five or six people. She took a deep breath to clear the heaviness in her chest. "People have heard wrong, Millie. I left because . . ." How could she explain something Millie would never understand? Better to give her the easier answer. "I left because I fell in love with an Englischer."

"But you didn't marry him."

"*Nae*. I have made some mistakes, but I didn't leave

because I hated anybody. I love the Plain people."
She sounded like an Englischer, one on the outside
looking in. *Ach, vell,* it was how she felt. "That's why I
came back."

Millie gave her a weak smile. "I'm *froh* to hear it."

A gray-haired Englisch woman with her glasses
hanging around her neck patted Mary on the arm
when Mary reached out her hand to dish rice onto
her plate. "When is your baby due, sweetie?"

"August sixth."

"Bless your heart. How wonderful."

Mary wasn't sure whether Millie or the other girls
standing next to her serving food might be offended
or embarrassed. Mary was neither. Despite all she'd
been through and all the promises Josh had broken,
she was thrilled to be bringing a new little soul into
the world.

Apparently, not everyone else was so excited about
it. Ada Herschberger and Treva Nelson appeared
next to her, one on either side, flanking her like
policemen charged with transporting a prisoner.

Treva smiled that angry, benevolent smile she had
used in school when she thought someone had stolen
her boyfriend or she couldn't get the pencil sharp-
ener to work. "Mary, I know you don't care what anybody thinks, but you're offending the Englischers,
flaunting your condition like that." She snatched the
spoon from Mary's hand as if expecting Mary to
smack her with it. "I'll serve rice. Why don't you go
do dishes with the other embarrassments like Bitsy
Weaver."

Mary clamped her lips shut, keeping the harsh
words in by sheer force of will. She refused to be
bullied, but she would never win anyone over if she

was obstinate. Then again, maybe she didn't care to win anyone over after all. Why would she want to be friends with Treva Nelson? Why would she want to live in a community where Treva was considered a *gute* and pious girl and Mary was the sinner?

Mary hated, *hated* to surrender, but what *gute* could come of demanding that Treva behave like a Christian? No *gute*, especially since Treva truly believed she *was* behaving like a Christian—getting rid of the sinners and all that. Mary would have to try another day and another way with Treva. That didn't mean she'd grovel, but she would try to behave as Jesus had taught.

She glanced in Millie's direction. Millie had taken to reading her rice again, not daring to stick her neck out for a pregnant girl who'd been gone for two years. Mary couldn't blame her. Mary couldn't blame anyone, and that was what was so frustrating. This is how these girls had been raised—not to be hateful, but to shun unrighteousness. They just didn't understand the difference.

Like the brilliant sun breaking through the clouds on a stormy day, Andrew Petersheim suddenly appeared in front of Mary. She hadn't even seen him come in. He didn't have a plate or a set of plastic silverware, which made it a lot easier for him to fold his arms across his chest. "The only embarrassment I see here is you, Treva."

Mary's heart leaped into her throat. Was Andrew coming to her defense? In front of all these people? Did she even want him to? Would they hate her all the more and punish Andrew too? Shock and agitation struck her dumb.

Treva frowned in confusion and slowly lowered

the spoon to her side, apparently unable to grasp that Andrew was chastising her. "Is there a problem?"

Ada's face grew one shade darker. "You can't cut in line, Andrew. Go to the back and wait your turn like everyone else."

"You don't make the rules, Ada," Andrew said, righteous indignation dripping from every syllable.

Ada glared at him. "Everybody knows that's a rule."

"I'm not here to eat," Andrew said. While he stared Treva down, Millie served rice and people sidled around Andrew as if he were a pothole in the road. "You need to apologize to Mary, Treva."

Treva's mouth fell open. Her eyes darted back and forth at the people in line. "Apologize? For what?" The words came out in a hiss. For sure and certain she didn't like all these Englischers listening in on their conversation.

Mary finally found her voice. "Never mind, Andrew. It doesn't matter."

Andrew stiffened his spine. "It does matter. Jesus said to love everyone. He said to treat everyone with kindness. Treva and Ada, you serve the devil when you are cruel to Mary."

Oy, anyhow.

Treva took her breath in sharply, and tears pooled in her eyes. "How dare you?" She pointed at Mary. "It is this one who serves the devil."

"You can believe what you want, Treva."

Mary took a step away from the table. "Andrew, please, let's go."

She could see the tension in Andrew's neck. He was as immovable as a lamppost. Treva slapped the tears from her face and flared her nostrils. It appeared there was no stopping either of them now.

"I will shout Mary's wickedness from the housetops," Treva said. "We must teach her humility because she won't humble herself. She's proud when she should be ashamed of herself."

"You should treat her as Jesus would treat her."

"Jesus would say, go away and sin no more. That's all I'm saying. Go away and sin no more. But Mary won't go away. She keeps showing her face."

"We are all sinners."

Mary had used that same reasoning on Andrew. He hadn't liked it. Treva didn't either. She blinked back more tears. "Some sinners are worse than others, and they should show some humility."

"You're a hypocrite, Treva," Andrew said.

Treva clapped her hand over her mouth to cover a sob. Even though Treva was a pill, Mary felt sorry for her. She reached out her hand, but Treva batted it away. She and Ada seemed to hang on each other for support as they marched away from the table. Ada had to strain her neck halfway around to give Mary a nasty scowl.

Millie and half of the other girls at the serving table stared at Mary as if she'd just kicked a puppy. The other half eyed Andrew, a mixture of disbelief and alarm on their faces. Andrew noticed the horrified looks, but he didn't seem to care. He lifted his chin a little higher and nodded to Mary as if the two of them had planned to humiliate Treva Nelson today.

Mary knew she should be grateful, but all she could muster was irritation and humiliation—the humiliation Andrew had been trying to save her from. Millie would have to serve rice all by herself. Mary couldn't stand there one minute longer.

Without a second glance at Andrew, she stormed out of the canopy and toward the stream that ran to the west of the property. It was a stupid choice to make. Her feet were sore, and there was no place to sit except on the ground, but if she sat on the ground she'd never be able to get up again.

So she walked as fast as she could, hoping that the exercise would calm her down and help her forget how angry she was.

She should have known he'd follow her. "Mary, wait. Are you okay?"

She didn't turn her head or slow her pace, but he caught up to her without even trying. Until she had the baby, she wouldn't be able to run away from anybody. Lord willing, no one would attempt to kidnap her. She walked about as swiftly as a duck on dry land. "I was just going back," she said, taking a deep breath. It had been a short walk, but she had pulled enough of her patience and grit together to go back in there and serve rice. She wasn't going to let Treva win, and no one would ever see her run away again when things got hard.

She wasn't surprised that Andrew was grinning like one of Bitsy's cats. "Treva finally got what she deserved."

She growled and tried to outpace him. "*Ach*, Andrew. No one deserves that. No one."

"But I thought you'd be grateful."

She threw up her hands. "If I don't deserve to be humiliated, then neither does Treva."

"But she was trying to embarrass you."

"She doesn't know any better, Andrew. You've ruined everything."

The grass stopped rustling behind her. She'd halted him in his tracks.

"I wanted to help. I couldn't stand by and let her treat you like that."

He sounded like Benji when he had thought Alfie was going to die in that tree. Pathetic and lost. She couldn't leave him like that, not when he thought he'd done the right thing. Sighing in exasperation, she turned back. "*Denki* for trying to defend me. You're a true friend."

"But you didn't want me to?"

She growled again. "I don't know."

"You're not making any sense. Are you mad at me or not?"

"Of course I'm mad at you."

He looked more confused than angry, but there was some irritation in his expression too. "Why? I told Treva what was what."

"She hates me more than ever."

"She doesn't hate you."

"A lecture is not going to soften her heart," Mary said. "She thinks she's right, and she's more determined than ever to see that she puts me in my place."

Andrew opened his mouth to argue and promptly closed it again.

"I'm sorry, Andrew. I am grateful that you tried to defend me, but you can catch more flies with honey than with vinegar."

"Honey? What do I know about honey?" He looked charmingly annoyed, like he wasn't sure who he should be mad at or how mad he should be or if he should even be mad at all.

Her lips twitched upward. He was so like his little *bruder* Benji—with the same dark eyes and an almost childlike eagerness to do the right thing. How could she stay mad at that face? "You've messed up a lot lately, but you were trying to help me. It was a true act of friendship."

"But I shouldn't have done it?"

She sighed. "I wish you hadn't made Treva cry."

"I wasn't mean."

"A little blunt. You called her a hypocrite."

Andrew's lips scrunched to one side of his face. "I didn't hurt her feelings. I made her mad."

"It doesn't matter. People will just see that you and I made her cry."

He scrubbed his hand down the side of his face. "*Ach.*"

"I shouldn't be so irritated, considering that you are one of my only friends in Bienenstock."

Light like a glowing fire leapt into his eyes. "I really want to be your friend. But I wouldn't be a very *gute* friend if I dropped our friendship because you irritated me."

"I irritate you?"

He rolled his eyes. "All the time. You're very irritating."

She giggled. "Well, at least you're honest. I'll try to be less irritating."

Andrew stepped slowly along the stream bank. Mary followed him. "You'll have to quit speaking your mind and start building up my confidence. It's irritating when you make me question the things I grew up believing."

"Like what?"

"*Ach, vell.* When you say things like Jesus died for your sins and that we are all sinners, it makes me rethink justice and mercy. I tend to want justice."

"We all want justice for everyone else and mercy for ourselves."

"That's what I mean," Andrew said, eyeing her in mock annoyance. "Now you're trying to change how I feel about mercy. It's wonderful irritating."

"I'm glad your comfort zone is teetering."

"Teetering? It's toppled over." He glanced down. "You're limping. Does your toe still hurt?"

"Everything hurts. My feet are killing me."

He motioned to a small rise of ground next to the stream. "Do you want to sit?"

She wanted to sit more than anything and not just because her feet throbbed with every step she took. She feared it would feel very nice to sit next to Andrew. "I won't be able to get back up."

"I can help you."

"Okay, but I'm getting heavier by the minute."

"I have muscles."

"I can see that," she said. He took her arm and helped her lower herself to the ground. This was a bad idea. Her *hinnerdale* was going to fall asleep.

Andrew sat next to her, maybe a little too close, but she wasn't planning on ever falling in love with anyone again, so what could it hurt? "What did I do wrong? With Treva," he said.

She leaned back on her hands and unfolded her legs out in front of her. "You did everything wrong, Andrew, but it isn't your fault. It isn't Treva's fault either. We can't expect her to behave in a way she doesn't understand."

"She should understand Christian charity."

"All she feels is Christian indignation." Mary stared at her toes. "Treva is one of the reasons I jumped the fence. *Vell*, Treva and the others like her."

"She was mean to you?"

"*Nae.* I was turning into her."

"I don't think that would have happened. You're nothing like Treva."

Mary sat up straight and clasped her hands together. "I didn't have a choice."

"Of course you had a choice. We all choose how we're going to behave."

"*Nae,* Andrew, I left because I didn't have a choice."

He furrowed his brow. "You were kidnapped?"

She giggled even though he hadn't meant it to be funny. Sometimes she longed to go back to that innocence. "They teach us in *gmay* that we must choose baptism or we will go to hell. But if there is no choice to say no, it's not really a choice."

"Of course you had a choice. You chose not to be baptized."

"Can you listen without arguing?"

The irritation crept back onto his face. "If I don't argue, you're going to try to knock me out of my comfort zone again."

"I'm not going to try to convince you of anything. That's what you did to Treva, and it didn't go well."

"Okay then." He rested his hands on his knees and studied her face as if he really wanted to hear what she had to say, without arguing.

She paused to make sure he wasn't going to interrupt her again. "What choices does a seventeen-year-old Amish girl have? She lives at home with no money of her own. She can choose to find a job, a tedious one, but if she wants to work for an Englischer, her parents discourage it. If she doesn't listen to her parents, she's naughty and rebellious and gets a stern talking-to from her *fater,* warning her that hell awaits troublesome daughters. She goes to *gmay* and gatherings, and she's expected to behave well so that one of those boring boys will ask if he can drive her home one night. She feels trapped and small and desperate because choosing to leave will only take her to hell. What kind of a choice is that?"

"I don't want to argue, but I can't believe that every Amish girl feels this way."

"Of course they don't. Most Amish girls look forward to this life, and they're very happy. Bitsy's nieces are so happy, I'm surprised they don't float everywhere they go. Your *mamm* is happy, isn't she?"

"*Jah.* Of course. Frustrated but happy."

"Most girls are pleased to let their parents map out their lives for them. Many girls never long for a life outside the community. But I did. That's why I felt so out of place, so disobedient. I prayed over and over again that Gotte would root this evil spirit from my breast, but He never did. I thought it was because I was too wicked for Him to take notice of me. But now I think it was His will that I leave."

"Leaving is never Gotte's will," Andrew said, before remembering himself and clamping his mouth shut.

Mary smiled. He was trying so very hard. "Never is a very long time and a very harsh sentence to pronounce on a seventeen-year-old girl." She sighed. "Sin is not Gotte's will, but leaving was not a sin."

He thought about that for a minute. "You are right."

"Gotte knew what was in my heart. With no real choices, I was in prison. I couldn't do it. I had to get out. If there is no choice to say no, it isn't really a choice. Saying no to the Plain life was the first real decision I ever made, my first real choice. And Gotte wanted me to make it so He could teach me that I truly did have a choice and He loved me no matter what choice I made."

"But think of all the people you hurt."

"Choices have consequences. Good and bad choices. Good and bad consequences. Gotte wanted me to learn that too. But fear of consequences should never keep you from making a hard choice." Should she mention that little chair at the auction? What had Alfie said? *He doesn't want Mamm and Dat to know about it.* Rebecca was passionate about peanut butter. Andrew was grappling with some choices of his own.

"How did you meet Josh?" he said, stiffening at the very mention of the boyfriend.

Mary gave Andrew a reassuring smile. It probably took a lot of nerve to ask about Josh. "Josh lived in Shawano, and he came to our produce stand every week one summer. The next summer, he came two or three times a week and then in August every day. Mamm and Dat didn't know, and maybe they wouldn't have cared. I was a wonderful obedient daughter. They didn't think they had a reason to worry. One day Josh bought all our produce just so I could get away early and he could take me to the lake." It had been a very romantic gesture. Mary had lapped up his attention like a hungry cat licked spilled milk from the floor.

Andrew cleared his throat. "Did you love him?"

Mary frowned. "I think it was love. Josh was handsome and exciting and Englisch, and to a girl like me, he was the freedom I longed for. It's hard to say whether I loved Josh or the possibilities I saw when I looked at him."

"So you ran away with him."

"Maybe I should have insisted he marry me. I don't know. I would have had fewer sins to repent of, but now I can only thank Derr Herr that I didn't marry him. What a mess that would have been, at least that's what Bitsy says."

"You went to Green Bay," Andrew said.

She nodded. "Josh's stepmother and his dad are divorced, but his stepmother adores him."

"You said you were happy. Why did you come back?"

She bit her upper lip. She wasn't going to tell him the whole, horrible truth. He wasn't ready for it. "I wanted to come home to have my *buplie*, surrounded by family and people who love me." She looked down at her hands. "It didn't quite work out the way I planned."

"But Bitsy loves you," he said, twining his warm fingers with hers. Her heart thumped against her chest like the bass drum in a rock band. "You know she'll cherish that *buplie* like one of her own." He traced the veins on the back of her hand with his thumb. "I thank Derr Herr every day for Bitsy Weaver."

"You do?" she said, a little too breathlessly.

"Because she took you in when no one else would. I'm sorry for that."

She pulled her hand from his. No good would come of holding hands with Andrew Petersheim. But she smiled at him so maybe his feelings wouldn't be hurt. "*Ach, vell,* I wouldn't have come to your house. I hardly know you."

"But I wouldn't have welcomed you if you had, and that is my shame."

She raised her eyebrows. "I don't wonder that your *mamm* might have let me stay yet. Benji says she takes in all kinds of strays."

Andrew chuckled. "I don't know whose *mamm* Benji is talking about, but my *mamm* would sooner shoot a stray than feed it. But you're right. My *mamm* would have welcomed you. She takes care of Mammi and Dawdi even though Mammi drives her crazy. But she might make you sleep in the cellar with the twins."

Mary shaped her lips into a sympathetic O. "The poor things. They must hate it."

"*Nae,* they think it's an adventure, like camping out every night."

"Camping doesn't sound fun to me, but I'm not an eight-year-old boy." Mary tilted her head back, closed her eyes, and let the fading sun warm her face. "*Denki* for defending me back there."

"Even if I made things worse?"

"Even then. I was ungracious before. What you did was wonderful kind."

"I made Treva cry, Ada gave me a dirty look, and now Treva hates both of us. Was it kind or stupid?"

Mary laughed. "I'm not going to answer that."

Andrew wished Mary hadn't made him sorry about what he'd said to Treva. Now he'd have to apologize, and the thought of telling Treva Nelson he was sorry was almost more than he could bear.

He had been standing in line with his family when he saw Treva and Ada hovering behind Mary as if readying for an attack. He'd cut in line just so he could overhear what Treva was saying to Mary. He hadn't heard everything, but he had heard enough to get his blood boiling. Every nerve seemed to catch fire at the thought of Treva mistreating Mary. He wouldn't stand for it.

At the gathering he had worried what his friends would think of him when they saw him talking to Mary. He thought he was being so courageous, so benevolent when he followed Mary into the house and got her a glass of water, but if he had truly been brave and truly a follower of Jesus, he would have shown a good example and helped Mary into the house, not caring what other people thought of him—only caring that he was behaving like a Christian.

And he'd just messed up again. How would Treva learn to treat Mary kindly when Andrew showed Treva nothing but disdain?

He didn't know what to do. The thought of people treating Mary poorly was unbearable, but he shouldn't have made Treva cry. Like Mary said, he'd only made it worse. The only reason he didn't jump up immediately and seek Treva out to offer an apology was because he was sitting next to Mary. A team of horses couldn't have pulled him away.

Mary kicked off her flip-flops and curled her toes around the short grass beneath her feet, favoring her right foot and her injured toe. Her ankles were swollen and her face carried the puffiness of a woman who was going to have a baby, but Andrew couldn't imagine that Mary could get more beautiful. She glowed as if lit from within by her own propane lantern. Was it this way with all women about to give birth? Was there anything closer to Gotte than bringing a child into the world? No wonder she looked like an angel.

The urge to kiss her seized him like a trap with razor-sharp teeth. He clamped his fingers around a clump of grass and held his breath.

Kiss her? He couldn't kiss her. Couples weren't supposed to kiss until they got married. The bishop made that clear with *die youngie*. Of course, everybody knew that everybody broke the rule, and if there was no choice to say yes, was it really a choice? He ripped the grass from the ground with all the force of his restraint. Her lips were so full, and she was so sweet. He was pretty sure kissing her would feel like heaven. Especially since Mary was an angel.

Andrew leaned closer to see if he could tell if Mary might be thinking the same thing. She had pulled her hand away from him earlier, but maybe that was just to steady herself on the grass. She *was* a little unsteady in general.

Before he got too close, a terrifying thought made him lean back. Mary had already been kissed by Josh, probably a thousand times. She'd be disappointed. Maybe she'd be repulsed. Maybe she'd be irritated.

He wouldn't measure up.

*Ach.* He didn't know anything, and she was a girl who already knew how to make a baby. *Ach, du lieva.* Heat traveled up his neck, over his face, and clear to his scalp.

Mary smiled at him as if she didn't notice that his cheeks were about to catch fire. "I should get back. And you should apologize to Treva."

*Jah*, he should apologize, but he was looking forward to it like a trip to the dentist. "Do you have to go? Treva seemed eager to serve the rice for you."

"That's why I have to go back. I can't let any of them think they've humiliated me. They'll think they have power over me that they don't."

"You know," Andrew said, daring to wink at her, "I

could refuse to help you up and then you wouldn't be able to go back."

Mary puckered her lips and raised an eyebrow, giving him a pretty good idea of what she thought of that suggestion. Her face made him chuckle. "I can always roll onto my hands and knees and crawl to the canopy. That wouldn't be humiliating at all."

"Andrew, Andrew!" someone screamed from behind them. Andrew turned, then stood when he saw who was calling him. Benji ran toward him at full speed with a pair of binoculars dangling from his neck and a . . . cell phone? . . . in his hand. Before Andrew could react, Benji crashed into him as if he were a football player trying to stop the entire opposing team. "Alfie is stuck in the shed."

Andrew braced Benji by the shoulders and gave him a severe frown. "What's he doing in the shed?" Those boys could find trouble without a map.

Benji scrunched up his face as if he was going to cry. "He was supposed to come out but the door got stuck. He's knocking and knocking and can't get out."

Andrew glanced at Mary, who seemed more amused than concerned. She loved his little brothers. Andrew was ready to give them the spatula. "Okay, show me where this shed is."

Benji erupted into a sob, raw and definitely real. "He already lit the smoke bomb."

Andrew's heart jumped twenty feet into the air. "He lit a smoke bomb?"

"It's orange."

Andrew swiftly pulled Mary to her feet, hoping he

hadn't injured her in his haste. "Show me, Benji. Hurry."

Benji took off like a bullet from a rifle, and Andrew followed, easily keeping up with his long strides. He didn't wait for Mary, didn't even stop to explain why. She understood. He saw the smoke before he saw the shed, though at first he wasn't sure what he was seeing. The billows rising into the air were bright orange, like a burning pumpkin.

Benji led him to an old gray shed standing against the wall of the equally gray barn, and there was definitely a smoke bomb. Thick orange smoke poured from under the door like a river of boiling apricot jam. Andrew thought he might be sick when he heard Alfie pounding on the door trying to get out. Alfie and Benji had already shaved a decade off his life, and Alfie was stuck in that shed.

Andrew didn't stop running until he reached the door of the shed and tried to yank it open. It was stuck tight. "Alfie," he yelled, "did you lock it from the inside?"

Alfie coughed and sputtered, the sound muted behind the door. "That's stupid. Nobody puts a lock on the inside of a shed."

Well, at least he didn't seem to care that he was in big trouble. Andrew growled as he yanked the door again. "Is there something blocking the door?" He realized that was also a stupid question the minute he asked it. The shed door was the kind that swung out instead of in.

The orange smoke scampered around Andrew's ankles and curled up his legs. He could taste a hint of it on his tongue, and the sharp smell stung his nose and eyes. Once again Andrew didn't know whether to be ferociously angry or hopelessly panicked. He couldn't give in to either emotion if he was going to keep his head.

"How did it get stuck, Benji?"

"I don't know. He shut it real hard."

The shed door might have slammed tight when Alfie went inside, but it was unlikely there was a lock on the other side. It must have been wedged shut, nothing more. Andrew clamped both hands around the door handle, braced his feet, and pulled with all his might. The door snapped open like a flag caught in the wind. A wall of orange smoke met Andrew along with Alfie, who threw his arms around Andrew and squeezed tight.

Andrew half led, half carried Alfie away from the smoke, which had almost already completely evaporated into the sky. With nothing to confine it, it was gone like a bad dream. Alfie coughed and squinted into the bright sun. "Well, that was stupid," he said.

Yes, it was.

Andrew wanted to spank him.

Something was still smoking. Grayish white smoke slowly curled out of the doorway. Andrew stepped into the shed. On the dirt floor next to the smoke bomb canister, a piece of newspaper was on fire. The smoke bomb must have gotten just hot enough to spark the paper. Andrew put the fire out with two stamps of his shoe and kicked the canister out of the shed.

A smoke bomb was one thing, but a real fire? Alfie could have gotten badly burned. He deserved any punishment Mamm could mete out. "Alfie," Andrew growled, holding up the half-charred piece of newspaper. "Look what you did."

Alfie frowned in puzzlement. "It's just a little piece of paper."

Benji hooked his arm around Alfie's shoulder. "Are you okay? It made really *gute* smoke."

Alfie's face was covered with a fine layer of orange dust and his already filthy shirt looked as if he'd been rolling in orange mud with the pigs. It was what a carrot would have looked like if it were an eight-year-old boy.

After making sure that Alfie could breathe and walk and see straight, Andrew squeezed Alfie's shoulder just tight enough so Alfie would know he meant business but didn't necessarily want to kill him. "What were you doing with a smoke bomb?"

Alfie brushed off his sleeve, which didn't remove one speck of dust, and grinned at Andrew. His teeth looked extra white against his orange skin. "Did you see the orange? Wasn't that cool?"

"Cool? Where did you get a word like *cool*?"

"Willie Glick's best friend is Englisch."

Andrew drew his frown deeper into his face. "It wasn't cool, Alfie. You could have suffocated or gotten burned."

Alfie glanced around him. "Where's Mary?" He gave Benji the stink eye. "Benji, you were supposed to bring Mary."

"I was going to, but you got stuck," Benji whined, "and she doesn't know how to run."

Andrew furrowed his brow. Where was Mary? Had he hurt her when he pulled so quickly? For sure and certain she couldn't move very fast, but she should have been here by now.

Alfie coughed and slumped his shoulders. "You were supposed to bring Mary."

As if she knew she was needed, Mary finally appeared with three water bottles cradled in her arms. Her eyebrows nearly took flight when she caught sight of Alfie. "Are you okay?"

Alfie regained his enthusiasm as quickly as he'd lost it. He sprinted to Mary and hugged her as well as he could with her big stomach and armful of water. She didn't seem to care that Alfie's color could rub off on her. "Andrew saved me," he said, moaning like a sad cow. Alfie was a *gute* actor, but not *gute* enough to fool Andrew. What did he want from Mary?

Mary puckered her lips into a sympathetic frown. "You poor thing. I'm *froh* Andrew was close."

"Andrew was wonderful brave," Alfie said, whimpering and carrying on. He took a deep breath and a fit of coughing overtook him. That wasn't pretend. Maybe they should take him to the doctor. He'd breathed in a lot of smoke. His lungs were probably as orange as his shirt.

"Are you okay, Alfie?" Benji said.

"I'm okay, but if it weren't for Andrew, I'd be dead."

Andrew raised an eyebrow. He had opened the door and stamped out a fire, but Alfie hadn't seemed grateful until Mary arrived.

Mary took a step back, looked Alfie up and down, and giggled. Handing him a water bottle, she said, "Have you ever read *Willy Wonka*?"

Alfie glanced at Andrew as if he might get in trouble for his reading material. "About the chocolate?"

"*Jah,*" Mary said. "You look like an Oompa Loompa." She threw Andrew a bottle and gave one to Benji. "I thought you might need these."

Andrew's throat felt as if it had been rubbed with sandpaper. He could only imagine what Alfie's felt like. That kid was going to turn Mamm's hair gray, and if Andrew didn't break out in some sort of post-terror rash, he'd be surprised.

Alfie took a swig of water. "If Jerry had let Andrew go up in that ladder thing, Andrew would have saved me from the tree too."

"Alfie," Benji said, pointing to Alfie's shirt, a look of deep concern on his face. "Mamm's gonna know."

Alfie looked down and jumped as if he'd scared himself. "Jiminy critters." He showed all his teeth and ran his fingers through his hair as if he was trying to pull it out. "Jiminy critters, Benji. What are we going to do?"

"I told you not to use the orange. It doesn't look like real fire."

"But orange is cool."

"Alfie," Andrew said in his sternest, most threatening voice, "why did you light a smoke bomb?"

Alfie paced in a circle like a caged animal. He was in big trouble this time, and he knew it. "I didn't light it."

"Who did?"

He was barely paying heed to Andrew. "You pull a string, and it just goes off. I'm not allowed to play with matches."

Andrew must be going crazy because the thought that Alfie would obey the no-matches rule actually made him feel better. But not better enough to forget his question. He didn't raise his voice often, but he wasn't going to get answers from Alfie any other way. "Alfie, tell me why you had a smoke bomb in the shed. Tell me right now, or I'll get Mamm."

Alfie stopped pacing and stared at Andrew as if

he'd just threatened certain death. His bottom lip quivered. "Don't tell Mamm. Please don't tell her."

"She's going to find out."

Mary took out a tissue and wiped some of the orange from Alfie's face. "We could sneak you to the stream and dunk you in. I bet the water would wash most of that away."

Alfie brightened immediately. "*Jah*, that will work."

"*Nae*, you don't, young man," Andrew said, in the voice Mamm used when she meant business. He didn't want to hurt Mary's feelings. She was especially tenderhearted when it came to Benji and Alfie, but Mamm needed to know about this. She was the only one who could put a stop to Benji and Alfie's shenanigans. "You're not getting away with lighting a smoke bomb."

"I didn't light it."

Andrew gritted his teeth. "Pulling a string or whatever it was. You're not getting away with it."

Mary cupped Alfie's filthy chin in her hand. "Alfie, why don't you tell us what happened and maybe we can talk about it."

Andrew nearly tossed his head back in disgust, but Mary was looking at him as if he had just put out a roaring fire with his bare hands. He wanted to impress Mary even more than he wanted to tell Mamm about the smoke bomb. He could at least let Alfie explain. Alfie would never be able to justify a smoke bomb, but Andrew should at least let him try. Mary had the impression that Andrew was a *gute bruder*. Would it hurt to let her keep on thinking that? "Okay, Alfie. Explain why you pulled the string on the smoke bomb."

"I didn't mean to get locked in."

"Alfie."

Alfie took a deep breath. "It's a secret."

"Alfie would never tell a lie," Benji said.

Andrew gave Benji a piercing look. "Why don't you tell me what happened, Benji?"

As if preventing the words from escaping, Benji covered his mouth. "I ca fell eedo."

Andrew gently pulled Benji's hand from his lips. "I didn't understand you."

Benji fingered the binoculars still around his neck. "I can't tell either. Nobody knows but me and Alfie and Dawdi."

"Dawdi? Dawdi can't even talk."

"That's why we told him our secret," Benji said.

Andrew took another look at those binoculars. They were definitely Dawdi's—Dawdi's hunting binoculars. Where had the boys found them? And why would Dawdi want them to light a smoke bomb in Zimmermans' shed?

Alfie stuffed his hands into his pockets. "Mamm has been acting strange."

Benji nodded hard enough to wrench his neck. "She brought us hot chocolate and told us she loved us."

"We don't know, but maybe she's going crazy. If you tell her about the smoke bomb, she might fall over the edge of the cliff."

Andrew knew manipulation when he saw it. Mamm was fine, even with Mammi Martha bringing home some new gadget almost every day. But Mamm did have her hands full, trying to take care of Dawdi and Mammi and the peanut butter business and two mischievous boys. Maybe Andrew could keep another secret for Mamm's sake. And for his *bruderen*. Mamm would give them what for if she knew what they had done. His brothers needed mercy just like everybody else.

*Ach*, Mary was getting to him. When had he ever before given ten minutes' consideration to mercy?

"Okay, boys," Andrew said halfheartedly. "I won't tell Mamm."

Benji and Alfie grinned like two cats in the cream.

"But I will tell her everything if you get in trouble again."

"We didn't mean to get in trouble," Benji said. "It was an accident."

Andrew remained firm. "I don't care. No fire, no smoke bombs, no trees, and no cats. And no of anything else. Do you understand?"

Benji pressed his lips together. Alfie nodded. "No getting in trouble." He looked at Mary. "Do you have any soap I can use in the river?"

"I can get some dish soap from the haystack supper."

Andrew didn't know how well the orange smoke dust was going to wash off. After all their efforts, Mamm might still find out.

"Is everything okay?" Jerry Zimmerman sauntered around the corner of the barn in Plain clothes. He obviously wasn't on duty today. Did that moan of displeasure come from one of his *bruderen*? Andrew couldn't be completely sure it hadn't come from him.

"I thought I smelled smoke," Jerry said, flashing that white smile Mary seemed to like. Jerry eyed Alfie, took a surprised step backward, and shot a questioning glance at Mary.

Mary smiled back. "We had a little problem, but it's all taken care of."

Alfie didn't realize that he was a walking announcement that something had gone horribly wrong. He strolled right up to Jerry and shook his hand like a friendly neighbor. "We're having a private talk with Mary and Andrew. Thanks, but we don't need your help."

"Andrew put out the fire," Benji said. "He's like a real fireman. Strong too."

Jerry eyed Benji. "Were you boys playing with matches?"

"*Nae*," Benji said. "You just have to pull a string."

"I'm glad to hear it." Jerry fished in his pocket and gave each boy a sucker.

Did he always keep a stash of candy on him to win over little boys? He was like the Englisch Santa Claus and the Easter Bunny all rolled into one. Andrew didn't like it, bribing children to get them to like you. Mary probably thought it was sweet.

"Never, ever play with matches," Jerry said. "You could burn down somebody's shed. Or even their house."

Benji nodded. "We know. It's a rule."

Jerry stared dumbly at Mary for too long. Mary stared back as if they were sharing a secret message with their eyes. Andrew ground his teeth together until they squeaked.

"*Vell*, since there is no fire, I better finish my supper." Jerry turned back. "Mary, maybe I'll see you when supper is over."

Mary nodded. "I'll be washing dishes."

"Okay."

"Why did he have to come over here?" Alfie said,

when Jerry disappeared around the corner. "He ruined it."

Maybe Jerry had ruined it, and maybe Andrew would be washing dishes with Mary until there were no more dishes to wash. Let Jerry try to ruin the fun then.

# Chapter Nine

"In here, Mary," Alfie said, pointing to the long room attached to the side of his house. A gas generator screeched and hummed outside the window. In many Amish businesses, the generator and other sources of power were banished to the outdoors so it wasn't so noisy inside.

Mary gave Alfie a weak smile as he opened the door for her. She could tell by the way her heart tripped all over itself that this was not a *gute* idea. It was not fair to Andrew, no matter how she felt about him. She liked Andrew Petersheim, liked him a lot, but she also liked her freedom. She couldn't have both. If she let herself care too much for Andrew, the choice would tear her in half. She'd rather stay in one piece, thank you very much.

Alfie and Benji wanted to show her how they made peanut butter. She could take the tour, but she didn't have to stick around and get caught up in Andrew's eyes or that captivating smile of his. He'd fixed her broken toe, but she didn't owe him anything, even if she was beginning to fear he had more power over her than she was willing to admit.

She refused to fall in love, even with Andrew Petersheim. Indifference would make her choice so much easier, but that sinking feeling in her chest wouldn't leave her, even when she tried her best to ignore it. Unfortunately for her, she was way past indifference when it came to Andrew. A peanut butter tour was a very bad idea.

Benji held the door as Alfie marched ahead of her into the long, ample room that housed their peanut butter business.

"Close that door," Rebecca yelled from the other end of the room. "You're letting in the flies."

Benji shuffled quickly into the room and shut the door behind him.

Alfie held out his hand like the woman on TV did when she was modeling a prize. "Here you go."

The peanut butter factory, as Benji had called it, was a long room attached to the east side of the Petersheims' house. Three long tables covered in bright white paper were set end-to-end running down the center of the room. Austin stood closest to her, pouring peanut butter from a large pitcher into the three dozen or so jars sitting on the table. Abraham stood at the middle table grinding peanuts with a food processor—powered by the generator outside. Andrew and his *mater* were at the far end of the room measuring and pouring oil into another, larger food processor. There were four industrial-size sinks against the far wall as well as stacks of empty boxes that used to contain peanuts. They all wore hairnets, which were a necessary part of food preparation, but they didn't look attractive on anyone. *Vell*, anyone but Andrew. He managed to look good no matter what he wore.

Andrew glanced up, tore the hairnet off his head, and bloomed into a smile that could have made a chicken lose all her feathers. Mary swooned with pleasure and irritation. Why did she have to like that smile so much? It wasn't like her to let herself get so attached in such a short time. How could she have been so careless?

Rebecca wore her hairnet over a green bandanna and the top of her head looked like a clump of broccoli. "Mary, how nice to see you. I didn't get five minutes to talk to you at the haystack supper."

*Ach, vell*, Mary hadn't talked to many people at the haystack supper, seeing as she had been occupied with Andrew and Benji and Alfie. First they had put out the smoke bomb, then they had taken twenty minutes to try to get the orange film out of Alfie's shirt. It hadn't worked all that well, but the shirt was so filthy to begin with, Rebecca probably hadn't noticed that it was tinged a dull shade of orange. Today, Alfie's shirt looked almost clean. He must be wearing Benji's shirt. Either that or he'd soaked his own shirt in a pot of bleach.

"Alfie and Benji wanted to show me where you make peanut butter. I hope you don't mind that I'm here."

"Not at all," Rebecca said. "We give tours every Tuesday."

"How *wunderbarr*. Do you have a lot of people every week?"

Rebecca scrunched her lips to one side of her face. "So far no one has actually shown up for a tour, but they told me if we put it on the Bienenstock city

website, we might get some takers. Five dollars a
person. But not for you. You are free."

"Are you sure?"

Rebecca nodded. "Friends never have to pay, and
after all the things you've done for my family, I'm in
your debt. Benji, wash your hands and don't touch
anything."

Mary didn't exactly know what she'd done for
Rebecca's family, unless she counted washing Alfie
while he was still in his shirt or bandaging Alfie's
arms, but Rebecca didn't know about either of those
things.

"Hallo, Mary," Austin said, standing up straighter
like a new father showing off his baby. "What do you
think of our peanut butter factory?"

"It smells wonderful *gute.*"

Rebecca's smile got bigger. "Andrew and I were
just starting another batch." Her gaze flicked in
Andrew's direction. "But maybe, Andrew, you'd like
to take a break and give Mary the tour."

Andrew slapped the measuring spoons on the
table. "For sure and certain."

"We wanted to give Mary the tour," Benji whined.
He managed to look dejected while slathering soap
all over his hands.

Rebecca pointed at Benji. "Do you have a food
handler's permit, young man?"

"*Nae.*"

"Then you're not certified to give a tour."

Andrew was as happy to see Mary as she was to see
him. Heaven help her, what was she going to do
about the mess she'd tangled them both into? "There's
not much to see," he said. "But I can show you."

Rebecca grunted. "Not much to see? You can be

sure this is the biggest organic, natural peanut butter operation in northeastern Wisconsin. How can you say there's not much to see?"

Andrew gave Mary a private smile. His *mamm* was very proud of their peanut butter factory. He took Mary's elbow and nudged her forward to the end of the room. "We buy the peanuts already shelled and roasted."

"It's a thousand times easier that way," Rebecca said, measuring oil into the food processor. "We grind them in here with some oil and salt."

Andrew grinned playfully at his *mamm*. "Are you giving the tour or am I?"

Rebecca smirked. "I was afraid you'd leave that part out. Benji, don't touch anything."

"But I washed my hands."

"Do you have a food handler's permit?"

"*Nae*," Benji said.

"Then I don't care how clean your hands are."

Andrew pointed Mary in Abraham's direction. Abraham smiled at her but didn't seem inclined to interrupt Andrew's tour. "We're making crunchy peanut butter today," Andrew said, "so Abraham roughly grinds a few peanuts that we stir in the peanut butter after it's done. Then Austin pours it into bottles and puts a paper seal over the lid. That's it."

"That's it?" Rebecca said. "You didn't tell her that we sell a hundred jars a month at Glick's Family Market, and another hundred at that Amish store in Shawano. After harvest, we're going to expand to Appleton. Benaiah will lease out more of our land for someone else to farm so the boys will have more time for peanut butter. Alfie, don't sniffle around the jars."

Mary watched Andrew out of the corner of her eye. He was smiling, but it was easy to see that the thought of peanut butter didn't thrill him the way it did Austin. Even reserved Abraham seemed more excited about the prospect of more peanut butter than Andrew. Andrew wanted to work with wood. Would he ever tell his *mamm*?

"Our kitchen is approved by the board of health, and the inspector told me it is the cleanest he's ever seen." Rebecca poured a bag of peanuts into the food processor. "Andrew, why don't you take Mary out and show her where we're going to add on."

That got Andrew excited. "Do you want to see, Mary?"

Mary smiled. "Of course."

Alfie took Mary's hand. "I'll show you my birds' nests. Mamm won't let me keep them in the house."

"*Nae*, Alfie," Rebecca said. "You're going to rub Dawdi's feet."

Alfie's mouth fell open. "It's not my turn."

"You're going to do it anyway, and Benji, you're going to give Mammi a scalp massage."

Benji scratched his head. "What's a scalp massage?"

"Use that special comb she bought yesterday."

"But I want to show Mary where I fell and had to get stitches."

Rebecca turned on the food processor. Combined with the generator outside, it made a terrible racket. "Obey your *mamm*," Rebecca yelled, "and let Mary and Andrew have some peace."

Alfie shuddered and made a face. "But, Mamm, I don't want to . . ."

Rebecca turned the food processor to high. "I can't hear you."

Benji and Alfie probably groaned loudly, but it was so noisy in there that Mary only heard a pitiful sigh. Mary ruffled their hair as they walked past. Benji smiled and waved. Alfie hunkered down into himself and marched out of the room.

"*Cum*," Andrew said, loudly enough for her to hear over the roar of the food processor. "I'll show you what Dat is going to build."

Andrew shut the door behind them. The noise lessened, but there was still the gas generator to contend with. "Dat is going to add to the building here and make it fifteen feet longer. Then we're going to get two more food processors and two more tables."

Mary hooked her arm around his elbow and pulled him far enough away that they could hear themselves think. She should have just thanked him for the tour, shaken his hand in a friendly, I'm-not-interested way, and walked home. It was unwise to be with Andrew. The more time she spent with him, the more time she wanted. And she certainly shouldn't have touched him. His warmth spread up her arm and into her chest like a river of melted chocolate. She didn't have the willpower to let go. Unwise, indeed.

Ignoring the voice inside her head that told her to go home and forget Andrew Petersheim, Mary steered him toward the barn. "I get the feeling you're not thrilled about expanding into Appleton."

Andrew curled one side of his mouth. "I'm sick of peanut butter. I almost wish I was allergic, then Mamm wouldn't expect me to help."

"You'd rather build furniture. At least that's what Benji says."

"Benji knows too much for someone his age."

Mary smiled. "He says he hears things when people don't think he's listening." She glanced at him. "Do you want to quit making peanut butter?"

He shrugged. "My *mamm* wouldn't be happy about it."

"You'd rather be miserable than make your *mamm* unhappy?"

He sighed. "I suppose so."

"But what kind of life would that be? If you spend it pleasing others, where is your happiness?"

"I can find happiness in making my *mamm* happy."

She pulled him to a stop. "I don't think you can, Andrew. You'd come to resent her in the end."

The lines around his mouth deepened. "But you chose to do what you thought would make you happy, and look what it did to your parents and your friends." He bowed his head. "I'm sorry. I shouldn't have said that."

"Why not? Of course you're right. I made my choices knowing that Mamm and Dat would be hurt, but even then I knew I couldn't live my life for them. You can't make everyone happy. You can't make anyone happy but yourself."

"That sounds selfish."

"Maybe it is, but if your *mamm*'s happiness comes at the expense of your own, you'll resent her. You'll resent your whole family and the peanut butter and your life."

He smiled weakly. "I already resent the peanut butter."

"Should my parents have given me money and helped me pack? Shouldn't they have wanted my happiness more than their own?"

"Maybe they thought they knew what would really make you happy."

She cocked an eyebrow. "Are you sure your *mamm* is convinced that peanut butter would really make you happy? You don't have enough power to ruin your *mamm*'s happiness, Andrew. The only life you have the power to ruin is your own."

"It's not that simple."

"I never said it was. It's the hardest thing anyone does—making choices and then owning the consequences. You may be making peanut butter for your *mater*, but you are the one who lives with the consequences. Your *mater* would want you to be happy."

"My happiness at the expense of hers?"

"If that's how you see it, *jah*. But she might understand better than you think that her happiness doesn't depend on you, just as your happiness doesn't depend on her. It would be nice if she was happy in spite of you, but that is her choice, not yours."

"But my actions do have the power to cheer her up or bring her down," he said.

"If I had stayed in the community, my parents would never have known that I wanted to run away, but I would have spent my life wondering what might have been. Trying to keep my parents happy would have made me bitter. I don't know if my parents would be happier today if I hadn't left, but they certainly wouldn't have appreciated or even known that I had sacrificed my whole life for them."

Andrew nodded thoughtfully. "*Nae*. They wouldn't have known."

"I would have died spiteful and broken without them knowing or caring about my sacrifice. I would have hated them, and they wouldn't have even known why."

"I think I understand." He smirked good-naturedly at her. "I *think*. Your thoughts are sometimes too deep for me."

"Not too deep. I've just been marinating in them for a very long time, maybe to make myself feel better. Maybe to make sense out of what I've done."

"Everything used to make more sense than it does now." Andrew opened the barn door, and they hesitated at the entrance, letting their eyes adjust to the dimness.

Mary breathed in the dampness of the air. This was one smell she'd missed in the city, the cool, sharp odor of an Amish barn. The scent brought back a thousand memories. "When I returned, I had hoped my parents would forget their anger and rejoice that I'd come home, but they didn't." She held her breath and let the pain wash over her. "They aren't happy I'm back. They're only sad I went away. They'd rather lash me across the face with their pain than shower me with their joy."

"I'm sorry," he murmured.

She forced a carefree lilt into her voice. Andrew needn't be burdened with her troubles. "I'll not complain that the path I chose ended up here. My parents choose their own happiness and their own misery. I can't force them to love me again. Maybe they don't even want to. I have caused them too much heartache."

"That's why I haven't told my *mamm*." Andrew looked around as if getting his bearings. "Why are we in the barn?"

She gave him a sly smile. "Benji says you sneak in here every night. I want to see your woodshop."

It was dim inside the barn, but she could still see the color travel up his neck. "It's not much."

"Will you show me?"

He shrugged. "Don't expect anything grand."

"I saw that chair you made. I expect to be astounded."

"Hah."

She followed him to the far corner of the barn behind a substantial stack of hay where two tables sat. The first table was small but made of sturdy wood, marked with the scars of Andrew's hard work. The second table was covered with a canvas tarp. Four small blocks of wood lay atop the tarp with pencil marks drawn into the grain. Mary ran her finger along the pencil lines of the closest block.

"I'm going to make a toy train for Benji and Alfie," Andrew said, his eyes studying her doubtfully.

"You're their favorite *bruder*, you know."

"It's only because I don't tell Mamm half the things they do."

She laughed. "They've got you wrapped around their little fingers."

He scrunched his lips together. "I fall for it every time."

"The best kind of friend is the one who can keep secrets."

Andrew's tools hung on the wall behind the table, each carefully mounted on its own set of hooks. The tools caught the light from the windows above. It was plain that Andrew took very good care of them. No rust, no wood shavings, no dust. It was apparent he loved his work—the work his *mamm* saw as a nuisance.

"Poppy's husband, Luke, has a lathe and a jointer

and a circular saw that he powers with a generator. I have no power, just some simple tools and elbow grease, so I use Luke's tools when I can."

"But I can tell you take your tools very seriously."

He wiped an invisible piece of dust from one of his saws. "I'm saving up for a sander. I might be able to hook up a generator out here. Mamm probably wouldn't care. Sometimes I go to Luke's shop and use his sander. It saves so much time."

Her heart did a little somersault as he reached above her head and pulled something from a high shelf she hadn't noticed. It was a canning jar half filled with gumballs sitting on top of a small box. "What is it?"

Smiling like a little kid, he handed it to her. "It's a bubble gum dispenser. You pull this handle, and one gumball falls from the jar and into the notch on the handle. Then you pull it out and eat it."

She pulled the handle straight out and was rewarded with a fat pink gumball. She couldn't have kept from smiling if she wanted to. "This is the most clever invention I've ever seen. And so useful."

He lowered his head and slid his hands into his pocket. Mary had always been quite taken with Amish humility. "I could sell dozens of those at the bazaar if I had the time to make them."

"Of course you could. I can see why you hide it on the top shelf. Alfie and Benji would eat all the gumballs."

Andrew twisted his lips into a funny grin. "I'm pretty sure they've already discovered it. Every time I come out here, three or four gumballs are missing— just enough so they're hoping I don't notice, but I guess it could be Dat who's the thief."

"Or Austin. He seems like someone who would like gumballs."

He shook his head. "For sure and certain it's Alfie and Benji. Two months ago, Alfie woke up with chewed gum plastered to his hair. The gum fell out of his mouth while he was asleep, and he rolled around in it. Mamm scolded him until the cows came home and then used store-bought peanut butter to get the gum out of his hair. Then he had to help her with the laundry for a month."

Mary turned the gumball machine around in her hand, looking at the smooth lines and square corners, the simplicity of the design. "You are truly a talent, Andrew."

"I could do so much more with better tools. Luke makes those collapsible baskets from one solid piece of wood. I could make toys and trinkets for the tourists along with furniture and cabinets."

He was so excited that Mary wouldn't dare remind him that his *mamm* had her heart set on peanut butter. Maybe he would figure out his life. Maybe he wouldn't. "It would be a *gute* business."

"*Jah.* A carpenter always has work."

She studied his face. Andrew deserved to always be like this, wildly happy and overly excited about wood and jigsaws and toy trains.

He must have seen some unreadable expression on her face. "What?" he said.

"It's easy to tell you love the wood."

He leaned against the wall and folded his arms. "I hear music when I'm working with the wood—slow, beautiful music like someone humming a hymn in a grove of trees. With peanut butter, it's always a rush to get more peanut butter into the bottles. Rush to get them to the stores. Rush to buy more peanuts. The wood almost begs to be worked slowly."

"Rushing only ruins it," she said.

"A tree takes decades to grow, stretching its arms to the sky from season to season, hunkering down during drought or frost, always holding out hope for spring. The tree's patience should be rewarded with deliberate care."

"You sound like a poet." Josh's stepmother loved poetry. She had poems hanging all over the house.

"I don't know about that. I just love the wood."

"Even this gumball machine is beautiful, and I saw your chair at the auction. You love the wood very much."

Andrew didn't seem to be breathing as he reached out his hand and smoothed the back of his finger down the side of her face. She didn't seem to be breathing either. His skin was pleasantly rough against her cheek, and his touch sent electricity tingling down her spine and back up again. She should tell him to quit. For her own sake, she needed to stop this growing attachment between them, not encourage it. Unfortunately, she had no will to form the words on her tongue.

He dropped his hand to his side, and they stood in breathless silence, staring at each other. Mary wouldn't have said a word for the world. She could wander through the quiet forest of his eyes forever. If she didn't ask any questions, he wouldn't have to answer. She could pretend that she'd never had another boyfriend, that she wasn't pregnant, that her life wasn't more complicated than a boy and a girl with their whole lives ahead of them. No peanut butter, no resentful parents, no ex-boyfriend, and no unexpected babies.

After staring at her for a long minute, Andrew seemed to come to himself. He smiled sadly and tucked an errant lock of hair behind her ear. "This was definitely more than the five-dollar tour."

She gathered enough of her wits to give him a reasonable response. "I'd like to say it was the million-dollar tour, but I can't afford that much."

He chuckled. "That was the ten-dollar tour. For twenty dollars, I walk the tourists home."

She tossed her head back like an irritated tourist. "I definitely can't afford you."

"You forget. Mamm said it was free. You might as well get the twenty-dollar experience since someone else is paying for it."

She didn't want to, but she couldn't keep a smile from sprouting on her face. "I might as well."

While they walked, Andrew told her funny stories about his *bruderen* and his *mammi*, and she shared fond memories of growing up. It was amazing what became dear to you when you stopped looking for the bad parts. They watched for bluebirds and wild-flowers, and kept an eye out for bees as they got closer to Honeybee Farm.

Andrew braved the hordes of bees and walked her clear up to the porch where he said goodbye and kept his eyes glued to her face as he backed slowly down the lane.

Mary slipped into Bitsy's house and took off her bonnet, feeling dizzy and giddy and oh, so foolish. She shouldn't have set foot inside the barn. Seeing that little corner of Andrew's world only made her like him all the more. Andrew was careful and considerate, kind to his *bruderen* and concerned about his *mater*. He had the uncanny ability to inspire her to talk and to make her feel that what she said was important. How many times had Josh complained that she talked too much? Maybe Andrew would grow tired of her if they spent enough time together.

Mary sat down at the window seat and ran her hand down Farrah Fawcett's silky back. Farrah Fawcett turned up her nose at Mary like she did with anyone who dared invade her window seat, but she let Mary pet her anyway. Bitsy came down the stairs carrying a lump of bread dough, with flour up to her elbows. "Did you have a *gute* time on your tour?"

Mary pressed her lips together and nodded. "*Gute* enough." She raised an eyebrow. Bitsy had a smear of flour down her cheek. "Were you kneading dough upstairs in your room?"

One corner of Bitsy's mouth turned up. "If you must know, Yost saw you and Andrew Petersheim cross our bridge, and I went upstairs to spy out the south window, but I didn't see much."

Mary felt as if the floor was slowly crumbling out from under her. "There wasn't anything to see."

Bitsy nodded curtly. "*Gute.* I don't allow kissing on my porch."

Mary forced a laugh even though there was nothing funny about it. "I can safely promise that Andrew will never kiss me on your porch."

"Does he prefer the barn?"

Leonard Nimoy, one of Bitsy's other cats, jumped up to the window seat and sidled onto Mary's lap.

Mary petted both cats so she wouldn't have to look Bitsy in the eye. "Andrew might like me as a friend."

"He likes you better than that." Bitsy set her dough on the counter and started kneading it.

Mary shrugged. "He might be interested in me as more than a friend, but he'll talk himself out of that soon enough."

"Why would he do a thing like that?" Bitsy looked up at the ceiling. "Lord, why do you keep sending *dumm* boys?"

"You know why, Bitsy. Amish boys do not want damaged goods as *fraas*."

Bitsy grunted. "Damaged goods? That's your *fater* talking."

"That's everybody talking. Andrew is kind and loyal, but he would never think seriously about someone like me. I've been with another man. I'm carrying Josh's baby. You know as well as I do that no man in the Amish community would ever consider marrying someone like me. Who wants to raise another man's child?"

"That's an awfully bleak reality you've invented for yourself, little sister."

"Not liking it doesn't change anything." There were always consequences.

Bitsy pounded on her bread dough like a judge with a gavel. "I don't spy on you as much as Alfie and Benji do, but I notice things. I warned you not to feed him, but Andrew Petersheim doesn't come around just for the food."

Mary shook her head. "He's nice to me, but I'm not worried about his feelings. Mine is the only heart that will be broken—whether I leave or I stay." She clamped her lips together. Oh, *sis yuscht*. She'd just admitted out loud how strong her feelings were for Andrew.

Bitsy eyed Mary as she kneaded her dough. "You can't tell me anything I don't already know. And after the haystack supper, it seems less and less likely you're going to stay—unless Andrew talks you out of leaving."

Mary didn't intend for her sigh to come out like a sob. "Andrew will go on just fine without me because he'd never really consider loving me anyway."

"Probably not." Mary couldn't tell if Bitsy agreed or was just humoring her. "But it will be wonderful hard to stay in the community and watch Andrew fall in love with someone like Treva Nelson."

"It would be better to leave," Mary said, "even if everything and everyone I love lives in this small square of Wisconsin."

"Oh, little sister, are you sure about that?"

"That everyone I love is here?"

"*Nae*, that it would be better to leave."

Mary studied Bitsy's face. Bitsy could be blunt and she always spoke her mind, but Mary had never heard Bitsy come so close to trying to persuade Mary to do anything. "It wonders me . . ." She bit her bottom lip.

"Go on. You can't hurt my feelings."

"*Ach*, Bitsy, my leaving has nothing to do with you."

Bitsy scrunched her lips together. "It's because you think Andrew will never consider loving you."

"*Jah*. He never will. But it's more than that. You saw them at the haystack supper. I'm not welcome here."

"I'm not welcome here either, but most everybody loves me."

"Then there are the boys who think that since

I've had sex, I'm willing and eager to have sex with anyone," Mary said.

Bitsy's expression turned stormy. "Who thinks that?"

"On Monday, Perry Glick cornered me in the harness shop, trapped me against the wall, and tried to kiss me."

Bitsy growled. "Where's my shotgun? I'm going to pay Perry Glick a visit."

"No need. Perry is accustomed to meek Amish girls, and I gave him a shock when I hauled off and slapped him."

Bitsy's eyes nearly popped out of her head. "I would have liked to see that. I would have liked to see that very much."

Mary couldn't help but smile at the look on Bitsy's face. "He pressed his hand against his cheek and started whimpering. I marched out of that shop as fast as I could."

"I hope his whole face swelled up." Bitsy looked up at the ceiling again. "Lord, please send Perry Glick a severe case of rectal itch." Bitsy washed and dried her hands, nudged Farrah Fawcett and Leonard Nimoy off the window seat, and sat down next to Mary. "You must have been terrified."

Mary shuddered just thinking about it. "Not terrified as much as angry. Perry thought he was justified in trying to take advantage of me because I'm a sinner or maybe because I'm pregnant out of wedlock or maybe simply because he thought he could get away with it."

Once again, Bitsy turned her eyes to the ceiling. "Just so you know, Lord, I'm going over there tonight to egg Perry Glick's house. Grant me speed and silence."

Mary giggled. "I could come with you and bring toilet paper."

Bitsy nodded. "We'll take Yost. He can throw a roll of toilet paper clear over the roof. He has a *gute* arm."

Mary was more confused than ever. How could she leave the best woman she had ever known? How could she leave Andrew when she was just beginning to understand her feelings for him? Maybe she just needed to give the community more time.

But how could she stay here when there was little hope that anyone would ever truly accept her? How could she go back to a world of acquaintances and strangers, where her morals were as old-fashioned as a horse and buggy and truth was twisted and warped to serve selfish desires? Where no one, not even Josh, cared one whit about a little Amish girl who didn't fit in anywhere.

Asking to see Andrew's tools had been a mistake. A big mistake.

There would be consequences.

And tonight, there would be eggs and toilet paper.

# Chapter Ten

Andrew plopped himself on the porch and quickly laced up his boots. He'd helped clear up the dinner dishes, and now he had a little time to work on his latest project. Mammi wanted everybody in at 7:00 p.m. for family reading time. It was her single-minded goal to fill that bookshelf sitting in the cellar, but it wasn't easy finding appropriate reading material for her family. She'd taken to buying books off the internet at the library. Mammi must have a secret credit card or something.

She'd bought Benji and Alfie each a children's inspiration book, which Benji and Alfie pretended to read every night during family reading time. Mostly they disturbed everyone else by whispering and poking each other. Of course, Andrew didn't mind being disturbed. *Martyrs Mirror* was grim and depressing, and Mammi Martha expected him to read it so they could have a discussion about it on off Sundays.

Andrew had been avoiding the apology he should have made to Treva Nelson three days ago. He should go to her house right now, but he only had one hour before reading time and he wanted to start cutting out Alfie and Benji's train. He could get one piece done if he was speedy, but he hated to rush anything with the wood.

"Andrew Petersheim, can I have a word with you?"

Sol Nelson stood ten feet from the porch with his hands folded across his chest and a firm scowl on his lips. Andrew's heart sank like a bucket of nails. There would be no working in the shop tonight, and Sol looked a little rigid for someone making a social call. Andrew didn't have to guess. Sol was here because of his *schwester*. Oy, anyhow, Andrew should have made that apology at the haystack supper, but he had been determined to stick to Mary like glue so Jerry couldn't get a chance to flirt with her.

Treva had stayed at the haystack supper only long enough to tell her pitiful story to everyone, and then she had gone home, Ada had told him, to nurse a migraine. He *had* gotten the chance to apologize to Ada, such as it was. Ada's husband, Junior, had stuck his nose in Andrew's face and told him to stay away from his *fraa*. Andrew couldn't blame Junior. He had kind of acted the same way in defense of Mary, though he hoped his breath was fresher than Junior's. Nothing chased a girl away faster than bad breath.

All Andrew's diligence with Mary hadn't done a lick of good. As soon as the dishes had been washed, Jerry had found her, and Jerry and Mary had strolled down by the stream together while Andrew and Bitsy dried pots and pans. At least they hadn't sat down together. Andrew was fit to be tied to a train track as it was.

Maybe Sol would pass on an apology to his *schwester*.

Maybe he would tear Andrew's hat in half. He looked unwaveringly cross.

Sol Nelson was slightly taller than Treva but wiry, where his sister was decidedly plump. They had the same pointed chin and dark eyes that flashed with righteous indignation. Treva was always out of sorts with someone or something. Sol seemed mildly irritated about half the time. Sol enjoyed playing volleyball and ping-pong, and he was actually fun to be with when Treva wasn't around to make sure he got offended about something. Treva was what Mamm called an eggshell person, someone who got her nose out of joint so often, her skin was said to be as thin as eggshells. If a friend didn't sit by Treva at *gmay*, she would ignore her for days and tell everyone how misused she had been. Treva's list of complaints and grievances about her neighbors was long and detailed, and sometimes she got Sol to go along with her.

Andrew had no doubt that he hadn't hurt Treva's feelings as much as wounded her pride. She had been hopping mad, for sure and certain. She had made sure that everyone at that haystack supper had seen her tears and had been told that Andrew Petersheim had been the cause of them.

"You made my *schwester* cry," Sol said, his hands shaking slightly. He obviously wasn't as confident or as angry as he seemed. "You used to be a *gute* Christian."

Andrew swallowed the irritation that crawled up his throat. He had been in the wrong, and Sol had every reason to expect an apology. "I shouldn't have said those things to Treva. I'm sorry."

Sol raised an eyebrow. "You're sorry?"

"*Jah.* I was angry. He who is angry with his brother is in danger of hellfire." Or something like that.

"Okay."

Andrew hated to leave it at that, as if Treva hadn't done anything wrong. His sense of fairness wouldn't let him turn the other cheek all the way around. "Have you ever heard the parable of the mote and the beam?"

"Of course. A hundred times at *gmay.*"

"I wasn't trying to be mean. I just told Treva to take care of the beam in her own eye before she tried to fix Mary."

"Treva doesn't have any beams," Sol said, as if that explained everything.

"She was mean to Mary."

Sol narrowed his eyes. "Treva is trying to help Mary, and you yelled at her in front of everybody."

Andrew bit his tongue, but the words came out anyway. "How is humiliation going to help Mary?"

"Someone must help Mary understand her place. Treva was only trying to help Mary feel some remorse. You told Treva she was a servant of the devil." Sol was yelling now, and his eyes flashed like lightning. "It was a cruel thing to say, and you don't know anything."

"I know that Jesus said we should love one another."

"Love one another?" Sol said. "We all love Mary. We love all sinners."

"Then act like it."

"Mary doesn't show any remorse. She acts like she's happy to be with child, and Perry Glick says she waved at him at the haystack supper, tempting him to join in her wicked ways."

Andrew clenched his teeth so hard, he gave himself a headache. How dare Perry Glick say that? He stepped forward until the toes of his boots touched Sol's. "I will not hear such talk about Mary. Jesus said to love one another."

Andrew felt someone brush against his side. "We'll hate you if you don't be nice to Mary."

Andrew looked down. Alfie stood on one side of him with his hands balled into fists and Benji stood on the other looking concerned and nibbling on his fingernail.

*We'll hate you if you don't be nice to Mary*, Alfie had said. How ridiculous were he and Sol, standing nose to nose, yelling at each other about love? Everything Mary had told him had evaporated as soon as he had decided it was more important to be right than to be kind. Andrew gazed down at his *bruderen*. What was he teaching them with his stubbornness?

Andrew took two steps back and shoved his hands in his pockets. "I'm sorry, Sol." He laid a hand on Alfie's shoulder. "We don't hate anybody."

To his surprise, Sol started to chuckle. "We're a fine pair of Christians, yelling Bible verses at each other like Pharisees."

"That's about right."

Benji started in on another fingernail. "Why do you hate Mary?"

Sol shook his head. "Nobody hates Mary."

Andrew tensed briefly before taking a deep breath and remembering what Mary said about flies and honey. Why should Andrew be upset with Sol and Treva? They were all sinners. He shouldn't condemn them just because they sinned differently than he or Mary did. Maybe their sins were worse than his. Maybe his sins were worse than theirs. Only Jesus knew that. Their job was to love and forgive each other.

Alfie looked up at Sol as if assessing his guilt or innocence. "If you don't hate her, then you should treat her better. Treva's not very nice."

Sol's smile faded. "We're doing what we think is best for Mary's soul."

Benji drew his brows together. "Are you in charge of her soul?" He looked at Alfie. "Who is in charge of my soul?"

Alfie scrunched his lips together. "Mamm. She washes our shirts."

Sol pressed his lips together, not entirely satisfied with Benji's innocent question. "We are all in charge of each other," he finally said. "We have to help each other be good."

Benji nodded. "The spatula makes me be good. Do you want to give Mary the spatula?"

Sol tried a little too hard to laugh, even though Benji hadn't meant it as a joke. "*Nae.* Of course not."

"She is going to have a *buplie*," Benji said, his brows drawn together as if he was thinking very hard about it. "She shouldn't get the spatula, especially cuz she hasn't done nothing wrong. She's real nice. She gave us a bee-sting cake once. And she stubbed her toe."

Sol's expression got darker and more troubled the longer Benji talked. There was nothing like the guileless simplicity of a child to touch someone's heart. Certainly all the yelling in the world couldn't do it. "For sure and certain she's wonderful nice," Sol mumbled.

"For sure and certain," Benji said.

Alfie wiped his nose on his sleeve. No wonder that shirt was always a mess. "You should be nice to every-body. That's what Mamm says. Even LaWayne Nelson. He's mean to the little kids at school, but we have to be nice to him and forgive him when he trips us on the playground."

Andrew's lips twitched sheepishly. LaWayne was Sol's little *bruder*. Alfie probably hadn't even made the connection. Probably. "Why are you boys out here?" Andrew said. "Aren't you supposed to be clean-ing your room?"

Alfie made a sour face. "Our cellar, you mean?"

"*Jah*. Mamm says it smells like something dead down there."

"There's lots of dead things," Benji said. "Spiders and a whole pile of moths by Alfie's lantern."

Alfie folded his arms and glared at Sol. "We heard you yelling through the basement window."

"So we climbed out and came to rescue you," Benji said.

Andrew tried not to act alarmed. "You climbed out the cellar window?" If his *bruderen* could climb out that window, there was no end to the mischief they could get into.

Alfie turned his glare on Benji. "We wanted to help if Andrew got in a fight."

"We weren't fighting," Sol said, even though they both knew that wasn't entirely true. At least their fight hadn't come to blows, wouldn't have come to blows. They were smarter than that.

Once again, Alfie had avoided his question, but Andrew wouldn't forget. Maybe he should install a lock on the outside of the window so the boys couldn't

escape from now on. Mamm would have a fit if she
knew. He messed up Benji's hair. "Go clean your
room. Sol and I will be nice."

Alfie wasn't convinced. "Okay. But yell to us if you
need us." He narrowed his eyes at Sol. "We have
some rope."

They had rope? Andrew was going to have to go
down there and clear out that cellar before the
twins caused a flood or burned down the house. Or
got arrested.

They wouldn't get arrested, would they?

Andrew wouldn't take anything for granted after
orange smoke, binoculars, and cats in trees. Those
boys had resources Andrew couldn't begin to guess at.

Alfie started for the corner of the house where
the cellar window was. "*Nae*, Alfie," Andrew said.
"Front door."

"Ah," Alfie groaned. "Mamm will catch us."

Andrew pointed insistently at the front door. "It's
safer than going through the window."

Benji stood as if unsure whether to side with Alfie
or Andrew. "We slid the bookshelf up to the window
so we can reach."

Alfie shot another glare in Benji's direction. "We'll
go through the front door and sneak downstairs.
Mamm won't notice."

The twins tromped up the steps and paused with
their ears against the front door, trying to hear where
Mamm was in the house. Alfie nodded to Benji,
jerked open the door, and they both rushed inside as
if making an escape in reverse. Sol laughed, more
naturally this time as he watched them go. His nag-
ging conscience was probably relieved. "The wisdom
of a child."

"I'm sorry I yelled at you. I'm sorry I made Treva cry."

"It's okay. Treva cries at everything. She uses tears to get her way."

Andrew motioned for Sol to sit with him on the porch steps. "We may never agree on Mary, but I hope that you and Treva will treat her with kindness."

"We will do what we think is best." He paused. "And it never hurts to be nice. I'll tell Treva. Maybe she can find another project besides Mary's soul."

Andrew didn't want to start another argument, but if he could just make Sol understand. "Jesus dined with sinners and publicans. He ministered to sinners. He called them his lost sheep. If we want Mary to stay and be baptized, we should treat her as Jesus would want us to treat her."

Sol leaned his elbows in his knees. "Mary's not going to get baptized."

"I hope . . . I think maybe she will."

Sol shook his head. "She isn't going to stay here."

"You don't know that," Andrew said, even though the doubt rose in his throat like bile. The more time he spent with Mary, the higher his hopes had risen that she might choose baptism. Might choose to stay. Maybe she had come to care for him as he had come to care for her. The dull ache of longing throbbed in the pit of his stomach.

Did she care for him at all?

"Mary came back because she needs the *gmayna* to pay her hospital bills when she has the *buplie*," Sol said. "She's using Bitsy and Yost because she couldn't fool her own parents into taking her in. As soon as she has that *buplie* and the *gmayna* pays her medical bills, she'll go back to wherever she came from and we'll never see her again."

"The *gmayna* doesn't have to pay her medical bills."

Sol sighed. "We try to take care of our own. Of course the *gmayna* will help with money."

"And you think that's why she came back? Because she couldn't pay for the *buplie* any other way? You . . . you think she'll leave?" The words shoved themselves from between his lips.

"I *know* she'll leave. She had no reason to come back unless her boyfriend kicked her out. He is the one who supported her in Green Bay. He kicked her out and she had nowhere else to go. She's using us to get what she wants."

Andrew didn't want to believe it. Mary had told him she came back because she wanted to have her baby in a place where people loved her. *Ach, vell,* that hadn't turned out quite the way she hoped. At least half of Andrew's neighbors were barely putting up with her. Why did she stay if she found no acceptance here? Was she truly as desperate as Sol thought? And where did that leave Andrew? After she had the baby, would she leave Andrew holding his broken heart in his hands?

Broken heart?

*Ach.* It was as if Alfie threw a grapefruit-sized stone at his head. Would he really be heartbroken if Mary left?

Sol frowned. "People are saying things about you, about why you are being nice to Mary." He cleared his throat. "Paul Glick says that Mary has led you into temptation. He says you're doing things with Mary that you shouldn't. She's pretty and obviously willing to do that kind of thing with a boy."

Not two minutes ago, Andrew had promised himself he wasn't going to descend into another argument with Sol, and now it took all his willpower not to give Sol a good shove off the porch. His blood raced scalding hot through his veins. He took a deep breath and spoke in a calm, controlled voice. "People shouldn't talk about Mary that way. None of it's true. If you aren't willing to believe in Mary, at least you should know *me* better. I would never do something like that."

Sol shrugged as if they were talking about his crops. "I don't believe the gossip. I'm only telling you what other people say. You probably don't realize what people think when you're nice to her."

"Gossip is a horrible sin."

Sol scooted a few inches from Andrew on the step as if he could sense the anger bubbling inside him, but he spoke as if he took no responsibility for the gossip. "I'm just telling you what other people are saying."

Funny how Sol seemed to think that gossip was something other people did.

Sol studied Andrew's face and scooted a little farther. "Look, Andrew, I know you like Mary. I used to like her too, but her kindness was an act. She left us without a word as soon as she could find a ride out of here. We can't forget how she betrayed her parents and the whole community. At heart, she's selfish and ungrateful."

Andrew clenched his teeth and clamped his fingers around the step he was sitting on. Sol and Treva didn't know Mary at all. They had reinvented her personality in the time she'd been gone. Andrew had barely known her before she left, but he knew she was smart and lively and kind. Jerry Zimmerman had known her, and his reaction upon seeing her spoke for itself. Andrew hated to admit it, but Jerry was a *gute* man. He would know if Mary had been selfish and ungrateful as a girl.

But what good would it do to try to convince Sol? They'd only get in another fight, and his *bruderen* would be forced to climb out their window again. They'd probably bring their rope this time.

Sol wanted to think he was doing Andrew a favor by telling him this, but he was only making him hotter and sweatier. "Mary has been in the Englisch world for three, four years. We can only imagine what wickedness she's gotten herself into."

"It's only been two years." And Sol had no doubt let his imagination run wild.

"It's hard to give up the Englisch way of life." Sol placed a hand on Andrew's shoulder as if he cared about him, but Sol couldn't quite hide his self-righteous glee. "Be careful that you don't misplace your friendship. She isn't going to stay. She's using you just like she's using all of us to get what she wants."

Mary had told Andrew that one of the reasons she left the community was because she was turning into a girl like Treva Nelson, proud, resentful, judgmental. He pinched his lips together and eyed Sol. Was this who Andrew had been before he met Mary?

He felt ill. Of course this was who he had been. He had warned his own *bruderen* to stay away from her, all because of his self-righteous confidence, as if he had never committed a sin in his life. It had only been a few weeks, but looking back, he didn't much like his past self. If it hadn't been for Mary, he'd still be in that place, maybe sitting here with Sol on the porch, congratulating himself on his own righteousness. He had resisted her mightily, but Mary had changed him with her exceptional grace, patience, and stubborn determination. He could never repay her for that.

Andrew would as soon pull out his hair than give ear to anything Sol said, but a seed of doubt had been planted in his head all the same—not doubt about Mary's goodness, but about her choices. Would she choose to leave the community after she had the baby? She'd left once before. It would be easy to do again. Would she value her freedom more than her ties to the community, her family, those she loved?

The ache in the pit of Andrew's stomach grew sharper. It shouldn't matter to him if Mary chose to leave. She had never figured into the plans he had for his life. But as he sat there trying not to yell at Sol, he realized it mattered very much.

"Don't get too attached to her," Sol said. "She's trouble, and she'll leave before you can tie that boot of yours."

Andrew looked down at his foot. He still hadn't tied his lace, and there was no hope for the woodshop now. He wished Sol would go away.

Andrew bent over and tied his boot, silently taking back the apology he'd given Sol.

Sol never even knew.

# Chapter Eleven

Matthew Gingerich was as nosy as an anteater and twice as obnoxious. He sat down next to Andrew on the bench and nudged his shoulder. "What is going on between you and Mary Coblenz?"

"What do you mean?" Andrew said, searching for a topic to divert Matthew's attention. How could Andrew explain Mary to anyone else when he wasn't even sure himself?

Almost automatically, Andrew gazed around the yard looking for her. *Gmay* was at the Coblenzes' house today—at the home where Mary had grown up and wasn't welcome anymore. Andrew had half expected Mary to stay away from services this morning, but she'd shown up in the buggy with Bitsy and Yost and lined up with everyone else when they marched into the house. *Her* house. Mary's parents hadn't said a word to her, and it wouldn't have been in keeping with the Sabbath to bar her from *gmay*.

Even though her parents pretty much ignored her, Andrew hadn't been able to take his eyes off Mary the entire service. She was so beautiful and so brave, sitting in her parents' home while her *mamm* turned her face away and her *dat* stared at her as if someone had let a pig into the house. Even though Andrew hadn't expected anything different, her parents' treatment made Andrew ache for Mary.

After services, the men had set up tables and benches on the front lawn for fellowship supper, and the men and boys were helping themselves to bread and spread, pickles and cookies.

"I heard you made Treva Nelson cry," Matthew said, stuffing another piece of bread into his mouth, "all because of Mary."

Andrew didn't growl, like he wanted to. He didn't even roll his eyes. He'd only just recently realized how active and vibrant the Amish gossip mill was and how much people liked to gossip. He had also recently seen how destructive and hurtful gossip could be and determined never to participate in it again. Couldn't people see how easily gossip could get out of hand? Couldn't they see that what one person thought of as the truth often got twisted beyond recognition?

"I made Treva mad," Andrew finally said. "But I didn't hurt her feelings." Was it even worth it to try to set Matthew straight? When he'd tried that with Sol, it had only turned into an argument. "She was being rude to Mary, and I told her so. But if it makes you feel better, I've apologized to Treva." And Sol, however insincere that apology was.

Matthew shrugged. "Why should that make me feel better? Treva can be wonderful mean. She once told my sister Mandy that she was fat."

"She did?"

"Mandy turned the other cheek, but I'm glad you set Treva straight. Forgiveness does not mean being cowardly. Sometimes we have to speak up when we see a wrong being done. Even the Lord Jesus cleared the temple when the moneychangers defiled it."

Andrew was grateful for any ally he could get. He'd always liked Matthew. "*Denki.* I appreciate that. I think people should treat Mary more kindly."

Matthew nodded. "*Jah.* People have been uncertain about her, but no one should ever be mean. My *schwester* says Mary was at the Kanagys' canning frolic. She's a wonderful nice girl, and I believe in repentance."

Andrew believed in repentance too. And second chances. And hope for a brighter future for Mary . . . and for him.

Benji came huffing and puffing up to Andrew's table. "Andrew, you've got to come. We need you."

Andrew pulled his brows together. "Aren't you supposed to be eating?"

"I finished already, and I need you to come. Fast."

This whole "dire emergency" business with Benji and Alfie was getting old. Andrew had just about come to the end of his patience. The problem was that, recently, Benji and Alfie's dire emergencies actually had been dire emergencies. Ignoring Benji could mean a broken arm or a burned shed or some other near-death experience. Andrew huffed out a frustrated breath and gave Benji the evil eye. "Why do you want me to come? Can't Abraham or Austin help?"

"It has to be you." Benji glanced at Matthew and grabbed Andrew's arm. "It's a secret."

Andrew didn't want to encourage Benji any more

than he already had, but Benji's secrets tended to be life-threatening. Besides, Andrew hadn't seen Mary in a while. This would give him a reason to find her. Maybe he'd get a chance to talk to her, to see how she was feeling about staying in the community. To see how she was feeling about her parents. He groaned and let Benji pull him around to the side of the house where no one could see them. This was not going to help him find Mary.

Benji squeezed Andrew's hand hard, almost as if this emergency was worse than all the others. "There's an Englischer yelling at Mary."

Andrew's lungs constricted. "Where is she?"

Benji pressed his lips together. "He's not really yelling. He's talking kind of angry, but it would be lying to say he is yelling."

"Where, Benji?"

"I always try to tell the truth."

Benji was the most exasperating boy in the world, next to Alfie. Andrew wanted to take him by the shoulders and shake the words out of him. Instead, he chose an understanding, sweet and loving smile on his face, as if he had nothing better to do than stand there and talk about telling the truth, even though he thought he might pop a vein in his neck. "I trust you, Benji. I know you always try to tell the honest truth. But where is Mary?"

"Alfie saw an Englischer drive up behind the barn, and then Mary saw him and sneaked away from the supper. Nobody saw her but Alfie and me. She frowned at the Englischer, and then they went inside the barn, and he started yelling at her." Benji traced his toe in the dirt. "Well, he wasn't really yelling, but Alfie told me to come and get you."

A major blood vessel was definitely going to pop in his neck. "They're in the barn?"

Benji nodded.

Andrew was halfway there when he turned back to Benji. "Stay here and go get Alfie."

"I can't get him and stay here at the same time."

"You and Alfie go back to the supper and leave this to me." Andrew didn't really have time to see if Benji would actually do what he said, but he'd have to trust his *bruder*. If Mary was in trouble, there wasn't another minute to waste.

He wanted to sprint but opted for a subdued jog just in case someone was watching him. The barn sat at the back of the Coblenzes' property next to a barbed wire fence and the pavement. A red car was parked on the other side of the fence off to the side of the road. Andrew's speed increased with his pulse rate. There was definitely an Englischer somewhere close by. Benji hadn't been wrong about that. He probably wasn't wrong about any of it. Benji knew more than anyone gave him credit for.

A slight movement off to his right caught Andrew's eye. It might have been a cat or dog tiptoeing behind the tall oak that stood next to the barn, or it might have been Alfie with a pair of binoculars around his neck and a pocketknife in his hand. Andrew was pretty sure it was Alfie, but he certainly didn't have time for that. He had to find Mary first.

The barn door was slightly ajar, and for sure and certain, Mary was in there talking to someone. "I'm not moving back in with you," she said.

"What are you going to do? Live on the streets? I'm not paying child support, if that's what you're after." A man's voice echoed off the ceiling of the barn, loud and clear. Andrew's heart jumped like a grasshopper. It had to be the boyfriend. Or, hopefully, the *ex*-boyfriend. Andrew thought he might be sick.

"Maybe I'll stay here." Andrew could hear the defiance in Mary's voice. No one could make her do anything she didn't want to do.

The boyfriend laughed. "In Amishland? Come on, Mary. You hated it here."

"I didn't hate it."

"Sure. That's why you left as soon as we scraped up enough money to buy a car. You never once wanted to go back in all the time we were together."

"Until I realized what kind of person you are." Mary's voice was rough and low, as if voicing a secret that only she and the boyfriend knew about.

"That's a load of crap, and you know it. You liked me just fine when I took you away from here." The boyfriend seemed to move farther into the barn. "But maybe you were just using me."

"Stay away from me, Josh," Mary said. "I don't want you here."

Andrew didn't know what was going on, but Mary's voice rose in pitch, and he wasn't about to let anything happen to her. He threw open the barn door. Mary had her hand pressed against the boyfriend's chest as if blocking an advance, her face a mixture of anger and distress.

The distress got Andrew's blood boiling.

The boyfriend snapped his head around when light flooded the space.

"Get away from Mary," Andrew growled, feeling brave enough to actually do something about it if the boyfriend gave him trouble. It was a powerful, terrifying feeling.

Scowling like he had a very nasty taste in his mouth, the boyfriend raised his hands and slowly backed away from Mary. "I don't want a fight, Amish boy. I just need to talk to Mary."

Andrew didn't realize his hands were balled into fists until Mary rushed to his side and wrapped her fingers around his arm. "It's okay, Andrew. Josh won't hurt me. At least I don't think so."

Josh lowered his hands. "Thanks for the vote of confidence," he said, a layer of sarcasm in his voice. He pulled a cigarette from his back pocket and stuck it between his lips.

Andrew's heart slowed enough for him to manage a rational thought. "Don't smoke in the barn. You'll start a fire."

Josh chuckled, but there was no humor in it. "Oh, the problems you have to deal with in Amishland. People can't even go out to have a smoke for fear of setting the crops on fire."

Mary and Andrew followed Josh as he sauntered outside ten feet from the barn, lit his cigarette, and sucked in the smoke. Andrew nearly coughed from the smell. How had Mary lived with that for two years?

"You shouldn't smoke around Mary. It might hurt the baby," Andrew said, earning a tentative smile from Mary and an I-couldn't-care-less look from Josh.

Josh tapped the ashes from his cigarette. "I don't want to be rude, man, but I need to talk to Mary. Give us some privacy."

Mary still had hold of Andrew's arm, and she squeezed tighter.

In spite of the boyfriend and the unpleasant look he was shooting in Andrew's direction, Andrew's heart soared. Mary needed him. Being needed was a heady feeling. "I'm not going anywhere unless Mary asks me to leave."

Mary breathed a barely audible sigh. "*Denki*," she whispered, looking up at him as if he'd saved her life. He'd never felt more noble, even though he hadn't really done that much. Mary turned to Josh. "Whatever you want to say, you'll have to say to both of us."

"Did you leave me to hook up with this Amish guy?" Josh practically spit the words at Mary. She squeezed tighter on Andrew's arm but didn't change the expression on her face.

"You know why I left," she said.

Josh pressed the heel of his hand to his cheek. "For crying out loud, Mary, do we have to go over this again? I said I was sorry. You Amish aren't supposed to hold a grudge. Can't you forgive me and move on?"

"I do forgive you, and I have moved on."

Josh blew smoke from between his lips. "That's not what I mean. You're the one who always talked about choices and consequences. I was afraid a baby would change us. Having a baby changes things."

Mary lifted her chin. "Don't you think I know that?"

"You're nineteen. A baby wasn't exactly in your life plan when we got together. You wanted to go to school." He let the cigarette dangle from his mouth as he stuffed his hands into his pockets. "A baby will tie you down. You'll have less freedom than you did when you were Amish."

Mary squeezed Andrew's arm even tighter. Freedom was the most important thing in the world to Mary. Was Josh getting to her?

Andrew wasn't certain about intervening, but Mary was clearly unnerved by the conversation. "Is there something particular you needed to say to Mary?" Andrew said. "Because we need to get back to the fellowship supper."

Josh glared at Andrew as if he were the devil himself. "If I had that haircut, I'd kill myself."

"Shut up, Josh," Mary said.

It was nice of Mary to defend him, but Josh's insult didn't bother Andrew. It wasn't anything he hadn't heard before. The local Englisch teenagers made fun of the Amish all the time, as if their multiple piercings and tattoos weren't ridiculous in their own way. What *did* bother Andrew was that Josh was getting madder with every word. The color traveled up his face like wildfire up a pine tree, and he bared his teeth like a dog on the attack. With his pulse throbbing in his ears, Andrew took a small step forward. If Josh's anger turned violent, Andrew would be ready to stand between him and Mary.

Josh frowned and turned away from Andrew as if he would never say another word to him again. "You don't belong here, Mary. You know it, and I know it."

"What about the baby?"

"Evelyn doesn't want the baby growing up around these religious kooks."

Mary's eyes went wide. "Evelyn? What does Evelyn

have to do with it?" She glanced at Andrew. "Evelyn is Josh's stepmother. We lived with her in Green Bay."

Andrew nodded, grateful that she wanted to include him in the conversation, like it was important to her that he knew.

Josh seemed to chew very carefully on his words. "Evelyn was furious I let you go like that, and she'll throw me out if I don't bring you back."

Mary's eyes went wide with indignation. "This isn't even about me or the baby. You're worried about losing your rent-free basement."

"That's not true," Josh growled. "I love you and so does Evelyn. She says I'm a deadbeat dad, and the baby hasn't even been born yet. But I'm not ashamed to admit I didn't want the baby in the first place."

"Yes," Mary said. "I know."

"Evelyn is worried about her stepgrandson, and she says I can't come back until I take care of it."

Mary huffed out a breath. "Forget it. I know what 'taking care of it' means to you."

Something hot flared in Josh's expression. "You can't be free with a baby, Mary. It would be better for everyone if you left it here for your parents to raise."

Mary lifted an eyebrow. "Better for you."

Josh had lived with Mary for almost two years, but he didn't even know her. Mary would never abandon her child like that.

Josh obviously thought he was being perfectly reasonable. "Put it up for adoption. It would give the baby a good, stable home with parents who could take care of him, and we'd be free to do what we've always wanted to do."

Mary dug her fingernails into Andrew's arm. He

didn't even flinch. If she needed something to hit, he'd give her his face. "I'm not going to put my baby up for adoption for your convenience," she said.

"It's not for convenience. It's for freedom. You've always wanted to be free. We'd both be happier without being tied down by a baby."

"Or a rent payment." Mary's glare could have lit one of Josh's cigarettes.

"That's not why I came, Mary. I want you back. I love you, and I know you love me."

Andrew held his breath. Did Mary love Josh? Mary had never told Andrew why she had left Josh. Maybe, like Sol said, Josh had thrown her out, and she'd had no choice but to come back to the community. Andrew didn't want it to be true, but that didn't mean it wasn't.

Mary released her grip on Andrew, folded her arms, and tilted her head to one side. "You'd take me with the baby?"

It was like a knife to the heart. Was Mary really considering going back to Josh? And where would that leave Andrew but completely lost? He should have paid more heed to Sol's warning.

"Of course with the baby. Evelyn will babysit anytime we want. She wants a grandchild." He didn't look up when he said it, so Andrew couldn't tell if he was sincere, even though the words sounded like poison when they came out of his mouth. Would Josh love his baby or simply treat her as a nuisance, or worse? No child deserved to grow up with a *fater* who didn't love her. Andrew bit his tongue on an accusation. It didn't matter what he thought, only what Mary believed. Andrew had never felt so heavy, as if the weight of all of Mary's choices pressed him into the ground.

Mary lifted her chin and stared at Josh with a fierceness Andrew had never seen before. "It was unfair of me to ask that question, Josh. It doesn't matter if you say you'd accept the baby. I'm not moving back. I don't love you anymore."

Josh threw his cigarette on the ground and stomped on it. "I made one mistake. One mistake."

"Don't yell at Mary," Andrew said, torn between indignation at Josh's temper and sheer relief that maybe Mary wasn't going to leave the community, at least not for Josh.

Josh eyed Andrew with unreserved hostility before spitting his venom at Mary. "Are you leaving me for him? Why don't you just get a puppy? The conversation would be more interesting."

"It's none of your business, Josh."

Josh circled Andrew like a lone wolf might circle its prey, but Andrew wasn't so easily intimidated. He pulled little boys out of burning buildings. He yanked broken toes back into place. Josh narrowed his eyes. "Don't get your hopes up, Amish boy. Mary will do anything to get what she wants. She pretended to love me just to get out of here. When that didn't work for her anymore, she came back."

Mary pressed her lips together and turned her head as if Josh had slapped her. The anguish on her face was so real, Andrew was surprised that she didn't cry out in pain.

"If you believe that," Andrew said, "then you don't know Mary at all."

Josh pulled another cigarette from his pocket.

"She'll use you to get her freedom, just like she used me. Has she asked you to leave the community and run away with her yet?"

"Of course not."

Josh seemed to pull all his rage into himself like a brewing storm. "I don't know who this guy is, Mary, but this life isn't for you. Don't you remember what it was like? You were a prisoner. Remember how your parents made you feel when you even had a thought of your own? How you were going to suffocate if you couldn't get out?"

"I remember," Mary said quietly, glancing at Andrew and placing a protective hand on her stomach. "I don't know what I want, Josh. But I do know that I don't want to go back with you. I've made too many mistakes already."

Andrew studied Mary's face. When he'd first met her, he had accused her of feeling no remorse for her sins. One look at the pain in her eyes, and he realized how wrong he had been. Mary was sorry for everything, and she still keenly felt the sting of her choices. Andrew's heart ached for her. Didn't she remember what she had told him? Jesus had washed her sins away. She could rejoice in that.

Josh pressed his lips into a hard line and glared at her, the anger raging in his eyes. "I'll sue for custody. I'll take your baby away from you if you don't come back."

Andrew's entire body tensed. Mary turned to stone beside him. "Would you really use my baby to control me the way my parents used the church?" Her voice shook with fear.

Josh squared his shoulders. "That baby is half mine."

"Yes, it is." Andrew felt her hands tremble around his arm. "But that would make you just like my parents—maybe worse, because my parents think they are doing what God would have them do."

Josh sensed he'd upset her. "Don't bring God into this. God would want my baby to have a father."

"As God wills," Mary whispered. Andrew suspected she was barely holding on to her composure.

He laced his fingers through hers. She could lean on him for strength. He wouldn't fail her. And he would not watch Josh hurt her anymore. "You need to leave now, Josh," Andrew said. "You're not welcome here, and coming from an Amish person, that's saying something."

Josh kept his gaze on Mary. "You better get yourself a good Amish lawyer because I'm coming for my baby."

Andrew thought he might spontaneously catch on fire he was so angry. He raised a hand and pointed to the oak tree. "My brother is spying on us from that tree over there. I just have to give the word, and he'll run to the house and fetch about twenty Amish farm boys who lift hay bales for fun. One of them could break your arm like a twig. Maybe you better leave before you make me angry."

Josh's gaze flicked toward the house. Everyone was in the front yard—not an Amish boy to be seen, but he got the idea. He pretended not to be the slightest bit alarmed. "Bring all the Amish boys you want. You don't believe in violence. They'd only try to stare me to death. Or maybe sing."

"Maybe," Andrew said, "but they might be willing to make an exception for you. We all get kind of testy when people smoke around our hay supply."

Josh didn't look scared, but he didn't exactly look comfortable either. He backed in the direction of his car. "Maybe you better unblock my number, Mary. I'll be calling about visitation. Soon." Josh took one last look at Andrew and without another word, strolled around the barn and out of sight. Mary folded her arms and took a few steps in Josh's direction, as if making sure he was really going. She turned and looked at Andrew. They stared silently at each other until they heard Josh start his car and drive off.

Without taking his eyes from Mary, Andrew called up into the tree. "Alfie Petersheim, climb down from that tree and go to the house this minute."

A groan came from a low branch. "How did you know I was here?"

"Go now, or I'm telling Mamm."

Andrew looked over his shoulder as Alfie let himself down from the branch and gave Andrew a pleading look. "But I helped you. You told him I was going to get help."

Andrew returned Alfie's plea with the meanest face he could make. Alfie promptly turned and tromped toward the house, looking back occasionally to see if Andrew was still watching.

When Alfie was halfway to the house, Mary sighed as if she'd been holding her breath and walked straight into Andrew's embrace. His surprise lasted a few motionless seconds, then he wrapped his arms around her and tugged her closer. It seemed the natural thing to do and so *wunderbarr*. She buried her face in his neck, and he felt wet tears against his skin. "It's okay, Mary. It's going to be okay."

"I never should have . . ." Her voice disintegrated into a sob, and he held her tighter.

"You of all people know that *should-haves* lead nowhere. Gotte wants who you are now and will turn it for your good."

She lifted her head. "Will He? What good can come of losing my baby?"

"Nothing. Nothing good can come of that, but Lord willing, it will never happen. Josh can't even afford to pay rent. Can he afford a lawyer? He's mad at you, but spite will only drive him so far. He might reconsider before he's even left the city limits." He brushed a tear off her face with his thumb.

She stifled another sob. "He hated the very thought of a baby. It's why I finally got up the courage to leave him. He wanted me to have an abortion." Her voice cracked. "Do you know what that is?"

Andrew nodded slowly as horror engulfed him.

"I knew," she said. "I knew for months that it wasn't going to work out with Josh, but I'd done so many bad things that I didn't know if I could come back. I didn't know where to go, so I stayed."

"You did the best you could. I can't imagine trying to live in the Englisch world. It's hard enough for Englischers—nearly impossible for an Amish girl."

She wiped away another tear. "In some ways I was freer than I had ever been. I could make my own decisions about work and school, I could wear anything I wanted, I could drive a car. But I went against Gotte and his commandments and put myself in bondage to sin. Josh and I are from different worlds. I realized I couldn't live with a man who doesn't believe what I hold most dear. I'd turned my back on so many things I believe in. When Josh insisted on an abortion, I knew I had to leave, no matter the consequences. There are some things I could never bring myself to do, not even for my freedom—especially for my freedom. I knew I couldn't do it if I wanted to live with myself. I've disappointed so many people."

"You haven't disappointed me. I admire you more than ever."

"You shouldn't. Josh was right. I used him. I used him to get me out of Bienenstock."

"Maybe he used you. You paid for his car."

She sighed. "Part of it. It's still mostly his. Even when I knew I couldn't stay with him anymore, I stayed because I needed a bed and I needed the work and a car. I used him for my own selfish desires."

Andrew rubbed the back of his fingers against her cheek. "There's nothing selfish about choosing to have a baby you didn't plan on or coming back to the community for your baby's sake, even when you knew you might not be welcome."

She blinked back more tears. "That's very sweet of you to say." She turned and gazed in the direction Josh's car had gone. "But I *have* been selfish, and that realization brings me much pain."

"But don't you remember what you told me? Jesus has forgiven you. You should forgive yourself."

Mary shook her head. "I thought I had, but seeing my parents today and talking to Josh has been like a kick in the teeth."

Andrew curled one side of his mouth. "You've been kicked in the teeth plenty. It's time to let it be and save that nice smile of yours."

"Easy for you to say," she said. "You have the best set of teeth in Bienenstock."

"My *mammi* would be very glad to hear you say that. She's bought us all special toothpaste. It tastes like dirt."

It melted Andrew's heart to hear Mary laugh after everything that had happened today. She suddenly gasped and grabbed Andrew's hand. "The baby is kicking." She placed his hand on her abdomen. "Do you feel it?"

Andrew decided not to even question the propriety of touching Mary's stomach. If she was willing to share something so intimate, he would take it as a gift and let his misgivings lie. He held his breath as he sensed the shape of a tiny foot under Mary's skin, a small miracle taking shape inside of her. His astonishment was almost palpable, like a thousand bright lights that he could reach out and touch. "It's *wunderbarr*, Mary," he whispered.

A smile grew slowly on her lips. "I know."

"Andrew!"

Andrew turned at the sound of his name and let his hand drop from Mary's stomach. Even though he was just feeling the baby kick, the *gmayna* wasn't likely to approve.

Benji stood about halfway between the house and the barn with his hands cupped around his mouth. "We need you real bad."

Andrew cocked an eyebrow at Mary. "My *bruderen* won't rest until they've driven me crazy."

She grinned. "It's nice to be needed."

Andrew could have stood there all day, gazing at Mary and feeling the baby kick, but Benji wasn't going to give up. Andrew inclined his head in Benji's direction. "Should we get back?"

"*Jah.*"

"Are you going to be okay?"

She grew more serious. He wished he hadn't asked. "When I first found out I was going to have a baby, I was terrified. I didn't think I could bear it. But now I think I'll turn to dust if Josh gets custody."

"Do you really think he'll try?"

She pressed her lips together. "It will be what I deserve."

Andrew took her hand and pressed it to his heart. "It seems physically impossible, but you are very *gute* at kicking yourself in the teeth."

She cracked a smile. "And you are very *gute* at making me feel better."

"We could spend an hour arguing about Gotte's love and Gotte's punishment, but I think you already know what Gotte would say, and Benji needs me real bad. We'll just have to leave it at that."

She smiled wider now, as if giving up on her teeth kicking. "Thank goodness for Benji. He's saved me from a very long and boring lecture."

"You better believe it."

# Chapter Twelve

Bitsy propped her hands on her hips and made herself into a brick wall. "Alfie Petersheim, you will not come in this house smelling like that."

Alfie, Benji, and Andrew stood on Bitsy's porch, peering expectantly into the kitchen while Bitsy barred their entrance. "I don't smell like nothing bad," Alfie protested, even though anyone within fifteen feet would have complained.

Bitsy was immovable. "Your incorrect English is correct. You don't smell like nothing bad. You smell like *something* very bad, like a rat with a rose in his mouth crawled up your neck and died on your head. That shirt could stand up and walk down the street by itself and probably do a little tap dance on its way."

Benji leaned around Bitsy and waved to Mary, who was standing behind Bitsy trying not to laugh. Mary waved back. Andrew stood a few feet back from his *bruderen*, probably because Alfie really did smell bad or because he wanted to pretend he wasn't with two eight-year-old boys. He was smiling so wide at Mary, he could have caught a lot of bugs in his teeth if the wind had been blowing.

"But, Bitsy," Alfie said, putting all his energy into an impressively high whine, "Mary invited us over to make peanut-butter-and-honey power balls, and how can she make them without the peanut butter?"

Benji scratched an itch at his ear. "Mamm let us take two whole jars."

If anyone knew how to put her foot down, it was Bitsy. Alfie's distress didn't even make her flinch. "I won't have you stinking up my kitchen. I'd have to burn a candle for days to get rid of the smell." She bent over and propped her hands on her knees so she could get a better look at Alfie. "I know your *mamm*. She's no slouch. Why hasn't she pried that shirt off your body and washed it already?"

"She only does laundry once a week, and Benji's shirt was in the wash today. This is the only one I have, and I keep it under my pillow for emergencies. I put it on and sneaked out while she wasn't looking."

"It should probably be burned," Bitsy said. "Do you still have the scabs?"

Alfie held out his arms even though nobody could see anything under his dirty sleeves. "Mamm would notice for sure."

Bitsy tapped her finger to her chin. "We'll just have to wash it while you make power balls." She held out one hand and pinched her nose with the other. "Take it off and give it to me."

Alfie's eyes got wide. "I can't make cookies half naked."

"You can't make cookies smelling like a bacterial infection either."

Alfie wasn't fit to make cookies at all. His shirt was

a mess, that was for sure and certain, but he also had a garden plot of dirt under his fingernails and what looked like mud caked in his hair. Mud or manure. Maybe that was why he smelled so bad. Mary sidled next to Bitsy. "Alfie, have you ever been upstairs?"

"*Nae.*"

"If you go up the stairs and down the hall, you will find a bathroom. Fill the tub and take a nice warm bath while we wash your shirt. You can find a T-shirt to wear in the big room with three beds." Alfie didn't need to know that it was one of her T-shirts. At least he wouldn't be "half naked."

Alfie's eyes were slits on his face. "Will you give me my shirt back?"

"After it's washed," Bitsy said. "And bleached. And fumigated."

"Do I have to take a bath?" Benji said.

Mary looked him up and down. "It wouldn't hurt."

Benji grimaced. "Do you have special rose soap?"

"*Nae.* Only regular soap."

He seemed to like that answer. "Okay. I'll take a bath too."

Mary bent over and helped Alfie when she could see he was having trouble unbuttoning his shirt. The fabric was stiff. "You boys need to wash your hair twice and use the little brush in the drawer to scrub your fingernails."

Alfie rolled his eyes. "Twice? Why do I have to do it twice?"

Nobody answered him, as if it should be obvious from the smells rising from his body.

Mary helped Alfie peel off his shirt. The scabs up his arms were getting smaller. They'd probably do much better if they were out in the sunshine more often, but that was too much to ask of Alfie. The boys ran upstairs, and Bitsy pinched the shirt between two fingers and held it away from her body.

Andrew came into the house. "Mamm makes them take a bath almost every night, but things have been hard with Mammi and Dawdi this week. She's barely had time to notice the boys live at our house."

Bitsy frowned. "They're old enough to know they need to take a bath. Don't let them get away with being lazy about it."

"You're right," Andrew said. "Alfie is afraid to take a bath in case Mamm sees him without his shirt on, and both boys hate the rose soap."

Bitsy directed a smug expression up the stairs. "Maybe he'll learn that keeping a secret is greater punishment than telling."

"Maybe he will."

Bitsy headed toward the washroom. "I'll scrub this shirt and leave it to soak in some bleach, but then I have to go to Walmart. Will you take it out after about twenty minutes? Lord willing, it will have time to dry."

"We'll hang it in the sun." Mary heard the water running upstairs. The boys had started filling their tub. Andrew had two jars of peanut butter in his hands. "You look like you're ready to make peanut-butter-and-honey power balls," she said.

"Or ready to sit and watch you make them."

She giggled. "And rob you of the experience? I wouldn't dream of it. These power balls are nutritious. If you get lost in the woods, they'll keep you alive for days."

"But what if I forget to bring my peanut-butter-and-honey power balls and then get lost in the woods? They won't do me any good."

"It's why you need to learn how to make them. So you'll never be caught without a bucketful."

A horn honked outside. "That's my ride." Bitsy walked past them from the washroom, grabbed her large flowered canvas bag, and headed out the front door. "The shirt is soaking. If the bleach doesn't help, you'll have to burn it. And do it away from the house."

Mary smiled and smoothed her hand down her stomach. The baby was extra active today, and it felt as if he was kicking Mary right in the ribs with his little foot. She winced and caught her breath.

"Is everything okay?" Andrew said.

Mary concentrated on taking deep breaths. "He's kicking hard today."

"Are you having a boy?"

Mary studied his face, a little surprised. No one in the community had cared to ask her that except Bitsy and her nieces. "Sometimes I call the *buplie* a he, sometimes a she, but I don't know what I'm having." She couldn't afford an ultrasound, even though the doctor had strongly recommended one.

Andrew's face flooded with concern. "How long has it been since you've seen a doctor?"

She held up her hand and grimaced as the baby kicked again. "I saw a doctor just last week." She paused to catch her breath. "She says everything is going fine, and I am right on schedule. Two weeks to go." Mary tried not to think about how she was going to pay the doctor, but she insisted on having her baby in a hospital, even if that meant years of debt. She'd made so many mistakes, and she would not be able to live with the guilt if she had the baby at home and something went wrong.

Bitsy had offered to help with the bills, but how could Mary ask any more of her than she and Yost were already doing, than she and Yost had already done—for Mary and for Jerry Zimmerman? Mary certainly wouldn't ask the *gmayna* for money. They resented her enough as it was, and she wouldn't give them any reason to think she had come home just so she could get them to pay for the baby.

Of course she wouldn't tell Andrew any of this. He couldn't do anything about it and would feel guilty that he didn't really want to help her. She wouldn't risk spoiling their friendship with her money troubles.

Her heart hurt just thinking about it. She was only prolonging the inevitable. Like as not, Andrew would stop coming around as soon as she had the *buplie*. He was twenty-four years old, and a friendship with someone like Mary would make the other girls in the district wary.

He was still looking at her as if trying to determine how healthy she really was. "Are you sure you're feeling well?"

"The *buplie* is wonderful ornery today. Maybe he'll be a wrestler." She winced again as the baby seemed to turn a full circle in her womb. "Can you fetch the oats? They're in the bottom cupboard, and I don't bend all that well."

Andrew pulled a chair out from under the table. "Here, you sit, and I'll bring the ingredients to you."

"I'll be okay." Another jab took her breath away. "Never mind. Hand me the peanut butter."

He hesitated, frowning like a largemouth bass. "Do we need to call the doctor?"

Mary took a deep breath and made a face at him. "I'll be fine. The honey is in the pantry. And the powdered milk."

He widened his eyes in mock horror. "Powdered milk?"

"Don't worry. You won't even taste it."

"Mamm used to make us drink powdered milk. I think it stunted my growth."

Mary made another face. "You're what, six two, six three? I think you turned out just fine."

His mouth relaxed into a smile. "I'm only six one. See. I should have been two inches taller."

Mary jumped at a loud, insistent knock. Andrew motioned for her to stay put and answered the door. Wallace and Erla Zimmerman stood on the porch, their faces as bleak as winter frost. Jerry's parents. *Ach.* A thousand heavy stones pressed on Mary's heart. He'd done it. Jerry had finally done it.

"I would have a word with Mary Coblenz," Wallace said, his voice ragged and unyielding as he stood with his hat in his hand, gazing into the house.

Andrew turned to her, an unspoken question in his eyes. Mary nodded. Wallace and Erla deserved to have their say, and she deserved to hear it. She folded her hands protectively around her baby.

Andrew invited Wallace and Erla into the house, but when he closed the door, they stood motionless, as if they didn't know what to do now that they were inside. "Do you want to sit down?" Andrew said.

The Zimmermans seemed frozen, like they hadn't heard him, staring at Mary as if she had all the answers they couldn't bear to ask. The pain in their eyes broke

Mary's heart. The anger in Wallace's expression took her breath away. "How could you?" Wallace said. "How could you do this to our son?"

Andrew had no idea what was going on, but bless him, he tried to make it better. "Please sit down, Wallace, Erla." His voice was perfect mildness, his expression full of calm. "Can I get you a cup of *kaffee*?"

Wallace banged his fist on the table, making everyone else in the room flinch. Mary held her breath as a sharp ache stabbed her stomach.

"There's no need for that," Andrew said, more firmly this time. He moved so he was standing between Mary and Wallace. "You can't come in here and treat Mary . . ."

"What do you know of it?" Wallace said, shaking an accusatory finger in Andrew's direction. "That girl convinced my son to leave us. He's gone off to New York."

Andrew glanced at Mary, doubt and confusion playing at the corners of his mouth. "What do you mean?"

"Jerry has left home then?" Mary said.

"You're the one who told him to do it." With a trembling hand, Wallace pulled a folded piece of paper from his pocket. "'*Dear Mamm and Dat, I'm sorry, but I can't live like this anymore. You don't have to worry about me. Mary Coblenz gave me some money for travel, and I have a job waiting for me in New York with a nice family willing to take me in.*'"

Erla covered her mouth with her hand and whimpered softly. Mary ached to embrace her. If only Erla knew how Jerry's words tore at Mary's heart too. But she stayed firmly planted in her chair and took the blame they thought she deserved.

Wallace kept reading. "'*I know how much this will hurt*

*you, but please try to understand. I have to find my own path and make my own choices. I must choose my own happiness and not live only for yours. I'm sorry, and I love you.'"*

Andrew snapped his head around to look at her, his eyes flashing with fierce accusation. "Mary," he hissed, "you gave him money?"

Bitsy and Yost had provided the money since Mary didn't have a cent to her name, but she didn't want the Zimmermans to be mad at Bitsy too. "He needed bus fare."

"What have you done?" The raw pain on Andrew's face couldn't have made it any clearer. He blamed her too.

"Andrew, it's not what you think. I—"

"We welcomed you into the community," Andrew said. "Is this how you repay us?"

Of course he wouldn't let her try to explain. Why would he? He was an Amish boy, raised to believe there was only one right answer to every question, set in his ways like the rest of them. His chest heaved up and down as if breathing was an effort, and his eyes flashed with the righteous indignation she'd seen so many times before in so many different pairs of eyes. "I trusted you. How could you do this to me? To them?"

In that instant, her hopes shattered like delicate glass on a stony path. After all they'd been through together, after she had bared her soul to him, didn't he know her better than to think she'd betray the whole community? A shard of that delicate glass pierced her heart. Andrew knew her too well. She'd confessed how selfish she was. He knew how she'd used Josh because she wanted her freedom. Maybe he was only just now seeing who she really was.

She felt dizzy. She had made so many mistakes, but helping Jerry was not one of them. She hadn't betrayed the Zimmermans or the community or Andrew. She had helped a friend. And no matter what anyone thought, Gotte had forgiven her for her sins.

The only mistake she could chastise herself for was believing that Andrew was different from every other Amish boy in Wisconsin. What a fool she had been! He would never let himself love her, but she thought that maybe in the past few weeks he had seen past her sin and into her heart.

*Nae,* he believed like the others, even if his true feelings had taken longer to reveal themselves.

Wallace crumpled the paper in his fist, propped his hand on the table, and leaned toward Mary. His face was a map of grief, withered and inconsolable. "Jerry hasn't been the same since you came back. He's restless and dissatisfied with the life Gotte gave him to live. Ada Herschberger says she saw you whispering with him at the haystack supper, and Martin saw Jerry here last week. You talked him into leaving, didn't you?" When Mary didn't answer, Wallace snapped at her. "Didn't you?"

Mary wrapped her arms more tightly around her stomach and glanced at Andrew, silently pleading for his help. He offered none, just stared at her as if she was a perfect stranger who'd been caught stealing his tools. "*Nae,*" she said. It wasn't any use trying to explain. Wallace was too angry to believe a word she said, Erla too distraught. Andrew, too resentful.

"That's why you came back," Wallace said. "To persuade him to leave and meet you in New York, and you gave him the money to do it."

She wouldn't be able to convince the Zimmermans

of anything. Wallace had already made up his own version of the story. What did it matter if Jerry had been thinking about leaving home ever since he was sixteen, long before Mary had even left, long before she had returned? Jerry had tried to talk to his *fater* about leaving, but Wallace wouldn't hear him, didn't even want to understand. Jerry had come to Mary for support. She'd given him her truth and maybe some courage to actually go through with it, but she couldn't blame herself for that. She couldn't even feel bad about the money. Jerry would have hitch-hiked to New York, and Mary couldn't bear to think of him in that kind of danger.

Jerry had made his own decision.

But Wallace blamed her.

"I've never been to New York," Mary said.

Wallace pushed himself from the table and glared at Andrew. "Jerry yelled at me yesterday. Yelled at me when I gave him correction. What has this world come to? 'Honor thy father and thy mother that thy days may be long upon the earth.'"

Andrew nodded earnestly. "Jerry should have come to you for guidance instead of going to Mary. She led him astray." Andrew turned his face to her but wouldn't meet her eye. "She thinks she is so wise, but she has brought shame and pain to the whole community."

Mary gasped quietly as the shock of betrayal slapped her across the face and the pain in her womb tore through her body. Andrew couldn't have hurt her more if he'd ripped out her heart and thrown it on the sidewalk.

It was clear what he thought of her. Mary Coblenz was not only the vilest of sinners, but she led her unsuspecting friends along the path to hell with her. She must be avoided. She must be shunned. She must be driven out.

"I'm . . . I'm sorry Jerry hurt you. So very sorry." What else could she say? She wasn't sorry Jerry had finally found his courage, and she rejoiced that he was free from his *fater*'s firm hand.

Wallace turned on her and spit out his words. "Stay away from me. Stay away from my family. If you have any shame at all, you will leave our community and never come back. Jerry's soul is on your head. You will suffer twice the damnation."

Reeling as if she'd suffered a blow to the head, Mary breathlessly clutched her stomach and rose to her feet. She couldn't look at Andrew and keep her composure, so she leaned on the table for support and locked gazes with Wallace. "I am deeply sorry that you are upset. If it eases your pain to blame me, then you can blame me. But I didn't do anything wrong."

"You can deny all you want. I know the truth." Wallace nodded to Andrew. "We all know the truth."

Saturated in pain and heartbreak, Mary could barely concentrate on Wallace's accusations. "Is there anything else you want to say?" she said, unable to raise her voice above a whisper. She wanted nothing more than for all of them to be gone.

Wallace shoved his hat on his head. "You're not welcome here, Mary Coblenz. Go back to where you came from."

Wallace turned his back on Mary and ushered Erla out of the house ahead of him. He slammed the door behind him and made the front window rattle.

Immediately after, Mary heard footsteps coming

down the stairs. Praise Derr Herr the boys hadn't witnessed that horrible commotion. Benji, then Alfie in her Twenty One Pilots T-shirt, came bounding down the stairs as if they were running from a wolf.

Benji threw his arms around Mary as best he could. To her surprise, two fat tears rolled down his cheeks. "Are you okay, Mary? Did they hurt you?"

Mary tried to appear calm and relatively cheerful, but it was nearly impossible to smile with her heart shattered on the floor. She smoothed her hand down his damp hair. "I'm . . . I'm okay, Benji."

"We sneaked and listened at the bottom of the stairs."

"Benji!" Alfie scolded.

Benji didn't seem to care that he'd just revealed their secret. He released Mary and looked up into her face. "They was very mean to you."

Mary's knees buckled under her, and she plopped herself into her chair before she fell over. Propping her elbow on the table, she covered her eyes with her hand, suddenly weary and broken. "Today is not a *gute* day for making cookies, Benji. I need to go lie down."

She felt Benji's cool hand against her cheek. "Are you okay, Mary?"

Andrew finally spoke. "We need to go now."

"But can we make peanut-butter-and-honey power balls tomorrow?" Alfie said.

Andrew folded his arms and looked anywhere but at Mary. "We'll see."

Benji wasn't so easily sidetracked. "But, Mary, you don't feel good. We could make some chicken soup. Andrew knows how."

"*Nae*, I don't," Andrew said.

Mary adored Benji and Alfie. She didn't want to hurt their feelings, but she had to get Andrew out of her house this very minute. With her head still cradled in her hand, she said, "Andrew, will you please take your *bruderen* and go home?"

"Ah, Mary," Benji groaned. "We want to take care of you."

Alfie scrunched his lips together. "What about my shirt?"

Andrew lunged like an uncoiled spring. "I'll get it." He was gone in less than a second.

"Benji," Mary whispered. Another pain seized her and rendered her momentarily unable to speak.

"What's the matter, Mary?" Alfie said, finally realizing something was wrong. The look of excruciating pain on her face probably tipped him off.

"Benji, my phone is upstairs on top of my dresser. Will you get it for me? Quickly, please."

Benji and Alfie raced each other up the stairs, clomping as if they were wearing heavy boots. Lord willing, her phone had enough charge to make a call. She silently chastised herself for not being more careful about that, now that the baby was so close. Too close.

She could hear the water running in the washroom, Andrew rinsing the bleach from Alfie's shirt. The twins stampeded down the stairs, and Alfie handed Mary her phone. Fourteen percent power. That would be enough. She entered the number and held her breath as it rang and rang. "Please be home," she murmured. Patti answered after what seemed like a hundred rings. "Can you come and get me?"

"Is it the baby, sweetie?"

"Yes."

"Woohoo, I'll be right there."

It was a sad state of affairs when your driver was more excited than you were about having a baby.

Mary nearly dropped her phone as another pain tightened around her abdomen. She was supposed to be timing contractions, but all she could do was endure them. She breathed in and out, moving her hand in a circle around the spot that hurt the worst. Benji and Alfie stared at her like she was something interesting and a little frightening on television.

"She's sick," Benji whispered to Alfie.

"She's going to throw up," Alfie whispered back.

Mary wanted to laugh and cry and scream at the same time. There had been nothing ever like this kind of pain, nothing like this kind of fear, gripping her like an iron hand and squeezing her throat until she couldn't catch her breath.

Would the baby be all right? What if he died? What if she died? Would anybody care? *Ach*, how she wanted the comfort of her *mamm*'s soothing embrace or even Bitsy's blunt reassurance right now. The pain in her heart was as unbearable as the pain in her body. Benji and Alfie were dear and so very sweet, but they couldn't help her.

She was alone.

And so afraid.

Andrew marched from the washroom with the damp shirt in his hands. Aunt Bitsy had managed to turn it shiny white, though why Mary noticed something like that was anybody's guess. She swiped the moisture from her cheeks so Andrew wouldn't gloat or lecture her or tell her she'd gotten what she'd deserved. She just wanted him to go away.

From the looks of it, he wanted the same thing. He didn't even slow his steps, heading straight for the door and presumably freedom. Or perhaps he was running from danger, not taking any chances that Mary Coblenz could corrupt him in a matter of minutes. "*Cum*, boys," he said, opening the door. "Let's leave Mary in peace."

"What about the peanut butter?" Alfie said, as if his *mamm* might want it back.

"Leave it."

Alfie grinned and made a pretty good try at a wink for Mary. "That means we'll be back to make power balls."

In one swift motion, Andrew tucked Alfie's shirt under his arm and scooped both jars of peanut butter from the table. He wasn't planning on coming back. "Let's go." He didn't say it kindly, and both boys ran to his side as if he'd cracked a whip in their direction.

Mary stiffened in her chair as another pain stole her breath. Please, dear Lord, let them leave so she could writhe in pain without an audience.

Benji wrapped both hands around Andrew's fingers and yanked as if he was pulling a drapery cord. "We can't leave, Andrew. She's sick."

"*Ach, nae,*" Mary gasped. "Please go. I'm right as rain."

Andrew's gaze snapped in her direction, but he looked away almost as quickly. "She's fine, and we're going."

It was all Mary could do to keep from moaning in pain. Ten more seconds and she could scream if she wanted to. "Goodbye, Benji and Alfie. We'll see you soon." *Go away. Go away now.*

Andrew opened the door, but Benji pulled on Andrew's arm with all his might. "We have to help Mary." When Andrew resisted, Benji reared back and kicked Andrew in the shins.

"Ouch, Benji! Stop that. What's the matter with you?" Another man might have slugged Benji for insolence, but Andrew wouldn't raise a hand against his *bruderen.* He wouldn't raise a hand against anybody. Mary was grateful for that, especially when Benji was just watching out for Mary.

She wished he wouldn't.

Benji let go of Andrew, went to Mary's chair, and knelt down at her feet. "Mary needs our help."

She wouldn't for the world wound Benji's tender heart, but she had to get rid of Andrew. With great effort, she leaned forward and forced a smile onto her face. "I love you, Benji, but you need to go."

"I can't, Mary. You're wonderful sick."

"Please go, Benji. Please just go."

A single tear rolled down his face and dripped off his chin. "Please don't make me."

Unable to do anything but concentrate on the pain, she laid a hand on Benji's head. "Okay, Benji. Okay." Like the doctor had told her, Mary breathed in through her nose and out through her mouth until the pain subsided, trying to ignore the three pairs of eyes staring at her.

The unbearable tightness faded, and she squeezed her eyes shut as a sigh of relief escaped her lips. If this pain was what she was in for, it might be worth another five years of debt to get an epidural. How had her *mater* done this six times? At home. How would she be able to do it at all? She wanted to cry, to burst into tears and sob in Bitsy's kitchen, but Andrew still hadn't left yet, and she wasn't going to give him the satisfaction.

She opened her eyes to see Andrew studying her face. The disdainful lines of his mouth had softened slightly. The hard set of his chin looked more like determination than resentment. At that moment, she could have almost believed he cared for her.

"You're in labor?" he said.

*Ach,* how she wanted him to leave and stop looking at her like that. She knew how he really felt. "I called a driver. She'll be here very soon."

"What does labor mean?" Alfie said, waving his damp shirt back and forth like he was fanning a fire.

"It means I'm going to have the baby soon. Someone is coming to take me to the hospital." She faked a lovely smile for Benji. "So you see, there's no reason for you to stay. I'm going to be fine."

Benji didn't budge. "When Dawdi had a stroke, Mammi Martha sat with him every day in the hospital and held his hand. She said she didn't want to leave him, even though he didn't know she was there. She said it's what you do for someone you love."

Mary couldn't argue with that. Besides, she would have burst into tears if she'd tried to speak.

Benji went to the fridge and pulled out the milk. "Do you want a drink? It's *gute* for the baby."

"*Nae.* I want Andrew to take you home now."

Andrew pressed his lips together. "I'm not going anywhere."

Benji nodded as if he and Andrew had agreed all along. "We're not leaving you."

Alfie hooked arms with his *bruder* and almost made

him drop the milk. "I'm staying too. It will give my shirt more time to dry."

"I'll be fine." Why wouldn't Andrew leave? He shouldn't let his *bruderen* make him feel guilty. It was obvious he didn't want to be there, and she didn't want his pity, didn't want his contempt, didn't even want his concern. She hated herself for the thought, but what she really wanted was ammunition—another reason to turn her face from the community. If even true-hearted Andrew couldn't offer her grace, then there was no hope for anyone else, and after today, she wasn't about to give them another chance.

Benji set the milk on the cupboard, obviously still hoping Mary would change her mind about having a drink. "Do you want a sandwich? I know how to make peanut butter and jelly."

Alfie nudged Benji in the ribs. "Don't feed her. I think she's going to throw up."

They all heard tires on gravel. Benji and Alfie jumped on the window seat, nearly stepping on Farrah Fawcett in an effort to see out the window. Farrah Fawcett turned her nose up at the twins, jumped from the window seat, and disappeared into the pantry, completely uninterested in the drama and heartbreak going on in the kitchen.

"It's the car," Alfie said.

Mary reached out to the boys. "There's a blue bag by the side of my bed. Could you get it for me?"

Again the boys raced up the stairs. Mary rose slowly to her feet, and another labor pain immediately seized her. Gasping, she doubled over and pressed her hand into the table for support. Andrew didn't hesitate to come to her and take her arm. She tried to push him away, but the pain was too great and his grip was firm. "Can you walk?" he said.

She held up her hand. "Wait until it passes."

She breathed in and out, though she couldn't see as it helped anything. It didn't soothe the pain and made her feel a little dizzy. Andrew rubbed his hand up and down her arm, but she refused to take any comfort from him. He was only acting out of obligation. He was no kind of friend.

The boys were down the stairs before the pain subsided. Alfie shoved the bag in her direction. "Not now," Andrew said. "Can you take it out to the car for Mary?"

Alfie was still waving his shirt around like a flag. He'd get that thing dry or put out somebody's eye trying. "We'll take it out. Come on, Benji."

"I call shotgun," Benji said, grabbing the bag from Alfie and running out the door.

Alfie was right behind him. "Mary gets shotgun. Don't you know anything?"

The pain finally became bearable. "I'm ready," Mary said, even though it felt as if that baby was going to fall out at any minute. She hated the thought of depending on Andrew for anything, but she hooked her arm around his elbow. She couldn't get to the car without him.

She avoided his gaze as he helped her to the door, unable to bear the resentment that was surely alight in his eyes. She would not, could not think about Andrew or his *bruderen* or Jerry Zimmerman right now. She couldn't think about Josh suing for custody or Evelyn wanting Mary's baby all to herself. She was holding the pieces of herself together with sheer willpower. Right now, she would be strong for the baby, and only the baby.

They had crossed the threshold and stepped onto the porch when another pain seized her. It wasn't supposed to be happening this way. Weren't they supposed to be like ten minutes apart or something? Mary stopped in her very slow tracks and sucked in a breath.

"Are you okay?" Instead of the bitterness she expected, Mary saw fear in his eyes and anxiety pulling at the lines of his mouth.

"I don't know," she whispered.

Andrew nudged her hand away and scooped her into his arms in one swift motion. She gasped and instinctively hooked her hands around his neck before remembering that Andrew couldn't stand the sight of her. Pressing her palms against his chest, she made a weak attempt to get him to put her down. "I'm okay."

He ignored her, tightening his strong arms around her and carrying her down the steps. She wanted to resist his warmth, but she had no strength to fight it. Resting her head against his chest, she listened to his ragged breathing and inhaled his heavenly scent of roses and cedar as he carried her to the car. Benji was sitting in the front seat with the car door open. "Benji," Andrew growled.

Benji immediately jumped out. "I was just getting it warm."

Andrew set her on her feet, and she shakily slid into the car.

Patti sat behind the wheel in a salmon tank top and yoga pants. "Sorry, sweetie. You caught me right in the middle of a downward dog."

Andrew opened the back passenger door. "Climb out, Alfie. You can't come."

Mary leaned against the headrest. Thank Derr Herr Andrew knew enough to keep his *bruderen* out of it. Mary couldn't have mustered the energy to tell them no. It would be wonderful awkward at the hospital if she arrived with two eight-year-olds in tow.

"Aw, why not?" Alfie moaned, but he was already sliding out of the car. He must have known it was a lost cause. "My shirt isn't dry yet."

"Keep waving it around in the sun," Andrew said. "By the time you get home, it will be dry."

Benji's voice cracked in about a hundred places. "But, Andrew, we can't leave Mary."

Andrew laid a firm hand on Benji's shoulder. "I'll take care of her."

To Mary's surprise, Andrew slipped into the back seat in Alfie's place. "You're not coming," Mary said, too distraught to be polite.

"I won't leave you." His voice was as hard as a block of ice and just as cold.

Mary wanted to weep. She needed her *mamm*. She needed Bitsy. She'd even settle for Treva Nelson. She didn't need Andrew's pity or his duty, but she was tired and spent and she had to save what fight she had in her for the baby.

Patti glanced doubtfully from Andrew to Mary. "Where's Bitsy, sugar?"

"Walmart."

"How are you feeling?"

"Not so good."

"Okay, I'll speed." Patti must have decided that it would take too much time to try to make Andrew see reason. She turned the car around and sped down the lane, kicking up dust behind her like a tornado.

Mary glanced to her left as they crossed the bridge. Alfie and Benji stood where Andrew had left them, Alfie waving his shirt in the air as if giving them a sendoff, Benji wiping at his eyes but never looking away. She would miss those boys something wonderful when she left the community for good.

Andrew didn't say a word all the way to the hospital. Mary was hardly more talkative. Patti would occasionally ask her how she was doing, and Mary would try not to sound too desperate. It didn't help that Andrew was sitting behind her, probably glaring at the back of her head. He shouldn't have come. He was making everything worse.

Patti pulled up to the emergency room door. "Andrew," she said, "go find someone to bring a wheelchair."

Mary wanted to protest that she didn't need an embarrassing wheelchair, but she could feel her stomach tightening in another labor pain. If they got a wheelchair, Andrew wouldn't feel obligated to carry her.

Andrew jumped out of the car while Mary started in with her useless breathing. Patti pursed her lips sympathetically and patted Mary's hand. "What's Andrew Petersheim doing here?"

Mary grimaced. "He just happened to be at Bitsy's when I went into labor."

"Try to relax, honey. Tightening up just makes it worse." Patti squeezed Mary's hand. "I hope you don't mind me asking, but how long has this been going on between you and Andrew?"

Mary's heart ached with longing—which was

completely ridiculous. This was Andrew Petersheim they were talking about. She was finished with him, and he was definitely finished with her. "Nothing is going on," she finally said.

Patti blew a puff of air out from between her lips. "Nothing? Mary, that boy is so in love with you, he's ready to explode."

"He's not. He told me I betrayed the community."

"Well, for goodness' sakes, Mary, he's Amish and set in his ways. It takes the patience of Job to deal with Amish people."

Mary stared at Patti in disbelief. "You don't like the Amish?"

"Of course I like the Amish. I love the Amish. Some days, I wish I was one of you, but you have to admit you're a stubborn lot, always thinking you're right and everybody else is wrong. You just have to be patient with Andrew. He's a *gute* boy. He'll come around."

"I don't think so."

"Well, if you're going to break his heart, let him down gently. He's a nice boy. I hate to see him get hurt."

Mary sighed. "There's no chance of that. We used to be friends, but he doesn't want anything to do with me now."

"Okay," Patti said. "I won't argue with a woman in labor, but when the time comes, he'll need a lot of forgiveness. Mark my words." Andrew arrived with a nurse and a wheelchair. Patti leaned over and gave her a kiss on the cheek. "It's going to be okay, sweetie. Andrew will take care of you. I'll run to Walmart and get Bitsy. As soon as I find her, I'll call you."

"My phone is dead."

"I'll call the hospital."

The nurse wheeled Mary up to labor and delivery where they immediately put her in a private room. Andrew didn't say anything, but he didn't leave her side either. She had to get rid of him. There was no way she was letting him watch her deliver this baby, no way she was letting him pretend to care about her, no way she would be made a fool of. "I don't want you here, Andrew," she said harshly. He needed to know that she couldn't care less about him or what he thought of her. She could show just as much disdain as he could.

He hovered near the door to her room, unsure of what to do. "I told Benji I'd make sure you were okay."

"Go, Andrew. I know what you think of me, but I will not let my baby feel your contempt." Mary didn't even try to stifle the sob that escaped her lips. Let Andrew rejoice that she was finally feeling the full weight of her choices, but let him be smug from a distance. Right now, his self-righteousness was too heavy a burden to carry.

"Contempt?"

The nurse handed Mary a gown and whispered softly in her ear. "Do you want that man to leave, because if you do, we can make him leave. It's the law."

"Yes," Mary said, gasping in relief and pain.

The nurse drew herself up to her full height of about five feet and marched to the door. "Sir," she said, "I must ask you to leave. Patients and hospital staff only allowed in this room." Mary knew that wasn't entirely true, but at that moment, the nurse was Mary's favorite person in the world.

Andrew furrowed his brow, no doubt torn between

his promise to his *bruderen* and his desire to get away from Mary as soon as possible. "Can I wait outside?"

"The waiting room is out those double doors and down the hall to the left."

"Go home, Andrew." *Go and have a happy life. I never want to see you again.*

He looked at Mary as if he cared about her. "If you need anything, have them come and get me. Anything."

She didn't even glance in his direction as he left, but the loneliness nearly choked her. She concentrated on her breathing and let her sorrow wash over her like a summer cloudburst. She'd rather be utterly alone than have Andrew standing there, reminding her of what she'd lost.

Though she hated to admit it, it was a loss she'd never get over.

# Chapter Thirteen

Andrew hissed, dropped his hammer on the barn floor, and shook his hand several times to try to ease the pain. He should never work with the wood when he was distracted. He always ended up smashing a fingernail or drawing blood. The problem was that he'd been distracted for a week, and there was no end in sight. If he couldn't get Mary Coblenz out of his head, it wouldn't be safe to pick up a power drill ever again.

It irritated him that he should be the one to feel bad when Mary was the one who'd done something terrible. If she wanted to ruin her own life, that was her business. Andrew wouldn't stop her. But he couldn't forgive her for tearing the Zimmerman family apart.

His chest shouldn't feel this hollow. It shouldn't hurt to breathe. He was glad to be finished with Mary. She'd brought him nothing but embarrassment. Some of *die youngie* wouldn't talk to him anymore, and he knew for a fact that Sammy Zook and Junior Eicher had gone smoking behind Eicher's barn and hadn't invited Andrew—not that he was friends with Sammy or Junior, and he certainly wouldn't have smoked, but still, he got left out of a lot of stuff these days because of Mary.

Now that Mary was out of his life, he could get back to normal, maybe start courting some nice girl who would never dream of jumping the fence or getting pregnant or having a boyfriend like Josh. It would be better now that he wouldn't see Mary ever again.

But how much longer before things would get better?

Mary had seemed so small yet so feisty sitting at Bitsy's table wincing in pain but keeping her calm, even after Wallace Zimmerman had yelled at her. Seeing her there, so vulnerable and alone, Andrew's chest had tightened with longing for something he didn't even want. Even as angry as he had been, he couldn't leave her when he understood what was really happening. And when he'd held her in his arms, it felt as if she belonged there, like a missing piece that had finally been found.

By the time they had gotten to the hospital, his heart had softened considerably. He felt sorry for her, the poor girl who was so alone and had just burned her last bridge in Bienenstock. She had been so brave, and he felt himself aching to protect her, to make sure no harm came to the baby.

But any tenderness he might have felt for her was gone. Mary couldn't be trusted. She had betrayed the entire community, and Andrew felt like a fool. A fool who was going to lose a fingernail.

The barn door opened, and Andrew heard the

shuffling of feet. Two pairs of eight-year-old feet.
Alfie and Benji had pretty much avoided him for a
whole week. He'd come home from the hospital and
announced that they weren't going to Bitsy's farm
ever again, and if Benji and Alfie disobeyed him,
he threatened to tell Mamm about the tree and the
smoke bomb and climbing out the window. They'd
tiptoed around him ever since.

The twins came around the hay bales that served
as a sort of wall to Andrew's woodshop. Benji's wide
eyes sparkled in the lamplight, anxious and doubtful.
Alfie was holding a wad of money in his fist and looking quite sure of himself. Andrew frowned. By the
light of the lantern he couldn't be sure, but the skin
above Alfie's upper lip looked discolored, as if he was
trying to grow a moustache.

"What happened to your lip?" Andrew said.

Alfie instinctively put a hand to his face. "I can't tell."

Benji nodded. "It's a secret."

"I think you better tell me."

"You'll tell Mamm."

Andrew's heart sank. He'd been very disloyal to
his *bruderen* just to gain their cooperation. He knelt
on one knee to get closer to eye level. "I won't tell
Mamm."

Benji's bottom lip trembled. "You said you'd tell
her all those things we did."

Andrew shouldn't have been so hard on Benji and
Alfie. They meant no harm to anybody. "I shouldn't
have said that. I've already agreed not to tell any of it,
and I won't."

"Even if we go over to visit Mary?" Benji asked.

Andrew kept his casual expression in place and

nodded slowly. "I already told you I wouldn't tell Mamm, and it wouldn't be honest to go back on what I said." There were other ways to keep his *bruderen* from Mary's house.

"Tell him about your lip," Benji said.

Alfie sheepishly shifted from one foot to the other. "I've never shaved before. I wanted to know what it felt like. It just felt like a paper across my skin, except I cut my lip."

Andrew looked closer and noticed a small nick near the corner of Alfie's mouth. "You . . . cut yourself?" Visions of blood and severed lips made Andrew dizzy. He was tempted to tell Mamm even though he'd just said he wouldn't. "Alfie, do you know how dangerous that is? You could have really hurt yourself. You could have given yourself a scar."

Alfie brightened. "That would have been neat."

"Not if you'd cut your lip off. Girls don't like to date boys without lips."

"I don't care about that. I want a scar."

"You'll care a lot in about ten years." He laid a hand on each of his *bruderen*'s shoulders. "I want you to promise me that you won't try to shave again until you get whiskers. At least ten years."

"But Mammi says in the Bible it tells us not to swear at all," Benji said.

Andrew pursed his lips. "I think this one time would be okay. Razors are sharp, and doctors are expensive. Mamm would not like to pay a doctor to sew you up."

"I could do it myself," Alfie said.

"*Nae*, you couldn't. And neither could Benji. Mamm would probably yell at you for three weeks."

Alfie slumped his shoulders. "Okay. I won't shave again. It made my lip hurt."

"I can see that. You should put some ointment on it."

"But then Mamm will know," Benji pointed out.

"She'll think you have a sore lip. That's all." Andrew loved his *bruderen*. He really did, but he was just about finished keeping secrets for them. He wasn't their *mater* and didn't want the job.

Benji nudged Alfie again. "Ask him the other thing."

Alfie held out his fistful of money. "Benji and me want to hire you to build something for us."

Andrew glanced at the money in Alfie's hand. It looked a little more substantial wadded up like that, but it couldn't have been more than five dollars. "What do you want me to build?"

"We want you to make a crib for Mary's *buplie*. Willie Glick says she sleeps in a drawer."

Benji wrinkled his face like a prune. "Mary doesn't sleep in a drawer."

"Not Mary," Alfie growled in disgust. "The *buplie*." Alfie turned back to Andrew. "We're willing to pay."

Andrew's heart pounded against his chest at the very mention of Mary's name. Lord willing she was feeling better, even though her life didn't really concern him anymore. She hadn't wanted him at the hospital, and he had paced in the waiting room until Bitsy arrived. Then he'd gone home, glad he hadn't wasted more of his time. He'd heard Mary had delivered her *buplie* later that night while Andrew had been in the barn working his wood. He was grateful he hadn't spent his whole day at the hospital.

Andrew didn't know what to say to his *bruderen*.

An outright refusal wouldn't go over very well. "How much money do you have?"

"We can pay you six dollars today, and seven more when the tomatoes are ripe." Mamm had given Alfie and Benji a small plot in the garden to grow their own tomatoes. The boys sold them at their own little roadside stand every summer.

Andrew's heart sank through the barn floor. He couldn't make a crib for Mary's *buplie*. He was trying to forget Mary, not keep her fresh in his mind, and he'd see her face every time he worked on the crib. He gazed at his *bruderen*. Both boys still had their wide-eyed, freckled innocence. Andrew wouldn't quash that for the world, but he couldn't say yes, either, not if he wanted to learn how to breathe normally again.

As if sensing his hesitation, Alfie held the money closer to Andrew's nose. It was probably every cent they had in the world. "We can pay more if there's lots of tomatoes."

Andrew stood up and cupped his fingers around his neck. "I don't know if that's such a *gute* idea, boys."

Alfie held the money higher. "Why not?"

"Mary is . . . I don't know. I think you should make other friends."

"I don't need more friends." Alfie counted on his fingers. "There's Willie Glick, Vernon Schmucker, Petey Gingerich. The Masts and Eldon and his sister, even though we're just pretend friends. Mary and Bitsy, Yost Weaver and Jerry Zimmerman and Dawdi."

Benji ran his finger along the wood on Andrew's table. "Why don't you like Mary anymore?"

The question caught Andrew off guard, though

he didn't know why it should have. Benji never did anything expected. "I like her just fine," Andrew snapped, before thinking better of it. His *bruderen* weren't going to give up without a sincere answer and a truthful explanation. "*Cum,*" he said, then lifted both his *bruderen* to sit on his work table so they could talk man to man. "Mary left the community two years ago."

"Don't you believe in forgiveness?" Benji said.

"Of course I do." But he had been arrogant to think that he was the one to do the forgiving. Only Gotte could forgive Mary. Andrew's job was to behave like a Christian and show forth love.

Love.

He suddenly couldn't breathe. It wasn't a job to love Mary. It came as easy as peanut butter and chocolate pie.

He smothered the thought and the feeling and tried to remember what he'd been talking about. "Mary talked Jerry Zimmerman into leaving the community and gave him money to go, and she shouldn't have done that. His parents were very sad."

Alfie nodded. "We heard he was gone."

Scratching his head in puzzlement, Benji squinted in Andrew's direction. "Did she make him?"

"Make him what?"

"Did Mary make Jerry go?"

That was a silly, irritating, eight-year-old question. "Of course she didn't make him."

Benji switched hands and scratched the other side of his head. "Then why are you mad at her?"

The aggravation bubbled up inside him. He didn't

have time to explain every little obvious thing to an eight-year-old. "Mary told Jerry to go."

"She gave him an order, like a bishop?" Alfie chimed in. "Mary's nice, and she liked Jerry a lot. Why would she make him leave?"

"She didn't make him leave." Andrew resisted the urge to growl. What did the twins know about anything?

Benji eyed Andrew in confusion. "One time, LaWayne Nelson told me to eat a worm, but I didn't do it."

"LaWayne is a dumbhead," Alfie said.

Benji nodded. "Jerry didn't have to go, even if Mary told him to. It seems like maybe he already wanted to leave."

"Mary made it easier for him," Andrew said. "She talked him into it. He would have stayed if Mary hadn't been such a bad example. Then she gave him some money."

"That was wonderful nice of her."

Benji didn't understand the significance of what he'd said, but it was as if an invisible hand clonked Andrew in the head with the handle of his hammer and knocked some sense into him.

*Ach, du lieva* and oy, anyhow.

*That was wonderful nice of her.*

He really hated that his baby *bruderen* were smarter than he was.

Mary had agonized over her decision to leave for months, maybe years before she actually did it. Maybe she had wanted to ease Jerry's suffering and help him understand that it would be okay. That was the kind of person she was. She wanted to give Jerry the support she had never gotten.

Half the community was suspicious of her. Had Andrew really convinced himself that Mary could single-handedly talk Jerry into leaving? Wallace Zimmerman believed it, but his foolishness was born of grief. It was a ridiculous notion, and Andrew would still be believing it if it weren't for his *bruderen*. In a moment of shock and anger, he had forgotten that Mary was the most levelheaded, honest person he knew, kind to a fault, and inclined to nicely tell people what they didn't want to hear but needed to. For sure and certain, Mary had warned Jerry about choices and consequences, and if she'd given him a sisterly hug and wished him happiness as he was leaving, well then, she'd left Jerry with a *gute* memory to hold on to in New York. There was nothing wrong with that.

As long as it had been a sisterly hug.

Andrew shoved his hands into his pockets to keep them from trembling. How could he have been so blind? He loved Mary. *Loved* her. He knew that now with the certainty of all his mistakes. He should have stood by Mary when Wallace accused her, but he got caught up in the fear and pain of the Zimmermans, needing someone to blame as surely as they had. Hadn't Mary admitted to using Josh to get what she wanted? Andrew had let his doubts consume him, and Mary had been the one to suffer for it.

He hadn't trusted Mary, hadn't shown her the mercy she always showed him. What must she think of him?

He didn't have to guess. The pain in her eyes when

she told him to go home was plain enough. She hated him, and he was going to be sick.

Alfie studied Andrew's face. "We could maybe do twenty dollars."

"What if we sold the bookshelf?" Benji said.

"Mammi would find out." Alfie had never looked so forlorn. Those boys really disliked family reading time.

Andrew was even more forlorn. He couldn't bear the thought of losing Mary or the thought that if he did, it would be his own fault. He was so *dumm* sometimes. An iron fist tightened around his heart. What if Mary decided to leave the community because of him? What if she refused to see him so he could have a chance to explain? His heart felt as heavy as a table saw, with the table.

There was only one thing to do. He'd have to enlist some help. "I'll tell you what," Andrew said. "I will take your six dollars so I can buy some wood, and you can pay me the rest in favors."

"Favors?"

"I need you to help me."

Benji let Andrew help him off the table. "You need our help?"

"*Jah.*" Andrew swung Alfie from the table too. "I wasn't very nice to Mary last time I saw her."

Benji grimaced like a pickle. "We know. We heard you. You really messed it up."

"Sometimes you don't got any sense," Alfie said.

"I need you to get me into that house. I really need to talk to Mary, but Bitsy might point her shotgun at me, or Mary might tell me to go away."

His *bruderen* grinned mischievously at each other. "We can help," Benji said. "We have walkie-talkies."

Alfie poked Benji in the ribs. "You're not supposed to tell."

"We can tell him. He's on our side now."

Andrew felt worse already. He was truly in trouble when his best hope was two little boys with a pair of walkie-talkies, six dollars, and an undisclosed length of rope.

# Chapter Fourteen

"Ach, Mary. She is perfect, just perfect," Hannah Yutzy said, snuggling Elizabeth June and stroking her tiny fingers. Hannah, usually so loud and enthusiastic about everything, had lowered her voice to a whisper so as not to wake the baby. Mary knew that it wouldn't have mattered how loud Hannah was. Elizabeth June slept through everything. She only woke up to eat.

Mary brushed her hand across the dark fuzz on top of Elizabeth June's head, so soft she almost couldn't feel it. She had never known this much love existed, that she could be so completely head-over-heels with a small pink bundle barely bigger than her heart. But there it was, and there was no going back to who she had once been.

Mary sat on the sofa with Hannah while the other women talked and laughed and worked on Elizabeth June's first baby quilt. The quilt had been Bitsy's niece Lily's idea, but Mary was astounded at how many women had come to help tie it. She didn't think there were this many people who cared about her in the whole world, let alone in her small Amish community.

Serena Beiler, whom Mary had met at the haystack supper, had come, even though she and Mary barely knew each other. Ada Herschberger must not have been able to warn Serena away. Hannah Yutzy and her sister Mary were there along with Frieda's *mamm* Edna, Lily, Poppy, and Rose—Bitsy's nieces—and Ruth Miller. Andrew Petersheim's *mamm* had dropped by for a few minutes to see the baby, but she said she had to get back home to help with her father-in-law. Even though Rebecca had been affectionate and more than kind, Mary was relieved she hadn't stayed. Mary didn't want to guess if Rebecca felt the same way about Mary that Andrew did—that Mary had betrayed the whole community and didn't deserve a place here.

Mary tried to put both Rebecca and Andrew out of her mind. She didn't need the heartache, not when all she wanted was to care for her baby and provide a loving, beautiful place for her to grow up.

The other women crowded around the baby quilt, each taking a few stitches, each waiting for her turn to hold the baby. After having endured Ada Herschberger and Treva Nelson, Mary was almost surprised that she felt nothing but love from each of them.

Serena didn't seem the least bit indignant that Mary had given birth out of wedlock. She threaded her needle with pink yarn. "Mary, did you name Elizabeth June after Bitsy?"

"*Jah,*" Mary said. "And June is my *mamm*'s name." She tried to ignore the twinge of pain that greeted her every time she thought of her *mater*. Mary had hoped that her parents would set aside their pride and at least want to meet their granddaughter, but neither of them had been over to see the baby. They already had seven other grandchildren from legitimate marriages. Maybe they couldn't make room in their hearts for an illegitimate one. And Jerry's leaving a week and a half ago couldn't have helped matters. There were some in the community more set against Mary than ever. That group probably included her parents.

But apparently, not any of the women who'd come to help make a quilt for Elizabeth June were outraged by Mary's behavior. The acceptance she felt from them made her want to weep in relief. It was a reminder that there were many, many good people in the community. Maybe she hadn't been looking hard enough.

"Will you call her Bitsy?" Serena asked, squinting into the eye of the needle. She was having trouble with that yarn.

"I don't know," Mary said. "I thought of Lizzy or Eliza or even Bitty, but the one that seems to fit her the best is ElJay." She glanced around at the faces turned to her. "It's . . . it's not really a proper Amish name, but I kind of like it."

Poppy had made one stitch in the blanket. She wasn't much of a quilter. "That's outrageous," she said, stabbing her needle into the fabric and giving Mary a wide smile. "I like it. It sounds like a girl who could show the boys what is what."

Serena nodded. "I like it too. There are only so many normal Amish names to go around. No one would ever have to wonder which ElJay they were talking about."

Hannah giggled, until she remembered that she held a sleeping baby. She inhaled mid-giggle and closed her lips. "I think it's the perfect name. She sounds like a rapper."

Lily looked up from her yarn. "A rapper? What is a rapper?"

Bitsy smirked. "Someone who wears his pants around his knees and can't carry a tune."

Hannah giggled, more quietly this time. "My *bruder* James is in *rumschpringe*. He has about a thousand songs on his smartphone. Rap is a kind of music."

"It depends on how you define music," Bitsy said.

"I think LJ is the name of a rapper." Hannah furrowed her brow. "Or maybe it's Cool LJ or something like that. I don't listen real often because Mamm won't let him play it in the house. She says it kills her plants."

Mary loved how cheerful Hannah always was, as if life was the greatest thing that could happen to anyone. "ElJay it is then. I think she'll like it."

"And if she doesn't, she can always change it," Bitsy said. "I nearly changed my name to Hyacinth, but nobody could pronounce it."

Serena had managed to sew her finger onto the quilt. "Oh, dear. I am not very *gute* at this." She took the scissors and snipped what little sewing she'd done. She glanced up at Mary. "Will you stay here with Bitsy, Mary? Or do you think you'll move on?"

Mary could sense the deep curiosity behind the question, but no malice or judgment. "I hate to be a burden on anyone, but I'm going to have to stay for awhile." She felt her face get warm. "I don't really have anywhere else to go."

Bitsy blew a puff of air from her lips. "Farrah Fawcett is more of a burden than you are. You know you are welcome as long as you want to stay."

Serena eyed everyone sitting at the quilt and a blush painted her cheeks crimson. "I'm new here, so you can tell me if I'm being rude. I don't like gossip and would rather get the real story from the real person. I just wonder about you, Mary."

That got everyone's attention. Mary gave Serena an encouraging smile. "I'd rather that people talk to me than about me."

Serena nodded and cleared her throat. "Ada says you jumped the fence and your parents wouldn't let you back into the house. I just . . . I wanted to know, but you don't have to tell me if I'm prying. I don't want to be known as the nosy neighbor."

Hannah giggled. "My *mamm* already has that title. No need to worry."

Mary didn't let the question hang in the air. She truly wanted people to understand. She wanted friends, not just acquaintances, and she would never make true friends without being honest. "It's true. I jumped the fence two years ago and lived with an Englisch boy. I came back, but my *mamm* and *dat* didn't want me back in the house. I hurt them very badly."

Serena pushed away from the quilt and sat next to Mary on the sofa. "*Ach*, Mary, I'm so sorry. That must have been very hard for you."

"It was. But I don't blame my parents. They did what they thought was best."

Serena patted her hand. "We all try our best, but

few of us know exactly what really is best. I suppose that's why we have to forgive each other."

"*Jah*," Mary said, pleasantly surprised that there was someone else who thought the way she did.

"It's the same in my marriage." Serena looked at Frieda's *mamm*, maybe because she'd been married the longest. "I was upside-down in love with Stephen, but now I find I have to forgive him all the time." She squinted as if thinking very hard. "Maybe I'm doing something wrong."

"You're doing it just right," Edna said. "Marriage is tolerance and forgiveness and hard work."

Hannah frowned. "Is it possible to be happy too?"

"That's what happiness is," Edna said. "You fight and you forgive and you work to make it better. Nothing worth having is easy."

Serena smiled with her whole face. "*Ach*, I'm glad to know it isn't just me. I love Stephen something wonderful, but for sure and certain he makes me hopping mad sometimes."

Everyone laughed.

Bitsy pointed at Hannah with her needle. "I hear you may have a husband soon."

Hannah nearly choked on her own spit. "Me? I don't particularly have my eye on anybody."

"But I hear there's about five boys who have their eye on you."

Hannah giggled as if that was the funniest thing she'd heard all day. "There are boys around the donut stand all the time, but it's because they like my donuts, not me."

"What about you, Mary?" Serena said. "I saw you at the haystack supper with Andrew Petersheim. Do you like him?"

Mary suddenly felt a hundred pounds heavier. What did it matter how she felt about Andrew? "He . . . I don't think he's interested."

Serena obviously thought it was a topic that made Mary happy. She pumped her eyebrows up and down. "He looked very interested at the haystack supper."

Mary reminded herself that she would rather have people talk to her than about her. She sighed and drew in a breath. "Andrew was here when Wallace and Erla Zimmerman came over." No one was looking at their quilting now. "Andrew thinks it's my fault Jerry jumped the fence. He said I betrayed the community."

Serena formed her lips into a silent O.

"That boy is never allowed in this house again," Bitsy said, winding a ball of yarn.

"Wallace is wonderful mad," Lily said. "He thinks the *gmayna* should shun you, even though you haven't been baptized."

"But how can Andrew blame you?" Hannah said. "Jerry has been thinking about leaving for years. We could all see it."

Mary didn't have an answer to that, except that Andrew hadn't really been her friend from the beginning. He was eager to side with the Zimmermans because he'd always seen Mary as a hopeless sinner, someone who wouldn't hesitate to sin again when she got the chance. Oh, he'd been nice to her, but he hadn't really liked her or believed her sincerity. He certainly hadn't trusted her.

Serena lowered her eyes. "I'm sorry. After I saw you together at the haystack supper, I assumed . . . but I heard he went with you to the hospital."

"Only because he and his little *bruderen* were the only ones here when I went into labor. Andrew isn't so heartless as to leave me like that, even though I told him to go away."

Rose worried the yarn in her fingers. "You told him to go away?"

"*Jah.* He was mad at me. I didn't want his sharp looks to add to the pain. As soon as I got to the hospital, I told him to leave. He was glad for it."

Bitsy grunted. "I had to push him out of the waiting room and threaten him with a visit from the toilet paper fairy before he'd leave. You wouldn't have wanted him to watch you deliver that baby anyway."

"Well," Poppy said. "I think it's despicable."

"That boy can't see past the end of his nose." Bitsy cut her yarn. "I've always thought so."

Mary was immediately sorry. She had painted too harsh a picture of Andrew. As Serena said, everyone did their best. Andrew had grown up Amish. His loyalty and heart were in the community. Of course he would side with them before he sided with an outsider. He had hurt her deeply, but that didn't mean he didn't have a *gute* heart. He just didn't have a heart for her. She was hurt, but she shouldn't be so vindictive. Andrew would be a neighbor to these women long after Mary was gone. "It-it was very kind of Andrew to get me to the hospital," Mary stuttered. She should be grateful, even though every minute in the car was torture. "We just don't see eye to eye."

Everyone in the room stared at her, and the air crackled with sympathy and righteous indignation. It was an exhilarating feeling to know that so many Amish women were on her side, but she felt bad all the same. She had been unfair to Andrew, and she should have known she couldn't smooth it over with a few kind words as an afterthought. Sometimes, her tongue ran away from her mouth.

A very loud, very urgent knock came at the door. Poppy abandoned her needle to answer it. She wasn't all that dedicated to the baby quilt, even though she tried very hard.

"Is Bitsy here?"

Mary craned her neck to look out the door. Benji Petersheim stood on the porch with no hat, dirt streaked down his cheek, and his hair sticking up in three different places. He looked as if he'd been in a wrestling match. Or a tree climbing contest. "What is it?" Mary called from her sofa.

Benji looked inside, grinned, and waved at Mary as if that was the reason he'd come.

Poppy smoothed Benji's unruly hair. Two of the three tufts sprang right back up again. "You want to see Bitsy?"

Bitsy sighed and handed her needle to Mary Yutzy. "Can you finish this row for me? Then we can roll." She lumbered to the door as if she had arthritis in her hips, though Mary knew for a fact that Bitsy was healthier than most of the people in the community. "This had better be important, Benji Petersheim, because I've got eight women in here with sharp objects in their hands, and some of us are running thin on patience."

Staring up at Bitsy and scratching his nose, Benji shifted from one foot to the other. "Well, you see, Bitsy . . ."

"Yes?"

"There's something I need to show you."

"What is it?"

"I can't explain," Benji said, speaking slowly as if he was making it all up as he went along. "You need to come see."

Bitsy's sigh was so long and loud, she might have been a car with a stuck horn. "Where are we going?"

Benji scrunched his nose. "You know your bee-hives?"

She narrowed her eyes. "*Jah*, I know my beehives."

"Then come see."

Clearly out of patience but with a bucketful of af-fection for Benji, Bitsy snatched her bonnet from the hook. "This is so I don't scare the bees with my orange hair." She finished tying her bonnet and paused to look at Benji. "Will I need my shotgun?"

Benji was ecstatic at the possibility of a shotgun. "You should bring it."

Bitsy glanced back at Mary with a wry twist of her lips, picked up her shotgun, and took Benji's hand. "If I'm not back in an hour, call the police," she said and closed the door behind her.

The women around the quilt laughed. Mary wasn't quite sure what had just happened, but Benji looked too much like his *bruder* for Mary's peace of mind.

Another knock at the door came not three min-utes later. Poppy, who had given up on the quilt, an-swered again.

"Poppy. *Ach.* I didn't expect to see you."

Mary's heart leapt into her throat, along with her stomach and half her small intestines. *Ach*, she should have known. Whenever Benji showed up, Andrew was never far behind.

"Who did you expect?" Poppy said, not even trying to mask the hostility in her voice. Whenever Poppy saw injustice, she had something to say about it.

"I . . . need to talk to Mary."

*Ach, du lieva.* Her large intestines came up to join the small ones.

Everyone at the quilt fell silent, turned their eyes toward the door, and froze like icicles in January.

Poppy half closed the door. "Maybe you should come back later. We're having a quilting frolic."

"I don't think I can manage it," Andrew said.

What did that mean? Had he broken his legs or something?

"Please, Poppy. Can I talk to her?"

"Okay. If you're going to make a pest of yourself." Mary could almost hear the glee in Poppy's tone. Andrew was going to get his comeuppance, and Poppy was looking forward to seeing it.

Mary couldn't muster any satisfaction. Why had Andrew come? Was he trying to torture her?

Poppy opened the door all the way and motioned for Andrew to come in. He stepped into the kitchen and stopped cold when he saw eight pairs of eyes staring at him. His face turned bright red, as if it had suddenly caught fire. He glanced back at Poppy. "I thought you were exaggerating to get me to go away."

"It's your own fault you didn't believe me."

Instead of turning about and marching out the door like she expected, Andrew stood perfectly still, staring at Mary as if she was the only person in the room. It was terribly awkward and aggravatingly unnerving. What did he want from her?

"Well, look at the time," Serena said, her gaze stapled to Mary as if Mary were a clock. Serena jumped from her seat and grabbed her bag from behind the sofa. "Stephen will wonder what became of me."

Lily met eyes with Rose. "We'd better go. The baby

will want to eat, and Dan has to milk before too long." They both looked at their sister.

Poppy seemed to expel all the air from her lungs. "Okay. I'm going too." She poked her finger into Andrew's chest. "Be nice, or I'll hear about it."

Andrew frowned but didn't say anything.

Hannah handed ElJay back to Mary, and she and her sister were gone before Mary could even form a thank-you on her lips. Mary almost wished she had a stopwatch. Her friends had cleared the room in less than two minutes. It was quite a thing to behold. Unfortunately that left her alone with the one person she'd rather not see again. She needed a conversation with Andrew like she needed a bladder infection.

Andrew wasn't comfortable or happy. That was easy to see by the way he held himself, like a man being fitted for trousers with pins sticking out in every direction. His dark eyes were cold and deep like a winter's sky, and she had to turn away. Everything hurt too much.

"May I . . . see the *buplie?*"

Mary tightened her arms around ElJay in an effort to protect her own heart. She didn't want to let Andrew hold her baby, but she'd be cruel not to let him look. No one, not even Andrew, should be denied the joy of seeing such a beautiful baby. "If you wish," she said. Who knew what Andrew really wanted?

It was a pleasant surprise when he went to the sink and washed his hands. He didn't know she wasn't going to let him hold ElJay, but he was still trying to be sanitary. He sat next to Mary on the sofa, too close, and sort of held out his arms as if expecting Mary to hand the baby to him, which she didn't. He pretended she hadn't just slighted him and nudged his pinky into ElJay's hand. She curled her fingers around his but didn't even stir. Mary now truly understood the expression "sleeping like a baby."

"She's beautiful, Mary," he said.

"*Denki.*" Mary gazed at ElJay. She was the perfect excuse not to have to meet Andrew's eye.

"My *mamm* said the delivery went well."

"Well enough." She wasn't inclined to have a conversation with Andrew. Let him have a look at the baby and go away.

"You were wonderful brave."

"*Denki,*" she said coldly, "for all your help." If she had been feeling sweet and charitable, she would have told him she couldn't have done it without him, but they both knew she would have gotten along just fine—probably better. If Andrew hadn't been there, Mary and Patti would have had a perfectly lovely conversation on the way to the hospital, and for sure and certain Mary wouldn't have fallen to pieces in the delivery room.

"Mary?" he said. "Mary, please will you look at me?"

She did her best to pretend that she hadn't heard the pleading desperation in his voice. Glancing up at him, she gave him a polite smile that she would have given one of her customers at the bakery when she worked there.

He pressed his lips together. "You have every reason to be mad and hurt."

"I'm fine."

"I was terrible to you, and I'm sorry."

Mary wasn't about to let him wheedle his way into her heart again, no matter how sincere he seemed or how *gute* he smelled. "We all make mistakes."

"I didn't mean any of those things I said. I just . . . I was taken by surprise. I felt so sorry for the Zimmermans."

"I'm glad you didn't feel sorry for me. I hate pity."

"As your friend, I should have defended you," he said.

"I forgive you."

He studied her face and frowned in frustration. "You do not, and going easy on me only makes it easier for you to shut me out."

Mary felt something crack inside her. Maybe it was her endurance. Maybe it was the last piece of her heart. "Well, let's make sure we never make it easy for me," she snapped. "It's got to be hard for me because I deserve it."

"That is not what I mean."

"Don't raise your voice. My *buplie* is sleeping."

He ran his fingers through his hair. "I'm not raising my voice." His volume sank to a near whisper. "Mary, I'm asking your real forgiveness, not just the words you think I want to hear. I am so ashamed of how I acted. Please, tell me you forgive me."

She found the low softness of his voice unnerving, but she wasn't going to be moved by it. "You have nothing to be sorry about. At first I was upset, but you reacted exactly the way any normal Amish man would react. It was unfair and unwise of me to think you would behave like anyone but the person you were brought up to be. I know better than to expect any mercy or understanding from your kind."

He stared at her in disbelief, not a trace of anger on his face. "My kind? Mary, you're one of my kind."

She sighed in longing and surrender. "I used to be, Andrew. As soon as ElJay is old enough for daycare,

I'm leaving the community. There is nothing left for me here."

His eyes grew wide as if she had slapped him. "But . . . Mary . . . you're making friends. Look at all the women who were here today."

"They're very sweet, but you and Wallace made it very clear. I am not part of this community, and I never will be. It was foolish of me to believe it could happen."

Pain burned in his eyes. "I already told you. I didn't mean a word of what I said. Please give me another chance."

"Why? So you can break my heart again?" She hadn't meant to say it that way. It sounded like he'd already broken her heart once. "What I mean is that I trusted you, and you failed me. I won't give you a chance to do it again."

He moaned softly, closed his eyes, and pressed his fingers to his forehead. "I can fill a whole silo with things I should have done. I have been *dumm* and frightened and angry, but I would never forgive myself if . . ." He wrapped his fingers around her wrist. Her skin felt hot where he touched her. "I love you, Mary. You have to understand. I don't see you as just a friend. I love you. Please don't leave."

Mary could barely breathe. The heat from his fingers spread up her arm. Wouldn't it be *wunderbarr*? *Ach*, how she wished it was true. "You don't love me."

"What kind of thing is that to say? I know my own heart."

"I was someone new, someone wounded and broken, and you thought you needed to save me. Maybe you thought you were doing your Christian duty to be my friend. Maybe you thought you could change me."

"I don't want to change you. I love you just the way you are."

"Then you should have trusted me. Your loyalty was planted solidly with Wallace that day. I saw it in your eyes. Where is the love in that?"

With his agitation growing, he stood up and started pacing around the room. "I've been weak and foolish, Mary. But I will never do anything again to make you question my love. At least I'll do my very best."

She hated to say it out loud, but Andrew was getting carried away. It had to be said. "Where can love lead us, Andrew?"

"What do you mean?"

"You might as well admit it. You may think you love me, but you would never marry me." Why did her voice crack? This was nothing she hadn't already accepted. "Amish boys do not want girls like me for *fraas*."

He acted as if he had no idea what she was talking about. "Why not?"

"Don't pretend you don't know, Andrew Petersheim. I have been with another man. I will not be pure on my wedding day. What a disappointment for my husband on his wedding night." She let the sarcasm drip from her lips and pulled ElJay tighter to her chest.

She was puzzled by the look of bewilderment on his face, as if every word from her mouth shocked him to the core. Hadn't he considered this before now? Or maybe he was shocked that she would be so blunt about it, bringing up something that went without saying.

He drew his brows together until they were almost touching. "Why do you kick yourself in the teeth like that?"

"Because everybody else does." Her voice trembled, and she looked away from his sapphire-blue eyes, resenting him for making her lose her carefully guarded composure.

He slid closer to her on the sofa, his sense of urgency apparent in the way he clasped his hands together. "Haven't you heard a word I've said? I love you. *Love* you. None of that matters to me."

"It should."

"Do *you* think it should matter, or do you think *I* believe it should matter?"

"You're an Amish man. Of course you think it matters."

Andrew's gaze pierced right through her skull. "Do I? Or do you just have a low opinion of me? Can you honestly believe that what you did in the past would make me reject you? I've met Josh. I know what you did with him, and I know why you did it. I know you were lost and searching for freedom, for someone to show you a little affection."

Her heart fluttered to life like the soft wings of a butterfly. Did he truly believe what he was saying? How could he? She didn't want to believe him, except Andrew wasn't a liar. He wouldn't say the words just because she wanted to hear them. It felt as if a cool breeze blew through the room.

"A man who would reject you because of your past sins doesn't deserve you," he said.

The corners of her mouth twitched, as if her mouth wanted to smile without her permission. "And you do?"

"Do what?"

"Deserve me?"

He studied her face, and something shifted in his eyes. "*Ach, vell*, I don't deserve you either, but I'd be a fool to spurn you because of things you did in the past." He bowed his head to hide a hopeful smile. "Besides, you make beautiful babies."

"Yes I do."

He slid his finger into ElJay's again. "Do I . . . do I have a chance with you, Mary? Or is it too late?"

Mary couldn't look at him for fear her heart would either burst with happiness or break in despair. She had dreamed of this moment more than once, Andrew declaring his undying love, her throwing her arms around him in unfettered joy. But she hadn't allowed herself even the tiniest sliver of hope. Now that the moment was here she was so confused, she almost wished it away. It was so much easier to hold on to the hurt, to let them drive her away, to give her no choice but to leave. Andrew had just made her decision infinitely harder.

The longing on his face made her want to weep. "Do you want to hold the *buplie*?" she said softly.

"I do."

She gently placed ElJay in Andrew's arms. He supported her head in the crook of his elbow and traced his finger around the curve of her little ear. "You've held a *buplie* before," she said.

"*Mamm* needed a lot of help with Benji and Alfie."

"Of course. No wonder you're so patient with them."

He played with ElJay's little fingers before moving his gaze to Mary's face. "You didn't answer my question."

She lowered her eyes. "I know."

"Is there any chance for me?"

Mary sighed. "Don't take this the wrong way, but I love you."

She couldn't look at him, but she could hear the hope in his voice. "Is there a wrong way to take that?"

"Yes, Andrew, there is." Mary got up the courage to look at him and breathed in a thousand new worries. "I may choose to leave. We both might end up brokenhearted."

"It doesn't have to be that way," he said, losing any hint of a smile. "There is a place for you here. I want to marry you. If you truly love me like you say you do, isn't love a good enough reason to stay?"

She stood and pretended to examine the stitches on the quilt. "I've known it for weeks, you know."

"Known what?"

"That I love you."

"I'm glad to hear it," he said, the hesitation evident in his voice. "I've known it for weeks too, even though I didn't want to admit it."

"I'm going to be honest with you, Andrew."

"I wouldn't want it any other way."

"Loving you, loving anyone, makes me vulnerable. I can never be truly and completely free if I give you my heart. Look how easy it was for you to hurt me. I don't know if I want to give you that much power over my life."

He nodded slowly. "Loving someone can hurt. It

can also be the most *wunderbarr* thing in the world. Don't you think it's worth the risk?"

She ground her teeth together. "But what about your feelings? If I stayed in Bienenstock and married you, would I be doing it because I love you or because my *buplie* needs a *fater*? Wouldn't you forever wonder if I was using you the same way I used Josh? I love you too much to do that to you, Andrew."

"I know your heart. How could I wonder such a thing when everything about you is love?" Andrew said. "If you were that desperate for a *fater* for your baby, you would have gone home with Josh, and you wouldn't be thinking about leaving now."

"But even you can see how selfish I'm being. I can't help it. I could never be happy if I felt I was living in a cage. I want my freedom. I want my choices. I sound like a spoiled child, but I have to be honest with myself." Mary hated showing Andrew so much of her weakness, but she had no other explanation left but the truth.

Instead of seeming offended, Andrew studied her face with nothing but compassion and heartbreak in his eyes. "What is freedom to you, Mary?"

"It means making my own choices, not being forced to do anything."

"Do you feel like you're being forced to love me?"

"*Nae*, but loving you forces me to make certain choices, like staying in Bienenstock."

"I know you don't like me to argue with you, but even if you love me, you have the freedom to leave and the freedom to stay. Staying is no less a choice than leaving."

"I suppose that's true."

"When you were younger, you saw your life here as

a prison, but were you any freer when you lived with Josh?" Andrew said.

"I don't know what you mean."

"If you stay here, you won't have to wonder where your next meal is coming from or your next paycheck. You'd be free from uncertainty. You'd have the freedom to belong to the community and the freedom to be with your family—to live among people who care about you, though they haven't always shown it. If you leave, you'll be among strangers. Of course you'll have the freedom to work, but you won't have the freedom to work anywhere you want. You'd have to earn enough money to get an education first." He covered ElJay's hand with the blanket. "You'll be forced to put the baby in daycare or leave her with Josh's stepmother so you can work to support yourself. Will you feel forced to move back with Josh so you can afford to eat? You'll be making your own choices, but those choices will be limited. How good is freedom if you can't be with your baby?"

She caught her bottom lip between her teeth and stood up. "You're making quite a bit of sense."

His smile didn't reach his eyes. "*Ach, vell,* I've been spending a lot of time with you. Against my will, you've taught me some sense." Andrew stood and laid ElJay in the little bassinet that served as her bed. He was so tender with the *buplie*, it almost broke Mary's heart. Andrew would make a *wunderbarr fater*.

After seeing ElJay settled, Andrew came to Mary and wrapped his long fingers around Mary's upper arms. He gave her the saddest smile she'd ever seen. "I'm going to leave before I snap like a twig, but I want you to be sure you know what your choices are.

I love you, but I would never use that love to force you to do anything."

"I know." If she made the wrong choice, she'd have no one to blame but herself. It had always been that way.

He traced his finger down her cheek. "You feel as soft as the baby."

"*Denki*." Warmth traveled up her neck, and she clasped her hands together so he wouldn't notice the shaking.

"I want you to choose me so bad it makes my teeth ache, but this is your choice. Make it for you, not for me."

She thought of Josh, threatening to take ElJay away if Mary didn't go back to him. How different he was from Andrew. Mary didn't deserve someone so deeply *gute*. How could she bear to break his heart? "*Denki* for being so calm," she said.

He scrunched his lips together. "My insides are roiling like a washing machine in a tornado." He stared at her lips for what seemed like an eternity. She wanted him to kiss her so badly she thought she might faint. He took a deep breath and tore his gaze from her face. She could almost taste her disappointment. It was better this way. A kiss from Andrew would only muddle her thinking.

"I hate to leave you, but Benji can only keep Bitsy occupied for so long and I'd rather not die by gunshot."

Mary forced a laugh from between her trembling lips. "I don't think Bitsy would shoot you."

"She marched into the waiting room at the hospital and told me if I wasn't out of there in thirty seconds, she'd come after me with her shotgun."

"Oh, dear."

Andrew grinned. "I love her for her devotion to you. I might have shot me too after what I said to you."

"You know I forgive you," she said.

"I know. *Denki*." He glanced out the front window. "But Bitsy hasn't. It's better not to be here when she comes back." He paused and pressed his lips together. "I love you, Mary. Never doubt that. But I don't want to pressure you or make you feel worse." Pain traveled across his face. "Plain and simple, I won't set foot on Honeybee Farm until you ask for me."

Mary almost stopped him right there. She loved him. Wasn't that enough? Maybe it was and maybe it wasn't. She'd only just found his love again. She had to be sure. With a growing ache in her chest, she nodded her agreement and let Andrew walk out the door.

It was the hardest thing she'd ever done.

# Chapter Fifteen

"Alfie Petersheim, don't make me come over there. Shabby work is the sign of a shabby mind." Mamm always said that, but even Andrew wasn't quite sure what she meant. What exactly was a shabby mind?

Mamm had Alfie and Benji scraping the gunk off the bottom of the chair legs in the kitchen—the gunk that collected when the chairs were pulled in and out from the table. It was something that happened every six months. The gunk got scraped whether it needed scraping or not.

"Don't rush it, Alfie," Mamm said, wiping out the oven she'd just scrubbed to shining. "You know I'm going to inspect your work."

"Aw, Mamm," Alfie groaned. "Why do we have to do this? Nobody ever looks at the chair feet."

"It doesn't matter who looks. I can't sleep at night knowing they're dirty, just the way Gotte knows all the sins in your heart even if no one else can see them."

Dat was outside doing chores, but Mamm had drafted the rest of the boys for their biannual kitchen cleaning duty. Abraham was wiping down walls,

Austin knelt on the floor scouring the linoleum with a scrub brush, and Andrew had just started oiling the cabinets. The twins did the same job every six months but were bound to graduate to the gunk under the fridge in a year or two.

It had been three days since Andrew had seen Mary, and every day he didn't hear from her felt like a whole year. It had been the right thing to do, telling her he'd wait for her to contact him, but the waiting was torture. He loved her. If he could see her smile every day for the rest of his life, he'd never want for anything else. The thought of her leaving left him breathless.

He hadn't been able to eat much of anything for days, because every time he thought of losing Mary, a wave of nausea knocked him over. At night, the loneliness overwhelmed him, making it impossible to sleep, and his legs had started twitching involuntarily when he was lying in his bed. It was a sure sign he was falling apart. Lord willing, Mamm wouldn't notice anything wrong with him. He couldn't shake the feeling that he'd brought all this suffering on himself, and he was ashamed to own up to it. No need for the family to know how foolish he'd been.

Well, except for Dawdi. Dawdi knew everything. Andrew poured out his heart to Dawdi every day while he helped Dawdi with his exercises.

Andrew dabbed the polishing oil on his rag and wiped the cupboard door with much more vigor than he felt. Mamm deserved a clean kitchen, and she didn't need to know how badly Andrew was hurting.

Shabby cleaning was the sign of a shabby life.

Earlier, he had helped Dawdi with his exercises, and then Mammi had helped Dawdi down for his morning nap. Now Mammi strolled into the kitchen from the bedroom, propped her hands on her hips, watched everyone clean. "Rebecca, why aren't you using the special rags I bought last week? They're microfiber. They'll do a much better job on that oven."

"Truer words were never spoken," Mamm said, not even looking up from her oven cleaning or setting aside the ordinary rag she was using.

Mammi searched through Mamm's kitchen drawers. "Where did you put those rags, Rebecca?"

"They're on the bookshelf in the cellar," Benji volunteered. Andrew didn't miss the look Mamm gave him.

Mammi didn't seem to care how those special rags had ended up in the cellar or who had put them there. "Be a good boy, and go get them. I can't do stairs anymore."

Benji glanced at Mamm—who didn't glance back— and ran down the stairs. Alfie set down the butter knife he used to scrape gunk and started to follow Benji. If Benji got out of three minutes of work, Alfie was determined to get out of the same three minutes. "You keep scraping, young man," Mamm said.

Alfie nearly ran down the stairs anyway, but he couldn't very well pretend he hadn't heard Mamm without getting in big trouble. He stopped short at the top of the stairs. "I need to help Benji."

Mammi sniffed the air. "I don't think you've been using the special rose spray." She sniffed again. "In fact, I'm sure you haven't. You stink to high heaven." She took a couple of steps closer to Alfie and regarded him with her bifocals. Her eyes got wider than the special platters she'd bought for Mamm to use at Thanksgiving. "Look at that shirt! Rebecca, have you seen Alfie's shirt? He looks like he's been raised by wolves."

Mamm narrowed her eyes in Alfie's direction. "Truer words were never spoken."

"Haven't you been using that bluing I special ordered from the dry cleaners?"

"It's my favorite shirt," Alfie said, as if that made everything all right.

He took one step down the stairs, but Mammi was quick for an old woman. She laid a hand on Alfie's shoulder, pulled him back into the kitchen, and turned him to face her. "He's a mess, Rebecca."

Mamm stuck her head all the way into the oven. "Truer words were never spoken."

Mammi tugged Alfie to the kitchen sink. "Hand me the rose water spray, Alfie. I can't bend over like I used to." Alfie grimaced, reached into the cupboard under the sink, and retrieved the bottle of special rose water. Mammi clucked her tongue. "It's almost full. I told you boys you need to use it twice a day."

Austin and Abraham sort of turned their backs on Mammi and got very busy cleaning the kitchen. Andrew knew for a fact that nobody used that rose water except for him, and he sprayed it on himself because Mary said she liked it. But he didn't tell Mammi. Abraham and Austin would glare at him for trying to be the favorite grandson.

Mammi sighed. "Hold still, Alfie dear." She started at the top, spraying Alfie's hair until rose water dripped from his locks onto Mamm's clean floor. Mammi spritzed the back of Alfie's neck then made him turn a full circle while she soaked his shirt. The soaking succeeded in making Alfie's shirt smell worse, like a wet dog rolled in manure.

Mamm's head seemed to retreat deeper and deeper into the oven until her forehead must surely have been touching the back wall. Mamm was wonderful particular about a clean oven.

By the time Mammi was finished with him, Alfie looked like a drowned rat, sagging with water and humiliation. Mammi reached out her hand to pat him on the head but must have thought better of it. "Go upstairs and dry off," she said, as if it was Alfie's own fault for being wet.

Alfie slumped his shoulders and dragged his feet in the direction of the stairs.

"Don't use the *gute* towels," Mammi added as she watched Alfie go.

Benji tripped up the cellar stairs with the special cleaning rags in his hand. Mammi barely noticed him. She grabbed her bag from the hook by the door. "Where's Benaiah?"

"He's in the barn," Austin said.

Mammi opened the front door. "He's taking me to Glick's to get Alfie a new shirt. And then to the library so I can order a few things off the internet. I just discovered that Amazon will deliver right to our door."

Andrew was pretty sure he was the only one who heard the stifled groan coming from inside the oven. Mammi closed the door behind her, and Mamm pulled her head out of the oven. "Alfie Petersheim," she called, "enough toweling off. Get down here and finish your job."

Alfie called back from upstairs, but no one understood what he said.

Mamm pushed herself away from the oven and stood up. She smiled as if she couldn't have been more delighted or more annoyed. "Benji, take the special rags back to the cellar. And make sure you put them away neatly. I won't have your bedroom looking like a junkyard." She rinsed her hands at the sink. "Austin, as soon as you finish that floor, I want you to wipe out cupboards." Andrew admired how Mamm always seemed to be moving forward. It was almost as if Mammi had never come into the kitchen this morning.

Alfie and Benji came back into the kitchen at the same time, and without another word, picked up their butter knives and continued scraping gunk. Alfie had obviously taken a towel to his head with zeal. Tufts of hair stuck out in every direction.

Mamm rinsed out her rag and knelt down in front of the oven again. "After the kitchen is clean, the rest of the day we're doing peanut butter. Austin ordered extra peanuts for the Labor Day rush."

Andrew's heart sank. He'd never heard of such a thing as the Labor Day rush. How would he finish Mary's crib if he had to do peanut butter all day? He had to finish that crib. It might be the thing that made Mary decide to stay forever. This wasn't just a baby crib, it was a matter of life and death. He had to skip the peanut butter, just for today. He cleared his throat. "Mamm, I need to finish something in my woodshop. Can . . . can Austin and Abraham do the peanut butter?"

Austin made a face. "We can't do it by ourselves. There's like a hundred pounds of peanuts out there."

Abraham glanced at Andrew but didn't say anything. Like Benji, he always knew more than he let on.

Mamm swiped her rag across the bottom of the oven. "You've been in that woodshop the better part of two weeks, Andrew Petersheim. Abraham did your milking yesterday. I need you to help with the peanut butter today. We can't do it without you."

And there it was. They couldn't do it without him. Mamm depended on him. Mamm needed him. He couldn't disappoint his *mamm*. She'd be heartbroken if he quit the peanut butter business. She'd never forgive him for letting her down.

But what about his heartbreak if he lost Mary?

The weight pressing into his chest got heavier and heavier until Andrew thought he was going to suffocate. *You can't make everyone happy*, Mary had said. *You can't make anyone happy. You can't ruin your* mamm's *happiness, Andrew. You don't have that much power. The only life you can ruin is your own.*

Mary knew it better than anyone. Instead of staying miserable, she'd made a choice to seek her own happiness and didn't blame anyone else for the consequences. She was the bravest person he knew. She always told the truth, even when it hurt.

*It's the hardest thing anyone does—making choices and then owning the consequences, but I think your* mater *would want you to be happy.*

Andrew set his rag on the counter, squared his shoulders, and let Mary's courage give him strength. He hated the thought of hurting Mamm, but he had to find his own happiness or wallow in resentment and regret for the rest of his life. "Mamm, I'm sick of peanut butter."

"Aren't we all," Mamm said, scrubbing at a stubborn spot on the oven as if she hadn't really understood the significance of what he was saying.

*Ach, vell.* He hadn't really said it.

"Mamm, I'm quitting the peanut butter business."

Abraham turned to stone and stared at Andrew as if he had grown an extra arm. Austin cocked an eyebrow. Benji and Alfie froze like popsicles.

Mamm finally quit scrubbing and pinned him with the stink eye. "*Nae*, you're not. We need your help today."

Andrew's heart knocked against his chest like a galloping horse. "It doesn't matter if you need my help or not. I want to be a carpenter. I'm quitting peanut butter today. Right now."

Mamm narrowed her eyes and got to her feet, clutching the rag in her hand as if trying to squeeze every drop of oven cleaner out of it. "Is that so?"

Andrew couldn't catch his breath, as if he'd run five miles in a minute. Mamm was definitely not happy, but he wouldn't turn back now. "*Jah*. I don't want to make one more batch of peanut butter. Ever. And there's another thing. I love Mary Coblenz and I want to marry her, no matter what you say. No matter that she jumped the fence or had a baby, and there's nothing you can do to talk me out of it. Even if you kick me out of the house, even if you never speak to me again, I love Mary and I hate peanut butter."

Alfie's face lit up, and he turned eagerly to Mamm. "Would you really kick Andrew out of the house?"

The lines on Mamm's forehead piled on top of themselves as she folded her arms and stared Andrew down like a cat on a mouse. They all held their breath, waiting for her to erupt. And she did. "Well, it's about time."

"It's-it's about time?" Andrew stuttered.

"You've been sneaking around this farm like a

ferret, no doubt hoping I wouldn't catch on to you, like I don't have a brain in my head or eyes to see past my own nose." She crossed her arms and leaned in. "What you boys don't realize is that I see everything. I'm smarter than you think, and you couldn't put one past me if you had the fastest horse in the state."

Benji nudged Alfie with his elbow. "She's kind of like the bishop."

It was clear that Mamm was just getting started, and Andrew wasn't sure how she'd react if he dared to speak, but he had to know. "So . . . so you know I want to be a carpenter?"

She threw up her hands. "Of course I know. You spend every spare minute in the barn trying to build things with a hammer and that tiny saw. Your tools are disgraceful. I would have given up months ago, but you just keep plugging away at it. It's like building a bridge out of toothpicks for all the good it does you. You have some money in the bank. You should have bought better tools months ago."

"I thought you wouldn't like it."

She frowned at him. "Well, maybe you never asked."

"You're not mad at me?"

Mamm erupted again. "Of course I'm mad. To think you'd choose wood over peanut butter just about gives me a seizure, but I can't make you like peanut butter, and if you cut your finger off, you'll have no one to blame but yourself."

Benji had been nibbling on his fingernail, and Andrew could tell he was thinking deep thoughts. "Mamm," Benji said, dropping his knife on the floor and standing up, "I have something to tell you."

Alfie pinched his lips together. "You don't have anything to tell Mamm."

Benji lifted his chin. "I want to be brave and honest like Andrew." He took a deep breath and promptly burst into tears. "Mamm, I broke my piggy bank and borrowed Dawdi's binoculars."

Mamm tilted her head to one side as if to get a better look at her son. "And are you sorry, young man?"

"*Nae*," Benji sobbed. "I'm not sorry at all, even if I get in trouble."

The hint of a smile sprouted on Mamm's face, but she forced it back and replaced it with the stern look of an indignant *mater*. "Does anyone else have anything to confess?" She looked straight at Alfie. "You know I'll find out. I always find out."

Nobody made a sound, except for Benji, who was whimpering softly into his hand. Alfie diligently scraped his chair foot as if he wasn't even part of the conversation.

"Mamm," Abraham said, "last week I spilled a whole tub of salt on the floor. I swept it up and threw it away without telling you."

"I know," Mamm said. "I heard it when I emptied the garbage."

Austin cleared his throat. "I accidentally ordered too many peanuts, and that's why we have to spend the rest of the day doing peanut butter. But I don't mind. I mean, I love making peanut butter. I'll never quit our business."

Mamm patted him on the cheek. "You'll be a comfort in my old age, for sure and certain. But if Andrew agrees to build my coffin, I'll probably forgive him before I die."

"Thanks a lot, Mamm," Andrew said, rolling his eyes. It wasn't hard to see that Mamm had already forgiven him. She was a little frustrated, but she was also happy for him. He'd seen it in her eyes right before she'd yelled at him. He felt lighter than he had for three days. If he had known what her reaction was going to be, he would have left the peanut butter business three years ago. He wanted to smack his palm against his forehead. That's what he got for making assumptions.

She hadn't said anything about the other thing, the Mary thing. Maybe in all the excitement, she'd forgotten. Maybe she'd wake up in the middle of the night and suddenly remember.

Mamm scrunched her lips to one side of her face, folded her arms, and looked nowhere in particular, especially not at Alfie, who was scraping chair feet as if there was a fire behind him, his shirt damp with rose water and sweat. "You boys have shown a lot of courage today. It makes me proud to know I didn't raise any scrubs. I raised you boys to be men, and that's exactly what you've become. Real men own up to their mistakes, even when they know their *mamm* might be mad. *Gute* men don't hide from the truth. They fight for it."

She was laying it on a little thick, but maybe it was because Alfie could be a tough nut to crack. Growling, Alfie slammed his knife on the floor. "I climbed Bitsy Weaver's tree and got stuck, and they had to call the fire department, okay? Are you satisfied?"

Mamm calmly raised her eyebrows. "Anything else?"

"I scraped my arms on the tree, but I didn't want

you to find out so I wore this shirt to cover the scabs." He tried to unbutton the shirt, but the fabric was too stiff.

"So you've been wearing a long-sleeved shirt all summer because you didn't want me to find out about the tree."

"Willie Glick won't play with me because he says I stink." Alfie's anger turned to distress midsentence. Big tears escaped his eyes and rolled down his cheek.

Benji took Alfie's hand. "I helped, Mamm."

Alfie wiped his face with his filthy sleeve. "We bought walkie-talkies and spied on Andrew and Mary, and then we set an orange smoke bomb in the Zimmermans' shed and I almost died."

Benji nodded. "He turned orange."

Alfie seemed determined to confess everything. "I climbed lots of trees, even though Jerry Zimmerman gave me a sucker and told me not to. And we climbed the bookshelf and sneaked out the window."

"And we gave Mary ten dollars because she needs money for her baby," Benji added.

Andrew melted like warm chocolate on top of a cake. The twins had given Mary money?

Mamm knelt down and put one arm around Benji and one around Alfie. "I'm so glad you're safe. I worry myself sick about you all day long." She pulled the boys to her and squeezed tight. Both Benji and Alfie cried into her neck, and she rubbed their backs and whispered comforting words into their ears.

After a few minutes, Mamm released them, and each boy pulled a handkerchief from his pocket and blew his nose. Mamm had trained them well.

Never be without clean underwear and a pressed handkerchief.

Alfie sniffled into his handkerchief, wiped away the last of his tears, and got a little cocky. "I guess you don't know everything, Mamm. We showed you."

It was never a *gute* idea to tell Mamm you thought you were smarter than she was. Mamm stood up so fast, she could have taken flight. "You showed me? You showed me?" She shook her finger in Alfie's direction. "You didn't show me anything, Alfie Petersheim. How many times does a fire truck come to the neighborhood? I heard about the whole thing not ten minutes after it happened."

Benji's eyes were as wide as saucers. "You knew?"

Alfie frowned at Andrew. "You said you wouldn't tell."

Mamm gave Alfie the smelliest of stink eyes. "*Ach*, young man, Andrew didn't tell me a thing." She turned and glared at Andrew. "And you have some very serious explaining to do."

Andrew grimaced. "I . . . I didn't . . ."

"I don't want to hear it," Mamm said, leaving no room for debate or explanation. "Annie Weaver got the whole story from Aunt Beth, and she came over before you boys even got home." She bent over and met Alfie's eye. "You wore that long-sleeve shirt all summer just to hide the scabs. I bet it was hot and uncomfortable."

Alfie could be as stubborn as Mamm. "Not too hot."

"Oh, not too hot? You smell like the sewer and your friends won't play with you. I'd say you've been well punished for your sins."

"I didn't mean to get stuck in that tree, Mamm."

"I'm talking about your sins of omission, like not telling your own *mater* that you almost died."

"I thought you'd be mad."

"Of course I was mad. Who wouldn't be mad? And let me tell you something, bub. If you so much as *think* about buying a smoke bomb ever again, I'll turn family reading time into family reading day."

Alfie and Benji looked positively horrified.

"And if you ever steal one of Bitsy's cats again, I'll make you clean toilets for a year."

Benji bit his bottom lip. "We didn't steal. We just borrowed it."

Andrew was stunned. Mamm truly did know everything. He had no idea about any stolen cat, unless Mamm was talking about that ugly thing that Benji and Alfie brought home several weeks ago. Andrew had gone with them to Bitsy's to take it back and met Mary. One of the best days of his life.

Mamm was adamant. "No more climbing bookshelves, no more hiding in trees, no more smoke bombs, and no more stolen cats. Is that clear?"

"Aw, Mamm. We can't do anything," Alfie said.

Mamm nodded curtly. "You can take that shirt off and burn it."

Alfie brightened. "Can I use the firepit?"

Mamm pinched her lips together. "Bury it. Out by the compost."

Benji took in a quick breath. "Alfie, we could dig a cave."

"Never mind," Mamm said. "We're throwing it in the trash." She knelt down and helped Alfie unbutton his shirt. "What lessons have you learned from this rigmarole, Alfie?"

"What's a rigmarole?"

"Just tell me what you've learned."

Alfie shifted his weight, no doubt trying to come up with something that would save him from another scolding. "I've learned that I need more long-sleeved shirts."

Mamm sighed. "That's not it. You've learned that when you try to keep secrets from your *mamm*, you end up wearing long sleeves all summer and being shunned by your friends. And you've learned that you can't hide a fire truck or an orange smoke bomb."

"I suppose so."

"And you've learned that your *mamm* loves you, even when you do something bad, and you can tell her all your problems and sins because she already knows and will understand."

"And yell at us," Benji said, trying to be helpful.

She peeled Alfie's sleeves away from his arms and examined the barely noticeable marks where Alfie's scabs used to be. "It was a wonderful nice thing to do, giving Mary money like that."

Alfie pressed his lips together. "It's so she can buy food for her baby. Andrew's making her a crib."

"I know." Mamm always knew. Andrew would never doubt again. She patted Alfie's arms. "Go put some aloe on this. And get those arms out in the sun. You look like a sheet."

Alfie's wide smile made his freckles seem darker. "You mean I don't have to finish the chairs?"

"Of course you have to finish the chairs. But then go outside. I don't need you underfoot." Mamm wadded Alfie's shirt up and tossed it in the trash can. "Austin and Abraham, you'll need to finish Andrew's cabinets.

He's going to show me this crib that everybody is talking about."

"Everybody?" Andrew said.

"Well, Alfie and Benji. I understand they paid for it."

Mamm hooked her elbow around Andrew's and tugged him out the back door, but she headed in the opposite direction of the barn.

"Mamm, the crib is in the barn."

"I know. I've seen it. It's a fine piece of work, Andrew. Mary will love it."

He expelled a despondent breath. "I hope so."

She led him to the corner of the house next to Alfie and Benji's cellar window. "I think Benaiah will have to put a lock on the outside."

"For sure and certain."

Mamm sat down on the ground and leaned her back against the house. "*Cum,* sit."

Andrew sat next to her and crossed his legs.

"Now, Andrew, I know you think I was distracted, but I want to talk to you about that other thing you said in the kitchen."

He swallowed hard. "About Mary."

"*Jah.* Sometimes I think I've raised bright young men, and other times I'm sure I've raised idiots."

Andrew nearly choked. "What?"

"You've sat on this farm for three whole days when you should be over at Bitsy's place talking Mary into marrying you. What in the world are you thinking?"

"You . . . you don't care if I marry her?"

"Care? Andrew, if you don't marry that girl, my heart attack will be on your head."

Andrew studied his *mamm*'s face. "But . . . but . . .

some of the *fraaen* were saying that they wouldn't want Mary for their sons. She's . . . well . . . she has a baby."

Mamm blew a puff of air from between her lips. "Stuff and nonsense. The ones who really know Mary aren't saying that. You've got to quit listening to the gossip, Andrew. It wonders me why you are sitting here talking to me when you could be over at Bitsy's with Mary. She's going to need a little convincing."

Andrew felt the pain and uncertainty of their last conversation all over again. "I told her I wouldn't go back to Honeybee Farm until she invited me back."

Mamm's mouth fell open. "Why did you go and do something stupid like that?"

"I don't want to put any pressure on her. She doesn't even know if she's going to stay in the community."

"Well, she'll leave for sure and certain if you don't do anything to talk her out of it. Girls want to be chased, Andrew. How can she know how much she loves you if you stay away? You should know that. I didn't raise any thick children."

"I don't want her to feel like I'm trying to force her," Andrew said.

"From what I've seen of Mary, you can't force her to do anything she doesn't want to do. Do you love her?"

"More than anything."

"Then you need to make her sure of your love. She won't choose you if she's not sure. Mary needs somebody to fight for her. You can't fight from a mile away."

"What if I make a pest of myself?"

"The smallest pest can bring down the mightiest oak."

"Whatever that means," Andrew said.

Mamm smirked. "The bark beetle never thinks a tree is too big to eat."

"This is not the best comparison, Mamm. Bark beetles kill trees."

"I'm just saying that the early pest catches the worm."

Andrew chuckled. "It's getting worse."

She poked him in the ribs. "Go now, before I give you the spatula."

"I need to finish the crib first."

"For goodness' sake, Andrew, how long will that take?"

"A couple of hours. And I need to take Alfie and Benji with me."

Mamm sighed in resignation. "I had hoped to make them spend the day thinking hard on their sins, but you don't have much of a chance with Mary without their help."

"Oh, ye of little faith."

"They've been trying to get you and Mary together for weeks. What do you think the walkie-talkies were for?"

Andrew stared at his *mamm* in a dumbfounded stupor. "How . . . how could they have known I'd fall in love with her? She's not my kind of girl."

Mamm pressed her lips together in frustration. "Benji has an uncanny sense about such things. I don't like it. He's going to get himself and his *bruder* into all sorts of trouble."

Andrew raised an eyebrow. "He's like you, Mamm. He got it from you."

Mamm's eyes grew wide. "You're right. I always know more than my sons think I do." She got to her feet and pulled Andrew with her. "Why are you still lollygagging? Finish that crib and go talk Mary into marrying you."

Andrew was already halfway across the yard. "Tell Alfie and Benji."

"I'll make sure Alfie wears a shirt, but the rest is up to you."

# Chapter Sixteen

Mary planted a kiss on ElJay's cheek. "Today is ElJay's due date."

"I'm wonderful glad you're past delivery," Bitsy said. "It was a trial." Bitsy came from the kitchen and held out her hands for ElJay. "All done eating?"

"All done," Mary said, handing her precious bundle to the one woman Mary could always count on, no matter what.

Bitsy was ElJay's official burper. As she'd told Mary, Bitsy couldn't feed the baby, but she'd use any excuse to hold her as much as possible. Mary sat back and watched as Bitsy draped ElJay over her shoulder and walked around the great room, bouncing her gently and patting her on the back. There was a thin line of dried spit-up down the back of Bitsy's navy-blue dress, from the shoulder to the hem, from earlier this morning. Bitsy didn't believe in burp rags.

Bitsy had opened every window in the house, trying to coax a breeze into the room. The birds whistled their tunes, and Mary was certain she could hear the humming of a million honeybees from

Bitsy's distant hives. This was a *gute* place, a place where Mary could be quite content for the rest of her life. She leaned her head back against the sofa and tried to push away the anxiety that seized her. The rest of her life seemed like such a long time.

Mary didn't even look when she heard a buggy pull in front of Bitsy's house. There had been a constant string of visitors since she'd brought ElJay home from the hospital. They always brought something to eat and their warm hearts to share with Mary.

Mary pressed her hand to her heart. She had tried hard to talk herself out of loving these people, but she couldn't do it anymore. There were still some who avoided her, like her own parents, but there were so many others like Serena Beiler and Hannah Yutzy who genuinely cared about her and truly wanted to be friends. Mary couldn't push them away as easily as she had wanted to believe.

But even if no one had come to see her after the *buplie* was born, Mary would still be bound to the community by Andrew himself. She loved him with every breath she took.

Bitsy was holding the *buplie*, so Mary answered the door. Her heart tumbled over on itself. Mary's *mamm* stood on Bitsy's porch holding an envelope and looking as uncertain as if she'd just gotten off the boat in a foreign country. "Mary, I . . . didn't expect you to answer. I thought Bitsy . . ."

Mary swallowed past the lump in her throat. Mamm had come to see Bitsy. "She's holding the baby," Mary said, unsure how to cross over the wasteland that stood between her and her *mater*.

Mamm fingered the envelope in her hand. "I just

came to drop this off. It was misdelivered to our house."

She handed it to Mary. It was addressed to Mary from Evelyn Giles, Josh's stepmother. "*Denki*," Mary said, trying very hard to keep bitterness from creeping into her voice. She had forgiven Mamm weeks ago, hadn't she?

Mamm brushed her hands down her dress, as if she'd finally finished some burdensome chore that she never wanted to do again. "I need to go."

Mary didn't hear Bitsy until she came up right behind her. "June Coblenz, if you don't get in here and meet your new granddaughter, I'll consider you the most heartless woman in the whole *gmayna*."

Mamm seemed to wilt under Bitsy's stern gaze. "I can't stay. Adam is expecting me."

"Adam is expecting you to mete out just punishment to your daughter. For once in your life, bite your tongue and come hold the *buplie*."

Mary half expected Mamm to storm down the stairs and drive her buggy away at top speed. Instead, she lifted her chin and stepped tentatively into Bitsy's house.

"Sit down, June," Bitsy said when Mamm seemed to have no intention of bending in any direction.

Mamm sat stiffly in the chair, and Bitsy handed her little bundle to Mamm. Mamm held ElJay as if she'd never touched a baby before and stared out the window as if actually looking at ElJay would mean some sort of surrender. Mary's heart ached. Bitsy shouldn't have bothered trying to force Mamm to love her grandchild. She would not be moved.

Bitsy took Mary's hand and pulled her to sit on the sofa. Bitsy's warmth and unyielding backbone gave her more comfort than Mary would have expected. They sat in silence, watching Mamm stare out the window, seemingly heedless of the wiggling baby in her arms.

It took all of Mary's restraint not to cross the room and snatch her baby away from her *mater*. Mamm treated Mary's greatest treasure like an armful of laundry.

Mamm's lips began to tremble. She stared faithfully at the window as her whole frame began to shake. Then a tear rolled quietly down her stony cheek. ElJay made one of her little baby noises, and Mamm looked down at her. A small sob escaped Mamm's lips, which came out more like a gasp of air. "She's the most beautiful *buplie* I've ever seen," she whispered, before she disintegrated into a pile of tears and clutched ElJay to her chest.

Mary couldn't speak. Bitsy didn't try. They sat in silence and let her *mater* cry until she couldn't cry anymore.

Mamm kissed ElJay on the cheek and looked up at Mary. "We should have read the prayer book more as a family."

"What?"

"Not a day goes by that I don't wonder what I could have done better. If I'd kept a cleaner house or taught you better or not worked you so hard, maybe things would have been different. I failed you, Mary."

"*Ach*," Mary said. "I made my own choices. It doesn't mean you were a bad *mater*."

"*Jah*, it does. You wouldn't have left if I'd done something different. I ask Gotte's forgiveness every day."

There was so much pain in her voice. Mary couldn't

stand it. "Mamm, you are not to blame. This was all my doing."

Mamm pulled a tissue from Bitsy's box and wiped her nose. "You hurt us, Mary."

Mary could feel Bitsy getting antsy beside her. "You may have been hurt by Mary's leaving, but that doesn't mean you have to hurt Mary in return." Bless her, Bitsy always said what needed to be said, no matter who she offended.

Mamm eyed Bitsy as if she'd just said something crazy. "We would never hurt Mary."

"You barred her from her own house."

"Of course we did. She showed up at our door as if nothing had happened. As if she wasn't with child. As if she hadn't broken our hearts and run off with that Englischer. Mary has to learn that she can't treat people that way." Mamm pinned Mary with a piercing, indignant eye. "We couldn't let you come back home. We had to teach you a lesson. There are heavy consequences to sin. We wanted you to suffer them."

Bitsy held perfectly still, even though Mary could feel her anger taut as a wire. "What do you think, June?" Bitsy said. "Has Mary suffered enough to satisfy your bloodlust?"

Bloodlust? That was harsh but totally lost on Mamm. She hadn't lived in the Englisch world like Mary and Bitsy had.

"We asked you not to take her in," Mamm said. "You cheated Mary out of a chance to learn a lesson."

Mary knew all this about her parents, but she couldn't seem to stop her hands from shaking. Bitsy noticed. Her eyes filled with concern, and she gave Mary's hand a squeeze. "It's time for you to go, June," she said, leaping to her feet.

"*Jah-jah,*" Mamm stuttered, realizing she was being dismissed but unsure what to do about it. She was the one who had told them she couldn't stay.

Bitsy took ElJay from Mamm's arms as quickly and as gently as she could. "Please don't come again unless you can act less like a badger and more like a *mammi.*"

Mamm was so surprised at the sudden turn of events that she walked out the door without even an argument. Apparently she remembered one more thing she had to say before she left. She turned and pointed at Mary. "Repent now or suffer Gotte's wrath. It's your choice."

Bitsy cradled ElJay in one arm and slammed the door with the other. Mary had no doubt that if she'd had three arms, she would have picked up her shotgun. She rocked ElJay back and forth as if to comfort her, even though she was fast asleep. "That was a lovely visit. We should do it again sometime."

Mary was too upset to laugh, but she wanted to. "Let's do it again soon."

"I'd better put ElJay down before I accidentally squeeze too hard." Bitsy laid ElJay in her bassinet, stood up straight, and stretched back her shoulders. "I shouldn't have said that thing about the badger. Now I'll have to take her a cake and apologize."

"You don't have to apologize. We were all a little upset."

Bitsy waved away her suggestion. "I don't mind. I'm always apologizing for something. It's why I bake so much." She sighed and sank to the sofa. "I hope you know that just because I think your parents should take you in doesn't mean I want to get rid of you. I'd just as soon have you here than anywhere else. I was trying to make your *mamm* own up to her stubbornness."

"I know, but I can't stay here forever."

"I'd say you can, but I know you better than that. Are you still chewing on the idea of freedom versus Andrew?"

Mary settled into the sofa next to Bitsy. "I love him, Bitsy, but I don't know if that will be enough in the end. I want the freedom to make my own choices."

"And you don't think you can do that if you're baptized?"

"Andrew says that in some ways I'd be freer here."

Bitsy nodded. "I'm not especially fond of Andrew, but he's right about that. You may not get to wear Calvin Klein jeans, but you wouldn't be stressed out trying to make ends meet or trying to fit into a world that you can't really make sense of. You wouldn't have to leave ElJay with Evelyn while you seek your fortune."

"I don't need a fortune. I just need enough for me and ElJay."

Bitsy propped her elbows on her knees. "No offense, Mary, but you've been gnawing on that bone for far too long. It's plain to everyone that freedom isn't the most important thing to you."

"*Jah*, it is. After all I've told you, you know it is."

"If freedom was the most important thing to you, you would have chosen to rid yourself of this baby months ago, like Josh wanted you to." Bitsy looked up at the ceiling. "Dear Lord, please keep Josh away from any and all other girls. He needs to grow a brain first."

Mary gazed at ElJay sleeping in her bassinet. She was less than two weeks old, and already Mary couldn't imagine life without her. She felt ill at the thought of what Josh had wanted her to do.

Bitsy grimaced, and Mary sensed she was trying to smile, as if to temper what she'd said about gnawing on a bone. "Freedom is wonderful important to you, for sure and certain, but love is what drives you. Your love of a tiny speck of a baby overcame your need for freedom."

Mary's heart flipped like a pancake. "But maybe with ElJay, I can have love *and* freedom."

"I don't think so. If that's how you want to define freedom, isn't it the same thing with Andrew?"

"*Nae*, because the minute I get baptized, I'm no longer free," Mary said.

"That's about the most ridiculous thing I've ever heard. Your definition of freedom changes from minute to minute." Bitsy glanced up at the ceiling, but she didn't talk to Gotte again. "You say you want freedom."

"*Jah*."

"Freedom to do what?" Bitsy asked.

"Freedom to live life how I want to."

Bitsy drew her brows together. "Well, little sister, how do you want to live your life?"

Mary thought about that for a minute. "I want to live my life with joy."

"Well then. There's your answer." Without another word, Bitsy went to the kitchen, and it sounded like she was rearranging her pots and pans.

Mary fell silent, unable to form a complete thought or a complete sentence. Bitsy always thought she made so much sense, but Mary had no idea what her answer was supposed to be. How were joy and freedom connected? Could love exist without freedom or freedom without love?

Bitsy banged pots and pans around for another few minutes while Mary sat on the sofa, her world swirling in chaotic circles around her head. "What did your letter say?" Bitsy said.

Mary picked up the envelope. "I forgot." She had hoped, prayed, that Josh would give up the idea of custody, but maybe he hadn't. Maybe this was already a summons from his lawyer. Her hands trembled as she stared at the writing on the envelope. She would move to Canada and live as an outlaw rather than give up her baby. So much for her freedom, Bitsy would say.

The walls seemed to close in on her. She had to get out, if only for a few minutes. "Bitsy, will you watch ElJay while I go outside for some air?"

"Under the apple trees is especially nice this time of year."

Mary put on her bonnet and stepped outside. She hadn't been out since she'd had the baby, and the air smelled sweeter than she remembered. With the letter clutched in her hand, she took her time getting to the orchard. She'd given birth less than two weeks ago. She wasn't up for anything but a slow stroll just yet.

The trees were brimming with big, beautiful apples, not quite ripe. The smell of sweet apples ripening on the tree was intoxicating. Ten beehives sat on the other end of the orchard in the shade, and the honeybees going in and out were as thick as a cloud.

Mary closed her eyes, took a deep breath, and opened the envelope. Instead of something official and sterile, there was a handwritten letter inside decorated with hearts and stars in Evelyn's distinctive hand. *Dear Mary, I sent Josh to find you, and as usual, he managed to mess up the whole thing. The short and long of it is, I want you back. To be honest, I like you more than I like Josh and would just as soon kick him out if he wasn't related. He has agreed to move to my upstairs bedroom. (It was either that or move out.) That leaves the entire basement for you and the baby to live in, rent-free. I don't even know if you had a boy or a girl, but I can't wait to see my grandbaby and give him some loving. Please move back. I'll pay for your schooling and tend the baby anytime you want. And if you're worried about Josh, he started dating a new girl last week. He barely remembers you. I hope this makes you happy and not sad. He was never really good enough for you. Call me! Evelyn.*

Mary breathlessly read the letter three times. Evelyn was offering her more freedom than she ever could have imagined. She wouldn't have to work while she went to school. She could study to be anything she wanted, and Evelyn could take care of the baby. She was big and loud and motherly and got alimony payments once a month.

If this was the best Mary had dared hope for, why did she feel nothing but dread? Why did Evelyn's letter make her want to sprint into the house and gather ElJay into her protective embrace?

She knew why without having to ask. Bitsy was right. Mary already had her answer. Where but here with Andrew would she have the freedom to live her life with joy? Where but in this community of lovable, flawed, *wunderbarr* people could she practice and perfect love in herself?

She had the freedom to choose, and she chose a life with Andrew.

Her heart hummed like a beehive at the height of spring. She chose ElJay and Andrew and the Amish and a life full of love.

"She's over here. Pancake." Mary snapped her head around. Benji Petersheim trudged through the orchard with a pair of binoculars around his neck and a walkie-talkie in his hand. He pressed a button on the side of the walkie-talkie. "Come to the apple orchard. You'll see us. Pancake." His grin was as wide as the sky. "They're coming. We brought you a treat. Mamm thought it would soften you up."

Mary thought she might burst. Wherever Benji went, Andrew wasn't far behind. "Why do you say *pancake?*"

"You have to say a code word to tell the person on the other side that you're done talking. Alfie says *over.* I say *pancake.* It's more delicious." Benji squinted into Mary's face, even though they were in the shade of the apple trees. "Are you going to marry Andrew? We all want you to marry Andrew."

Her heart was like a freight train now. "I'd like that very much."

"Alfie keeps asking if you're going to get married, and Andrew keeps telling him to be quiet. It saves time when somebody already has a *buplie,* that's what Alfie says. Alfie wants you to marry Andrew because he hates the cellar. I want you to marry Andrew because you're my favorite girl ever, besides my *mamm*."

"That's so sweet," Mary said, her voice cracking like a green log in the stove. If she said any more, she was going to cry.

Alfie ran through the trees carrying a walkie-talkie and a plastic bag full of tan balls. "Mary, we was looking all over for you. We made you a treat. Mamm said they would soften you up." Alfie opened the bag. "We didn't eat one cuz Mamm said we had to save them for you."

"Can I have one?" Benji said.

"Benji," Alfie hissed. "They're for Mary."

Mary thought her lips would fly off her face she was smiling so hard. "What are they?"

Alfie pulled a soft ball out of the bag and handed it to Mary. "Peanut-butter-and-honey power balls."

Benji nodded. "Since we didn't get to make them that one day you were having your baby."

"And that's not all," said Alfie. "We and Mamm made power balls and Andrew made a crib, but you can't take it in the house yet because the varnish isn't dry and it stinks."

"Andrew made me a crib?"

"Well, he made ElJay a crib, but it was really for you."

A thrill of pleasure ran down Mary's spine. She didn't know what to say, so she took a bite of a peanut-butter-and-honey power ball. "Mmm. Wonderful *gute*. Try one."

Benji reached for the bag, but Alfie pulled it away. "I told you, Benji. They're for Mary."

"I want to share them," Mary said. "Take as many as you want. You deserve it."

Benji pulled four power balls from the bag and stuffed one into his mouth. "They're *gute*, Alfie."

"Okay," Alfie said, as if surrendering to the inevitable.

She'd been expecting him, but Mary thought she might faint when she caught a glimpse of Andrew strolling toward her through the apple orchard. He was so handsome and so good and strong that she wondered why she had ever questioned where she should be.

How could she have kept him waiting, wondering all this time? How could she bear the pain of one more second apart? The tenderness of a thousand heartaches and the longing of a thousand dreams washed over her. She burst into tears at the sight of him and ran into his arms as if she had always belonged there. Being the intelligent man that he was, he didn't ask questions, just wrapped his arms around her and let her weep.

They stood like that for several seconds before Andrew wiped a tear from her cheek. "I love you, Mary," he said, and she could feel the wild rhythm of his heartbeat beneath his shirt. "No matter what you have to tell me at this moment, I love you."

"Are you okay, Mary?" Benji said.

She sobbed into Andrew's shirt. "Josh never made me cookies."

"Didn't he have any recipes?" Benji asked.

"Mary," Andrew said, a tenderness in his voice that only made her want to hold on tighter. "I know I said I'd stay away, but I couldn't bear to be away from you."

"Mamm told him to come," Alfie said.

Andrew palmed Alfie's forehead and playfully shoved him backward. "We're not talking about Mamm right now."

Alfie protested with a snort and pushed Andrew back. "Well, she did."

Andrew smoothed his fingers down her face, pain alight in his eyes. "You've decided, haven't you?"

Her heart fell to her toes. Andrew thought she was going to leave him. She had to put him out of his misery immediately. She laced her fingers with his. "Andrew, I know you like your freedom, but would you consider marrying me?"

He opened his mouth but couldn't seem to form any words. She didn't wait for him to try. She laid a hand on his chest. He slid his warm hand over hers. "In case you need convincing, I have a lot to offer. I have the most beautiful baby in the world and a very *gute* recipe for peanut butter chocolate pie."

"You do have a beautiful *buplie*," he said.

Alfie whispered to Benji, loud enough for the whole orchard to hear. "I told you the baby would save time."

"I also have a cell phone and a whole bag of peanut-butter-and-honey power balls." She got on her tiptoes to whisper in his ear. "Will you marry me, Andrew? I'm crazy about you."

In answer, he caught her mouth with his and kissed her like a thirsty man at the edge of the desert. She kissed him back with the same ferocity, drinking him in, wanting more with every breath.

Andrew was a much better kisser than Josh, even though she suspected it was his first kiss—maybe because Andrew loved her with a good and pure heart.

But she would never again compare Andrew to Josh or anyone else in her past. The only thing she would take from that place was ElJay. Andrew was her future, and she never wanted to look back.

Neither of them could ignore the giggling coming from their small companions. Alfie made a gagging noise, and Andrew laughed, breaking the connection and pulling away from her slightly, but they still clung to each other as if they'd wake up from a dream if they let go.

"Mamm says no kissing until you're married," Benji said.

Andrew smiled at his brother. "Mamm never has to know."

Benji rolled his eyes. "She always knows."

Andrew didn't seem too concerned that his *mamm* might find out he'd been kissing. He bent his head and kissed Mary again, and it was like an orange smoke bomb with stars and sparkles going off in her head.

She really could let him kiss her all day, but there were small, impressionable children in the area, and she'd rather do her kissing in private. She pulled away from him and gave him her brightest smile. "I'll take that as a yes to my proposal."

His laughter was the most beautiful sound she'd ever heard, next to anything that came out of ElJay's mouth. "A thousand times yes. I should have expected that you'd be the one to ask."

"*Ach, vell,* you were trying not to pressure me. I might have been waiting until Ascension Day."

"How did you make up your mind about me? About us?"

She took his hand. "I saw you coming through the trees and couldn't resist how handsome you are."

"I'm not that handsome, and you were very confused three days ago."

"Evelyn offered to pay for me to go to school."

He furrowed his brow in confusion. "But wouldn't that have made it easier to leave?"

"*Jah*, but it also made my choices more clear. Evelyn offered me freedom, but what is freedom without love? Choosing one path means leaving everything on the other path behind. I can't imagine my life without ElJay, but I realized I couldn't imagine my life without you either. I love you too much to settle for partial freedom and half the joy."

He kissed her on the cheek while the twins' backs were turned. "You always think deep thoughts. I don't understand half of what you said, but I got the part where you said you love me. I'll spend the rest of my life making sure you don't regret your choice."

"Just spend the rest of your life loving me, and I'll never want for anything more."

He raised an eyebrow. "Not even freedom?"

"I chose freedom when I chose you."

Benji and Alfie stood with their backs against one of the apple trees. They'd managed to polish off half the bag of peanut-butter-and-honey power balls. Hopefully, they hadn't made themselves sick. "Are you two getting married?" Alfie asked.

Andrew grinned. "We are."

Alfie and Benji jumped up and down and hugged each other as if Mammi had just cancelled family reading time. Alfie's eyes were as bright and twinkly as stars on a summer night. "When are you getting married?"

Andrew slid his arm around Mary. "As soon as possible."

Alfie nodded his wholehearted approval. "August tenth is a *gute* day for a wedding."

Mary giggled. "Four days from now?"

"You can wear your pink dress and we can have power balls for dessert."

"The only other thing we need is fireworks," Benji said.

They should always let the eight-year-olds plan the weddings. Everything would be so much easier.

Andrew ruffled Alfie's hair. "But don't tell Dat and Mamm yet. I want to surprise them."

Alfie rolled his eyes. "Don't bother. Mamm already knows. She always knows."

# Connect with Us

Visit us online at
**KensingtonBooks.com**
to read more from your favorite authors, see books
by series, view reading group guides, and more.

for sneak peeks, chances to win books and prize packs,
and to share your thoughts with other readers.

facebook.com/kensingtonpublishing
twitter.com/kensingtonbooks

## Tell us what you think!

To share your thoughts, submit a review,
or sign up for our eNewsletters, please visit:
**KensingtonBooks.com/TellUs.**